A Town Afraid

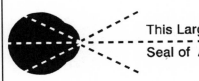
This Large Print Book carries the
Seal of Approval of N.A.V.H.

A TOWN AFRAID

JACK BALLAS

THORNDIKE PRESS

An imprint of Thomson Gale, a part of The Thomson Corporation

Detroit • New York • San Francisco • New Haven, Conn. • Waterville, Maine • London

THOMSON
━━━━━✦━━━━━ ™
GALE

LIBRARY OF CONGRESS CATALOGING-IN-PUBLICATION DATA

Ballas, Jack.
   A town afraid / by Jack Ballas.
     p. cm.
   ISBN-13: 978-0-7862-9594-4 (hardcover : alk. paper)
   ISBN-10: 0-7862-9594-5 (hardcover : alk. paper)
   1. Large type books. I. Title.
PS3552.A4673T69 2007
813'.54—dc22   2007008268

Published in 2007 by arrangement with The Berkley Publishing Group, a member of Penguin Group (USA) Inc.

Printed in the United States of America on permanent paper
10 9 8 7 6 5 4 3 2 1

A Town Afraid

1

Bill Tenery bent his stiff bones enough to swing his leg over his horse's rump, stepped from the saddle, tied his horse to the hitching rack and walked in under the boardwalk's roof. A sweep of his left hand removed his hat. He brushed snow from his shoulders, flicked the thong from the hammer of his handgun and pushed through the heavy saloon door.

He had no reason to think trouble awaited him in this town. In towns he'd left behind he'd not had reason for trouble to find him — but it had. While walking to the bar, he pulled his sheepskin back and hooked it behind the handle of his Colt.

Although only mid-afternoon, he thought a water glass of rye whisky would help push the frost out of his bones, then he'd find the hotel, get a room and sleep the clock around. He told the bartender what he wanted, turned to look at those in the room and knew the trouble he hoped to avoid stood in the middle of the floor facing him.

Two men stood there. He'd never seen them before, but he'd seen their kind, and seen the look on their faces.

Without being aware of it, he closed his fingers around the glass the bartender slid toward him with a backward move of his left arm. He locked gazes with the man closest to him, a tall, hatchet-faced man in Eastern dress. "You men got business with me?"

"We been expectin' you, gunfighter. You're the one the Saddle Horn sent for. Now we're gonna extend your trip a little farther — all the way to hell."

Tenery had no idea what they were talking about, but what he did know was that there wasn't anything he could say that would get him out of this. He looked at the two men he thought would bring it to him first. There was another. He'd seen him slip into the crowd, which was now pushed back against the wall trying to get out of the way and yet trying to see all that went on. The man lost in the crowd was the one Tenery worried about.

He flicked a glance along each side of the room. If his eyes had rested on the man's face, Tenery would not have recognized him

— so he looked for his Eastern dress. He dared not take his look off the two men in the middle of the room long enough to study those along the wall. He pinned the man who had spoken with a hard, penetrating stare. "You talkin' to me, mister? I haven't been sent for by anyone, and I don't know who, or what, this saddle horn is you said something about."

"You're a damned liar. We knew there'd be one o' your kind show up sooner or later. That outfit ain't one to do their own fightin'."

Tenery went quiet inside, but the tendons in his neck pulled against his head, and a hard, painful knot formed between his shoulders. His mouth dried up enough that he thought he could spit cotton. He didn't know what they were talking about — but the man had called him a liar. No one did that without an apology, or they paid for it. "Mister, you just now called me a liar. You can either apologize or see if you can shoot your way outta the box you've put yourself in."

"I think perhaps we'll shoot our way out." While still getting the words out of his mouth, the man's right hand sliced inside his coat.

Tenery had guessed all three of his opponents would be wearing a shoulder holster. With the man's move toward the inside of his coat, Tenery, without thinking, swept his hand down and up. His .44 bucked twice, once at each of the two men in front of him. He didn't give either of them another look; he had the third man to worry about.

A spear of fire hit his left side, knocking him into a turn to face the crowd standing rigid along the wall. His eyes picked out a man with a handgun pointed at him. Smoke still curled from the barrel. Tenery thumbed off a shot, turned the muzzle of his Colt back to the first two and thumbed off a shot into each of them — just in case one of them might still cause him trouble.

They lay on the floor. He was certain that neither of them was any further danger, but he made sure. He swung his gaze back to those along the wall. The man who had stood there, gun in hand, had disappeared.

Tenery wanted to look at his side. He knew he had taken a hit, could feel the hot blood running down and stopping at his belt, but his Colt revolver had had only five shells in it, the hammer resting on an empty when he started; now, five shots later, it again stood on empty.

His eyes swept those along the wall while

he shucked the empties and pushed in six fresh cartridges. The third man must have run. He wasn't among those standing there. "Those two have any more gutless friends among you?"

No one stepped forward. He'd come in for a drink, the one his left hand still grasped. He tilted it, drained the glass, held it for the bartender to refill, knocked it back, tossed a half-dollar to the bar and walked toward the door.

Before he could pull the door toward him, a cowboy standing just inside said, "Mister, I wuz you, reckon I'd make tracks outta this here town, they's more o' them like those you put lead in." Then he stepped closer to Tenery. "Git outta here an' take the right fork in the trail. 'Bout seven miles out is my outfit's headquarters. Know you done took some lead. They'll take care o' you." He made as though to turn away, then twisted back. "Soon's I make sure they ain't none o' that bunch tries to follow you, I'll try to catch up."

Tenery nodded. "Much obliged. Case I can't stay in the saddle, look for me along the way." He pushed his way out the door, walked to his horse and toed the stirrup, but it took him two tries to swing into the saddle. He shook his head and stared at the fuzzy outlines of the buildings along the street. Snow showed signs of banking along their sides. *Gotta get somewhere and take care of this bleeding, or I won't make it one mile, let alone seven.*

He reined his horse toward the fork in the trail the friendly puncher had told him about, only about a hundred yards beyond the last store. He stopped, unbuttoned his shirt, wadded its tail into a ball and pushed it against the hole which showed inside his long johns.

Back in the saddle, he wondered why he should trust the cowboy, then decided he had seemed, acted and dressed like a Westerner. Besides, he had no other choice; if he didn't get help soon he'd never again need it. He nodded to himself and kneed his horse ahead.

The farther he rode, the less sure he was that he'd make it. Snow blinded him. Loss of blood caused his muscles to feel like a wet dishrag. His strength flowed from him. Objects ahead and to the side danced and waved in the fading light, blurry one moment, then disappearing. He slid from one side of his saddle to the other. He thought to tie himself on the horse, but knew if he moved he'd fall off. He wrapped his fists around the saddle horn and gripped with all his might. If he fell, his loss of blood along with the plunging temperature would be a sure way to freeze to death. He tightened his grip on the horn. His side hurt worse with each step of his horse, and with each step his mind slipped in and out of consciousness. Much farther and that cowboy had better not be far behind or there'd be no reason for him to catch up.

Hours, days, weeks maybe, he saw the golden glow of lantern light ahead. He'd trusted the cowboy in town this far. Win, lose or draw, he'd trust him one more time. Maybe they would take care of him where those lights shined. His horse plodded on, setting his own pace, seeming to realize his rider was hurt.

Only a few feet from the tie rail in front of the main house, Bill heard hoofbeats from behind. He stopped his horse, then thought the building farther along might be the bunkhouse. He urged his horse ahead, but when he stopped again and tried to lift his leg over his horse's rump he couldn't move.

The hoofbeats came alongside. Tenery slanted his eyes to the side. He thought if he turned his head, his whole body would turn and he'd fall. The cowboy from town left his horse on the run and grabbed for the reins of Tenery's horse. At the same time he yelled over his shoulder, "Git somebody out here. They's a hurt man 'bout to fall off'n 'is horse. Cain't handle 'im alone."

Three men ran from the building Tenery had thought to be the bunkhouse. They tried to help him from the saddle, but he wouldn't release his grip on the saddle horn. Bill squinted to see them better but his eyes wouldn't focus.

The man standing to the left side of his horse tried to get him to turn loose of the horn, but his fingers wouldn't relax. "C'mon, cowboy, let them fingers turn loose. I got you in case you topple this side. Grant'll catch you if you fall the other way."

Tenery still clutched the horn as if his life depended on it. The puncher to his left pushed his fingers under each of Tenery's and peeled his fingers back one by one, then the man to his right did the same thing with his other hand. Bill had been fighting sliding off into the deep pit of darkness that surrounded him most of the way from town; now he figured to hell with it, and let himself give in. He slipped into the arms of the man on his left side.

Gently, Rufus Bent, foreman of the Saddle Horn Ranch, held his arm around Tenery's shoulders until he could get one arm under

14

the crook of his legs, then told Slim Cannard, the puncher who had trailed Tenery from town, to go to the big house and get Miss Penelope. "Tell 'er we got us a bad hurt man an' need 'er help."

Cannard headed for the ranch house. Penny, as all the hands called her, met him only a few feet from the front door. "What's the ruckus about, Slim?"

"Man's hurt, got shot in town. I seen it all. Rufe needs you to help us tend to 'im." He fell in beside her, almost running, as they hurried toward the men carrying Tenery's limp body.

Under their heavy load, the men staggered to the open door of the bunkhouse. Rufus yelled for anyone inside not properly dressed to put on clothes, the boss was on the way in.

Their words came to Tenery as though they talked into an empty barrel. He opened his mouth to say something, but what he tried to say wouldn't come out.

The men handled him as though he would break. They lowered him to the first empty bunk they came to. This was the first time Tenery allowed himself to relax since leaving town. Pain still paralyzed his entire left side, but he somehow knew these people would not further harm him. He let go of the world and sank back into the black void.

Hours later, he realized he was warm for the first time that day. He must have had the drink he'd wanted to warm his insides and then gotten a room at the hotel. He opened his eyes only a slit to see where he was. An angel bent over him, a beautiful angel. *I must be dead,* he thought.

Then he tried to roll to his side. The pain that flooded his entire body brought back all that had happened. He couldn't be dead. Dead, he wouldn't hurt so much. "Ma'am, don't remember meetin' you, but wherever I am, I'm sure glad to be there if you're as pretty as I'm believin' right now." His voice came out in little above a whisper, but his eyes showed him as pretty a blush as he'd ever seen.

"Sir, you can't be hurt as badly as I've thought, or you couldn't think of such malarkey."

He opened his eyes wider. Yep, she was as pretty as he'd first thought. "Not malarkey, ma'am. I always tell the truth. Found it keeps me outta trouble — most always."

"Tell you what, cowboy, it didn't serve you well in town if what Slim Cannard said is true." She pulled the blanket up under his chin, smoothed the wrinkles from it, then

16

looked into his eyes. "Since I know Slim right well, I believe him. You've lost a lot of blood. Gonna feed you broth until you get better, get your strength back, then we're gonna talk more about what happened to you, and why."

He slipped into sleep while she talked.

Penny stood beside his bunk and stared down at him. His boots were not unduly worn, his clothes were not ragged, his holster and side gun were almost new, not what she'd expect of a gunfighter's weapons. Slim had told her the men who'd brought the fight to Tenery had accused him of being a gunfighter. She shook her head and studied his face. Handsome, she thought, very handsome, and what she'd seen of his body while tending his wound bespoke of much hard work and clean living. Although the scars suggested that he had seen violence. She again shook her head, torn between two emotions; first, she felt glad that he didn't appear to be that which he'd been accused, then disappointment washed over her that he might not be a gunfighter — she needed that kind of man.

She sighed. Whatever and whoever he was, she'd do her best to get him well. She glanced around. Her men huddled in a circle around her. She singled out her foreman. "Rufe, you reckon it'd hurt 'im too much to bring 'im up to the house? I can take care of him better there, and you men can go about your tasks without interference."

Rufe squinted at her a moment, then shook his head. "Ma'am, don't reckon that'd be a good idee. You don't know this man, don't know what he might be capable of. Uh-uh, don't think I could rest well knowin' you wuz up there with a stranger in yore house."

She chuckled. "Old friend, thanks for your concern, but that man lying there isn't in good enough shape to do me harm, and besides, I'd like one of you to stay there at the same time."

She turned her look to Slim. "Get your sleepin' gear. I'll have you stay with him until he gets better. Too, you can help me wait on 'im. Besides that, I want you to start at the beginnin' an' tell me exactly what happened and who brought the fight to 'im."

Slim nodded, went to his bunk and gathered what gear he'd need while up at the big house.

Rufe realized that any argument he had wouldn't change her mind. He nodded to four of the hands. "You men lift 'im gently an' just as carefully take 'im up to where Miz Penny tells you to put 'im down."

While the men struggled with Tenery's weight, Penny hurried ahead to make sure the guest bedroom was ready. Slim followed.

When the men had Tenery in bed and properly covered, Penny walked to his bedside, studied him and then pinned Slim with a look. "Slim, if that man even moans, or feels feverish during the night, come get me. Somehow I have a feelin' he's gonna be right important to all of us on this ranch."

Slim nodded. "Miz Penny, I don't even know the man's name, but somehow I took a likin' to 'im." He glanced at Tenery. "Don't b'lieve he's what them men o' Cord Rourk's called 'im." He grinned. "But I'm here to tell you, ma'am, even though he most likely ain't no gunfighter, he shore can handle that six-gun we put there by his bedside. Most times them what are good with their weapons ain't known outside o' their own hometowns."

Penny, still staring at Tenery, pulled her mouth to the side in a grimace. "Know what, Slim? If he's good as you say, I think I'll try to keep 'im around a little while. But we ought to get to know 'im 'fore we make up our minds about 'im one way or the other."

"Yes'm, think you're right 'bout that," he replied, "but I done made up my mind. I b'lieve he's one o' them men you don't want ta mess with. If you do, then you done bought yourself a heap o' trouble." He nodded. "Yep, done made up my mind. I like 'im."

She chuckled. "Hope you're right, cowboy." She stopped, frowned, sniffed and nodded. "Coffee's ready. Want a cup?"

She was gone only a few minutes, and came back with two cups, steam rising from their tops. She handed him a cup, stared at him a moment, took a sip of her coffee and shrugged. "I've got time, you do too, so tell me exactly what brought on the gunfight this man had in town."

Slim looked into his cup a moment, took a sip, touched the pocket where his bag of Bull Durham tobacco rested, then quickly dropped his hand to his side.

"Oh, go on an' smoke, cowboy. Know a cup o' coffee doesn't taste right without tobacco smoke to go with it. Papa used to tell me that."

His face flushed a bright red to go with his hair. He grimaced, pulled the tobacco sack from his pocket and fashioned a quirly.

He put fire to it, then nodded. "Ma'am, they brought it to him. He tried to avoid it, even asked them to apologize for the way they talked to him. They didn't." He then told her everything that happened. When finished, he shook his head slowly. "Ma'am, that there man probably ain't no gunfighter, but I'm tellin' you I done seen a few real gunfighters an' that man lyin' there could beat 'em all. He's that good."

She again glanced at Tenery. "I hope he's everything you say, Slim. Gonna keep 'im here if he'll stay for what I can pay 'im."

"Aw now, ma'am, me an' the boys'll let our pay go fer a while if keepin' 'im here'll put Rourk an' his bunch in their place."

Penny sighed. "We'll talk about that when all of us are present. Think I'll turn in. Slim, be sure to call me if he feels feverish."

She glanced at Tenery, remembered his words that he thought her pretty and felt her face turn hot. She'd never met such a brash man before — but, for a reason she didn't stop to analyze, his words brought a quickening of her breath.

The next morning, Bill Tenery opened his eyes to bright sunlight. The snow had stopped. Without thinking, he twisted to roll over. The muscles along his left side knot-

21

ted and pain screamed at him from every nerve end, wracking his entire body. It all came back to him — all except leaving the saloon and the ride to the Saddle Horn.

He squelched the desire to move again to see where he was. Instead, he opened his eyes wide, worked his look to the side and up and down. The room was well furnished with a sturdy frontier chest of drawers, and what he could see of the bed was of the same type, all oak. The windows were curtained with an attractive valance and drapes down the sides. He mentally shook his head. This was no hotel room. He'd stayed in rooms this nice while in Washington, D.C., but none in the West.

Before he pushed his mind to remember further, the face of the girl he'd seen the night before came into his head. Had he imagined her? He'd been in and out of the real world during his ride out of town. Then he saw the lanky cowboy who had directed him how to get to where he had a hunch he'd ended up. The kid slept in a straight-backed chair. Tenery realized then that he had not imagined the girl. She was real. Was she the wife or sister of the cowboy sleeping only a few feet from him? For some reason, Tenery hoped she was neither.

"Hey, fella, wake up and help me to that

chair you're sittin' on. You crawl into this bed an' get some regular sleep. Know you must be stiffer'n a board sittin' there like that."

Slim opened his eyes, blinked a couple of times, then turned his look on Tenery. "Damn! Miz Penny's gonna skin me alive for goin' to sleep when I'm s'posed to be takin' care o' you."

"You took care of me when you steered me in this direction, cowboy. Reckon I really lucked —" He cut his words off. The girl of the night before came through the door carrying a tray with two steaming cups on it.

"So you're awake. Thought maybe you'd like somethin' to build back all the blood you lost. One o' these cups is chicken broth, the other's coffee. You're gonna drink the broth first."

Tenery turned his eyes to Slim. "She always this bossy?"

Slim chuckled. "Reckon so, but she's got the right. She *is* the boss."

Tenery cocked his look back to Penny. "Ma'am, don't think we properly introduced ourselves; I'm Bill Tenery. Sorry for lyin' here like this, but don't think I can stand yet."

"Don't you dare try to stand. I'm Penelope Horn, an' that long drink o' water sittin' in that chair is Slim Cannard. He's been lookin' after you durin' the night." She took the broth from the tray. "He *has* been taking care of you, hasn't he?"

"Why, Miss Horn, I don't believe I've gotten a wink of sleep all night he's been so attentive; fluffin' my pillow, straightenin' the covers, askin' me if I needed anything."

Penny frowned and looked at Slim, then back to Tenery. "Two things wrong with what you just said: first thing is that I detect a bit of joshing in your tone; second thing is, Slim's been sittin' there squirmin' like a boy tryin' to think of something to say to the first girl who ever looked at him."

Tenery chuckled. "Ma'am, let me just say that I didn't want for anything durin' the night. He set me on course for your ranch and checked my back trail to make sure no one followed."

He cocked his look toward Slim. "Anybody follow me?"

"Tried to but you might say I sorta changed their mind. Funny how a couple o' shots whinin' by yore ear can change yore whole outlook on life."

Tenery shook his head, then looked at Penny. "This the Saddle Horn?"

She nodded.

Tenery placed his hand on the mattress

and eased himself to a more comfortable position. "Miss Horn, those men in town accused me of bein' a gunfighter. Reckon Slim told you that, an' I'm tellin' you I'm *not* a gunfighter. They also said you'd sent for me. When I denied *that* accusation they called me a liar. Reckon I took charge of the party then."

Penny took his empty broth cup from him and handed him the cup of coffee. She frowned. "Tenery? That name's familiar. You have any kinfolk hereabout?"

"Yep. My mother and father have a ranch just north o' the Shoshone reservation. Papa negotiated with Chief Washakie for permission to settle there. Fact is, I'll bet half o' Papa's crew are Shoshone warriors.

"I've not been home for nigh onto ten years now. That's where I was headed when I ran into that trouble in town." He sighed. "Seems like everywhere I go I run into trouble."

She took the cup from his hand. "I'll go warm this; know it got cold while you drank your broth."

She was gone only a few moments; when she returned and gave him the cup, steam rose from its top. "What'd you do, get antsy to see the other side o' the hill and leave home? You talk like they made you go to school — if there was one nearby."

"Ma'am, if we're gonna talk very much, let Slim help me sit up, then we can talk 'til you get all your questions answered."

Penny shook her head. "No, we're gonna wait'll you get a good bit better, then we'll talk. Slim can get you comfortable, then I want you to get more sleep."

Slim helped him slide down in the bed, then Tenery looked at Penny. "Miss Horn, I'm not tellin' you your business, but judgin' by the way those men acted in town, think I'd post a couple of men out yonder a ways to make sure you don't get any trouble outta them."

"Already done, Mr. Tenery. I was reared in this country too, an' lately the Crow an' Lakota have been the least of my worries. Now you get some sleep. I'll check on you later." She looked at Slim. "In case you didn't get enough sleep sittin' in that chair, you better go to the bunkhouse and get some shut-eye too."

Cannard's sheepish look answered her accusation. He gathered his gear and headed out.

As soon as he cleared the door, Tenery looked at Penny. "Ma'am, that young'un stayed awake longer'n I thought he would. He's a good man."

She chuckled deep in her throat, a husky, pleasant sound. "I know, Mr. Tenery, I know."

She came to the side of his bed, placed her hand on his forehead and nodded as though satisfied. "No fever. Get some sleep. You stay free of fever the rest of today an' I'll fix you a good breakfast in the mornin'."

Before she reached the door, he breathed deeply. She smiled to herself. He was the only man she'd had in the house since her father passed away. The neighbors had ceased to visit since Cord Rourk's outfit came into the county, bringing trouble with them. Even though Tenery lay there badly hurt, she felt safer, more secure. From Slim's report, it was likely neither Rourk nor his men knew Tenery had been hit.

She warmed dishwater, and while standing over the sink washing the few dishes there, she thought of the troubles the Easterner had brought in. She frowned. He wanted her ranch, there was no doubt about that. He'd tried to get her to sell — for a fraction of what it was worth — but she wouldn't have sold to him for any price. This was her home, the one she grew up in.

Too, about the same time he came into the country, the town's people had changed. She'd talked with a few of them. They were reluctant to discuss anything about business, and since Halbert's Mercantile had burned to the ground, they were more closemouthed than ever. That wasn't like them. They had all been friendly folk until recently. Her frown deepened. Everyone seemed afraid.

Then she thought of Bill Tenery. Guilt washed over her, but her idea took root. If Tenery was as good with a handgun as Cannard had said, he might be the answer to all the mess, plus his having shot three of Rourk's men put him in her camp. She'd have to get him well and see if he'd work for her, at the salary she could afford to pay. Her guilt really took hold.

She dropped the dishrag. "Oh my goodness. Here I stand daydreaming when I should be getting supper ready."

After getting out the things she intended to have, she went to Tenery's room to check on him. He still slept. She went back to the kitchen and sliced vegetables into the stew pot — onions, carrots, potatoes — which she'd brought up from the cellar earlier. The beans were already bubbling away in another pot. Even raw, the onion smelled good enough to eat as it was. She realized she was hungry, then thought how hungry the wounded man in her spare room must feel with nothing but broth since the day before. She decided if he had no fever she'd give him some solid food for supper.

Then she pondered why he should be away from home in the deep of winter. If they had a place where they could get three meals a day and a warm place to sleep, most riders would hole up during cold weather. Maybe there was trouble between Bill Tenery and his father. She'd wait until he talked about it; besides, it wasn't any of her business. But she still wondered.

2

Two days later Tenery stood at the foot of his bed, leaned into his side to ease the pain and put on his shirt. He had to sit on the edge of the bed to pull his jeans up. He'd tucked his shirttail in and buttoned his jeans when Penny came through the door.

"What in tarnation do you think you're doing, Mr. Tenery? You need at least two more days of healing before you should be up an' around."

Tenery shook his head. "No, ma'am. All I've done is rest, now I need to see if I can get some strength back. Know there's no way I can ever repay you folks for the kindness you've shown me, but I gotta try."

"You don't *gotta* try anything 'til you get well."

"Yes'm, I do. There's been a few o' the hands come in to see me, an' every one of them has talked about troubles you an' the townsfolk are havin'." He shook his head.

"Miss Horn, I don't know Cord Rourk, don't know what he's up to, but I'm tellin' you right now: I know the kind of men he's got ridin' for 'im, got scars to prove it, an' I've never seen a one of their kind I could cotton to."

Penny frowned. "Wish they hadn't said anything about our troubles." She shook her head. "Oh, I wanted to tell you 'bout them myself, then I wanted, needed, to ask something of you." She shrugged. "Think I'll wait'll you get better to ask. Now's not the time."

"Ma'am, it won't do harm to ask. I'm in your debt for what you folks did for me. Can't think of anything you could ask but what I'd try to do it."

"That's the point, Mr. Tenery. When I ask, I don't want you to feel you owe us anything. What we did, we'd do for anyone and expect nothing in return. Fact is, if I thought you'd agree to what I need on that basis — well, don't reckon I'd ask."

"Tell you what I'll trade for an honest yes or no to whatever it is you're gonna ask."

"What's that, Mr. Tenery?"

Tenery grinned. "You stop callin' me 'Mr. Tenery,' an' I promise to give you an honest answer. My name's Bill."

She stared into his eyes a long moment,

then gave him a slow nod. "All right, Bill, but that is only if you'll call me Penny." She chuckled. "You ever call me Penelope an' I'll figure you're madder'n a skunk-sprayed huntin' dog. Don't think I'd want to be anywhere close to you then."

"My mouth doesn't seem to fit around Penelope, so Penny it is. You've got a bargain."

"Coffee's made and in the kitchen. Since you're up and dressed, come on, sit down an' I'll fix us some breakfast. Reckon your mouth'll fit around eggs, bacon an' flapjacks."

"I been smellin' that aroma of good strong coffee for 'bout twenty minutes now. Figure that's what gave me the strength to shed that bed. Lead the way, ma'am."

An hour later, breakfast finished, Penny had picked up the coffeepot to fill their cups when one of the hands knocked on the back door and without waiting for a "come on in" rushed in, out of breath. "Miss Penny, Hank an' Jethro wuz out watchin' fer riders who didn't b'long to us. Somebody took a bunch o' shots at 'em."

She placed the pot back on the stove. "Either of 'em hit?"

Andy Brothers shook his head. "No, ma'am. Hank brought the news. Jethro stayed behind to send them on their way back where they come from." He glanced at the coffeepot then looked at Penny. "Think he's got 'em pinned down, but reckon they got *him* where he cain't git outta there neither."

Penny frowned, obviously pondering what to do. Without thinking, Tenery took charge. "Cowboy, you can have coffee later. Right now, go to the bunkhouse and get two or three men. Circle back to where they're holed up, get between them an' town — close in on their backside. Don't fire until you're well within rifle range, then flush 'em out." He took a swallow of coffee, then grimaced. "Aw heck, Penny, I stuck my nose in where it didn't b'long. Go ahead; tell 'im what you were about to tell 'im."

Andy stood there, shuffling from one foot to the other, looking from Tenery to Penny, obviously wondering whether to carry out the orders he'd just received.

Penny looked at Tenery a long moment, then shook her head. "No, Bill, we'll do it your way." She turned her eyes to Andy. "All right, Andy, you heard what the man said. Move out." Then before he could get to the door, she added, "Make sure the men take advantage of all the cover available."

Andy threw his "Yes'm" over his shoulder

as he left the kitchen's warmth.

As soon as the door closed against the icy draft that blew in, Penny pinned Tenery with a look that said, "All right, tell me why you took charge like you did?" Then she put her question into a statement. "Mr. Tenery, the way you reacted just now was as though you'd given an order and expected it to be obeyed without question."

Tenery frowned, wondered how to answer her, then nodded. "Penny, reckon I reacted from long trainin' an' experience." He shook his head. "Promise I won't do such again."

"Didn't ask you to promise any such thing, Bill. When you're ready I'd like you to tell me more about you."

He smiled and held out his cup. "Tell you a little now if you'll let me beg for another cup o' that coffee. It's 'bout as good as any I ever drank."

"All right, here's your coffee, now tell me."

Tenery frowned, stared into the cup of steaming liquid without seeing it, took a sip and nodded. "Told you earlier that Papa had a ranch down yonder north o' the Shoshone reservation; didn't tell you he an' his twin brother were graduated from the United States Military Academy at West Point in New York."

34

Penny smiled. "Bill, anything you want to tell me will be new. So go ahead."

Tenery sighed. "All right. Papa had General Grenville Dodge at the end of his bayonet during the War Between the States and spared his life. Papa fought on the side of the South, his brother, Vance, fought for the North.

"Anyway, he made a good friend of General Dodge — fact is he married the general's niece. So when I grew from a tadpole to a good-sized frog, he asked me how I would feel about an appointment to the academy, an' after I told 'im how much I had held that as a personal goal, he asked the general to try to get me an appointment.

"I got the appointment, graduated with honors, then was assigned to General Crook's command here in the West. Fought Indians, an' after a few years was reassigned to Washington. Didn't like the apple-polishing politicians there, so I resigned my commission and headed West. That was a year ago. This is as far as I've made it toward home. Seems like everywhere I've gone I've run into trouble. Fact is, there are those who have tagged me with the name gunfighter. Didn't want that reputation, but I got it and it's followed me. Don't know why, but it has." He took a swallow of his coffee and waited for her reaction.

Despite the seriousness of the conversation, Penny chuckled deep in her throat.

Tenery frowned. "What the heck's funny 'bout me gettin' tagged with a reputation I've tried to avoid?"

Penny's chuckle turned to an acid smile. "Nothin's funny about your story, Bill, but if you could have heard the way Slim told of your escapade in town the other afternoon, you'd know why it's followed you. I'll bet there's not a man in Elkhorn who hasn't told others about you, and they've told others until it's likely they've built you into a cross between Wild Bill Hickok an' Bat Masterson." She glanced at his now empty cup, stood and picked up the coffeepot.

"I don't think I'd worry about the reputation you've acquired. When people talk about gunfighters, they usually separate them into good an' bad. The bad are those who get tagged with the name gunman." She shook her head. "From what I've seen an' heard, you'll never get that name tagged onto you."

Anger welled bitter acid into his throat. "You say don't worry 'bout it, but hell — 'scuse me, ma'am — but it's gotten to where I can't stop in a trailside saloon for a drink without someone lookin' at me and

36

figurin' me for such. Then if they're hun-gerin' for a reputation, the trouble starts."

The sound of horses leaving the ranch yard brought a sharp crease to Tenery's forehead. "Hope none o' those men get hurt."

"I do too, Bill. They're all like brothers to me. Most of them came out here with Pa after the war thinkin' to ride on when they got here, but they stayed. The Saddle Horn wouldn't be here if it wasn't for them." She looked at his cup.

Tenery put his hand over it. " 'Nuff."

She frowned. "You've talked about your father, nothing about your mother. Want to tell me about her?"

He chuckled. "No, ma'am. Not now any-way. I'll tell you their story, an' more about me later. All right?"

She nodded and smiled. "Sounds good. Now I want you to go back to your room, lie down and rest."

Bill didn't argue. The loss of blood had taken a lot out of him. "Soon's anyone gets back, let me know. Need to know that they're okay."

She nodded.

Back in his room, Tenery thought to lie down for a few minutes, then get up and wait for the men to get back. That was what he thought to do, but he'd been on the bed only a few minutes before he drifted into deep sleep. He opened his eyes to mid-afternoon sun's rays slanting through the window. "Oh my gosh, Miss Penny's gonna tag me for a lazy bum. Better get outta here an' see how things went with those men who went outta here after the shooters."

"What in the world are you talkin' 'bout, Bill Tenery?"

His face warmed with the rush of blood to it. "Well, reckon I was just talkin' to myself. Got used to doin' that, ridin' alone across several states."

Penny walked to a rocking chair, patted its back and said, "Sit. I heard what you said and I'd never tag you as lazy or as a bum. Despite trying to show how tough you are you've been badly hurt. You need to rest and give yourself a chance to heal." She smiled. "I b'lieve your body took charge when you came back to your room and despite your desire to fight it off, when the mattress hit your back you went to sleep." She grinned. "An' I might add it was a mighty deep sleep." She nodded. "Did you good. Bet you feel a lot better."

"Yep. Gotta admit to that. Feel almost like I could do a good day's work."

"You try that an' I'll have the boys put

you in your saddle an' send you packin'.'"

He chuckled. "No, ma'am, don't reckon I'll try it." He frowned. "The boys get back? They didn't and I'll begin to worry."

He'd only gotten the last word out when hoofbeats sounded in front of the house. He nodded. "Sounds like 'em now." He picked up his gun belt and slung it around his hips.

Penny stared at him, opened her mouth to say something, then clamped it shut and watched while he tied the leather thong around his leg. She shook her head. "Bill, do you always prepare as though you're goin' to war?"

"Reckon it's kept me alive so far." He shrugged. "Ma'am, we don't know who rode in. 'Til we know they b'long to us, we better be ready."

"Sounds like you've joined my outfit an' you don't even know whether, or what, I can pay you."

He slanted her a look across his shoulder. "C'mon, let's see how the boys did out yonder." He settled his Colt in its holster, then ran his fingertips over the smooth leather. Someone had cleaned and oiled his gun belt and holster. The last he knew, it had been caked with blood. Slim must have been the one who took on the chore.

He had his hand on the doorknob when it opened toward him. Rufus Bent stared at him. "What the hell you doin' outta that bed? You gonna give yourself a chance to get well, or you want ta start bleedin' agin?"

Tenery felt a laugh bubble up from his chest, then grabbed his side. Laughing wasn't something a side wound would put up with. "Came out to see how y'all made out with the shooters."

Bent slanted him a sour look. "Wouldn't of come back if we hadn't took care of 'em. Tied 'em crost their saddles, slapped them broncs on their rump an' sent 'em toward home." He pulled out the makings and rolled a smoke. After lighting it, he cast Tenery a hard look. "You done stirred up a hornet's nest when you shot them men in town."

Bill pulled the side of his mouth down in an exaggerated grimace. "Didn't figure to bring trouble down on you folks, but when I was accused of workin' for you, then Slim sent me out this way, figure y'all sort o' adopted me into the crew — that is, if y'all will have me."

Penny stood there. Her head swiveled from Rufus to Tenery, then she gently turned Bill toward the kitchen. "C'mon. Rufe, you an' the boys c'mon back to the kitchen too. A fresh pot o' coffee's boilin' back there. We gotta do some talkin'. 'Sides that, I want ta hear more about those men you shot." She looked up at Tenery. "Bill, I need you there 'cause most o' this will involve you."

When they were all seated around the kitchen table and had full cups of coffee in front of them, Rufus looked at each man, then turned his look on Penny. "All right, Miss Penny, reckon I want ta hear how this involves Tenery." He sipped at the hot liquid, blew through pursed lips and pinned Bill with a look. "Reckon I want ta hear what she says much as you do." His face smoothed of worry wrinkles and took on a tender, caring look. He nodded. "You see, son, when we came West, reckon I had dang near as much to do with raisin' that girl as her ma an' pa had."

Without looking at the foreman, Bill nodded. "Figured as much." Then, looking at Penny, he said, "Ma'am, you've said most o' this involves me. Let's hear it."

She glanced at the still full coffee cups in front of the men before raising her eyes to lock onto his. "What I'm going to ask will require Rufus' approval."

Bill nodded. "Like it should be."

She sipped her coffee, looked at Rufus and

shrugged. "Well, don't reckon I'm doin' too well." She squared her shoulders. Her jaw set. "Might as well get it said. The way Slim describes you, he thinks you're as good with that handgun you wear as any he's seen. That brings me to what I want to ask. First off, I can't pay fightin' wages, but if Rufe agrees, I want you to work for the Saddle Horn." She sighed. "Well, there it is. I'd be ashamed to ask except I don't want any of my men getting' hurt. I think you can prevent that from happenin'."

"An' you don't give a damn if *I* get hurt?"

"Oh, Bill, of course I do, but somehow, unless there's a whole bunch you're facin' I think there's not enough of them to beat you.

"My men are all good with long guns, but handguns?" She shook her head. "None o' the men are gunfight—" She gasped. "Oh, Bill, I don't mean that the way it sounded."

Hot blood rushed to Tenery's head. He squelched the anger it brought with it. He smiled and from the feel of his lips the smile reflected the bitterness the name gunfighter always brought with it. "Miss Horn, I think I know how you meant it, and yes, I'll work for you — but there will be no pay, no money involved." He looked at Rufus Bent. "Mr. Bent, I'll need help in moving my gear

42

to the bunkhouse when you can spare a man to do it."

Penny opened her mouth as though to say something. Rufus held up a hand to cut her off. "Little miss, I think you've said enough for right now. And yes, I agree we need Mr. Tenery's help." He twisted to look at the man who'd ridden in so sorely wounded only a few days ago. "I'll have Slim bring your gear to the bunkhouse. When you feel up to it, you an' me need to talk. Want you to find a bunk an' crawl into it. You gotta get well." He twisted his mouth to the side in a grimace. "We'll talk 'bout where you fit into this outfit."

Tenery nodded. "I'll be in my room 'til Slim gets here." He swallowed the rest of his coffee, stood and left the room.

Bent turned his gaze on Penny, then looked at the two men he'd brought to the house with him. "You men, go on down to the bunkhouse. I'll be along shortly."

When they'd closed the door behind them Rufus turned to look at Penny. "Little miss, I hope you realize you've hurt that man, hurt 'im as much as any words could. From the look of him when you had your say, I figure he'd rather have had another slug tear at his flesh than have heard those words from you. Don't know why, but I b'lieve he'd not have been hurt so bad if anybody else had said them."

Penny sniffled and angrily swiped at her nose. She reached for a dish towel, wiped tears from her cheeks and eyes and blew her nose. Her eyes turned to Bent.

"Rufe, don't reckon there are words to tell you how sorry I am that I said what I did. That's a good, decent man, comes from a good family, an' from what he's said while we talked, he led an honorable life." She shook her head. "Think maybe I've let myself put the ranch an' you men above anything. Think I've gotten so I don't think of anything but y'all, the cattle an' tryin' to do whatever it might take to make things peaceful like they used to be." She turned such that Rufus couldn't see her eyes. She sniffled again, then leaned to place her head in her hands on the table in front of her and sobbed.

Bent walked around the table to pull her to her feet and put his arms around her. "Hush, missy. Now you dry yore pretty eyes, wash your face and go in there an' apologize to Tenery. If he's the gentleman I believe him to be, he'll accept your words — but he'll still move down to the bunkhouse 'cause it'd be the proper thing to do."

Tenery *did* accept her apology, and moved

to the bunkhouse, as Rufus had said.

For the next two weeks Tenery gradually worked his way back into health and strength. His wound still showed tenderness when he tried to do too much. When pain knifed through his side, he let up on what he was doing. Finally, soon after breakfast one day, he told Rufus he felt good as new. He picked up his gun belt, buckled it, slipped his Colt into its holster and shrugged into his sheepskin.

"You goin' somewhere, young'un?"

Tenery nodded, tying his holster to his thigh. "Figure to ride into town, talk to some of the people, see if I can come to any kind of conclusion as to what's caused 'em to change."

"They ain't gonna tell ya nothin'. I think whatever it is that's got 'em scared is somethin' that talkin' 'bout will only make worse."

"You reckon it's got anything to do with Cord Rourk?"

"B'lieve so, Tenery, but I cain't figure what it might be. I know most o' them folks in town. They ain't a coward among 'em. Why, hell, Penny's pa handpicked them he wanted to settle in Elkhorn, then he give 'em land to build their business on."

"*He* gave 'em the land? What gave him the

45

right to do that?"

"Tell you how it is, Tenery. When Roland Horn come into this here county, he made damned sure every inch o' the land he claimed, he had title to, and the papers signed an' in his possession." He nodded. "Yeah, he gave 'em the land, an' he had the right."

Tenery straightened from tending his holster. "Those folks might not tell me anything, but I want to take a good look at the town, see how it shapes up."

Bent shook his head. "If you was on the ranch payroll, I'd order you to stay here, if for no other reason but to keep you from gittin' hurt agin."

Tenery chuckled. "Not gonna do you any good to try to baby me, Rufus. Gonna do it my way."

Rufe nodded. "Figgered as much."

"Those city slickers o' Rourk's come to town often?"

Rufus nodded again. "I gotta say I ain't never been to town since Rourk supposedly bought that ranch he's on that there wasn't at least four o' them. They ain't never less than two o' them together."

Bill shrugged, and thumbed the thong over the hammer of his Colt to keep from losing it along the trail to town. "Think I'll

46

ride in an' take a look around anyway. After I get an idea what's goin' on, an' get an idea who might talk to me, I'll go back in."

Rufus looked hopefully at the ex-soldier. "You gonna let me send some men with you?"

"Nope, gonna play this hand alone 'til I know more. Right now, we don't know for sure that Rourk has a damned thing to do with the trouble that's being kicked up."

Bent sighed. "All right, boy, but you be careful, an' keep a good lookout to your backside."

Tenery nodded and went to the stable for his horse.

Six miles northeast of Elkhorn, Cord Rourk and six of his men sat around the kitchen table. All were dressed in Eastern garb. Rourk scrubbed them down with a hard look, his frown pulled his eyebrows together such that they almost touched. "I didn't bring you men out here to let one man run you to cover." He pulled the cork on the bottle of rye whisky sitting in the middle of the table, poured his coffee cup half full, then filled it to the brim with coffee. He took a swallow, shivered when the strong drink hit his stomach and sat the cup on the table in front of him.

"Three of you challenged 'im. He killed two, an' the third won't be worth a damn with a gun the rest of his life. The bullet that took Three Toed Charley broke every bone in his elbow. He'll never bend it again."

Ben McCall sat across the table from Rourk. He stared at his boss, then tried to swallow the lump in his throat. It didn't work so he talked around it. "Cord, I couldn't get my gun clear because of people jammed up against me. They were tryin' to stay out o' the line o' fire just like I was. Hell, I figured that gunslinger was a dead man facin' two men, an' one o' us in the crowd up against the wall. Didn't think he'd even suspect Three Toed Charley of bein' able to join those in the middle o' the floor.

"But I'm tellin' you, Cord" — McCall looked around the table to take in everyone there — "an' I'm tellin' the rest o' you: if you ever get a chance at that man, don't do any talkin', just pull your gun an' start shootin'. Don't give 'im a chance. He stood there at the bar, an' one second his hand was empty, the next a gun was in it spittin' out shots faster'n any two o' us could pull trigger."

"You afraid of him, McCall?"

McCall frowned, wondered how to answer Rourk's question, then decided he'd give his boss an honest answer. He swallowed at the knot in his throat and nodded. "Think you would say I got pretty good sense. That bein' the case . . ." He nodded again. "Yeah, I think maybe I am. Unless I had two or three o' our men with me. I b'lieve any one of us alone would die, an' not come close to gettin' the job done."

Rourk smiled, a hard smile, one without humor. He pinned McCall with an amused look, one that crinkled the corners of his eyes. "I stuck you with that question, Ben, because I knew I'd get an honest answer." He picked up the bottle and poured until his cup filled, then handed the bottle to the man next to him. "We'll all have a drink and talk about how we're gonna take care of this gunfighter."

Tom Lease sat directly across the table from Rourk. "Tell you, Cord, whatever our plans are, they better involve more'n one man takin' 'im on."

The cold smile he showed most of the time again crinkled the corners of Rourk's mouth. "I'm thinkin' the same way, Tom. When we go after 'im, I want ta make damn sure we get 'im." He pulled his chair closer to the table, then took a swallow of his stiffly laced coffee. "Before we get into tryin' to come up with a plan, I want ta know: any o' you ever heard of this man before?"

Jim Sore shook his head. "I've talked to a whole bunch o' the town people. I ain't found a soul yet who knows his name. That Saddle Horn rider Slim Cannard followed 'im outta town after the shootin'. Don't know whether he knows 'im or not."

Rourk snorted. "Damn! Don't like fightin' anybody or anythin' when I don't know what or who." He nodded. "All right for now. I want you men, and the rest of the crew, to find out who we're fightin'. When you do, we'll finish our plan. Don't want less than four of you in town at any one time. Got it?"

They pushed back from the table, tossed off the rest of their coffee and answered in unison. "Got it, boss."

On his ride toward Elkhorn, Tenery marveled at the beauty of the land and the fact that he'd not noticed it before, then he grinned inwardly. He hadn't noticed anything during the only ride he'd made over this trail before. The only thing he'd been aware of then was pain and the likelihood of passing out. Now he took notice.

The air, so cold it burned the back of his nostrils, had frozen any smells from it. The pristine white of the snow blanket, broken only by rock outcroppings, the dark green of pine thickets and the barren branches of aspen, brought to mind some of the charcoal drawings he'd seen back East: all black and white — but beautiful.

While admiring the beauty, his mind never veered from studying places readily adapted to ambush. His thoughts turned to wondering why he'd been tagged as a gunfighter; he wore his gun tied down, but so did others who only took that precaution to keep from losing it along the trail. It never entered his mind that the way he carried himself exuded quiet confidence that he could handle anything the world brought to him, a confidence that seemed to be the hallmark of gunfighters, ranch foremen, trail bosses — in fact, it was a way for meeting the world that most Westerners had. He pondered the problem a few minutes, wondering how he could change the perception of others, and finally shrugged. To hell with it. He'd never looked for trouble, but when it came his way he didn't dodge it. Papa had taught him that.

He rounded a bend in the trail. Elkhorn's main street stretched ahead of him, only a block and a half long. A nice town; one that people from the surrounding countryside should enjoy visiting. He intended to find out what stood in the way of their enjoyment.

He reined in at the hitching rail in front of the general mercantile, threw his leg over his horse's rump and stepped to the ground.

It took only a few moments to cover the distance from his horse to the glowing stove sitting in the middle of the store. He stood there, holding his hands close to the cherry red sides, feeling the warmth seep into his hands and body. Not until he'd warmed did he unbutton his sheepskin and twist to look at the man standing behind the counter, quietly studying him. Tenery smiled. "Wintry out there."

The man, sober-faced, nodded. "Usually is, this time o' year. Know who you are, but not by name. I know you by deed only. You're the one who shot and killed two o' Cord Rourk's men." His words were not an accusation, but simply a statement of fact.

"Yes, sir. Can't deny that, sir. They brought it to me, *and* called me a liar when I denied being a gunfighter. I don't take kindly to words like that."

The storekeeper continued his steady study of Tenery a few more moments, then with a slight smile extended his hand. "Cody, Trent Cody here."

Tenery grinned. "I must've passed inspection." He grasped Cody's hand. "Bill Tenery, an' I came in to buy some pipe tobacco. Hoped to hear a friendly voice in the bargain. Yours sounded friendly enough but sorta like you were holdin' back on a decision as to whether I was welcome in your town."

"If you're any kin to Chance an' Betsy Tenery, I reckon you oughta be welcome anywhere around here. Where you stayin', young'un?"

"First off, gonna lay claim to Chance and Betsy bein' my ma an' pa. Second, I'm stayin' out at the Saddle Horn. That's as far as I could make it after that Easterner hidin' in the crowd shot me."

"You couldn't have found a better place to hole up. I heard you mighta took a slug in that gunfight, but didn't know for sure 'til now." Cody glanced toward the door, then looked at Tenery as though he'd only that moment walked through the doorway.

"You say you want some pipe tobacco? What brand?"

Surprised by Cody's abrupt rudeness, Bill frowned, then glanced at the man who had entered the store — an Easterner.

"Make it a twist o' that rough cut." Tenery guessed from the storekeeper's change from the affable man who apparently knew his parents that for some reason Cody feared the Easterner — which meant the stranger was probably one of Rourk's men.

Tenery decided to act the way the storekeeper did, as if they hadn't had any conversation about anything before the city man came through the door. He asked what he owed for the tobacco, paid and left.

From the mercantile, he walked across the street to the Red Dog Saloon; there were no horses tied to the hitching rack in front of it, so maybe the big redheaded bartender might open up a bit.

His hope that the saloon might be empty this time of day proved correct. He grinned when he got to the bar. "Give me a water glass full o' that rye whisky you handed me the other day."

While he poured Tenery's drink the bartender looked over his shoulder. "Slim Cannard wuz here Saturday night. Said ya wuz out at the Saddle Horn gittin' well from where a chunk o' lead caught ya in the side." He nodded. "Figured you done took a bullet when ya left here. Cannard said that by the time you got to the ranch you were jest 'bout drained dry of all the blood in ya."

The bartender chuckled. "Didn't figger you wuz one to leave without comin' back to town to see what might a caused them to brace you like they done." He handed Tenery his drink. "People call me Red, Red McClain. Never could figger why they call me Red."

Bill shaped his face in what he thought was a puzzled look and said, "Danged if I can figure it out either, Red, but reckon I'll call you Red 'til I got it all thought out." They laughed.

Tenery knocked back half of the whisky in the glass, shivered and tilted the glass to drink the rest of it. "McClain, if you ever get to where you feel like you can talk to me honestly, we need to talk."

Before he finished his sentence, Red was speaking. "Tenery, we ain't gonna get that friendly. We do, an' people gonna git hurt." He shook his head. "Not gonna be responsible for such."

"You worried 'bout that tender body o' yours gettin' some holes in it?"

"Ain't worried 'bout me, ain't never been *too* worried 'bout me." He stood back from the bar and pinned Tenery with a no-nonsense look. "Now I done said enough. We gonna be friends, don't push it no further."

Bill nodded. "All right, if that's the way it's gotta be." He held out his glass. "We still friendly enough for you to sell me another drink?

Red laughed. "Always gonna be that friendly." He tilted the bottle above Tenery's glass.

They talked a few more minutes. Bill tossed a couple of coins to the bar top, then nodded. "See you next time I come to town."

He pushed through the heavy door, toed the stirrup and rode out of town. Not until then did he thumb the leather thong back over the hammer of his Colt and button his sheepskin up to his neck.

He thought about his visit while keeping a close look at everything surrounding him. He'd found out one thing for sure: the two men he'd talked with were not afraid for themselves, but they damned sure feared something. He pondered that aspect of his problem a moment, then saw movement out of the corner of his eye. He reined hard in toward the hill to his right, and with the first jump of his horse a huge bull elk burst through the edge of pines which had shielded him from the trail.

Tenery sighed, relieved that he hadn't more trouble. He pulled the corners of his mouth down in a grimace. He was glad it wasn't trouble, but wasn't ashamed of his evasive move; if anything, it forced him to be even more vigilant.

Another half hour and prints in the snow showed where a horse had crossed the trail headed to his left. He reined his horse to a stop to study the tracks a moment. Until now, the only tracks he'd seen were his own, those he'd made after he left the ranch for town. Maybe one of the Saddle Horn riders had come down this way to drive any drifting cattle back closer to ranch headquarters. He told himself that — but didn't believe it.

The horse tracks were going away from the slope of the hill. Tenery edged his horse toward the cover of the pines. Finally, deep into the copse of trees, he pulled his horse in and sat there frowning. He rubbed his side, which still gave him twinges of pain. He could do without another slug tearing at him.

He thought to tie his horse and follow the other horse on foot, then shook his head. Hell, he'd have to cross the expanse of ground bare of cover when he crossed the trail. Too, there wasn't much cover on the other side of the trail, and the snow had partially thawed and refrozen such that it had a hard crust. His feet breaking through that crust would make noise that could be heard a considerable distance in the quiet that pervaded the countryside.

He sat there, brow puckered, for several minutes, then dismounted, pulled his Winchester from its saddle scabbard, tied his horse to a pine branch sagging under the weight of snow clinging to its needles and backtracked to a bend in the trail.

He held the cover of winter-killed brush and single trees until he was around the bend far enough that he couldn't see the trail where he'd first seen tracks. He then crossed. He wished for moccasins, but cast that wish aside; moccasins would make noise breaking through the snow's crust same as his boots. He studied the ground around him. The brush had shielded the ground enough that there were bare spots. He mentally measured the spots for several moments, then nodded. He thought he could stretch his legs far enough to reach them. If his luck held, he might be able to find enough places bereft of snow such that he could also find the rider.

The man for whom he looked might be friendly, but if so, why hadn't he stayed on the trail? Of course, if he looked for cattle to push in closer to the ranch, he'd have left the trail. Tenery shrugged. He'd play it safe. With that thought he pulled his lips into a wry smile. How safe could it be trying to slip up on a man who might be intent on killing him?

With every step, he'd first study the terrain along the trail, each snowdrift, each rock, each tree; only then would he take his next step. The only man he could think of who might want to do him harm and knew he'd been in town was the Easterner he'd seen in Trent Cody's store. One man, the wrong man, knowing of his whereabouts was enough to make him dead. One man justified his caution.

He'd lifted his foot to take another step when the muscles between his shoulder blades bunched enough to cause pain. He lowered his foot and again scanned the snowbank between him and the trail. The Easterner he'd seen in the mercantile lay stretched out on the nearside of it; his rifle rested along the crest of the bank, his attention obviously focused toward town.

Tenery looked at him a moment, then moved his eyes to the side. A steady look was enough to draw the attention of the person at whom the stare was directed. He couldn't shoot the man in the back, and that was the only shot he had with the man flat on his stomach. He thought to make his presence known, and then shoot when the man turned. He mentally shook his head.

He couldn't do that either, but he couldn't stand here like this the rest of the day.

He lifted his rifle, rested his sight on the man and said, "You move an' I'll put a slug right in the middle of your shoulder blades."

The city man opened his hands and let his rifle fall into the snow. Tenery stepped toward him, the crusty snow crunching under his feet with each step.

"How the hell you get this close without me hearin' you?"

Tenery chuckled, a dry sound with no humor in it. "Been makin' my livin' doin' this for years. Leave your rifle where it is. I'll shoot if you make a move toward it. Reckon I oughta shoot you anyway but I gotta think 'bout it awhile. I've never killed a man without givin' 'im a chance."

"What kind o' chance would it be if you allowed me to try an' pull my revolver against you? That man you shot said he'd never seen anybody good as you with a gun."

"There're those who are better, but we're not talkin' 'bout that right now; we're talkin' 'bout what I'm gonna do 'bout you."

3

Jim Sore put one foot in front of the other. He cursed Tenery, cursed Rourk, cursed the West, then went back to cursing Tenery. The next time he saw the gunslinger, he'd pull iron — he wouldn't say anything, he'd just pull his gun and kill him.

Hours later, he rounded a bend and lantern light painted store windows only a hundred or so yards ahead. He headed for the saloon. He needed a drink; a gallon of drinks.

He stumbled to the boardwalk, lifted a leg and put his foot on the boards. He couldn't feel the walk when his foot made contact. He cursed again, lifted the other leg and shuffled to the door. His grip on the knob failed to turn it. His fingers tightened, the latch clicked and he pushed through the door.

He dragged one foot after the other to stand in front of the bar. Red McClain stared at him. "Wh-what the hell happened to you? You look like you been to hell an' back."

Sore stared at the bartender from under eyebrows only now beginning to thaw. "Don't want any conversation outta you. Gimme a bottle, a full bottle of that pig swill you call whisky."

Hot blood pushed to McClain's face, saliva boiled at the back of his throat. He wanted to smash the Easterner's nose back into his face but squelched the urge. He picked up a bottle from the shelf behind the bar and placed it on the shiny surface in front of Sore, then put a glass in front of him.

The bushwhacker ignored the glass. He bit down on the cork and pulled it from the bottle, turned the bottle straight up and swallowed until he gasped for breath. He sucked in a couple of huge gulps of air, then again put the bottle to his mouth. His Adam's apple bobbed five times; Red counted. A grin broke the corners of his lips. "You gonna drown you keep on tryin' to swallow the whole bottle at once." Then he laughed until Sore pounded the bottle to the bar — hard enough it should have broken.

"I want any garbage outta you, I'll knock

it out. Now shut the hell up."

Hot acid again boiled to the back of Red's throat. Blood pulsed at his temples. "You threaten me ever agin an' I'm gonna give you a chance to carry out your threat. You hear me, you city sewer slop?"

Sore stared at McClain a moment. The desire to give Red his chance to whip him shone in his eyes, but at the same time caution obviously pushed back his deepest want. Red outweighed him by fifty pounds, and it was all muscle. Sore snatched the bottle from the bar, threw a cartwheel to the surface and turned his back to the bartender. He shuffled to a chair at the back of the room and sat. He tilted the bottle once again, pulled it down and looked toward the door. It swung open, letting in cold which Sore hoped to never again feel. "Shut the damned door." His yell brought only a dry chuckle and the door opening wider.

Ben McCall, Rourk's favorite rider, laughed deep in his throat, then shut the heavy barrier against the cold. "Damn, reckon you're kinda touchy today, ain't ya?"

Sore stared at McCall, whom he'd never gotten along with. By now the whisky he'd put into his empty gut had a firm grip on his senses, and loosened his tongue. "Yeah.

Jest touchy enough to whip your butt if I hear another word outta you."

McCall's hand dipped in a lightening move to the inside of his coat. It came out holding a snub-nosed revolver. "Anytime, Sore, anytime you want to try, get at it. I'll blow another hole in that stupid head of yours."

The fuzzy edges of Sore's brain cleared enough to tell him he'd better back off. McCall wasn't a man to mess with. In addition to being fast as a striking rattlesnake with his gun, he was built like an oak stump; short but solid and powerful. Through bleary eyes he stared at the gunman.

"Aw hell, Mac, I've had a helluva day, ain't thinkin' right. Put your gun away. I'll buy ya a drink."

McCall's revolver disappeared as fast as it came to hand. He stared steely eyed at the drunk, then glanced at the more than half empty bottle. "I buy my own drinks." He walked to the bar.

McClain squinted at the gunman headed toward him. He filed what he'd just seen away in his memory. He'd have to tell Tenery about it. All was not as it appeared with the Easterners. He wondered if the rest of them were as hostile toward each other as the two who were now in his saloon. He'd have to find out before he said anything to the gunfighter. He wanted to do as Tenery had asked, but didn't want to get anyone else in the town in trouble. He took a bottle and poured McCall the drink he asked for. He had a lot to think about, and that meant a lot to worry about.

About seven miles to the northwest, Tenery urged his horse a little faster. He glanced at the horse he led and chuckled, imagining the shape Sore must be in since he'd set him afoot.

He took the horses to the stable, admiring the tack Sore had fitted his horse with, and put each horse in a stall along with fresh hay before heading for the bunkhouse. The cookshack butted up against the sleeping quarters. The smells of food washed out any thoughts he had of Sore, or any of Rourk's bunch.

While he filled his plate with a steak that hung over the edges, he felt Bent's eyes studying him. After heaping enough food on his plate to feed two men, he glanced down the long table, saw Rufus had an empty place on the bench beside him and went to it.

Chewing a huge chunk of steak, Bent growled out of the corner of his mouth,

"Have fun in town? Have anymore gun-fights? You figgered out how dumb it was for you to go into town alone?"

Tenery chewed, swallowed, then nodded. "Yep, had fun, but not in town. Yep, came close to havin' another gunfight an' yep, I been knowin' all along how dumb most o' the things are that I do." He sawed through another bite of steak and put it in his mouth.

Rufus scooted back on the bench and pinned Tenery with a look that would have gone right through him if it had been an arrow. "Came *close* to havin' a gunfight? What the hell you mean? You either had one or you didn't."

Bill glanced along the table and saw that every man there had his head and ears pointed at him. They all wanted to hear what happened. "Let me finish eating and I'll tell you what happened."

He ate as though he had the rest of the month to finish his meal. He allowed himself an amused smile inside, but the smile didn't pass his lips. Finally, when he guessed every man at the table was ready to belt him in the head, judging by the way they inched their way closer to each other, and as a result closer to him, he put his fork and knife on his plate and swept them with a

66

glance. Then he told what happened along the trail, and that he'd set Sore afoot. He laughed. "Bet that gunny's feet fit right in with his name — *Sore*."

Rufus shook his head. "Tenery, it ever enter that thick skull o' yours that every move you make sets you up to get yoreself shot all to hell?"

"Yeah, Rufus, reckon I've given that a lot o' thought. But I gotta tell ya, I don't know any other way to do things. Papa once told me if I got trouble to face it head-on, then to push as hard as I knew how." He shrugged. "Reckon that's exactly what I'm doin'. It's what I've done all my life."

Bent shook his head. "Reckon if I wuz yore pa that's 'bout what I'd of told ya. But dammit, I ain't yore pa, an' I sure as hell don't want you gittin' yourself shot to pieces again."

The meal over, each man at the table pulled out a pipe or corn shuck papers, packed their pipe or rolled a quirly, lit up and silently enjoyed their smoke; each was obviously absorbed in his own thoughts. Then, as if as one, they stood and went about cleaning their mess gear.

When Tenery had dried and stowed his gear, he pulled Rufus aside. "Bent, you reckon Miss Penny'll let me come up to the house? We gotta talk, an' she's gotta be part of it."

"Aw c'mon, Bill, you gonna let that lil old slip of the tongue stick in yore hide forever?"

Tenery shook his head. "No. I reckon I been dodgin' gettin' that name, an' worryin' 'bout it for so long that I let the mere suggestion that I might be a gunfighter stick in my craw." He gripped Rufus' elbow. "C'mon, let's go tell 'er what I've found, and what I suspect."

About the time Bent and Tenery headed for the house to see Penny, Trent Cody locked the front door of his store and headed across the street to have his before-supper drink. He wanted to talk with McClain too, if there were no Rourk riders in the saloon to see them.

There were no horses tied to the hitch rack in front of the watering hole. He wasn't surprised when he found himself to be Red's only customer. "Gimme a double of the usual, Red."

McClain frowned. "Never knowed you to have a double before."

"Ain't, but if this place stays empty like it is, you an' me's gotta talk. Figger a double'll give me the guts to talk."

Red snorted. "Ha! You got no need to

68

reinforce your guts, Trent. You got the same reason for playin' it safe that we all have. What you want ta talk 'bout?"

"Tenery. We gotta talk 'bout Tenery. He was in the store before he came over here. He didn't actually ask any questions, but he was ready to 'til I sorta closed off the conversation."

Red nodded. "Same here." He chuckled. "Fact is, when he left, I done the same thing you're doin'; I had me a good stiff double shot." He shrugged. "Reckon I done you one better; I had a water glass full."

The door squeaked. Red glanced at it and said under his breath, "The bull o' the woods just came in." Then in a normal voice, he said, "Evenin', Mr. Rourk. Wintry out, ain't it."

"Colder'n a well digger's butt in the Klondike." Rourk walked to the bar.

McClain marveled that the handsome blond man with the graceful walk had garnered the ill will of practically every man, woman and child in Elkhorn.

"Give me a small glass of your good bourbon. Keep the bottle handy, I might want another."

McClain poured from his private stock, placed the glass in front of Rourk, watched him knock it back in one gulp and poured another. "On the house." He hated to give the suave Easterner anything, but wanted to see what he had on his mind; Rourk visiting town was unusual.

The blond man sipped at the drink he now held. "Seen anything of that gunfighter who shot my men a few days ago?"

Red wondered whether to tell him that Tenery had been in, then thought of the two Rourk riders who'd argued in the saloon earlier. He nodded. "Yeah, he come in for a drink today. First time I seen 'im since the gunfight. He's mighty slick with that hogleg he has tied down to his leg."

Rourk's face flushed a bright red, made only more so by his fair skin. He'd apparently wanted to enjoy his drink, but his obvious anger caused him to toss the rest of his drink down and hold his glass for another. "No man shoots my riders and gets away with it. I'm going to keep a couple of men in here, my best men, best with a gun, and when he shows up I'll see that he doesn't ride out."

Red couldn't let the rancher's words go without challenge. "Gotta tell ya, that man come in here wantin' a peaceful drink. Yore men took it to 'im. He didn't want no gunfight."

Rourk stared at him, his face getting red-

70

der with each second. "You taking his side?"

McClain shook his head. "Nope, jest sayin' it like it happened, like what I seen, and what the room full o' folks what wuz in here at the time seen."

Rourk's easygoing, handsome face, now mottled red, twisted into an ugly mask. His eyes, usually sky blue, darkened to slate gray, hard as granite. "Any more opinions you have of that nature you'll keep to yourself." He turned his look to Cody. "That goes for you too, Cody."

Neither man answered.

The Easterner knocked back his drink, looked at the bottle as though thinking about having another, then turned his glass upside down on the bar. He fished a couple of cartwheels from his pocket, tossed them to the counter and walked out.

He'd no sooner left when a couple more of Rourk's riders pushed through the door. McClain looked at Cody. "Reckon we gonna have to wait to have that talk." He poured the storekeeper a glass of the "good" whisky, then filled a glass for himself. "This'ns on the house too."

Trent nodded his thanks. Red set a bottle on the bar for the two Rourk riders; when they took the bottle to a back table, he leaned toward McClain and said under his breath, "You know jest like I do, Rolly Horn ain't set no cowards up in business. We jest ain't got a way o' gettin' together to plan things without bringin' down trouble on them we care about."

Red nodded. "Gotta give that some thought. We come up with somethin' we'll talk 'bout it."

Cody nodded, then smiled. " 'Shamed o' myself for feelin' this way, but I wuz mighty happy to see young Tenery's still close by. That boy's hell on wheels. He don't take no pushin', not even a little bit."

Red pulled his brows together, his mouth a straight line. "Cody, we got no right to involve that boy in our troubles."

Trent shrugged. "I figure when them two thugs pulled guns on that boy he dealed himself in. Ain't told you this before, but I met Chance Tenery, Bill's pa, a few years back — helluva good man, but he never took no mess off'n nobody either. Seems like him an' Miss Betsy, seems like they raised that boy the same way."

He took a sip of his drink and cast McClain a crooked grin. "Red, I ain't gonna do nothin' to sway young Tenery into helpin' us" — his grin widened — "but I'll bet you the price o' one o' your bottles o' good whisky he's already made up his mind to take a hand in whatever trouble we got."

McClain gazed into his drink, rolled the glass around on its base, making a wet ring on the polished surface. He picked up a bar towel and wiped the bottom of his glass, then wiped the bar. He nodded. "Think you're right; ain't got a right to feel this way, but if he *is* dealin' himself in, I gotta say I'm right damned glad."

Seven miles northwest of where Red and Trent talked about what he might do, Bill Tenery sat across the kitchen table from Penny Horn and talked of the same thing. Every few minutes, Rufus Bent would nod in agreement with what they were saying, or he'd shake his head and frown into the depths of his half-empty coffee cup.

Finally, he straightened in his chair, twisted to look at Tenery sitting next to him, then gave Penny a no-nonsense look. "Penny, it jest flat-out ain't right for us to pull this boy into our troubles. He already danged near got hisself killed." He nodded. "Course, he didn't know 'bout us then, but he danged sure knowed 'bout us when he tangled with Sore. He —"

Tenery cut him off. "You haven't pulled me into anything that I wouldn't have gotten involved in anyway. When those two pushed a fight on me — that's when I got involved." Tenery took a swallow of coffee, then twisted his mouth in a wry grin. "Reckon it's time I accept, an' maybe earn, the title Miss Penny hung on me."

"Oh, Bill, please don't do me this way. I've apologized, several times; not goin' to anymore."

"Ma'am, I accepted your apology. I admit I'm downright skittish 'bout havin' that name hung on me, but along with that I know I'm right good with a handgun, rifle too for that matter. Know there are those out there better than me, but haven't run up against any yet." He grinned. "An' I'm here to tell you I don't hanker to."

"Sounds like you done made up yore mind to side us in our fight?" Rufus didn't wait for Tenery to answer, he looked across the table at Penny. "You got any o' that snakebite medicine left I brung back from town last month?"

Penny twisted her mouth in disgust. "Rufus, do you think I sit up here an' drink that stuff alone?"

"Aw now, Penny, I wuzn't suggestin' nothin' like that, I wuz jest hopin' 'fore we got into what me an' Tenery come up here for that maybe you'd let us sweeten our coffee with a wee bit o' that whisky."

She chuckled. "Since I'm not sittin' up here alone, think I'll sweeten *my* coffee at the same time." She went to the cupboard and stretched to the back of it to pull out a bottle of McClain's "good stuff." She placed the bottle in the middle of the table, sat and looked at Tenery. "All right, Bill, other than you tanglin' with Sore, what else happened?"

He frowned, glanced at Bent, then looked at Penny. "Can't say as how anything happened, it was what *didn't* happen that puzzles me. I tried to talk to both Cody and McClain 'bout the trouble I figure they're havin', but when I drove up on asking them 'bout it, they either changed the subject, or cut me off completely. Either o' you got any idea why?" He took a swallow of coffee, then shook his head. "Neither of those gents impress me as bein' shy on guts."

Bent poured a healthy portion of whisky into his and Bill's cups; at Penny's nod he splashed a liberal slug into her cup as well. He put the bottle back in the middle of the table, leaving the cork out of it. He took a swallow before speaking. "Gonna tell ya, Tenery, ain't neither o' them men lackin' iron in their backbone." He shook his head. "Don't know why they won't talk 'bout their problems, but seems like 'bout the time

Cord Rourk an' his bunch o' city thugs set up shop out at the Circle-R ranch, them folks in town, all o' them, pulled inside themselves." He tossed back the rest of his spiked coffee and reached for the coffeepot.

"Cain't say it ain't more'n jest coincidence, but 'bout the time Miss Penny told Rourk she wouldn't sell to him for any price, *we* started havin' trouble, an' the townsfolk shied away from us."

Penny nodded, took a swallow of coffee and choked, then tried to act as though she drank spiked coffee every day. "Too, I've noticed people who've been friends for years don't act as friendly toward each other as they once did. That's what worries me. Pa handpicked each one of those people he let settle on his land. He picked 'em as bein' the kind o' people who would fight for each other." She shook her head. "I can't figure it out, Bill."

Tenery sat and stared into his half-full cup. Finally he reached to his pocket, took out his pipe and packed and lighted it. "The Saddle Horn losin' any cattle?"

Bent shook his head. "That's the hell of it. Far's I can tell we ain't lost one cow —"

Penny cut him off. "Worse'n that; we ain't sold any either. We —"

"What Penny's tellin' ya, Tenery, we've

76

tried to drive two herds to railhead; each of 'em's been stampeded. Next day we rounded 'em up an' headed 'em back to home range." Bent nodded. "Yeah, we think Rourk's bunch is the ones who caused 'em to run, but they done it at night. We didn't have a chance at catchin' none of 'em."

Tenery pulled a great breath through his pipe, blew out the smoke and shrugged. "Don't make sense."

"Yes, it does, Bill. Each time we had to bring our herd back to home range, Rourk made me another offer for the ranch, and each time he lowered the price. He wants my ranch somethin' awful."

"Why? He's got his own ranch. I've not seen it, but it sounds like it's a pretty good-sized spread."

"Lots o' land, poor grass, dry cricks by midsummer." Rufe picked up the bottle and refilled their cups.

"How'd the people who owned it before handle the grass and water problem?"

Penny eyed her cup, then pinned Bent with an accusing stare. "Rufus, you're gonna drink this." She chuckled, and shot him a crooked grin. "I b'lieve that mightta been what you figured on doin' to begin with."

She looked at Tenery. "To answer your

question, they were good people, good neighbors. We let them graze an' water on our place." Her voice hardened. "If I see even one o' Rourk's cows on my range, I'll either drive 'em back to home range — or shoot 'em where I find 'em. Besides, the Edwards family never told us good-bye. I don't believe they would've sold out to Rourk and left. Got no way of provin' it, but I wonder if they sold out, or got run out."

Tenery wondered how such a sweet, beautiful woman could abruptly show steel in her backbone. He laughed. "Ma'am, I surely do b'lieve if Rourk could look in your eyes right now, he'd pack up his bunch o' city trash and get movin'. Whoooeee, Rufus, remind me to not ever cross this woman."

Rufus frowned, grimaced and shook his head. "Gotta tell ya, Tenery, you done learned somethin' the easy way. Be careful you don't *ever* git on the wrong side o' her."

"Rufus Bent, just for sayin' that, think I'll drink this drink you so generously poured, or maybe I'll pour it in the dishwater. It should clean the dishes right good."

"Aw now, hell, Miss Penny, surely you wouldn't do that. I wuz jest tryin' to tell 'im you're one wonderful woman, one to ride the river with."

Penny and Bill looked at Bent a moment, then at each other and broke into gales of laughter.

Tenery took another sip of his drink and nodded. "Yep, that's what I'm gonna do."

Penny stared at him a moment. "*You* apparently have decided what you're gonna do, but danged if you're given Rufe an' me a hint as to what it is; so now let us in on the big secret."

"Want you an' Rufe to sketch me a rough map that shows me how to get to Rourk's place an' how far it is from Elkhorn. Want to know the buildin' layout, what each structure is, about how far apart each is." He shrugged. "Reckon I need 'bout as much information as possible so I'll feel like I've seen it with my own eyes."

Rufus knocked back the rest of his drink and stared at Tenery as though he'd lost his mind. "You're crazy as a rabid skunk. I ain't lettin' no Saddle Horn rider stick his neck out by goin' to that ranch. He'd get shot 'fore he got a mile onto Rourk's range, an' if you think I'm gonna let *you* go up there alone I know yore brain's done got scrambled worse'n a fryin' pan full o' eggs."

"Bent, don't reckon you had your ears pointed the right way when I said I would join the fight against Rourk. I didn't say I would take orders from you, or anyone else." He waited a moment, expecting Penny to get her dander up when he said he'd not take orders from anyone. When she didn't respond to his words, he nodded. "Good, I just wanted to make that clear.

"Since I was no bigger'n a tadpole I grew up playin' with Shoshone boys. Our favorite game was playin' scout an' slippin' up on make-believe enemy like the Lakota and the Crow. Then in the Army there were several years where we had no scout — so I became one." He grinned. "I must've been a danged good one or I wouldn't be sittin' here talkin' 'bout it." He waited a moment. "An' I'm here to tell each o' you, I don't plan to take any of the boys with me — never did figure doin' so."

When he finished laying it out for them, he glanced at Rufus, then looked straight on at Penny. She sat staring at him, her lips slightly parted, eyes wide with sort of a scared look. "Bill, you'll get yourself killed. Don't b'lieve I could stand that. You've already been bad hurt. Please don't take such a foolhardy chance." She pulled her shoulders up in an exaggerated shrug, then shook her head. "I'm not doubtin' you're a good scout, and knowin' you, you're probably one of the best, but please listen to me.

I'm not tryin' to give you an order; I'm *askin'*."

Tenery forgot Rufus was in the room. Penny's hand lay on the table, palm up as though begging; he placed his big hand over hers and folded her small one into it. "Penny, I know it's dangerous, but I'm really not just blowin' smoke; I really am good at that game, and even if you approved me takin' the whole crew with me, I wouldn't do so. You see, what I have in mind is a one-man job. Any more would bring on a gunfight." He shrugged. "We need to know a lot more about that bunch before we take 'em on in a shootin' war." It wasn't until then that he became aware he still held her hand — and she'd made no effort to pull it from his. His face heated with the rush of blood, but he continued to hold her slim little fingers.

As though short of breath, her words came out soft. "All right, Bill Tenery, reckon you think you can do anything you set your mind to. I gotta b'lieve whatever you tell me 'cause I ain't got any other choice. Rufe an' I'll get busy on the drawin' you asked about." Her eyes, blue as a mountain lake, swam in unshed tears. Then apparently trying to cover her emotion, she pushed her heavily spiked coffee over to him. "You better drink this. Don't want Rufus gettin' so fuzzy-brained he can't help me."

"Aw hell, Penny, it'll take a lot more'n I done drank to make my brain not work good."

Tenery laughed. Penny joined him. Bent's face turned bright red.

Bill stood. "I better get on down to the bunkhouse, put the things in my bedroll I'll need in case I have to spend the night somewhere 'tween here an' Rourk's place. Fact is, it might be a good idea to take a little more time; that way I can get a fair look at the terrain around his ranch. Never know when that kind o' knowledge is gonna come in handy." He stepped toward the door, then said over his shoulder, "Rufe, bring me the paperwork y'all come up with when you finish. If it doesn't take you very long, I might leave tonight."

As soon as Tenery closed the door behind him, Bent poured his cup half full of coffee, then spilled whisky into it. He stared across the table at Penny. "Gonna have my say 'bout somethin', little miss."

"Know what you're gonna say, Rufus — an' it ain't gonna do you any good to say it."

He bristled. "Now how in hell you think you know what I'm gonna say?"

Penny studied his flushed face a few moments. She nodded. "You helped raise me almost much as Papa did. I know you can read me like a book, but, Rufe, this is somethin' I didn't ask for, an' it's somethin' I can't do a danged thing about." She hesitated, then said so softly she hardly heard herself, "Don't know as how I want ta do anything 'bout it." She cocked her head in a way she knew she always did when something meant a great deal to her. "You gonna tell me not get my feelin's all tangled up where Bill's concerned, ain't ya?"

He nodded. "Reckon you done took the bit in yore teeth on this one. Wish you hadn't. That boy's what them in any bunkhouse in the country would call 'all man,' but that ain't no assurance he's gonna have a long life. Don't want you sittin' up here hurtin deep inside with me not bein' able to do anything 'bout it."

Penny pushed back from the table, walked around it and put her arms around the burly old foreman. "Bless you, Rufe. I know you're thinkin' 'bout *me,* but you gotta see by now I'm not a girl anymore; I'm a woman grown. There are some things full-grown women or their best friends can't do anything about; this is one of 'em." She picked up his coffee cup and took a big swallow. Coughing, she put the cup back in front of him.

"If I knew what to do in order to make him realize that maybe I could be his woman, I'd do it, an' I wouldn't care whether it was a brazen thing to do. But I don't know anything about men — any man — so reckon I'm gonna have to be plain old me."

Bent chuckled. "Gonna tell you somethin', little miss, you bein' plain old you would put any man on God's green earth in a heap o' trouble."

"You're biased, old friend." She went to a drawer to pull out a pencil and paper. "Let's get busy."

Two hours later, about midnight by Tenery's reckoning, he rode out of the ranch yard. He went over the things he'd put in his bedroll: field glasses, moccasins, two blankets and a change of clothes. One saddlebag held coffee beans, a large slice of bacon, two tins of beans, and .44 shells. He stuffed his old beat-up coffeepot in the other.

He rode relaxed. Still on Saddle Horn range, his nerves wouldn't tighten, nor would his senses get on edge, until past Elkhorn.

He frowned into the cold darkness. Why

did he feel so good, so much at ease, knowing what he might face? His frown turned to a smile. He felt this way because he loved the challenge, the freedom, the danger. And even better, he had an abundance of confidence; his boyhood, the Academy, the Indian fights with the Lakota, the Crow, the Cheyenne — all had prepared him for situations such as this.

He rode easy until he approached Elkhorn. He reined in at its edge, and studied its dark windows. They reminded him of lifeless eyes staring into the dark. Even the empty snow-blown street looked as though human feet hadn't touched it. The only movement was when the wind picked up powder, twisted it into a swirl and carried it away in an insane, mindless dance.

He had hoped to see a light in the saloon. He would have stopped long enough to have a cup of hot coffee with Red. He shrugged. The time it would have taken to drink a cup of coffee was time enough to get a mile on down the road.

The few occasions when he'd seen riders from Rourk's ranch, he'd gauged them as soft men, men who wouldn't put themselves in any discomfort if they could avoid it. By his best guess, the temperature hovered close to zero. His chin was tucked behind the collar of his sheepskin; a soft, muffled chuckle escaped from lips he guessed to be blue from cold; *this* weather would cause discomfort.

Tenery wanted to find the cluster of ranch buildings before daylight and to find himself a sheltered place from which he could study the ranch headquarters and any movement about it. *He* didn't want to be the one to bring on his discovery, and maybe death.

The sky lightened only a few shades of gray at the time Tenery expected to see bright blue. *Gonna snow again, better for what I gotta do.* He thought to ride a circle around the ranch, close enough to bring the buildings into a comfortable distance for study with his field glasses.

He stayed below the ridgelines; there were enough brush and boulders visible from the ranch house that the only thing that would bring on discovery was prolonged motion. He moved a short distance at a time, and then only very slowly.

He studied every possible bit of cover, until he had a clear route of escape back toward the Saddle Horn. Then, about three-quarters of the way around Rourk's Circle-R, Tenery studied a rock outcropping with a few second-growth pines scattered about in front of where he thought to hunker. The rock formation stood on the downslope with the wind blowing from the other side of the ridgeline.

He put the boulders between himself and the ranch buildings, then rode to them. He slipped his feet from the stirrups and slid to the ground. He walked to each side of the rocks and looked toward the buildings below, making sure he could see each building without a tree blocking his line of sight.

When certain he could observe all around the headquarters, he scraped pine straw into a pile, went to his horse, pulled his bedroll loose from the pigging strings and freed his field glasses.

Then he sat and focused on the main building. He had no fear of sunlight reflecting off the lens of the long glass. The heavy clouds erased any fear of being discovered.

Only a wisp of smoke came from the chimney; probably from embers of the fire they'd enjoyed the night before.

He moved the glasses to focus on each building. The one he thought might be the bunkhouse also had a bit of wind-torn smoke, but not enough that a morning fire burned in the stove. The building he considered as the cookshack had no evidence of smoke. Tenery grinned. Hell, those city boys still huddled in their blankets.

A few large flakes settled on legs stretched in front of him. He hoped the storm worsened and continued. If he decided to stay here until dark, and get close enough to snake his way to the wall of the house, where he hoped he might hear some of their conversation, a continuing snow might cover his tracks enough that they wouldn't know they'd been spied upon. In any event, Tenery figured he'd better move as little as possible during daylight.

He'd been there about two hours before smoke billowed from the bunkhouse chimney, then a couple of men ran from it to what he believed to be the cookshack. Soon, smoke streamed from its chimney. He shook his head. "Damn! Those folks sleep 'til might nigh noonin' time." His muttered words buried themselves in the wool of his collar.

After perhaps an hour, time that breakfast should be ready, several men huddled in a bunch hurried from the bunkhouse to the cookshack. Tenery counted them. He needed to know how many men he'd face if and when he mounted an attack.

He wanted to determine how many men the Easterner had around him. They all appeared to wear city clothes, which made him think the kind of fighting he'd known since early boyhood would be foreign to them. That thinking caused him to consider waging war on them alone; if not, he'd decide how many and who of the Saddle Horn crew he'd bring into the fight. He hoped there weren't so many that he needed help.

By the time he thought all had left the bunkhouse he'd counted twelve men. He frowned. Even though he figured on fighting his kind of fight, twelve men, and possibly two or more staked out in Elkhorn, would be too many to gamble that he alone could handle them — unless he could figure a way to get two or three at a time isolated from town, their ranch headquarters or a chance of getting help. He'd have to give that some thought.

He sat on the pile of pine straw until his backside felt frozen; then he pulled his legs under him and squatted until he cramped; then he sat on the pine straw again.

Finally the sullen skies darkened to what he thought might be dusk, and night set in. Time to get busy. He thought another hour in his cramped vigil and he'd be frozen to a block of ice, at least frozen such that any movement would cause excruciating joint pain.

He studied the ranch house, tried to find

the side with the least windows. If he crossed the snowfield and anyone glanced out, he'd be silhouetted against the white background — an easy target. He gave the back of the house a long look, thinking the kitchen would be located there; and no one seemed to use the ranch's kitchen.

Two darkened windows, like the eyes of a dead man, stared into the yard, one mounted on each side of the back door. The side windows toward the front all glowed with a golden hue. If the crew gathered in that room he might find out what happened to the town's folks. They showed fear and weren't of the brand to fear.

Tenery stood and flexed his stiff muscles and joints. Soon bloodflow quickened to bring warmth. A few tentative steps assured him he could move with ease. He gathered his horse's reins in his left hand and circled toward the rear of the house.

When he was about a hundred yards from the back door, he tied the horse to a drooping, snow-laden pine branch. He thought to leave his Winchester in the saddle scabbard, then shook his head and pulled it free.

Snow had put a new blanket on top of the old. Powdery, it packed silently under his feet. Every muscle so tense as to cause pain, and his mouth dry enough he couldn't spit, he moved toward the back of the house. If anyone in the lighted room had the urge to use the outhouse, he'd be in the middle of a gunfight with his horse tied to a tree a hundred yards away.

His eyes glued to the back door for any sign of opening, he took long strides to get to the wall, his stomach churning harder with every step. His fears were justified.

Still about fifty yards from the house, the door swung toward him. He dropped flat on his stomach, rifle pointed toward the door. The man, head bent into the wind, never looked away from where he headed. Tenery didn't move. The Easterner would finish his business in the small, slab-sided little building and come out soon.

If Bill went ahead before he emerged, his tracks would show like a map to where he was. If he stayed where he lay, the man might head back indoors without glancing around. In only a few minutes that seemed like much longer, the tall, thin man came out, slammed the door hard enough to break it from its leather hinges and twisted the wooden latch. Head bent toward the ground once again, he went straight to back door and hurried inside.

Tenery let out the breath he'd been holding. Even with the sub-zero temperatures, he sweated. Not good. The sweat would freeze and he wouldn't be far behind it. Death would come soon thereafter. He had to get his body moving.

As soon as the kitchen door closed behind the man, Tenery stood stooped over and ran to the house, circled toward the lighted windows and squatted below the first one he came to. He glanced back the way from which he'd come. It wouldn't take long for his tracks to fill.

He hunkered below the bottom of the window a moment, but heard only a mixed mumble of voices. He raised his head higher, yet still couldn't hear clearly, so moved to the side and stood. Even now he couldn't make sense of the jumble of voices. He eased his head to the edge of the window.

The same twelve men he'd seen go to the mess shack sat in chairs scattered about the room, with two men standing in the middle of the floor. Rourk sat by the glowing cherry-red stove — and another person he'd not seen before, a pretty, blonde woman, sat next to the handsome Easterner. Tenery frowned. Was she a woman brought out here from the East, or was she from Elkhorn? He pondered that a moment while watching the two men.

They stood faced off against each other. Even though he could not make out their words, they were obviously shouting at each other, their fists clenched. In a moment, Rourk stepped between them and motioned each to a chair on opposite sides of the room. They still jawed at each other.

Tenery recognized one as Jim Sore. They acted as though they hated each other. He nodded mentally; that knowledge might come in handy before he finished his fight with them.

He hunkered below the window until his muscles again stiffened. The only information he'd gained was two men's dislike for each other, and the fact that none of them crawled out of their bunks at a decent hour. Then he got an idea that could cause them discomfort — a lot of it — but along with the idea came worry for the woman. He shrugged. She shouldn't have been there with the bunch he'd looked upon. In his mind, birds of a feather flocked together.

Hunched over he ran back to his horse, eyed the house a few moments more before jacking a shell into the chamber of his Winchester. He sighted on the foremost of the side windows, squeezed the trigger and heard the distant tinkle of breaking glass. He grinned into the frozen air and sighted on the window next to it, picturing the chaos happening in the front room.

He moved to the rear of the house and quickly took care of the two kitchen windows, then ran to the other side of the house and fired through the windows on that side. If the front had any windows he figured he'd leave them with their glass intact. He'd pushed his luck a long way by staying long enough to take care of the windows on three sides. He toed the stirrup and headed away, but not before firing three more shots through the now-shattered glass of the windows on the side which he now rode. He thought those last three shots might keep them hugging the floor long enough for him to get a safe distance, at least beyond rifle range.

4

Tenery headed for the mountains, this time hoping snow *didn't* fill his horse's tracks. He wanted that bunch of flat-landers to follow, and when deep enough in the mountains to bog down. He wondered about the woman he'd seen in Rourk's living room and hoped the Easterner wasn't stupid enough to bring her on the chase.

He rode another half hour until his horse had difficulty plowing through the ever-deepening blanket. He reined the big animal at right angles, rode about a hundred yards, then set his course back toward Rourk's ranch. On the way back, he made certain those following him could not see as far as the new trail he made — he wanted to blow the windows out of the bunkhouse. Sleep would come mighty hard for the crew freezing inside.

He thought he might be far enough ahead of them that they couldn't see him, but they could hear his rifle shots when he took care of the bunkhouse windows. He'd have to work fast, just in case they didn't bog down in the heavy snow. Even though his guts tied themselves in knots, he felt more alive than he'd felt in months. This was what he was born to.

Finally, the ranch buildings came into view, showing black against the white background. He urged his horse to step it up a pace, to no avail. The big animal had about spent all his strength, but tired as he was Tenery figured he could get enough out of the gelding to get to Elkhorn ahead of Rourk's bunch — unless they lost his trail in the mountains.

He closed to within comfortable rifle range of the bunkhouse, pulled his rifle free of its scabbard and methodically shot the windows from the side he rode on. Then circled toward the other side, shooting out the cookshack windows while he did so.

Something buzzed past his ear. He slapped at it, thinking it might be an insect or bee. But there were no insects or bees out in this weather. He glanced toward the mountains. A cluster of riders, barely in what he thought to be good rifle range, pushed their horses mercilessly through the deep drifts. They must be killing their mounts to keep this close to him. Despite that, his shoulder muscles tightened.

His stomach muscles pulled tighter, he shot out the windows on the blind side of the bunkhouse, circled the ranch house to put it between him and the riders and rode into the trees. Then he reined his horse to the south toward town.

Still about a quarter of a mile from the outskirts his horse stumbled. A knot swelled in Tenery's throat. His horse, about done in, would not make it much farther.

With every other step, the horse staggered, until he rode it through the stable door. He jumped to the ground and asked the old-timer if he'd loan him a horse until the next time he made it into town.

Quickly, he explained that Rourk's crew trailed him about three-quarters of a mile out. He knew that in telling the liveryman it was Rourk who followed him he took a chance. If the old-timer had the same fear of the Easterner the rest of the town's folk had he probably wouldn't cooperate.

The crippled-up old man fooled him. He chuckled, pointed to a stall and reached for the cinch on Tenery's saddle.

"Best horse I got. Take care o' him. I'll see if I cain't steer that bunch into thinkin' you done gone lookin' fer a drink, or maybe somethin' to eat." He chuckled again, more like a cackle this time. "Bet that bunch o' city slickers 'bout done froze. Hope so." He finished pulling the cinch straps tight, pushed Tenery toward the horse, then nodded. "Git gone. I'll grain feed your horse. He looks 'bout done in." He pointed toward the back door. "Go out that way. They ain't likely to see ya leave." He cackled again. "Tell Miss Penny an' that broke-down old Rufus howdy for me." He ran at a limping gait to the back door, swung it open and slapped Tenery's loaner on the flank. He closed the door behind him, just in time to hear a bunch of horses stop at the front.

Rourk pounded on the big double doors and yelled for the liveryman to open up. As soon as the door swung open, he waved his crew in and yelled at Hans Olerud, the old-timer, "That gunfighter come in here?"

Olerud nodded. "Yep, he done come in, left his horse an' went lookin' fer a drink." He scratched his head. "Seemed to be in a right big hurry to find a drink. Don't reckon I ever seen a man so thirsty."

Rourk waved his men toward the door. He and his men would find Tenery if they had to search every house in town. They headed for the saloon first.

As soon as the Easterner and his bunch

pushed through the door, Rourk scanned the few drinkers still in the watering hole. None at the bar was Tenery. His look went to the poker table, then he pinned Red Mc-Clain. "Where'd he go?"

"Where did who go?"

Rourk sucked in a deep breath, trying to squelch the anger bubbling in his throat. He failed. "That gunfighter. Know he came in here. Now where is he?"

Red drew his brows together and scratched his head. "Damned if I know. He ran in here like he wuz in a big hurry, knocked back a couple o' drinks like he wuzn't ever gonna get another, borrowed a pair o' snowshoes I had here behind the bar, flipped me a cartwheel, an' went out the door like a turpentined cat. Less'n you an' yore men got snowshoes you ain't gonna catch 'im."

Rourk stared at the bartender a moment, tried to push his anger down enough to think straight, and only partially succeeded.

"He head for the Saddle Horn?"

Red shook his head. "Doubt it. Miss Penny done told 'im she didn't want 'im around; said he brought trouble down on ever'body round 'im."

Rourk picked up the glass of whisky Mc-Clain put in front of him, knocked it back and stared at the empty glass a moment. "Where you think he might've gone?"

Red shrugged. "Damned if I know. From what I hear he's a pretty good woodsman. He might be anywhere out yonder in the hills." He nodded. "Yep, reckon he could make do with whatever he had with 'im, an' still stay ahead o' you an' yore men — even if all o' y'all had snowshoes."

Rourk frowned, and waved his men to a table at the back of the room. He turned his attention back to Red. "Give me a couple bottles, make it rye whisky. Gotta talk to my men."

When they pulled up to the table, Rourk poured the drinks. He swept them with a look that denied defeat. "We won't pursue the gunfighter any farther this time. Our horses are worn to a frazzle, we're damn near frozen and tired. We'll stay in town and head back to the ranch in the morning." His words got grunts of approval.

While Rourk talked to his men, Tenery rode his borrowed horse toward the Saddle Horn. Based on the attitude of the towns-people, he never would have guessed that the old liveryman and McClain had told some great, whopping lies to help him get clear of Rourk's bunch. But what he did know was that he rode a fresh horse while the Easterners were all mounted on tired ones, and he knew where he was headed while those chasing him would have to seek his trail. He carefully reined his horse where he estimated the snow as lying at its shallowest. Twice, riders from the Saddle Horn challenged him along the trail before he rode through the stable doors of Penny's ranch.

He stripped his horse, threw hay down from the mow and was rubbing him down when Rufus Bent came into the stable.

"Now, young'un, let me take over on that task, while you git on up to the house an' warm up a mite. Miss Penny's kept hot coffee on the stove danged near ever since you rode outta here. Let 'er know you're still in one piece." He took the gunnysack from Tenery and continued the job Tenery had started. "Now git on up there, young'un. Tell 'er I said to give you a right smart slug outta that bottle she keeps fer me."

Bill chuckled. "Damn, Rufe, you really got a silver tongue; you talked me into doin' both those things without a hitch. I'm not arguing with you. Gonna do just like you said."

Bent stepped back a couple of paces and swept the horse with a look, then did the same with Tenery. "This here's Olerud's horse. I don't see no holes in your hide, but somethin' tells me you done had a hard time of it."

Tenery nodded. "Not as bad as those who're chasin' me. Tell you 'bout it soon's you come for a cup o' coffee." He slapped the old foreman on the shoulder and headed for the house.

He raised his fist to knock, but the door swung open ahead of his fist. "Bill! Come on in." Penny put a steaming cup of coffee in his hand, looked him over from head to feet, then pushed him toward a chair. "Now you sit down." She chuckled. "Looks like you been rode hard an' put away wet."

Bill grasped the hot cup with both hands, warming them a bit before putting the cup to his mouth. "Ummm, you do brew a mighty fine pot o' coffee, Penny. Been hopin' all the way home there would be someone still up when I got here. Wouldn't have wanted to go bangin' round in the cookshack, wakin' folks up tryin' to get a pot o' coffee goin'."

"Bill Tenery, if you'd gone to bed without wakin' me, I'd have been mad enough to spit."

"Ooowee, don't think I ever want you gettin' that mad at me." His voice started out in a joking manner, but somehow it trailed off dead serious.

Her wide eyes brimmed with tears; her lips quivered. He had never wanted anything so much as he now did. He held his arms rigid on the table in front of him to keep from pulling her close, pressing his lips to hers, and calming her obvious fears for him.

"Bill, I don't believe you could do anything to make me that mad." She headed for the cupboard. "Gonna pour some o' Rufe's whisky in that coffee. Know he'd want me to do that if he was here."

"Fact is, he told me to tell you to do that. He's down at the stable finishin' takin' care of my horse. He'll come up soon's he's finished."

"Tell me what's happened. Rourk's outfit get you cornered anywhere?"

"Let me wait'll Rufe gets here an' I'll tell you both at the same time." He stood and went to the stove to pour Penny a cup. Hearing Rufe scraping snow off his boots outside the door, he took another cup off a peg and poured the old foreman a cupful.

When Rufe pulled out a chair and sat, Tenery put the steaming cup of liquid in front of him. Bent took a sip of his coffee, frowned, shook his head and glanced at the cabinet.

"What's the matter, Rufe, isn't the coffee good?"

"It'd be a hulluva lot better if you'd sweetened it with a wee bit o' whisky."

Tenery chuckled as Penny poured a jolt into each cup.

When she again sat, she looked at Tenery. "All right, you were gonna tell us what happened while you were gone."

Rufus nodded. "Bet it's gonna be a wing-dinger, or he wouldn't be ridin' one o' Olerud's horses."

Tenery laughed. "Reckon you're mighty close in your bet. First, I gotta tell ya that bunch is gonna sleep mighty cold 'til they get somethin' to patch the windows in the bunkhouse *and* the ranch house. I'll tell y'all what happened, starting with soon's I set up to watch 'em from the side o' the hill outside the ranch buildings."

He pulled his pipe from his shirt pocket, glanced at Penny for approval. At her nod, he packed it with rough-cut tobacco, lighted it, took a swallow of coffee and then told them everything that had happened.

When he finished, he took another swallow of coffee and shook his head. "Don't know what kind o' story Olerud told 'em. Hope it won't get 'im in trouble." He grinned. "They must have believed him

104

because I haven't seen hide nor hair of 'em since I left Elkhorn."

Rufe laughed, picked up the bottle and hit Tenery's coffee with another healthy shot. "Tell ya how it is, Bill: that old man can tell you three of the biggest whoppin' lies you ever heard, an' while you're makin' up yore mind that every word he told you is true, he'll launch into another one. You'll believe it too." He shook his head. "Naw, don't figger you oughta waste a single worry as to whether you caused him any trouble."

Tenery grimaced. "Knowin' what I've been doin' might cause y'all a heap o' trouble" — he shrugged — "but I figure you had trouble when I showed up." He took a long drag on his pipe. "Promise you one thing, though; I'll stay 'til the problem's buried — or I am."

"Oh! Don't you ever say or think such, Bill Tenery." Penny blushed a bright red. "What I'm tellin' ya is that you've made a whole bunch o' friends here on the ranch, an' I'll bet you've made some in town, even if they don't show it."

Penny's red face gave Tenery a sense of pleasure — unless he was drawing the wrong conclusion. He thought maybe the way he felt was not a trail only wide enough for a one-horse buggy. Maybe she had some feelings for him too, other than worry about him getting hurt.

He swallowed the rest of his coffee, stood and put on his hat. "Reckon I better get on down to the bunkhouse. Sleep is something I was beginning to think I'd never have a chance to catch up with, but right now I figure to give it a danged good try."

"Goodness gracious! Neither one of us has given you any consideration." Penny looked at Rufe. "Pour Bill another drink of your whisky so he'll sleep."

Tenery shook his head. "No, no more." He chuckled. "I guarantee you I'll sleep. Fact is, I'm leavin' right now so I won't be rude enough to go to sleep sittin' at your table, Penny. Thanks anyway." When he pulled open the door he said over his shoulder, "We'll talk more after breakfast. Maybe we can figure out what I better do next." He shut the door and headed for his bunk.

When the door closed behind Tenery, Penny pinned Rufus with a no-nonsense look. "Tell ya how it is, Rufe: we're not lettin' that man ride out of here ever again without some of our men backin' 'im."

Rufus pulled his mouth into a crooked grin. "You gonna be the one who stops 'im? You know damned good an' well they ain't none o' the boys or me gonna be able to stop 'im from doin' anything he sets his mind to."

She stared at the old foreman a moment. "Betcha he ain't one bit more hardheaded than me. Want ta bet?"

Rufus chuckled deep in his throat. "Little one, you know danged good an' well I ain't gonna take that bet." He knocked back the rest of his drink, stood and stepped toward the door. "Better see if them men who're s'posed to relieve those out on the trail have crawled outta their bunks."

Penny knocked the cork back into the neck of Rufe's whisky bottle and put it back on the shelf. "Dumb as those Easterners are 'bout this weather, I don't think any of 'em will stay out in it longer'n they have to."

Bent grimaced. "Little one, I think you're right," he said, "but I figger we just flat cain't afford to take a chance." He chuckled. "Whatever they do I'll bet not even the idea of sleepin' in a cold ranch house will sway 'em into stayin out in the weather tonight." He nodded. "Now I'm gonna get some sleep." He pulled the door closed behind him and headed for the bunkhouse.

Cord Rourk and his crew sat in the saloon

long after Tenery left town, and had finished six bottles of rye by the time Rufus Bent headed for bed. Bleary-eyed, Rourk swept his men with a glance. "We better call it a day. We won't find Tenery even if we go wanderin' 'round them damned hills the rest of the night. I think we better grab what sleep we can, an' get back to the ranch. I've got a lot of thinking to do before we go hot-footing it around the country chasing a man who knows what he'd doing in open country." He stood. "See you men at the café 'bout nine o'clock. Let's get to bed."

The next morning after eating, Rourk and his crew sat drinking coffee, each putting forth their ideas as to what they should do about the gunfighter. Cord accepted none of their ideas. He stood. "We'd better get on back to the ranch. We'll have to find something to patch those windows Tenery shot out."

Ben McCall pushed his hat back until Rourk could look into his eyes. "Boss, you hear those shots the gunfighter cut loose with on his way back to the ranch after we'd chased him into the mountains?" Rourk grimaced then nodded. "I'll bet you those shots finished off the rest of the windows — cookshack, bunkhouse *and* main house. We won't find enough stuff in the barn to patch more than two or three of them," McCall finished.

Cord Rourk stared at him. "You better hope you're wrong. Any material we got is gonna go into fixin' those in the main house. I believe you're all gonna sleep cold tonight."

Tom Lease sidled up to Rourk's side. "Got a idea. Somethin' to think 'bout at least."

Cord cast him a sidewise look, one he deliberately made contemptuous. "Well damned if it's not about time you had a thought worth thinkin' 'bout." He faced his hireling. "Well, c'mon. You got an idea, let's hear it."

Lease frowned, his face reddened. He obviously disliked Rourk, but the money he made here was too good to jeopardize. "Just thinkin', Rourk, we could tear out some of the stalls in the stable and use those boards to patch the windows."

The boss stared at the man a long moment, then nodded. "Well, damned if I haven't finally gotten a sensible idea out of at least one of you. We may have to do that." Then he thought of the woman he'd left at the ranch when the chase started. He shrugged mentally; what the hell, he hadn't asked her to come out there in the first place. If she froze, she'd brought it on herself.

The woman whose comfort Rourk so care-lessly shrugged aside shoved more wood into the stove and stood as close to its glow-ing cherry-red sides as she dared without catching her clothing on fire. Gretchen Thoreson thought with loathing how far she'd sunk since her husband, Gore, had been killed by a raiding band of Crow. She pushed aside her self-examination. She'd been lonely and when the handsome East-erner had come into her bakeshop to buy some sweet rolls, she'd deliberately set out to get his attention — but she denied to herself that she'd ever intended to let him have his way with her.

After the gunfighter shot out the remain-ing windows, she'd swept the shards of glass into a pile and emptied the broken glass into the trash. Then she gathered several blankets, stoked up the fire and slept on the floor next to the stove.

Now, wrapped in the blankets she'd huddled in during the night, and thinking Cord and his crew would soon return, she searched the cupboard for something to cook for them to eat. A frozen haunch of venison and a few tins of vegetables came under her searching look and settled her mind on preparing stew.

An hour or so after time for the nooning, horses pounded through the ranch yard and on to the stable. Soon after, Rourk and his men stomped into the house. None of them bothered to clean their feet before entering. Cord glanced at the stove, gave a nod and strode to it. Glancing into the pot, he nodded again and held his hands out to warm them. Gretchen shrank inside, felt something in the shriveled core of her emotions die. She'd not had a word of thanks, not a word of kindness, not a word of tenderness from the man for whom she'd almost dragged her morals in the dirt.

"As soon as I eat, I'm going back to town. You don't have to go with me, just lend me a horse," she said.

"Didn't have any thought as to going back with you." Cord turned to one of the men. "Leave your horse saddled. She can ride it back and turn it in to the livery when she gets there." He glanced at her. "Leave those blankets here, we're gonna need them."

She opened her mouth to give him a sharp retort, but held her tongue. Her attempt to gain companionship at whatever cost had proven that the cost was too high. "I don't think I'll stay 'til I eat. Show me the horse you're lending me."

Tenery groaned and rolled over, pulling the covers up under his chin. He lay there another few minutes, then cursed under his breath and threw the covers off. He had to think of his next move against the Easterner. He needed to give a lot of thought as to why a bunch of men he considered brave would knuckle under to a bunch of thugs.

Sounds from the cookshack indicated the crew had gone to eat breakfast. Bill glanced at the bucket sitting atop the big potbellied stove in the middle of the room. A bucket of cold water sat on the floor next to the stove. He swung his feet to the floor and went to the stove. He found a basin and mixed some of the hot and cold water and bathed as best he could, then shaved, took some of the white ash on the end of his finger and brushed his teeth. He then dressed and went in to eat.

Rufus Bent pushed away from his place at the table and walked over to sit by Tenery. "What kind of hell you got planned for Rourk today?"

Bill shook his head. "Don't know, Rufe, been wonderin' 'bout that myself."

"Tell you what I think, boy, I think you

need to take a day or two to rest." He shrugged. "Hell, man, you ain't give yourself a chance to really get well from that gunshot you took. Miss Penny will agree with what I'm tellin' you."

Tenery nodded. "You're probably right, but if I learned anything in the Academy it was to get the enemy on the run and don't let up." He grimaced. "Tell you what; let's go up to see Miss Penny, maybe 'tween the three of us we can come up with somethin'."

Tenery, Penny and Bent all offered ideas as to what action to take, then cast the proposals aside. Finally, Bill stood. "Think I'll ride into town. Maybe something will come to me as to what I can do."

At his words, Penny's face appeared stiff as cardboard. "I'll tell you what you can do. You can go in there and get yourself shot again; or, as weak as you are, the ride in that cold out yonder might give you pneumonia." Her face softened. "Oh, Bill, give yourself a chance. Stay here and let us care for you. A day or two won't make much difference."

He put his empty coffee cup on the table, stared into the bottom of the enamelware vessel, then looked from Penny to Bent. "Yeah, time might make a lot o' difference.

113

I gotta find out if anybody in town knows anything 'bout that woman I saw out yonder at Rourk's place." He pinned Rufus with a hard look. "You ever see or hear 'bout a woman out yonder? The stage ever bring in a woman Rourk might have met an' taken to his place?"

Before Tenery finished his questions, Rufus shook his head. "When you mentioned seein' a female out yonder, it surprised me. Ain't nobody in town ever mentioned it neither. Know Miss Penny ain't heared o' nothin' like that or she'd have said somethin' 'bout it."

Tenery pulled his bandana down around his head, over his ears, tied it under his chin, clamped his hat firmly to his head and said he was going to town and might spend the night there.

Penny, her lips trembling, uttered only two words: "Must you?"

Cold wind ushered in by the open kitchen door before it closed behind him gave her his answer.

During his ride to town, Tenery wished many times that he had taken Penny's advice. The cold forced its way into his lungs, his ribs ached and his face felt as though any change of expression would cause it to crack and fall off. He rode straight to the livery.

Hans Olerud swung the big doors open ahead of him. When Bill swung from the saddle he looked at the old man. "Brought your horse back. Been grain fed and kept in a warm stable." He crinkled his lips at the corners. "Anybody in town I need to be leery of?"

Olerud chuckled. "When that bunch rode outta here 'bout noon for Rourk's place, they looked like they'd seen all the cold an' ice they ever wanted to see. Didn't none o' 'em stay in town." He frowned. "Funny they'd all leave like that. Rourk usually leaves at least two here to keep watch."

Tenery cocked his head to the side. The question he had in mind to ask would not get an answer from any of the townspeople he'd met. He hoped the old man would give him something to sink his teeth into. "What'd he leave 'em here to watch? Why doesn't at least one man stand up to his bunch?"

Olerud continued rubbing his horse down. He didn't answer, and cast a look across his shoulder that said he wouldn't answer. His jaws clamped down on his chaw. He chewed furiously a couple of times, spit a stream into the dirt at his side and finally said,

"Sonny, ain't nobody gonna answer any questions like that. I wuz you, I'd leave well enough alone — you gonna git somebody killed, an' leadin' the pack o' them what gits killed will probably be you." He shook his head. "Done said all I'm gonna say."

Tenery stared at a horse apple lying in the middle of the runway and nodded, then looked at Hans. "Know what, old-timer? I got the men o' this town figured to have as much guts as any men anywhere. Don't know what's got all your jaws clamped tight, but I think one way or the other I'm gonna find out." He turned to leave. "Gonna go get a drink, might stay in town tonight so my horse'll have another night as your guest." He chuckled. "Reckon Rourk took all of 'em outta town to help fix the windows I shot out the other day. Tell you *that* story one o' these days." When he left the stable he still chuckled, leaving Olerud scratching his head.

When Tenery walked into the bar, Mc-Clain, without asking, poured a glass of rye whisky and put it in front of him. "Figgered you'd be out at the Saddle Horn warmin 'yore froze-up body by Miss Penny's fire. You been in town ever since you rode in a couple days ago?"

Tenery shook his head. "Nope. Only been

116

back a few minutes. Had to return Olerud's horse."

Red laughed. "Don't know what you wuz doin' with his horse. That bunch chasin' you figgered you left town on snowshoes."

"Snowshoes? What in the world would make 'em think that?"

Red shrugged. "Damned if I know. People get funny ideas sometimes."

Tenery knocked back his drink and held his glass out to be refilled. McClain said under his breath, "Tenery, I wuz you I think I'd stay outta sight much as possible. Don't think Rourk left anybody in town, but he might send a couple o' men back after they git done what he took 'em outta here to do."

Bill nodded. "Thanks, Red, I always keep my back covered — much as possible. Think for now, though, I'm gonna get a room an' sleep late in the mornin', maybe I won't crawl from the blankets 'til 'bout six."

He left word with the young man at the desk to bring a bucket of hot water to his room at six. A hot bath and shave would be something to look forward to. He didn't want to be at the barbershop with a hot towel over his face if some of Rourk's men returned.

The next morning when he stepped out the door of the hotel, his mouth set for ham, eggs and grits, the mouthwatering smells of fresh baked goods assailed his nostrils. His desire for ham and eggs took a back seat. He hadn't had bear-sign in months. He'd never gotten used to calling bear-sign doughnuts even while attending West Point.

His gaze swept both sides of the snow-packed trail some would call a street. Across the street and about three doors farther than the café, a neat, whitewashed small building squatted. The sign over the door named it The Saddlery. Tennery frowned, certain that the smells of baked goods came from there — but what did leather goods and fresh-baked breads have to do with each other? Despite his reasoning, he headed toward the small building.

He closed the door behind him, then stopped dead in his tracks. The woman he'd seen through the window at Rourk's ranch sat behind the counter reading a tattered and worn book. She looked up, smiled and put the book aside. "Yes, sir, what can I do for you?"

It took a second for Tenery to realize that she had no reason to know him. The only time he'd been close to her had been at the Circle-R, and even though he'd seen her, he was certain she'd not caught a glimpse of him. "Well, ma'am, I smelled that bear-sign soon's I stepped out the door of the hotel. That smell put my taste for ham an' eggs right out of my head. You got any fresh coffee to go with 'em?"

She smiled and clamped hands to hips. "Now why would any sensible woman cover the whole town with the smell of doughnuts, luring young men like you to her place, unless she had coffee to go with her fresh-baked sweetbreads?"

"Good. Set me out a half dozen an' a cup o' coffee to start with."

"My goodness, if you're that hungry, I'd better put on another batch."

Tenery shook his head. "No ma'am. Think this'll do me for awhile." While eating he studied her from under his hat brim. She was a very pretty woman about thirty-five years of age, ash blonde hair, blue eyes, beautiful complexion and a buxom but well-proportioned figure — the kind of woman most men would court. He wondered what she was doing running a bakeshop — or being close to a man such as Rourk.

"Ma'am, I saw your sign and almost decided a saddlery wouldn't have anything to do with baked goods."

"Tell you how I come upon that name. You want company while you eat?"

"Be pleased, ma'am."

She checked Tenery's cup, to make sure it was full, poured one for herself and sat across the counter from him. She took a sip of her coffee, then nodded. "During one of the last raids the Crow made against this town, the menfolk, every single one of them, went after the red hellions. The Crow put up a pretty good fight. One of the men who got killed was my husband. He ran this place, and back then it was a saddlery." She stared at him a moment. "Oh pshaw, you ain't interested in my troubles."

Bill nodded, surprised that he really was interested. "Yes'm, I surely am interested. Please go on."

She shifted her gaze from him to her cup, stared into it a moment, then nodded. "Well, you know there are but few things a woman can do to make a living. I chose two of them — baking and sewing — opened my shop in here and didn't bother to change the name my husband called it." She shrugged. "It makes me a livin', maybe not as good as some things would, but this way I can look at myself in the mirror without feelin' shame."

Tenery took a swallow of his coffee, reached to his shirt pocket for his pipe, then withdrew his hand.

"Aw, go on an' smoke. Know a man

enjoys his coffee more that way."

He chuckled. "You're right, ma'am, but reckon I better get into these bear-sign 'fore I think 'bout packin' my pipe."

They talked a few more minutes, then Gretchen — he'd learned her name was Gretchen Thoreson — looked toward the window and sharply drew in her breath. Her cheeks lost their rosy hue. She said to Tenery, "Sir, there's a man comin' toward the door, an' I b'lieve he means trouble. You can go out the back if you want."

He looked toward the window and saw Jim Sore approaching. He shook his head. "No, ma'am. Think I'll stay right here. If he wants trouble, you stay outta the way — get over there against the wall."

Jim Sore pushed past the door and into the room. "Seen ya come in here, Tenery. Cord's gonna be mighty pleased when I tell 'im you picked a fight with me and lost."

As soon as he'd seen Sore, Tenery had put his back to the wall. From where he stood, he could watch both the front and back doors. He chuckled. "Tell you what, Sore. Know you thugs always travel in pairs. That bein' the case, when your partner comes through that back door, I'm gonna blow your damned head off — then I'll take care of him." While he talked, his right hand made a flicking motion; suddenly, his Colt pointed at Sore. "If I was you, I'd yell for 'im to stay where he is, or to come in with his hands empty an' held shoulder high."

Sore didn't need a second round of advice. "Tom, don't come through that door! He's already got his gun out an' ready."

Tenery nodded. "You're a lot smarter'n you look. Now, with the tips o' your fingers pull that gun from under your arm an' drop it to the floor." He wagged the barrel of his Colt toward the floor. "Get it done right now."

Sore stared at him, his look more poisonous than the fangs of a rattler. "Gunfighter, you ain't got enough eyes in your head to keep us from getting' you. You've already stepped on enough toes in our bunch that there's not a one of us who don't want your hide."

"You better do like I said an' drop your gun, or there'll be one less of you I have to worry 'bout. Do it!"

While talking he tried to keep a sharp watch on the windows. Sore dropped his weapon and held his fingers spread. "Now what, gunfighter?"

"Now you can step out that door, walk to the middle of the trail, call your friend to you, then together walk to the north end o' town. Give me a chance to get outta here."

Tenery stood where he was, watching out the window, until Sore called his friend and walked away. Then he went back to the counter and picked up a doughnut.

She poured them each a cup of hot coffee, then sat on her stool across the counter from him. "Mr. Tenery, I'll not pretend that I haven't heard of you; everyone in town has, and I'm certain you've seen me before although I didn't see you."

She looked into his eyes, then nodded. "You saw me out at Cord Rourk's ranch. What you saw has probably caused you to judge me — at least you've formed an opinion as to what kind of woman I am. I ask you not to do that. Given more time I might have turned out guilty of what you've already made up your mind is true."

She shrugged. "I'm lonely and Cord's a handsome man who can be charming when he wants to be. He showed me what kind of man he really is when they came back from chasing you. In a way, you kept me from making a terrible mistake." She swallowed and dropped her gaze to the countertop. "It'll be hard for you to believe, but that's the truth."

"Ma'am, I'm not one to judge people," Tenery replied. "You're right. I had already formed an opinion of what you and Rourk meant to each other, but that's in the past, and what I think or don't think is not important now."

He took another bite of doughnut, swallowed coffee with it. "You warned me when Sore came toward the door. You could have let him walk in on me. I thank you. As for what went on in the past between you and Rourk? Well, that's none of my business, and in the event you're worrying about me telling here in town what happened out at the Circle-R, that's something I wouldn't do even if my suspicions were true."

She sighed. "Thank you, Mr. Tenery." She stood, went to the front door, peered down the trail and turned back to him. "Those two are going into the livery. How will you get your horse?"

He slanted her a crooked grin. "Mrs. Thoreson, reckon knowin' where they are gives me a leg up. You still gonna let me go out your back door?"

"Yes, but please be careful; there might be more of them waiting for you."

He shook his head. "Don't think so, but ma'am, I'm always careful." He eased his gun in its holster, tipped his hat and went out the door. As soon as he stepped into the open, he moved to the side, then ran a

124

zigzag course to the back of the mercantile.

He opened the back door and ducked inside; a wintry blast followed him. Trent Cody looked up from a stack of sacked flour he was in the process of rearranging.

"Well, Mr. Tenery, you always come in people's back doors?"

Tenery chuckled. "Only when I'm tryin' to keep my hide in one piece."

"Rourk's men after you agin?"

"I wouldn't say 'again'; I'd say 'still.' They haven't let up tryin' to get me under their guns since I first came to town."

Cody threw him a wry grin. "Don't seem like they're havin' too much luck."

"Luck? Yeah, reckon that's the only tag you could brand it with. I been lucky, they've been unlucky — so far," he said.

"You act like there're some o' them chasin' you now."

Tenery shook his head. "Not chasin' me. They're waitin' for me down at the livery."

"What you gonna do?"

"Figure to go down there; give 'em their chance."

Cody lifted another twenty-four-pound sack of flour, placed it on top of the stack. "Tell you what, Tenery, they's a door into the stable at the side, toward the back. Not many ever use it; don't reckon they's many who know 'bout it. It opens into a storage room. That might give you the edge."

Tenery frowned. "Cody, you people seem willin' to help me, but when I start askin' what's goin' on, every damned one o' you cut off the conversation like it never started." He shook his head. "Damned if I can figure it."

Cody stared him in the eye, a hard, penetrating look. "Leave it alone, Tenery. You don't, you're gonna get some good people killed." He shook his head. "Don't think I could stand that."

Tenery squinted into the older man's face. "Don't understand, but I got the right to wage my own war against that bunch o' thugs." He nodded. "Thanks for what you told me. Maybe I can thin 'em down a little more."

"Go out the back, swing north a ways before you cross the trail to come back to the livery. Then be gawdawful careful."

Tenery slanted him a crooked grin, pulled open the door and disappeared into the icy blast.

He kept to the backs of the stores, ran into the woods and headed north until about a half-mile north of town, crossed the trail into the woods on the other side, and headed back to town. He needed his horse, but his horse stood in the livery and to get him he had to get past two of Rourk's henchmen. He stopped, pulled into his mind a picture of what Cody had told him of the stable's structure. He nodded to himself, thinking he knew how he'd handle it.

5

Tenery, careful to push his feet through the snow crust as silently as possible, moved to the side door Trent Coty had told him about, scraped banked snow from its bottom, lifted the latch, pulled the hinged door toward him and slipped into the dark room.

He carefully closed the door, then stood there in the darkness to allow his eyes to adjust. This room had much less light than the stall area, which had a couple of windows, and the huge double doors in the event they were open.

Satisfied that he could see well enough, he slipped to the door which opened into the animal area and ran his hand down it to determine which side opened and whether it had steel or leather hinges. It had leather. He sighed. Good! Leather was less likely to make a noise than seldom-used steel. His hands searched for a latch and found it. Slowly he lifted it while gently pulling the door open, an inch, another; finally he got an opening wide enough to squeeze through. But first he searched as much of the stable as he could see from where he stood.

He shrugged mentally. If he couldn't see them, maybe they couldn't see him. He eased through and stood still a moment. Then just when he was about to move to a stall next to the room, Hans Olerud broke the silence. "Who you men waitin' in here for? I ain't had nobody come in here all day — too cold, I reckon."

"Shut the hell up, you old bastard. We told you to keep quiet when we came in here. Get back to your livin' quarters."

Tenery grinned into the murky darkness. He had no doubt but what the old livery-man had deliberately caused them to talk so they would give their location away. Bless that old soul. He was not a coward, but fear gripped him for some reason other that that of harm to himself.

He waited until he heard the door to Olerud's room at the other side of the runway close with more force than was necessary. That too was the old man's way of saying he was out of the way and for Tenery to go ahead and do what he had to do. Nope, that old man was no coward *or* fool. Now he knew within a foot or two where his prey stood, but how in tarnation could he get behind them? He didn't want to kill them unless he had to — nor did he want to get himself shot again.

He stood there in the wan light trying to think of some way to avoid a killing, then gave it up. They came here to get him any way they could. He could find nothing that said he owed them any degree of consideration.

He stared at them, wanting to see where they trained their gazes. Finally he determined that one looked toward the double doors in back and the other looked toward the front. If he moved, he felt certain the one looking toward the back would see the movement. After thinking on that for a few moments he decided to hell with it. He couldn't stand there all day. He wanted, needed, something to toss to the other side of the runway. His eyes came to rest on a shovel stuck in the dirt floor about six feet in front of him. He mentally shook his head. Before he could reach it, he'd be shot to ribbons.

Then, as he usually did when thinking, he rubbed the back of his thumb along the tops of the cartridges stuck in his belt loops. He grinned. Slipped a couple of them free, letting them fall into the palm of his left hand, at the same time drawing his Colt. In a lightening move, he tossed the brass-encased cartridges against the wall at the other side of the runway.

The two thugs spun toward the noise, firing blindly. Tenery stepped farther into the runway. "Over here." While he uttered the words his thumb pulled back and slipped the hammer as fast as he'd ever fired. He put two chunks of lead into the Eastern trash closest to him.

As that one fell he triggered off a couple of shots toward Tenery. A streak of fire burned through the muscle along Tenery's left shoulder. He thumbed off another two shots toward the man closest to the front. That man, knocked back against the wall rolled off shot after shot, but his gun muzzle shifted further and further toward the floor. He fired once more when his body crumpled into the floor's manure.

Tenery knew he had two shells left in the cylinder of his .44. He stood there watching for movement from either of them. The one closest to him moved his pistol to line up with Tenery and pulled the trigger again — before the ex–army officer could get off another shot. Another streak of fire burned through his right leg, then his leg went numb. Deliberately, he aimed at the thug and fired his fifth shot. The man's body jerked, stiffened, his gun fell from his hand. Tenery held his Colt ready for another shot, but neither man moved.

"You through raisin' hell out here, Tenery?" Olerud called.

"Yeah. Come on out, old-timer." His last word came out with a groan.

"You hit, boy?"

"Yeah. Leg an' shoulder."

"Stay still. Let me take a look at you."

Tenery wanted to give in to the pain, but he knew townspeople would show up soon and he didn't want the gunmen found where Olerud might take the blame. "No, Olerud. We gotta get these men outta here 'fore anybody shows up. Think we gonna have time to get rid of 'em. The folks hereabouts will keep low 'til they're danged sure the shootin's stopped."

"Hell, Tenery. I cain't lift either one o' these men."

"You gotta, old-timer. I'll help you much as I can. Don't want Rourk or his men comin' after you. C'mon, let's get at it."

Olerud saddled and bridled the horses of the two men. With Tenery braced against the side of each horse, lifting as much as his wounds would let him, and with the liveryman pushing each body upward, they managed to get the bodies across their saddles.

"Tie their hands to their feet under the horses' bellies, then send them out the back door. I'll slip back into that room I came outta. Don't want anyone but you to know I've been here." Tenery groaned and leaned against a stall. "Act like you heard shots but don't know where they came from, certainly not from in here."

"Damned if I'm gonna let you git in that room not knowin' how bad you're shot."

Tenery nodded. "You damned tootin' are. Now get those horses out the back door. Get rid o' all those folks who're gonna be askin' questions, then come in an' see if you can't bandage me up a bit. Then I better head for the Saddle Horn. Penny'll doctor me 'til I get back on my feet."

Tenery couldn't catch all the old man said, but it sounded like "Danged hard-headed Army officer, jest like all o' them I ever knew. Think they know everything." Despite the pain, Tenery chuckled. The numbness was wearing off and pain pushed at his guts. His muscles tightened, trying to ward off every streak of burning hurt that stabbed through him. He watched while Olerud opened the back doors wide enough to slap the horses through. Satisfied that they'd beaten the questioning people who would be converging on the stable, he went back in the room with the side door, stripped off his bandana and wrapped it around his leg.

He pulled the kerchief tight, tied the knot and waited for the yelling people outside to converge on the stable. Soon, after only a few moments, Olerud yelled, "What in tarnation you folks yellin' 'bout outside my business? You should oughta be out yonder findin' out who wuz doin' all the shootin' I heered from in here."

Somebody said, it sounded like Red McClain, "Hell, Olerud, I woulda bet my saloon them shots come from inside yore stable. You sure you're all right?"

"Ain't no reason I shouldn't be all right. Now git on with findin' out who done all the shootin', an' why."

Somebody else, it sounded like Andy Brothers from the Saddle Horn, commented, "Bet my saddle it wuz Bill Tenery. He come to town ahead o' me. Rufus sent me in to make sure he didn't need help in case he run into trouble." The man — Tenery was now sure was Brothers — laughed. "I figgered when Rufus sent me in it wuzn't a matter o' *whether* Tenery wuz gonna run into trouble, it was *when*. That boy could find trouble in church on a quiet Sunday mornin'."

Despite his throbbing leg and shoulder, Tenery chuckled at the way Olerud had handled the crowd. That old man could lie with the best of 'em. At the same time, he thanked every deity he'd ever heard of for Rufus Bent sending Brothers to town to look out for him. After a bit, the sound of voices dwindled.

A few moments later, Olerud opened the door and slipped into the room. "You all right, boy?"

"Hell no, I'm not all right. I got two chunks o' lead in me." He stifled a groan. " 'Fore you take a look at how bad I'm hit, see if you can corner Brothers before he leaves town. Gonna need 'im to ride along with me — keep me in the saddle in case I can't make it."

The liveryman searched around, found a lamp, struck a lucifer on the seat of his jeans and put fire to the lantern wick. "Tenery, I ain't leavin' here to look fer nobody. You need somebody to ride to the Saddle Horn with you, I'll do the job in case Brothers has done left town." He picked up the lantern and brought it close to Tenery's side. "Sit down on that nail keg there next to you while I take a look."

Tenery, the room beginning to swim before his eyes, gladly sank onto the keg. "Wait a minute, Hans. Feel like I'm gonna pass out."

Hans put his gnarled old hand to the back of Bill's head and pushed down. "Put yore head down 'tween yore knees. It'll bring the blood back to yore head."

Glad to comply with the old man's direction, Tenery sat bent almost double a few moments. His head cleared. He stayed bent a few more moments, then slowly straightened. "All right, Hans, I'm okay now. See where that lead is and if it went all the way through. I sorta think neither slug stayed inside me."

Olerud reached to his side, pulled his bowie knife, and slit Tenery's jeans from waist to bottom. He parted the cloth, looked at the front and back of the bloody thigh and grunted. He motioned for Tenery to shrug out of his sheepskin, then sliced the sleeve of Tenery's shirt. Not until he'd taken a close look at the meaty part of the shoulder did he look into Bill's eyes. "Ain't neither one o' them slugs still in you. Now you sit still while I go to my livin' quarters an' git a jug I got stored there. I gotta find some clean cloths to bandage you with too."

Tenery was glad Olerud had a jug of

whisky for two reasons: he wanted a couple of good swallows, and he wanted some of it poured into the open flesh wounds. He gave the old man a tight grin. "I'm not goin' anywhere, Hans. Bring the whisky even if you don't have anything to bandage me with."

While the liveryman was out of the room, Tenery's thoughts turned to Penny. After her begging him not to go in town, he was certain she'd raise all sorts of hell when he again came in all shot up. Those thoughts turned to the woman herself and he said: "You're one beautiful woman, Penelope Horn." He studied his feelings a few moments, and thought he'd better again tell her how pretty she was. Something that important needed to be said often. Olerud's return broke into his thoughts.

"Found the whisky *and* clean rags. Gonna fix you up right good now." He placed the jug on the ground at Bill's feet. "Gonna clean the blood away from these holes first."

Tenery shook his head. "Nope, *first* you're gonna hand that jug up to me and let me take a few swallows of its contents. *Then* you can clean those holes."

Olerud chuckled, picked up the jug and handed it to him. "Shoulda thought o' that myself." After Tenery took a couple of healthy swallows and handed the whisky back to him, Olerud took a couple of belts himself and wiped his mouth on his sleeve. Sloshing one of the rags with the strong liquid, he sponged gently at the shoulder wound first. After cleaning the area around the wound he poured some into the long gash.

Tenery clamped his jaws tight, but despite the tight jaws a loud groan escaped him.

Olerud frowned and shook his head. "Sorry, young'un, knowed it wuz gonna burn worse'n fire, but it'll keep it from festerin' later."

From the shoulder, he turned his attention to the hole in Tenery's leg. After wrapping a bandage tightly around Tenery's leg, he chuckled deep in his chest.

"What's so funny?"

Still chuckling, Hans shook his head. "You reckon the reason most o' us men stay healthy is 'cause the whisky we put down our gullet keeps us pure-dee-fied inside?"

Tenery laughed, groaned, then gripped his leg. "Damn, Olerud, don't make me laugh when I'm hurtin' like this."

The liveryman handed Tenery the jug of whisky, gathered the unused rags and stepped toward the door. "Git off that keg an' lie there on the floor. Gonna see can I find Andy Brothers if he ain't done left town." He shook his head and grinned. "Figger as how since he's here, he's gonna danged well stop in Red's place an' have a couple slugs o' whisky 'fore he gits back in the cold an' heads back to the Saddle Horn."

Tenery gathered his muscles to stand and move from the keg, groaned and again sat. Before trying to again get to his feet he pinned Olerud with a questioning look. "Hans, don't you folks have any law in this town; a marshal or somethin'?"

Olerud grimaced. "Yeah, we got us a town marshal, but 'bout all he's good for is to gather up the drunk ranch hands on Saturday nights an' lock 'em in his root cellar 'til the next mornin'." He shrugged. "We ain't got no jail; never had no need for one 'til Rourk brought his bunch in here. Still don't need one 'cause ain't nobody ever caught one o' them Easterners doin' nothin' wrong, an' they danged shore ain't nobody gonna come forward an' accuse one o' 'em of anything."

"It just flat doesn't figure. I've met several of the men of this town and haven't met one yet I'd consider a coward." Tenery pinned Olerud with a look hard as granite. "That includes you, old-timer." He pulled

139

the corners of his mouth down in an exaggerated grimace. "Can't understand why someone doesn't step forward an' tell what's happenin' an' who's behind it."

The old man's jaws knotted, his mouth thinned to a slit and his eyes hardened enough to look like agates. "Leave it the hell alone, Tenery. We got enough trouble without you causin' more."

Tenery stared at Hans a long moment. "All right, Olerud, but I'm tellin' you right now: I got my own war with that bunch an' I'm not lettin' up 'til I take care o' those who keep comin' after me. Maybe I'll be takin' care of the town's troubles at the same time."

The old man shook his head. "They's too many of 'em, boy. You gonna get yourself killed 'fore you kill 'em all."

"Hope it doesn't come to that, Hans. Figure if I can, I'll take 'em one or two at a time, lock 'em up somewhere 'til maybe we — an' I include the whole town in that 'we' — can think of what to do with 'em." He pulled the cork from the jug and took a couple of swallows. "Know they got the townsfolk buffaloed, but nobody has ever told me what they're doin'. There has to be somethin' more an' I can't figure what it is."

The old liveryman said, "Ain't nobody gonna tell you what they're doin'." He chomped down on the cud of tobacco tucked between his cheek and gums, chewed furiously a couple of times, than spat a brown stream onto the floor. "I've knowed ever'body in this town since Roland Horn brought us in here an' give us land to settle on. He didn't bring in no cowards, an' they ain't one in this town today." He shook his head. "Ain't gonna be neither."

Tenery had hoped Olerud would tell him something considering the help he'd given him in getting rid of those thugs he'd shot, but like the rest of the townspeople, he clammed up when it came to talking about the troubles. Tenery shrugged.

"I could bring you in some blankets an' take care o' you right here, Tenery. You ride out to Miss Penny's an' that leg's gonna start bleedin' agin. You gonna be in bad shape if that happens."

"In bad shape already, but I'm not gonna be the cause o' you gettin' killed in case Rourk's men come snoopin' around."

Olerud chuckled. "Boy, I figger I could tell 'em a big enough whopper that they'd leave me alone."

Tenery pulled his mouth to the side and shook his head. " 'Tween you an' Red Mc-

Clain I think you're the most accomplished liars I ever ran across, but this is somethin' I'm not gonna deliberately put either o' you in a bind for doin'. Now find Brothers an' tell 'im not to come down here 'til after dark. Don't want anyone seein' him; besides, there's one person in this town I haven't made up my mind about, and that person might be loyal to Rourk."

"Who's that, boy?"

Tenery shook his head. "Not gonna say 'til I know I have it figured right. I'd be doin' that person a bad injustice if the word spread around, and I was wrong."

Olerud stared at him a moment, then nodded. "Glad you're gonna play the hand that way, son. Wouldn't think highly of you if you done otherwise."

Rourk and his remaining ten men huddled around the big potbellied stove in the middle of the room. They'd finished nailing boards taken from the barn to the shot-out windows, but the boards were a poor fit, and the cold north wind whistled through the cracks. They talked about what they'd do to Tenery when they caught him, but much of it was bluster.

Cord Rourk swept them with a glance. "He's made fools of every damned one of you, me included. Don't know where he stays when he's not in town. From what I hear he stays clear of the Saddle Horn. They don't want anyone bringin' more trouble to them. We gotta find who's hidin' 'im; make 'em sorry they ever heard the name of Tenery."

One of the men, Fran Martin, cocked his head to the side. "Horses comin', Boss. They ain't movin' very fast. I'll take a look."

Martin pulled his coat tighter around him and went to the door. Outside he peered toward the sound of hooves, squinted, then yelled, "Two men slung across their saddles! You men come out here an' help me get 'em off!"

The rush of footsteps brought everyone to the side of Martin. They stared at the two horses slowly plodding toward them, then ran toward them.

When they'd untied the ropes binding the hands to the feet of the two bodies, pulled the stiff corpses from the horses and laid them in the snow, they stood there staring at the men who had been their bunkmates only hours before.

"Tenery again." Rourk's voice came out tight, with a trace of fear. His men looked at him and the face of each reflected the same emotion — fear.

He scanned the group of men standing around him. "We're going to put a stop to this. He's killed the last man of us."

"How we gonna do that, Boss?"

"We're gonna go to town and turn it upside down 'til we find that bastard. Then we're gonna drag 'im down to the livery an' hang 'im from the hayloft's loading arm." He made a chopping motion with his right hand. "An' when we hang him we're gonna hang the person who's been hidin' 'im."

Ben McCall shook his head. "We ain't gonna find 'im, Rourk — not in town. Ain't a person in that town who has enough guts to buck our bunch. He might be usin' the Saddle Horn, but I don't think so." He frowned. "We got those townspeople scared to death. They ain't gonna cross us, an' that girl out at the Saddle Horn ain't gonna put any of her men in danger. Most o' them's been with her ever since her pa died."

Rourk's lips thinned, his mouth pulled down at the corners. "Well, you smart bastard, where the hell you think he goes after he shoots one of you?"

McCall stiffened. "Tell you somethin', Rourk, an' you better listen good. Don't you ever call me a bastard again. If I knew where he goes, I ain't sure I'd want to be the one to corner 'im."

Rourk's eyes squinted. "You scared of 'im, McCall?"

"Not one damned bit more than you are, Rourk." He nodded. "But yeah, think maybe I'm scared of 'im, but I'm here to tell you right now, I ain't one bit more afraid than you or the rest of this bunch. That man's hell on wheels with a gun, any kind of gun — an' he ain't afraid o' any of us. If it ain't fear, you could say I'm mighty leery of facin' him an' any man here who says he's got the guts to stand up to him, right out in the open, is a liar — you included."

Rourk's hand went to the top button of his sheepskin. "You callin' me a coward?"

McCall's face felt like parchment. "You don't want ta brace me, boss man, you ain't good enough. Now drop that right hand away from the top o' your coat 'fore I get the idea you gonna try to get that thirty-eight outta your shoulder holster."

Rourk dropped his hand to his side, then swept the rest of his men. "Any of you men feel the same way as McCall?"

Tom Lease nodded. "B'lieve every one of us thinks like Ben, Rourk. We ain't loyal to you — hell, we ain't even loyal to each other. We're loyal to what we're gettin' outta this setup. We stop gettin' — we stop doin'." He swung his gaze to take in all of them.

"Think we put all our cards on the table, you know where we stand. I believe I'm sayin' it the way any of you would say it?"

They nodded in unison.

McCall knew that as of this meeting out on the frozen ground of the Circle-R, Rourk had lost control. "Tell you how it is; we'll continue to operate the same way we been doin, 'cept you ain't callin' the shots. You're still accomplishing what you figured when you brought us here from the East, and we're still profiting from it." He looked at the men, then nodded. "There's only ten of us left, and I'm declarin' right now, if Tenery kills any more of us, I'm headin' East." He shrugged. "Now you know how I stand. *And I ain't ridin' to town to look for Bill Tenery.*"

Lease turned toward the door, then turned back. "We better put these bodies behind the barn 'til spring thaw. Ain't none of us can dig a hole frozen as the ground is. Let's go in an' have a drink. I ain't goin' to town lookin' for nobody."

Just as Olerud had thought, he found Andy Brothers standing at the bar in McClain's saloon. He pushed his way to his side. "Buy you a drink, cowboy, then I got somethin' I want ta tell ya."

146

"You buy me a drink an' I'll listen to anything you gotta say." He chuckled.

Hans flicked a finger toward the bar in front of Brothers. "Give 'im another of whatever he's drinkin'. I'm buyin'." Seeing that McClain nodded, he twisted toward the cowboy and said in almost a whisper, "Come down to my place soon's it gets good dark. Got somethin' you might be interested in."

Andy, so brief that Olerud wasn't sure he'd seen it, nodded. Then said, also in a whisper, "Be there."

Hans knocked back his drink, ordered another, and at the same time bought a full bottle. When he picked the bottle up and slipped it inside his belt, he told Brothers he better buy one also.

When he got back to the stable, he looked down the trail toward the Circle-R. Seeing no one riding into town, he pulled open the door and went in. He went directly to the room in which he'd left Tenery. "It's me, boy. Don't shoot. Know you got that there forty-four pointed at this door."

"C'mon in, old-timer, you find Brothers?"

Olerud pulled the door closed behind him and nodded. "Jest like I thought; he wasn't gonna leave town without a couple o' drinks." He chuckled. "Hell, he needed *somethin'* to thaw the ice outta his blood after that ride into town. Speakin' of thawin' blood: figgered after we used so much o' my whisky on yore hell-raisin' hide you'd pay fer this bottle I brung from McClain's place. Figgered you might want a drink 'fore you headed for the Saddle Horn."

"You think Andy'll buy a bottle to take with us when we leave town?"

Hans nodded. "Done took care o' that. He's got a bottle tucked inside his belt right now."

Olerud stayed with Tenery until he thought it might be getting dark enough that Brothers would show up, and, not knowing whether the cowboy knew about this room, he went to his sleeping quarters to await him. He had not long to wait.

The small door at the side of the big double doors swung open and Andy came in. "Hey, Hans, where you hidin' out in here?"

"Right here, you danged fool, you want the whole town to know you come down here?"

"Aw heck, Olerud, ain't nobody out in this cold. Where you got Bill hid out?"

Hans nodded his head toward the door to the room he had Tenery stashed in. "You gonna have to help me get 'im in the saddle.

He's done got hisself shot up some." He frowned. "On second thought, I got a buckboard out back. If we loaded 'im in it, don't reckon it'd cause 'im to start bleedin' as quick as sittin' his saddle."

Andy nodded. "B'lieve you're right." He then shook his head, obviously in wonder that anyone could get into so much trouble. As he entered the room where Tenery lay, he said, "Tenery, you know damned well Miss Penny's gonna raise all sorts o' hell with you for gitten yourself shot agin."

Tenery, a master at sarcasm, drawled, "Well, tell you how it is, Brothers. On the way in town I got to thinkin', wonderin', what could I do to upset Miss Penny. Then I thought of it. I figured, hell, I'll see if I can't get myself shot a couple o' times. That'll get 'er really boilin' mad at me."

"Aw, Bill, you know what I mean. She cares a whole bunch what happens to any of us. She cares so much she lets it out by tongue-lashin' us. She don't mean nothin' by it, but she needs to let her feelin's out someway. Reckon she takes that way of lettin' us know how she feels. She does all of us the same way."

For some reason Tenery felt deflated. Brothers' words took away the idea that he was special, and he wanted to be special to her for some reason he hadn't figured out — yet.

He rolled to his side and looked at Ol- erud. "You don't mind, old-timer, saddle my horse and let me get outta here."

"Know we done gone over this before, but you gonna start bleedin' somethin' awful. You better stay here, or at the very least I'm gonna have Andy take you outta here in the buckboard."

Tenery shook his head. "Hans, you know damned well if Rourk or his men find me here it's gonna cause you a heap o' trouble." He shrugged. "Nope, not gonna bring any more trouble down on you. Hitch up the buckboard an' let Brothers get me outta here."

Olerud left the room muttering, "Danged fool don't let 'imself do nothin' that might help 'im get to healin' good."

Tenery agreed with the old man, but he would rather get shot again if it would keep Olerud safe.

In about a half an hour, he and Brothers were on the trail for the Saddle Horn.

Olerud led Tenery's and Andy's horses along the backs of the stores and on out of town until a bend in the trail hid the main street from view. He pulled off the road, into some trees, and waited. Soon the rattle of trace chains and bump of wheels came to his ears. He stayed where he was until he made certain it was Brothers and his buckboard making the noise.

He rode into the trail, edged by the wagon, and tied the horses to the tailgate. "Ride 'bout slow as you can. Don't cause that young'un no more hurt than he's already got."

Brothers raised his hand to show he understood; then slapped the reins against the back of the horse.

Olerud turned his steps back toward town. When he came even with McClain's saloon, he went in the back door. In only a moment he stood at the bar. Seven others stood there with him.

Red stared at him a moment, poured a glass of whisky, put it in front of him and said, "Don't figger you done drank that bottle you took outta here this afternoon, but yore nose is red enuff to tell me you're mighty cold." He nodded toward the glass. "That'n's on the house. Need to talk to you a little bit in private soon's you down that."

Hans knocked back the drink and nodded toward McClain's office. Red opened the door and turned to face the liveryman. "That yore buckboard I seen leavin' town

151

with Brothers sittin' in the boot?"

Olerud nodded.

Red gave him a hard stare. "Old friend, you gonna get yourself killed? If not yourself, somebody else is gonna die."

Hans gave the bartender a hard, straight-on look. "You tellin' me you'd of done somethin' different?"

"Naw, don't reckon I woulda done a dang thing different, but you cut it mighty thin when you stood there this afternoon an' swore that shootin' wasn't in yore barn."

Olerud shrugged. "Didn't know nothin' else I could of done. Tell 'im the truth an' I'd of got some o' them killed; didn't want that to happen." He grinned. " 'Sides that, they ain't another danged man in this town, 'cept one, can lie any better'n me an' you know who that is."

Red chuckled. "Reckon you're right. Now tell me what happened."

Olerud started with Tenery slipping into his storeroom, then told McClain how he'd warned Tenery that an ambush had been set for him; that Tenery had taken a couple chunks of lead and had killed the two Rourk riders. Then he told him how they'd gotten rid of the bodies. "Tenery's gonna get the blame for the whole thing when them horses get out to the Circle-R."

McClain nodded. "Based on what he's done before, I figger it like you. He's done caused that bunch a whole heap o' trouble an' reckon he's gonna keep on doing it 'til they kill 'im, or he wipes all o' them out." He shook his head. "Don't figger he's gonna stay that lucky."

Hans stared straight on into Red's eyes. "It ever occur to you that the results of what he's doin' ain't luck?" He chomped down hard on his tobacco, then nodded. "Tell you how I got it figgered, McClain. That boy's a fightin' man like damned few this or any other country ever seen."

Red chuckled. "Hear tell the Army sent 'im to Washington an' put 'im behind a desk an' he jest flat couldn't stand it. He requested to be sent back out here to the West — they refused, an' 'cause o' that they lost themselves a future general.

"He graduated from that school at West Point 'bout as high as any who ever went there. His pa went to the same school, but fought for the South durin' the War 'Tween the States." He frowned and shook his head. "Figgerin' that's the truth, wonder how he ever got into West Point?"

Hans, looking pretty smug, pulled the corner of his mouth to the side. "Tell you how he done it, Red: when the railroad wuz

pushin' West, Bill's pa, Chance Tenery" —
he nodded — "yeah, you've heard of him.
He's a fightin' man too. Anyway, his pa went
to work for General Dodge, the man who
bossed the buildin' of the railroad. Chance
Tenery ended up marryin' the general's
niece; so when he asked the general to get
his son appointed to the military academy,
he done it. *That's* how Bill Tenery got to
West Point."

McClain shook his head. "Dang! Things
shore do work in funny ways. So Bill's the
son o' *that* Tenery." He pinned Olerud with
a questioning look. "How you know all
this?"

Hans chewed on his tobacco a couple of
times, looking for the spittoon in the corner.
He cut loose, hitting it dead center.

"You gonna miss that there bucket one o'
these days, *then* you gonna clean up the
mess."

"Ain't missed yet, clean it up when I do."
Hans laughed. Then he said in a serious
tone, "You wonder how I know all this? Well
I'm gonna tell ya. I knowed who that boy
wuz soon's I heared his name. Ain't told
nobody 'til now; fact is, never had reason to
do so 'til you asked me 'bout 'im." He
grinned. "Tell ya somethin' else: I worked
fer 'is pa there on the railroad, helpin' 'im

build bridges, trestles an' culverts." He nonchalantly puckered his lips and spat toward the spittoon again.

McClain rolled his eyes toward the ceiling. "Makes me feel better knowin' all this, but bein' the best fightin' man in the world ain't gonna steer a chunk o' lead away from 'im."

Olerud nodded. "That's why we gotta help 'im any chance we get."

"I agree, old friend. We gotta do that, an' still not cause the people o' this town any trouble."

The liveryman nodded. "We got two big problems, Red. Reckon we just gotta do what we think's best."

Red nodded.

Rufus Bent watched Penny walk to the window and again pull the curtains aside. She looked up the trail. Her shoulders slumped. He frowned, a pang shooting through his chest. He wished there was something he could do to make his *almost* daughter stop worrying about that young'un, then he realized that he worried about as much as she did. He tried to settle her feelings anyway. "Little girl, that young man's gonna be all right. Fact is, I figger Andy's done found 'im an' they decided to stay in town 'til daylight. They'll be along soon's Brothers can get that hardheaded young man on the trail. Now you quit worryin' that pretty head o' yours."

"Oh, Rufus, you say that but I know you too well. You're as much worried as I am."

"Well heck, honey, if I'm gonna worry, they ain't any need for both of us to do it. Come on over here to the table an' let me pour you a cup o' coffee."

When seated with a steaming cup in front of her, she pinned Bent with a questioning look. "Rufe, you think we oughta tell Bill what Rourk's bunch is doin' to the townsfolks? Think we should tell 'im what he's doin' to us also?"

The old foreman frowned, obviously giving her question a lot of thought. Finally, he shook his head. "Don't think we oughta do either one. We tell 'im an' it's gonna make 'im madder'n hell — might even cause 'im to go in town an' get 'imself shot to pieces agin."

"Oh. Rufe, I didn't think of that." She shook her head. "We won't tell him. Let's see what has happened in town. Maybe then we can figure what to do."

They talked deep into the night. Around two o'clock Bent threw a question at her she had wondered about herself. "Penny, know how you feel 'bout that boy. What you gonna do when he figures he's gotten even with Rourk's bunch an' packs his bedroll and rides off?"

Penny stared into his eyes a long moment. "Well, Rufe, if he does that, I figure I'll just pack my own bedroll an' follow him 'til he pays some attention to me."

Bent looked at her a moment and finally let his lips crinkle at the corners, then a laugh erupted from the bottom of his chest. When he could stop laughing, he wiped tears from his eyes, shaking his head, and said, "Damned if don't b'lieve you'd do exactly that."

Never looking away from him, or smiling, she shrugged. "Believe it, Rufe. There ain't many men who come this way. But one came this way that if I could have chosen, he's the one I would have picked."

Rufus twisted his mouth to the side. "Little one, I guarantee you I won't stand in yore way. I like that boy mighty good." He took a sip of his coffee, then cocked his head, obviously listening. He looked at Penny. "Wonder who'd be drivin' a wagon around this country in the cold this time o' night?"

Penny replied, "Don't know, but I'll bet my saddle whoever it is has a whole bunch o' trouble behind them, otherwise they'd have made camp or stayed in town." She stood. "Better go see what we can do to help."

As soon as Rufus opened the door, Brothers reined to a stop in front of him and Penny, but she knew they had trouble as soon as she recognized the two horses tied to the buckboard's tailgate. She ran to the wagon's side, then yelled over her shoulder, "Rufe, get some of the boys out here; Bill's got 'imself hurt again." Without waiting for anyone to help, she climbed to the bed.

Before she could ask Brothers what had happened, Tenery growled from beneath a pile of blankets, "Don't ever hitch a ride with that cowboy sittin' atop that seat. Know danged well he hit every bump an' rut in the trail on purpose. Know he did it on account of you sendin' 'im in to check on me."

"Oh, Bill, what happened? Where're you hurt?"

"Shot. Shoulder an' leg. Better let Rufe take care o' me; Olerud slit my jeans from waist to ankle."

"Bill Tenery, I don't care if he took them slam off of you. Soon's the boys get you in the house, I'm gonna see how bad you're hurt, then *I'm* gonna take care of you."

"Olerud already did a mighty good job of cleanin' an' dressin' each hole in me. All I need right now is a cup of hot coffee with a wee mite o' whisky to help me thaw out. Better pour Andy a pretty stiff drink at the same time." He rolled to his side, groaned and pushed himself to sit.

"Gotta get these blankets back to Olerud soon's I'm able to ride again. Gotta get his buckboard back to him too."

"You let me worry 'bout that. As soon as we get you taken care of I want to know what happened."

Tenery nodded. "Just get me in outta this cold an' I'll tell you the story."

It took only a few minutes to get him in and settled on blankets by the fire. He looked around the room and said, "Danged if I don't b'lieve I've been right in this same place before." He shook his head and grinned. "Must've been dreamin'."

"Bill Tenery, you know you weren't dreamin'. You get yourself shot up again an' I'm gonna have Rufus take you to the bunkhouse, and there you'll stay."

He slanted his look to Bent. "You gonna let 'er mistreat me like that, Rufe? Dang, looks like I've worn out my welcome already."

"Boy, you ain't never gonna wear out yore

159

welcome 'round here. It's jest that you cause the little missy so much worry you gonna cause her hair to turn white."

This gave Tenery the opening to say what he'd thought to say while lying in Olerud's room. He stared into Penny's worried eyes. "Rufus, I don't care what color her hair turns; she'd still be the most beautiful woman I've ever seen."

Her face turned a pretty pink. Then, not breaking her gaze, her face sober, she said, "That's the second time you said that, cowboy. Seems to me you'd have found some way of showin' the way you think by now."

Tenery knew his face had turned red from the feel of the heat. He broke his gaze from hers and looked at Bent, then the three or four men from the bunkhouse. "Reckon I been thinkin' 'bout that, but here with all these men standin' round, grinnin' like mules eatin' briars, don't reckon I'm gonna say anything more. Now if you'll get me a cup of coffee, spiked pretty stiff with whisky, I'll let Bent take a look at how good a job Olerud did on cleanin' me up an' dressin' these holes in me. After that, I'll tell y'all what happened in town."

They listened and drank coffee while he told them what had happened.

Finally, Hank glanced toward the front window. "Don't know 'bout y'all, but I figger Bent's gonna be findin' things fer us to do soon's we eat breakfast. It's done got daylight an' ain't none o' us had a wink o' sleep."

Penny pulled her gaze from Bill to her crew. "Oh my goodness. You men go to your bunks. I'll take care of Bill." Her look shifted back to Tenery. He had closed his eyes and obviously slept.

Bent argued with her a moment that he'd take care of the ex-soldier, but she'd have none of it. Bent and the crew headed for the bunkhouse.

Gretchen Thoreson pulled her chair closer to the stove. She frowned, wondering what she'd do if word got around that she'd been seeing Rourk. She valued her good name, and through loneliness had *almost* allowed herself to ruin it. She thought of Tenery and judged that he would honor his word, that he wouldn't say anything — but Rourk or one of his men might.

Her thoughts turned to Penelope Horn, the only woman in or close to town who was young enough to understand her feelings. She and Penny had been good friends until Cord had taken over the Circle-R. She wondered if she could rekindle their friendship. She bit her lower lip until she realized she had made it sore.

She had no idea what she could do. Should she go to Penny and tell her of the awful mistake she'd almost made? Would her friend turn her back on her? Would she even understand how a woman felt after having her man close to her at night, and then abruptly losing the intimacy of touch, sound, feeling, talk? She thought about whether Penny had ever had feelings or thoughts about the relationship a married couple had with each other. Would Penny understand?

Rourk and his crew passed a bottle around until it was empty, then got another from the case and continued drinking. The Circle-R owner only sipped at the bottle each time it came to him. He studied his men, thinking if he got them drunk enough he might talk them into going to town and doing what he'd suggested — turn the town upside down in hopes of finding Tenery. The likelihood some of them might get killed didn't bother him. He intended to stay behind. Besides, he had to think of something that would force Penelope Horn to sell her ranch, or abandon it. He needed time away from his crew; time to think, plan, plot. He stared at the drunken lot lying around the room and disgust invaded him. They'd never amount to anything, all they worried about was where they could get the next woman, or another bottle.

His mind turned back to Penelope Horn and her ranch.

He wondered if he could, in some way, incite the Crow to attack the ranch; that is, if they could get around Elkhorn without bringing the townspeople out in force to fight them. He shook his head. That wouldn't work. If he got the Crow riled up, they'd attack *all* whites. He shivered. He might be killed, wounded or captured in such a situation.

He didn't like this desolate country, but it was the quickest way to acquire what he wanted — money. The Saddle Horn along with the Circle-R would be a prize plum that he might sell for enough to make him financially independent. That was the only reason he'd come out here. These stupid hicks — farmers, ranchers, miners — could never match wits with a man who had spent his life outthinking others.

His thinking went to the Indian tribes that had been wiped out with smallpox. He shook his head; there was no way to introduce the disease without jeopardizing himself. That plan wouldn't work either.

He could take his men to the Saddle Horn headquarters and wipe out all on the place. No. He realized he could not command the loyalty of even one of his men now, especially since they would not gain one red cent from such an act.

Besides, that girl, or rather, her father, had gathered fighting men to the ranch — and they would be loyal. Every one of her men, according to the way he'd heard it, had fought beside Roland Horn in the Civil War, had come out here with him, then stayed. Rourk shook his head. He had not one man to whom he could attribute that degree of loyalty or bravery. He took another drink, this time a healthy couple of swallows. To hell with it; he'd join his men in their stupor.

Penny sat in her rocking chair only a few feet from the sleeping ex-soldier. She stared at him, watching the rise and fall of his chest, bare except for the bandages swathing his shoulder. If giving the ranch to Rourk and moving away was an option, she'd do it, but that wouldn't work for several reasons. First, she couldn't do that to the men who'd helped raise her. Second, Tenery was fighting his own private war with the Easterner. When they'd attacked him on his arrival in Elkhorn they'd declared war on him — in his mind. Third, if she left, she'd be abandoning the people she loved — the townspeople. She had no idea why they had not banded together to fight Rourk. It wasn't like them to meekly accept whatever he was doing, but she knew when she found out what the reason was, it would make sense.

Tenery stirred, moaned and turned to his back. Penny hurried to his side, placed the palm of her hand on his brow and nodded; not feverish. His eyes opened. He stared at the ceiling a moment then cut his eyes toward her. "I been asleep long?"

She shook her head. "Only long enough to help your wounds mend." She stood. "Lie still and I'll get you a cup of coffee; then I'll feed you."

"No, you won't feed me. I'm not a baby." He smiled. "If I was a baby I don't think I'd be lying here thinkin' what a beautiful woman you are." He moved his eyes enough to look around the room. "The men all in the bunkhouse?"

She nodded. "I ran them off. They didn't get a wink of sleep last night. They need the rest. Why are you askin'?"

"I have a few things I want to say an' don't

165

figure it's anybody's business but yours an' mine."

She looked into his eyes, hoping the things he had to say were the things she'd wanted to hear since first seeing him.

"Penny, this is harder than I thought it would be. I'm not used to saying things like this; fact is, I never said them — to anyone."

She had been holding her breath; it exploded from her lungs. "Well, for goodness' sake, say whatever it is you want to say. I won't bite — promise."

His face turned a bright red; she could see it through his sun-and-wind-darkened face. "Well, what I been wantin' to say is, I've told you twice now how beautiful I think you are. I reckon I've seen a few women I thought that about." He shrugged. "None could compare with you."

Her breath softened to small gasps. She wanted to drag the words from him, words she ached to hear. "Thank you, Bill. Did you have anything else you wanted to say?"

He nodded. "Yes'm, reckon I want to say I think you're pretty all the way through, think you're the woman I want to —"

The door squeaked on its hinges. Rufus poked his head in. "Anybody want some coffee? Jest made it fresh."

The "damn" that forced its way from

Penny was unintended, but said it all.

Rufus glanced from one to the other of them. "I come in at the wrong time?"

Tenery stared at him a long moment. "Bent, you're the damnedest, most inappropriate critter I reckon I ever met." He looked at Penny. "Reckon I won't let what I was gonna say rest. It's somethin' I gotta say no matter what you think of it." He looked at Rufus. "How 'bout pourin' me a cup o' that mud and hit it with a splash of your whisky?"

Penny gave Bent a hard look. "Do the same for me, Rufus. Maybe it'll make me feel better."

Bent nodded. "Reckon I did come in at the wrong time. I'll come back later."

"Reckon I'll have plenty of time to have my say 'fore I get well from these holes in me." He looked at Penny and grimaced. "Talk to you later."

Penny gave him a straight on look. "*That* is a promise I guarantee you you'll keep."

Bent pushed his way inside, carrying a tray with three cups and the coffeepot, along with the jug of whisky.

Gretchen pulled a chair to the window and sat staring out at the bleak, gray snow. She swept the town with a glance. The only people remaining in this world that she knew and loved were in those weathered clapboard buildings — only now did she look at them and think of those who were inside. Her selfishness had caused her to cling to thoughts of Rourk. She shook her head. She would seek out Penny, see if she could help her understand her actions, even though she thought no one knew of her indiscretion. She had admitted to herself her foolishness, now she wanted to explain what she'd almost done and seek understanding. She glanced along the snow-laden trail once again. Rourk and two of his men were entering the far end of the rutted street.

She watched until they reined in at the hitch rail in front of the Red Dog Saloon. From where she sat, the way they swung from their saddles and staggered after stepping to the boardwalk indicated to her that they already had taken on more alcohol than would allow for good thinking. She hoped Rourk would not come here after drinking more. Her hope was in vain.

She sat there until the gray gloom of day turned to snow-lit darkness. She stood, realizing she'd not eaten since the day before. She'd been so wrapped up in her problem, one she'd brought on herself, that she'd forgotten to prepare anything to eat. She went to the kitchen and put wood on the coals.

Cord Rourk stood at the bar. He scanned the men standing along its length; then looked at McClain. From Red, he twisted to look at a back table where his two men sat. Not a damned one of them gave a happy hoot in hell what happened to him. He sneered to himself. He didn't care anything about them either; them or anybody else. Cord Rourk was the only thing in this world of import to Cord Rourk. The rest of humanity could fry in hell as far as he was concerned. He knocked back his drink and held his glass out for another, downed it.

His thoughts turned to Gretchen. He wanted her. He'd not been able to get her in his bed, and he intended to do just that. He didn't give a thought to her as anything but a way of satisfying his physical hunger. He'd go see why she'd left his ranch in such a huff. He ordered and downed another drink, paid what he owed and headed for Gretchen's bakeshop.

When he tried the door, it failed to yield to his pull. He knocked, and waited. After a few moments, Gretchen's voice behind the locked door said she was closed for the day. "Don't give a damn 'bout you bein' closed. It's me, Cord; open up."

"You're drunk. I don't want to see you like that. In fact, I don't want to see you in any shape, at any time. Go away."

Hot blood rushed to his head. Who the hell was this hussy to talk to *him, Cord Rourk,* like that? He drew back his foot to kick at the door, then dropped it back to the boardwalk. Maybe he could sweet talk her. "Aw c'mon, I only had a couple drinks. I need to talk to you. Talk 'bout us. What I can do for you."

"There's nothing you could ever do for me. Now go away."

He thought to break through the door and beat her highfalutin butt 'til it was raw. Then through the whisky fog in his brain he realized where he was: in the middle of town — a Western town. No matter that he'd kept the town under tight control. The way things stood, no one could pin any of his men's activities on him. *But,* if he touched a woman, every man in this squalid little settlement would come after him with guns. He stood there a few moments, still pondering whether to force his way in, then thought better of that idea and turned his steps back toward the saloon. He needed a drink — a lot of drinks. McClain's joint had no women, but it had whisky — enough of it to kill the cravings for a soft body in bed beside him.

When he unsteadily walked through the door, Red noted the red face that the weather could have caused, but the weather would not cause the swollen arteries in Rourk's neck and forehead. Only anger would do that.

McClain wondered what had put a burr under the city man's saddle. He opened his mouth to ask, then clamped his jaws together. He didn't care what caused Rourk's anger as long as it didn't cause him to vent his feelings on any of the townspeople. He had a gut full of the man and the trash he'd brought into town with him.

He thought to see if he could gather the men of the town together and run the Rourk bunch out of town. He pondered that idea a moment, then shook his head. He'd get friends killed; men with families. He couldn't do that. Another idea entered his mind; one as repugnant as his first thought. Why not let Tenery get well and take care of a few more of them? He shook his head; the boy had already suffered enough at the hands of the city bunch.

Rourk broke into his thoughts, "Gimme a

bottle, gonna get drunk, drunker'n hell."

McClain reached for a bottle, then drew his hand back. "You've had enough, Rourk. Any more and in your frame of mind you're gonna go lookin' for trouble."

"Don't need a damned dumb bartender to wet-nurse me. Gimme a bottle!"

McClain lowered his hand to the underside of the bar. His fingers curled around the walnut stock of the twelve-gauge Greener he kept there for occasions such as this. He'd never, since he opened the doors of his business for the first time, thought he'd ever need to point it at a man. He knew better now.

He picked the shotgun up. "Dumb as you think I am, I learned how to use this lil old scattergun a long time ago. Don't think I've fergot how." He waved the barrels toward the Easterner's friends sitting at the back of the room. "You go on back there, sit down an' don't cause me any trouble, otherwise I'm gonna see can I cut you in two with this. I hear tell if a man takes both barrels in his gut he'll jest flat come apart in the middle."

Rourk took in the twin barrels staring at him and turned white, then a sickly grayish color. The hand he'd held out to take the bottle he'd ordered shook like an aspen leaf in a strong wind. Without a word he turned and stepped toward the back.

He said over his shoulder, "McClain, you just made the biggest mistake of your life."

6

Rourk snatched a chair away from the table and plopped himself into it, and picked up the bottle from the middle of the table. The cork had been pulled, so he put the jug to his mouth and swallowed until he needed breath. He slammed the bottle to the table, gasping, then swept the two men sitting there with a hard look. "Get up there to the bar, drag that redheaded bastard out to the middle of the floor an' beat the livin' hell outta him."

Ben McCall stared at Cord then shifted his eyes to look at Tom Lease. Lease gave him a slight shake of the head. McCall's lips wrinkled into a smile, but his eyes remained cold as the winter wind. "You want that man's butt kicked, do it yourself. He ain't done nothin' to either one of us."

"W-w-what do you mean? I told you what to do — now get it done."

Lease pinned the suave city man with a

look that couldn't be mistaken. "Tell you how it is in case it didn't enter your skull out there at the ranch. You ain't givin' any of us orders." He shook his head. "By that, I mean we're gonna still run our little game; you've got your things to do, we're all still gonna make money outta it — *but you ain't callin' the shots no more.*"

Rourk stared at Lease. He'd misjudged the man; in fact, thinking back to the scene at his ranch, he realized he'd misjudged the entire bunch he'd gathered in the East to help him set this rotten little town on its heels. He felt his dream of owning the town as well as the Saddle Horn Ranch slipping away. He'd better soften his approach for a while until he could come up with a plan that would give him control of his men again — fear was the only thing he knew would rein them in. He dropped his gaze from the hard look Lease held him with. "Aw hell, reckon I'm mad at the world. That bastard over yonder behind the bar just bucked me usin' a scattergun. Ain't gonna let 'im get away with that." He shook his head. "Nope, nobody bucks Cord Rourk an' gets away with it."

His whisky-fogged mind turned to planning how to bring fear to those he'd gathered around him. Even drunk he realized he needed a clear head to tackle *that* problem. He sat there feeling the stares of the two men, stares which had only hatred in them. To hell with them. His thoughts again turned to Gretchen. He wanted her. He'd have her. *Now!*

Gretchen sat at the table by the window. She ate slowly, not aware she was chewing every bite until it was liquid. Movement at the door of the saloon drew her attention. Rourk emerged, hung onto the door a moment, then staggered to the edge of the boardwalk, where he fell off. He stayed on his hands and knees for a few moments, shaking his head, then pushed to his feet and angled across the street. He weaved from side to side — a couple of feet with each step — heading toward the bakery.

Gretchen watched a moment, dropped her fork onto her plate and went behind the counter. A Winchester .44 and a twelve-gauge Greener hung from pegs on the wall at eye level. She pulled the shotgun down, broke the action, checked to make certain both barrels held a shell. Snapping the action closed, she went to the door. She knew she didn't have to be real accurate to hit whatever she pointed it at. She had only a few moments to wait.

"Open this damned door or I'll kick it open!" Rourk's slurred words were clear enough to show anger, and loud enough to attract the attention of anyone walking along the frozen street. But no one walked the street in this weather.

Gretchen flicked her gaze up and down the trail hoping to see someone, anyone, come from one of the stores. Empty. Her stomach churned. She wondered if she could pull the trigger on another human being. But that thing standing outside her door was no human. Cord Rourk was an animal. Her hands shook. Her finger poked through the trigger guard seemed like a thing with its own mind, it shook so hard. She swallowed to rid her throat of the bitter bile that bubbled there.

"Rourk, you kick that door even once an' I'll pull both triggers on this shotgun I'm holdin'." Her voice quavered such that she wondered if he'd understood her.

Rourk laughed, a nasty sound deep in his throat. "You don't have the guts to unload that scattergun at me. Now open the damned door."

She brushed her thumb across both hammers, making sure they were eared back. Abruptly, she calmed, stopped shaking. Her finger on the triggers tensed. She knew she'd pull the triggers if he put a foot against her front door.

Then she wondered about the window — would he think to break it? She wanted to know where he stood outside of the door; if she fired she wanted to make certain she put the shots where they'd do the most damage.

She worked her way to the side of the window to locate him. He stood directly in front of the door, his right hand ready to open it. She waited.

Even though she was expecting it, the jarring sound of his boot hitting the door caused her to jump backward — but at the same time she pulled both triggers of the Greener.

A hole the size of a dinner plate opened in the lower panel. Simultaneous with the appearance of the hole a moan and a loud curse came at her. She broke the action, removed the spent shells from the barrel and shoved in two more. Only then did she slide back to the window and peep out.

Rourk lay on the boardwalk, both legs pouring blood from his thighs. *Now* there were people on the street. It seemed to her they came from the doorway of every store. She pulled a chair to the middle of the floor in front of her door and sat.

The first voice she recognized was that of Trent Cody. "Miz Gretchen, you all right?"

She went to the door, lifted the two-by-four length of wood that barred it from its rack and pulled the door open. "Yes, Mr. Cody, I'm just fine." She glanced at Rourk. Her voice calm, still holding the shotgun, she asked, "He gonna die?"

Cody stared at her a moment, then nodded. "Figger if we don't get 'im to the doctor right soon he ain't gonna make it."

Still in that deadly calm voice, she said, "Let 'im bleed to death."

It was then that Red McClain pushed through the people gathered there. "Naw now, Miz Gretchen, you don't want ta have that on yore mind the rest o' yore life." Red swept the crowd with a searching look. "Don't reckon the doc's showed up yet." He looked at Hans Olerud. "See can you stop that bleedin', Hans. Better not move 'im 'til we get it stopped. Cain't send 'im back to his ranch until he mends some, then we'll have some o' his men take 'im back out there."

Suddenly the calm left Gretchen and she shook and trembled such that she couldn't stop.

McClain had seen reactions like this before, many times. He looked at Cody.

"Run over to my place an' bring me one o' them jugs o' good whisky. This lady's gone into shock, she's pale as a fresh-washed bed-sheet."

Making sure Trent responded to his order, Red went to Gretchen and pulled the Greener from her hands. He had to uncurl each finger from the stock and then gently but carefully pull her finger from the trigger guard. Holding the shotgun in his left hand, he pulled her to her feet and guided her to the rocker she always sat in when there were no customers. He wet a dish towel in the pitcher and bathed her forehead until Trent Cody pushed his way through the crowd.

Red took the bottle from him and poured a stiff shot, about two fingers in a water glass, then held the glass to her lips. She coughed, then raised her face to Red's. "Gotta tell somebody why I did this. Ain't proud of it, but I gotta tell it — the reason for my doin' it." She nodded. "B'lieve you or Hans are the only ones in this town who would understand why I did it."

He shook his head. "Ma'am, we gonna let that old dog lie 'til we take care o' Rourk, *and* until you get settled down."

Gretchen stared at him a moment, then nodded. It was then that Olerud said they could move Rourk to the hotel.

■ ■ ■ ■

Penny had refused to let Tenery move to the bunkhouse. She insisted that if she let him move he'd take on chores that would start him bleeding. She would make sure he healed properly before allowing him to do anything.

He was certain she had no idea what being close to her every waking minute of every day did to him. He'd had time alone with her but never got the courage to tell her what he was about to say when Rufus barged in that night. Now, they sat across the breakfast table from each other, each with a full cup of coffee.

Penny took a sip and looked over the rim of her cup at him. "Bill, why are you looking for a fight every time you see one of Rourk's men?"

"Not lookin' for a fight with 'em. They always bring it to me — then I *have* to take 'em on. Wish they'd leave me alone, but then I wouldn't have any idea why the townsfolk seem afraid of 'em. Not a man there that I figure doesn't have guts enough to buck 'im." He shook his head. "Can't figure it out, Penny, an' I've given it a lot o' thought." He gave her a straight-on look. "I think you know what's goin' on. Why can't you tell me?"

She held his gaze a moment, then lowered her eyes to stare into her cup. "Bill, I really don't know, but I'll tell you this: those people in there aren't cowards — not a single one of them. They aren't fightin' 'im or his bunch for a very good reason. My reason is simple: He wants my ranch an' I believe he'll do anything to get it. If I could get proof of the things he's done I'd write Washington and try to get a U.S. marshal out here." She pulled her shoulders up around her neck. "But, Bill, I ain't got a shred o' proof to give a lawman."

Tenery locked her in a no-nonsense look. "Gonna tell you how it is, ma'am. I'm not a lawman; we're a long ride to anywhere where we might find one, an' by the time a letter could bring the law in here I think it might be too late for the town — and for you."

He took a sip of coffee. "So far, I've responded to attacks on me, haven't tried to dodge any o' those city slickers, even when I might of been able to avoid a fight; figured if they wanted to bring it to me I'd take care of it. So far it's been my fight." He shook his head. "That's not true anymore. Now it's *our* fight."

Penny leaned toward him, a scared look on her face and in her eyes. "Oh, Bill, I won't let you take on my fight. You've already been terribly hurt by those men. I — I couldn't stand it if you got hurt again."

He studied the look she gave him. Was it a look of caring? Was she scared for herself, or her men, or was she genuinely afraid for *him?*

He knew he'd been piercing her with a look he'd give a soldier on the battlefield. He softened his gaze. "Penny, unless you run me off, you won't be able to stop me." He lowered his gaze, took another swallow of coffee, then his voice so soft and low he wondered if she could hear him, he said, "You see, I'll be fighting for *you.* Don't have any reason to believe you'd care 'bout me, but I care 'bout *you,* a whole helluva lot." He sat back in his chair. "Not gonna ask how you feel about me — not now. Gonna take care o' this job I've cut out for myself first."

She sat there, her eyes wide. She opened her mouth as though to say something, but no words came out.

Aw hell, he shouldn't have told her about his feelings without at least courting her first, but dammit, he reckoned he'd done this like everything else he did — just bulled into it headfirst, that was the way his adopted father, Chance Tenery, had taught him. "Aw, Penny, I shoulda waited to tell you."

She stood, her eyes still wide and staring at him. She walked around the table, leaned over and wrapped his shoulders in her arms. "Cowboy, you just saved me from makin' a hussy outta myself. I already told Rufus I was gonna act against the way he and Ma and Pa raised me. Told 'im I was gonna chase you down the trail to say how I felt if you didn't say anything first." She leaned over and kissed his cheek. "If you'll stand an' turn around we could make our first kiss one to remember."

She didn't have to say that twice; Tenery held her in a bear hug while he smothered her eyes, cheeks and lips with his.

The hinges on the back door squeaked. Rufus Bent stepped into the room. "Well, hot dammit, looks like I waited jest right this time!"

Red McClain and Hans Olerud told Trent Cody to see that Rourk got settled into a hotel room, that they would stay and see that Gretchen settled down.

Cody gave them a hard stare. "Don't give a damn if Rourk bleeds to death, but I'm

184

here to tell ya, I want Miz Thoreson to not feel any shame for what she done. Know she must have had a good reason for doin' it."

Red nodded. "Know you're right, old friend. Me an' Hans'll stay here 'til she calms down. Don't know why she fired on 'im, but that's her business."

Gretchen waited until the townspeople cleared out, then she looked at the two men who had stayed with her. "Want ta tell you gentlemen what brought this whole thing on, shamed of it, but I'll tell ya the truth of it."

Red shook his head. "Ma'am, you don't owe us no explanation. Knowin' him, an' knowin' you, I reckon anythin' you'd say would make me b'lieve you had every right to shoot 'im. 'Sides that, he wuz drunker'n a skunk when he left my place."

Olerud fidgeted a moment, then looked at McClain. "Red, you an' Miz Thoreson don't mind, figger I'll head on back to the livery." He shuffled his feet again. "Reckon I ain't used to dealin' with no feeemale folks what's all upset like she is."

Red stared at Olerud a moment. "You ain't much of a friend, Olerud. You gonna leave me to see can I calm Miz Thoreson down?"

Olerud nodded, slowly. "Yep, McClain, reckon that's 'zackly what I'm gonna do." He pulled the door toward him and hurried out into the cold.

Red stared at the door a moment, then turned his look on Gretchen. "Ma'am, reckon after I git you all calmed down I better get that door patched up so you won't freeze in here tonight."

"Mr. McClain, if you'd just nail a board or two over that hole I'd surely be obliged to you. I ain't very good at fixin' things."

Red noticed her cheeks had color in them again. "Miz Thoreson, I'm gonna fix that door like it oughta be fixed, don't reckon I could sleep very well if I thought 'bout you lyin' over here freezin'."

"Sir, I'd be obliged if you listen to what I got to say. Figure while I've got the nerve I better say it. I wait for you to fix that door I might lose what gumption I got."

He pulled a chair over in front of her. "All right. Seems like what you gotta say is mighty important to you so I'll listen."

She lowered her eyes to stare at her tightly clasped hands resting in her lap, then she looked at him straight on and stood. "I'll pour us a cup o' coffee, get you a few doughnuts, then I'll tell you."

Red realized she took this way of pulling

herself together, settling her nerves. He waited.

She pulled over a stool, put his coffee on it along with a plate full of doughnuts, then again sat in her rocker. "Tell you, Mr. McClain, you folk're treatin' me like a lady. I ain't an' you'll b'lieve me when I get through talkin' to you."

Red shook his head. "Ma'am, ain't nothin' you can say gonna change my mind 'bout you bein' a lady."

"Listen to me first, then tell me them words."

He nodded. "Go ahead."

She started with how she felt after her husband got killed. She shook her head. "Gonna sound like I'm makin' excuses, but I ain't. Jest want ta tell ya what I done an' why."

She told him about practically throwing herself at Cord Rourk; about being at his ranch when Tenery attacked the Eastern bunch; the way Rourk acted that brought her to her senses before she did anything to drag her morals in the dirt. She gave him a straight-on look. "Mr. McClain, after I lost my husband I knew loneliness like I never dreamed existed, so almost I let myself do things no lady would ever do." She shrugged. "Gonna say it again; I ain't makin' excuses. I jest want ta tell you; a woman who'd almost do what I almost done ain't no lady."

Red took a bite of doughnut, followed it with a swallow of coffee, then pinned her with a firm look. "Miz Gretchen, you're a lady far as I'm concerned, an' if the whole town knew what I know now, they'd say it the same way I'm sayin' it."

Gretchen blinked to try and hide the tears, and forced a smile. "That's mighty kind o' you. Somehow it seems important that you think well of me."

Red grinned. "Ma'am, reckon if that's all you gotta worry 'bout you ain't got a worry in the world. Tell you somethin' else, Miz Gretchen, what you jest finished telling me, ain't nobody in this town gonna ever know. You ain't got a thing to be ashamed of. I figger they ain't a spankin' new widow woman in the country who would feel or maybe do any different than you done."

He stuffed the last half of doughnut in his mouth, looked at the hole in the door and said, "Reckon I better get busy an' get yore door fixed or you gonna be mighty cold tonight."

Red headed for Trent Cody's store. He thought he'd find a new door to fit Gretchen's place.

■ ■ ■ ■

Penny looked at Tenery, her cheeks hot, and knew that anything she said to try and throw Rufus' thoughts off of what was obvious would be useless. So she shrugged, looked him in the eye and said, "Well, Rufe, reckon Bill just saved me from makin' a hussy outta myself. Ain't gonna have to chase 'im down the trail after all . . ."

Thinking to avoid causing Penny any more embarrassment, Tenery pulled his mouth to the side in an exaggerated grimace. "Gotta tell ya, Rufus, you got the damndest sense o' timing of any person I have ever seen. Now you just turn your back and let me be the cause of Penny's cheeks turning an even brighter red than they already are."

Bent, obviously as embarrassed as Penny, turned and grabbed the doorknob. "Mighty sorry, young'uns." He pulled the door toward him.

"Aw hell, Rufe, come on in, pull up a chair, we'll have a cup of coffee while I try to find out how you feel 'bout your almost daughter an' me carin' 'bout each other."

"Wh-why, hell, young'un, reckon if I'd of picked somebody myself, don't reckon I could of done better."

Penny put another cup on the table, then pinned Tenery with an "I told you so" look. Then, while still looking at Bill, she said, "Rufus, what brought this on was, Bill said he was gonna take up our fight with Rourk. I told 'im as how I thought it'd kill me if he got hurt again — he didn't let me finish. He told me he cared for me a mighty lot." She picked up the coffeepot and poured them each a full cup.

"Well dammit, reckon this calls for a pretty good slosh o' whisky in our coffee."

Tenery frowned at the old man. "Bent, reckon I'm gonna have to buy you a full jug next time I'm in town. Might save you bustin' in on Penny an' me next time I take 'er into my arms."

Rufus stared at the tall soldier and growled, "Aw hell." Penny and Tenery guffawed.

Without being asked, Bent opened the cabinet door, pulled the bottle off the top shelf, put it in the middle of the table and sat. "Reckon we gonna talk 'bout you takin' on our fight, young'un." He splashed a bit of whisky into each cup, then shook his head. "You ain't takin' on our fight. Ain't gonna watch my Penny die a slow death every time you take a bullet."

Penny looked at Tenery. "Bill, I'm not the

190

only one at this table who dies a little bit every time you get hurt. Rufe'll admit to feelin' mighty strong 'bout you too." Her face again glowed a bright pink. " 'Course, his feelin's are a bit different than mine."

"Damn, I surely do hope so, ma'am. Don't think I could stand to huggin' an' kissin' that old man."

Bent and Penny looked at each other a moment, then laughed until tears came to their eyes.

McClain, despite vowing to fix Gretchen's door as good as new, found that Cody didn't have the materials in stock to get the job done the way he wanted. He patched it such as to make do until the order he placed could arrive. When finished, he looked at her a moment. "Sorry I couldn't get it fixed like I wanted to, but I'll guarantee you soon's the stuff comes in I'll git the job done right."

She handed him a cup of coffee. "Sit. Mr. McClain, don't know why you're bein' so nice to me, but I want you to know how much I appreciate it."

"Aw pshaw, ma'am, wasn't much, fact is, I figure you gonna be a mite chilly in here tonight." He took a sip of coffee, glanced at the window and nodded. "Now looka there, it's done got night. You ain't had a chance to fix supper so why don't you come to the café with me an' we'll see what they got to eat tonight?"

"Mr. McClain, if you ain't in a big hurry to eat, reckon I'm gonna fix you some supper right here."

Red opened his mouth to refuse her invitation, then thought that maybe it would be a good idea for her to have someone to do for until she settled down more. Being alone after what she had been through might not be a good idea. He nodded. "Why, ma'am, reckon I ain't had a home-cooked meal in a mighty long time. You can put up with me for a little longer I shore would enjoy havin' supper with you if you figure I won't be in the way."

"You get in the way, I'll just shoo you aside 'til I get things done."

After they'd eaten, Red helped clean up. He offered to spread a pallet in the front bakery if she felt nervous after all that had happened. She assured him that she was all right, so he went back to his saloon. Once there, he poured himself a full glass of whisky and sat behind the bar staring into its depths.

Damn but it had been good sitting there talking to a pretty woman after a meal as good as any he'd ever eaten. He shook his head. He'd sure like to see if she'd let him take her to the café for dinner sometime soon, but that might seem to her that he had not believed her version of what had happened out at Rourk's ranch. Nope. He'd better wait a while before he asked her to have dinner with him.

He picked up his drink and took a small swallow. His mind shifted to the happenings of the day. Was it time the townspeople arched their backs and bucked the Rourk outfit? Could they do it without getting wiped out by the Eastern thugs? He pondered that until a man off one of the ranches came in and ordered a drink while still brushing snow from his shoulders.

While Red had the bottle tilted over the cowboy's glass, Olerud came in. "Dang, McClain, figgered you wuz gonna spend the rest o' yore life over yonder at the widder woman's place. I done been here twice hopin' to see if you got her settled down. She seem to be all right after puttin' that double load o' buckshot into Rourk's laigs?"

Red chuckled. "Hans, that woman's jest flat got gumption." He picked up the drink he'd poured himself before the cowboy came in, took a swallow and put it down behind the bar. "Cody didn't have the stuff

193

I needed to fix her door so I patched it up the best I could."

The cowboy knocked back his drink and held his glass for a refill.

McClain gave the man more whisky, then eyed Olerud. "Hans, it wuz kinda late when I finished messin' with her door so I asked 'er if she'd let me take 'er to eat supper at the café." He shook his head. "Know what she did? Well she sat me down while she cooked supper. It shore wuz enjoyable."

The cowboy stood, tossed a coin to the bartop and left.

Red waited until the heavy wooden door shut tightly, then looked at Hans with a heavy frown creasing his forehead. "All right, you ain't made several trips to see me in that weather out yonder 'less you got somethin' on yore mind. What you thinkin' 'bout?"

Olerud turned and swept the room with a look that in Red's opinion was half scared and the other half determined. He swung his look back to McClain. "Tell you how it is, old friend: Miz Gretchen blowin' Rourk's laigs out from under 'im mighta blowed the top off'n the outhouse." He motioned for Red to pour him a drink.

Red did so. "You thinking the same way I'm thinkin'? You thinkin' we got more

194

trouble now than we had before?"

Hans nodded. "Reckon that's 'zackly what I'm thinkin'.'"

Even though no one had come into the saloon, McClain cast a look around anyway. He shook his head. "Don't see as how we could have *more* trouble — but you might be right. You reckon now that Rourk's gonna be outta things for a while we oughta try to git the townsfolk together an' have a talk?"

Olerud frowned, then shook his head. "Been studyin' on that an' I ain't come up with nothin'. Seems like the more I argue with myself 'bout what we oughta do, the more reasons I come up with as to why we shouldn't. What you think? Know you done give this a lotta thought too."

Red drew his shoulders up around his neck in an exaggerated shrug. "Damned if I know, Hans. Know one thing, though: I'm gonna git me another Greener, load it with buckshot an' keep one at each end o' the bar. Ain't gonna git very far from one o' them."

Olerud's face seemed to take on more wrinkles and his mouth sagged at the corners as he frowned. "I ain't packed a gun in years — not since that last hoss throwed me an' I had to quit cowboyin' — but next time you see me I'm gonna have a handgun on me."

McClain nodded, slowly. "Miz Gretchen mighta forced us into somethin' 'fore we're ready." He shrugged. "What I mean by that is, I figger we're gonna have to git folks together, form a plan, not go into this blind — we gotta know what we're doin', an' everybody has to know what each one's gonna do."

"Well hell, McClain, she mighta done that, but from what I'm thinkin' she's done give us the best chance we ever had to be able to *get* people all in one place without causin' all hell to break loose. They's one other thing I'm thinkin': I shore wish we could git that young'un to help us, you know the one I mean. Young Tenery."

"No damned way I'm ever gonna be responsible fer that young'un takin' lead in our cause. He's done come mighty close to buyin' the farm a couple o' times." Red shook his head. "Wouldn't ask any man to do that."

"Know you're right." Olerud sighed. "But it shore would feel a lot better knowin' we had his guns with us."

Red filled their glasses and they stood there, absorbed in their own thoughts.

■ ■ ■ ■

East of the Absaroka Range and south along the Wind River Range, Chance and Betsy Tenery sat next to each other in front of their huge stone fireplace.

Chance tightened his arm around her shoulders. She moved closer to him and laid her head on his shoulder. They had never lost the fire and love for each other through the years.

They had watched Billy grow to be a man; watched Mopeah, a respected warrior, make him a Shoshone warrior and name him Coyote Man after a fight with a band of Lakota Sioux; said good-bye when he left home and headed for the Military Academy. They loved him as much as though Chance were his real father, and Betsy had birthed him from Chance's seed. But in truth, Billy had been a waif whose real mother and father had been killed by the Lakota. Chance had taken him in. Later, he and Betsy had been married and they reared Billy together.

Chance snuggled his cheek against the top of Betsy's head. "You wondering the same thing I am?"

Her nod rubbed against his shoulder. "It's

197

been months since that letter when he said he was leaving the Army, couldn't stand the apple-polishing of the Washington military and was going to head home as soon as he had his discharge in hand."

Chance tightened his arm again, but Betsy couldn't get any closer. "Honey, I've thought long on it. If I thought Mopeah would look for him, stay outta trouble and bring him home, I'd ask him to go lookin'."

Betsy was silent for several moments, obviously giving Chance's suggestion thought. "Would that be fair to Mopeah? He'd have to cross the Crow lands, perhaps go deep into Lakota country while he checked white settlements along the way." She straightened and twisted to look at Chance. "I know it isn't right, but there are still many whites who think all Indians are the same. They shoot first and look to see who they might have killed afterward."

Chance grunted. "You're right. Bad as we want news of Billy we'd probably be sending Mopeah to his death." He sighed. "Reckon I'm to the point of graspin' at straws." He shook his head. "I could go — leave Yancy here to keep you safe."

Before he finished his suggestion, Betsy shook her head. "Chance, we both know that Tetlow would give his life before he'd

198

let anything happen to me, or the ranch. And every Shoshone warrior would help him — but I reckon it all boils down to the fact I want *you* here with me."

She snuggled against him again, then, her voice quiet but hopeful, said, "You think there are still wanted posters out for Yancy Tetlow?"

Chance chuckled. "Honey, the day he rode in here, probably long before that, I figure the law had forgotten about Yancy. Even if there are some who might remember him, the law wouldn't want him; he says he never killed anyone. I believe him. There's a law on the books that some crimes over seven years old, short of murder, are not ones that're tried. The law is known as the statute of limitations. Why? What're you thinkin'?"

"Why don't we send Yancy? He loves Billy almost as much as we do, and remember he helped raise him from the time you all escaped from that outlaw nest of Carsten Blade's."

They sat like that, neither saying anything, until a tiny, timid voice broke the silence. Betsy said, "Think on it, Chance, think on it. You, Yancy, Mopeah, half the Shoshone tribe and I have all been lookin' for Billy to show up for months now. Any one or all of those I mentioned would quit doing whatever they had set themselves to doing and head out to find our son. They all love him. The Shoshone think of him as one of them."

Chance chuckled. "They have good reason to think that way. By the time he left for the Army, I figure he was more Indian than white."

She nodded. "Do like I said, Chance, and talk to Yancy — see what he thinks."

Chance nodded, stood and picked her up. "Think we could think on it better in bed." Her only answer was a girlish giggle.

7

Bill Tenery packed his belongings, which Rufe and the boys had brought to the ranch house when he came in shot the last time. He took them to the bunkhouse, despite Penny protesting that he needed to heal more. She finally agreed that it was for the best in that she wasn't certain she could handle being that close to him each day *and* each night.

After another three days, Tenery told Rufus he wanted him to go with him to see Penny.

Again seated at the breakfast table, Bill pinned them each with a no-nonsense look. "Got you two together so I wouldn't have to say it twice. I'm goin' in to Elkhorn, gonna find out what those folks are afraid of. Gonna talk to McClain an' Olerud, get them to talk to me." He sat back in his chair, then continued, took a swallow of coffee which Penny had poured when he and

Rufus came in. "When I find what's got 'em so scared, I'm gonna come back here, get healed good, then I'm gonna go back in there an' have a meeting with *all* the town folk. But when I go back in I figure to have a way to fight their problem."

"Their problem? Why do you feel you have to fight their fight?"

Tenery stared at Penny and said, "Way I have it figured, I know *your* problem, and if we can find what they're afraid of we'll be able to pull it together an' come up with the best way to fight 'em." He nodded. "Fact is, I think their problem is pretty well tied to ours. I figured to let y'all know what I'm thinkin' an' at the same time let you know that I'm goin' in there. I shouldn't be gone more'n two or three days."

Rufus chomped down on his chew, stood, went to the back door, spit and again sat. "When you leavin'?"

"In the morning."

"You still won't let me send a couple of the boys with you?"

Tenery shook his head. "Way I got it figured, I can get in town, take care of what I need to and leave without drawin' much notice." He shrugged. "That's the way I'm gonna do it."

Chance Tenery put his cup down, went to the door and yelled toward the bunkhouse, "Yancy, Mopeah, Adam, come on up! We need to talk." He went back to the table and sat next to Betsy.

She glanced at him, and a quirk of a smile crinkled the corners of her lips. "Well, I guess you've made up your mind to talk about who's going looking for Billy."

"Aw now, honey, you know danged well I'm gonna be open-minded about who goes."

Betsy chuckled deep in her throat and nodded. "Sure, Chance. You'll be open-minded as long as they agree with what you've already decided."

Before she could say more, Mopeah pushed through the front door, followed by Yancy and Adam. Betsy stood and put three more cups on the table.

Adam picked up the coffeepot and filled all the cups. He looked at Chance. "Well, partner, what we gonna talk 'bout this time?"

Chance swept them with a look. "Reckon it's time someone went lookin' for Billy." He frowned. "Know y'all been lookin' for him to ride in, and probably most o' the Shoshone tribe's lookin' for the same thing."

The three said in unison, "I'll go."

Chance shook his head. "Betsy and I talked about that. Mopeah might get killed by some Indian-hating white man. Adam's wife is about to have their baby any day now." He turned his eyes on Yancy.

Tetlow squirmed. "Much as I'd like to see 'im, I'd most likely git myself arrested 'fore I got past the first town."

"Yancy, that old dog won't hunt. The law probably forgot about you more'n ten years ago. The statute of limitations says that — short of murder — a man can't be tried for his crimes after a certain number of years." He took a swallow of coffee. "Now tell me the real reason you don't ever go to town, not even down to South Pass. Hell, you have the boys bring you back a jug or tobacco when they go to town."

Tetlow squirmed even more. His face blushed to a bright red. "Chance, I jest plain don't like towns."

"Hogwash! What's the real reason? Tell me, Yancy, right now."

Tetlow stared into the bottom of his now empty cup, moved his look from Betsy, to the big Shoshone warrior Mopeah, then to Adam, hoping one of them would get him out of this. They didn't. He squirmed again, wishing he could disappear. He didn't. He took a deep breath. "All right, gonna tell ya what I been fearin' ever since you let me come to work fer you." He stared at the table, switched his gaze back to Chance. "You reckon I could have a drink o' yore whisky? Gotta get the guts to tell you this."

Chance frowned, stood and pulled a bottle of rye from the cupboard. "Yancy, I don't know what could be so bad you haven't told us before this." He tilted the bottle over a glass Betsy had put on the table along with four more.

Yancy knew his hot face was red as a fall sunset. And even though he tried, tears overflowed and trickled down his cheeks. He gulped his whisky and placed the glass back in front of him. He nodded. "Gonna tell ya like it is. Ever since you let me come in here after the fight we had with Blade's men over yonder in the hole I been scared to death you wouldn't let me stay. Figgered if'n I went into town you'd know you could get along without me." He shook his head. "Y'all, the Shoshone, Adam an' his wife" — he shrugged — "ever' danged one o' you done got to be family to me. Don't think I could stand it if'n you run me off."

Chance glanced at those around the table.

Every eye he looked into swam with tears threatening to spill down their cheeks. He went to the other side of the table and grasped Yancy's shoulders in his big hands. "Tetlow, gonna tell you something. You're as much a part of *our* family as anyone could be. Billy, Betsy, Adam, Mopeah, me — hell, you old outlaw, every danged one of us love you like a brother." He shook his head. "Don't know what in the world could have ever given you such an idea. Don't b'lieve anyone ever said anything to indicate we don't want you around."

Yancy took a swallow of his drink and followed it with a sip of coffee. He shook his head. "Tell y'all like it is, I got raised up by a uncle when my folks died within a month o' each other."

He shrugged. "Didn't have nothin' but a horse doctor out there in that Tennessee countryside, he never knowed what killed 'em.

"Anyway, my uncle never paid me no nevermind less'n I didn't git my chores done by sundown. If I didn't, he'd beat me with a harness strap 'til the blood came out." He stared at his hands, clasped tightly in his lap. "Reckon I stood the work an' the beatings long's I could, then I run away. I wuz thirteen at the time.

"When I run away, they wuz three growed-up men took me in. They wuz rustling cattle, an' seemed to figger me to do the same. We got caught.

" 'Fore the sheriff could get me locked up, I grabbed a hoss an' run like the devil." He looked at them, pulled his mouth down in an exaggerated grimace. "I tried robbin' stages, stores, whatever I figgered might have a few dollars, but I swear to you, I never shot nobody durin' any o' those hold-ups.

"Then I heard 'bout Mr. Blade an' his place in Jackson Hole." He shrugged. "I went in there an' he let me stay." He looked at Chance. "That's where you found me an' where I fell in love with that little boy o' yores. Reckon Billy wuz the real reason I helped y'all escape, an' when you said I could work fer you it seemed like the clouds of heaven opened up an' let me in." He shook his head. "Reckon I been afeered ever since that you wouldn't keep me around."

Chance glanced around the table. Not a person had dry eyes, not even the battle-hardened Shoshone warrior, Mopeah.

Chance cleared his throat, trying to get rid of the huge knot stuck in it. It didn't do any good. He took a drink of whisky — *that* helped. He pinned Yancy with a "don't argue with me" look. "Look around the table, Yancy. If you think their tears, or mine, are caused from not giving a damn 'bout you, you just flat aren't as smart as I think you are." He shook his head. "I'm tellin' you right now — you have a home here with us as long as you live."

Yancy stared into his drink; then he looked at each one of them. "Y'all really mean what you done told me, don't you?" He sat back and chuckled, then turned it into an outright laugh. "Sunuvagun, reckon I can go to town, do what all o' you do, but best of all, I'm gonna be the one who gets to ride outta here lookin' fer Billy."

Chance stood to grab a can from the shelf above the stove and pulled a wad of bills from it. He stuffed the paper money in his pocket while he shook out a handful of gold coins, all double eagles. He put them in front of Yancy. "This isn't comin' outta your pay. I have every cent of your pay written down in my time and wages book. The only thing you've ever drawn from it is tobacco and whisky money when one o' the boys were gonna ride into South Pass City." He replaced the paper money in the can, the can on the shelf.

He looked at his friends, then at Betsy and grinned. "Reckon this calls for a drink."

When his look again rested on Tetlow, he said, "Soon's you find Billy, an' bring 'im home, I want you to do something with your money. You must have accumulated at least nine years' wages." He chuckled. "Hell, if you don't draw it out soon, I'll probably have to give you the ranch to get even."

Yancy's face turned red again. "Aw, Chance, all I need's tobacco an' whisky, some new jeans once in a while." He grinned like a schoolboy trying to start a conversation with the first girl he'd ever met. "Why heck, now that I done found out y'all ain't gonna run me off, I don't figger I need nothin' y'all ain't done give me." He stood. "Reckon I better git busy an' roll my b'longin's. Figger I can put a few miles behind me 'fore sundown."

When he went out the door, Chance pulled his handkerchief from his back pocket, wiped his eyes, blew his nose and muttered, "Who would've ever figured him thinkin' such."

Miles to the northeast, in the first town one would approach from the Shoshone reservation, Rourk gingerly eased his legs over the side of his bed. If he didn't make the effort to get strength back in his injured limbs, didn't get back to his ranch and see if he couldn't regain control of his men, he'd lose everything he'd gained since coming to this godforsaken part of the country.

He frowned. Suppose he *couldn't* control his men? He thought on that a few moments, then nodded to himself. He still knew men back in New York who would do anything for a few dollars. He'd write Branch Whitcom to round up ten or fifteen of 'em and come out. He'd gamble on their coming; he'd send railroad fare for that many men.

In the middle of Rourk's thoughts, Charley Farnum, the hotel's owner, opened the door and brought in a tray of food. He put it on the washstand.

"What kind o' slop you bring me this time?"

Farnum stared at him a moment. "You don't want it, I'll take it back." He pinned Rourk with a hard look. "I take this back, you can get off your crippled ass an' get your own food after this."

Rourk returned his look. He'd add this bastard to the list of those he'd get rid of soon's he could get a gun. He'd burn the buildings they died in down around their dead bodies — the first one he'd get rid of was that damned woman who'd shot him. "Leave the slop you brought me. I'll eat it."

He pulled his legs back to rest on the bed. "Move the washstand over to my side, an' when you come back for the tray bring me a pencil and paper."

Farnum looked at him a moment, turned and left the room.

Two days later, his letter written to New York and put on the stage by Farnum, Rourk mustered enough strength to shuffle to the window. He stared down at the wind- and snow-swept trail. A rider, hat pulled low on his forehead, chin tucked into the collar of his sheepskin and hunched over his saddle horn, rode on past the saloon and reined in at the livery. Cord frowned; the rider looked vaguely familiar, but any rider out in this weather, dressed as any with any sense would be, would look familiar. He shuffled back to his bed.

Bill Tenery, the rider Rourk had seen, pulled his right foot from the stirrup preparing to climb from the saddle when the big door swung toward him. Olerud held the door open against the wind and waved Tenery in. "Don't sit out here in a cold saddle. Act like you got some sense."

"Damn, glad to see you too, Hans."

"Aw hell, Tenery, I'm always glad to see

you; tells me you ain't managed to git yore-self killed when I ain't lookin' at ya." He pulled the door closed and opened one of the stalls for Bill to ride into. "How you doin' since gettin' shot the last time?"

Tenery nodded. "Reckon my bein' here tells you that."

Olerud squinted at him while he climbed stiffly from the saddle. "What in the name o' tarnation brung you outta that warm bunkhouse into this weather?"

Bill shot him a cold smile. "You an' Mc-Clain brought me outta that warm bunk-house. The three of us gotta have a meetin'. We're gonna do some serious talkin', then I'm gonna ride back out to that warm bunkhouse an' let the good Lord help me finish healin, an' *then* I'm gonna come up with a plan how to solve your problem."

"Don't b'lieve I'm gonna like the answer to this question, but I'm gonna ask it anyway. What makes you think we gonna tell ya anything more'n we done in the past?"

Tenery frowned, clamped his jaws tight, then said, " 'Cause I'm gonna squat right there in Red's saloon 'til y'all tell me what I want ta know. I'll keep you there if I gotta hold my Colt on you."

Olerud shook his head. "Knowed I wuzn't

212

gonna like yore answer." He cast Bill a puzzled look. "From the way you talk, you ain't heared what's done happened here in town since you come in last time."

Tenery shook his head. "Nobody's been to town since I was last here. What's happened?"

"Ain't tellin' you nothin' 'til we set down 'crost a table from McClain. We gonna hear what you come in town fer, gonna think on it a few minutes, decide what we gonna do; an' durin' all that confab we'll tell you 'bout what's done happened here in town."

Tenery nodded. "Fair enough." He pulled his sheepskin tighter around his shoulders. "Gonna go down to Red's place an' knock back a couple o' tall drinks, an' maybe a cup of hot coffee. Soon's you quit for the day, come on over an' we'll talk."

Olerud chomped down on his chew, then worked his jaws furiously and spat. "Still don't think neither one o' us is gonna like what you gonna say."

Tenery stepped toward the door. "Don't give a damn whether either one of you likes it but you're gonna listen — then I'm gonna listen real hard to what y'all tell me."

He ducked his head, opened the door and headed into the wind. In only a few moments he pushed through the door of the saloon. Only one person stood at the bar.

"Haven't been many times I didn't have to elbow my way close enough for you to hand me a drink, Red."

"Danged weather's gonna cause me to go broke, Tenery. Bet I ain't had ten customers all day."

"Well, Olerud'll be up here soon's he quits for the day. I told 'im I wanted 'im up here so the three of us could talk — an' I guaran-damn-tee you we're gonna talk 'til I get the information I rode all the way in town to get."

"Don't know that I'm gonna like what you gonna ask us."

Tenery nodded. "Those are about the same words Olerud used, but like it or not, I'm gonna ask, an' 'tween you two I'm gonna get the answers I rode in here for."

The one other person at the bar tossed a coin to the polished surface, flipped a hand up in farewell and left. Red followed him with his eyes until the door closed behind him. He shifted his look to Tenery. "All right, now tell me what you want to know."

Bill shook his head. "Not sayin' anything until Olerud gets here, then I'll have my say. Only gonna say it once, then I'm gonna spend some time listenin' to what y'all tell me."

"What makes you think we gonna tell ya anything?"

Tenery grinned. "Tell you what, Red, ask Hans that question when he gets here. He'll tell you why you're gonna talk to me." He took a swallow of his drink. "And I'm tellin' you right now, I meant what I said."

An hour, maybe two, went by without any more being said. Tenery had a couple more drinks and a cup of coffee.

Finally, the old man pushed through the door and slammed it shut, shivering. He walked to the bar, his hand held out. Mc-Clain put a drink in it, then grinned. "Reckon you was in need o' that drink."

He pulled an unopened full bottle of rye from under the bar, went to a table and put it and three glasses next to it; then he went to the door, slipped the wooden timber in place and came back to the table. "All right, we're here. Ask yore questions."

Tenery went behind the bar and poured himself a cup of coffee. He looked over his shoulder. "Either o' you want a cup?" At their head shakes, he brought his cup to the table and sat. He packed his pipe, lit it, and pinned each of them with a "don't wriggle outta this" look.

He puffed a couple of times and nodded. "All right, here it is. I know what Rourk is tryin' to do to Penny: he figures to get her ranch any way he can. I'm not gonna let that happen. Now, I'm gonna ask you once, only once, an' I better get an answer."

"What you gonna do if we don't give you what you want?" Red said belligerantly.

Before Tenery could answer, Olerud cut in, "Red, he done told me he'd pull that there hawgleg an' use it on us if we don't talk." Hans pulled the cork on the bottle, poured himself and McClain a drink and said, "Danged if I don't believe 'im."

Red looked through slitted lids at Bill. "Ask yore question."

Tenery looked straight on into McClain's eyes. "Like I told the two of you once before, I don't figure even one man I've met in this town for a coward. There's something Rourk's men have said to you that makes all of you pull in your horns; I want ta know what it is, then we're gonna do somethin' 'bout it."

Olerud squinted one eye almost closed and stared at Bill. "You say 'we,' young'un?"

Tenery nodded. "I said 'we.' "

The old man cackled and slapped his knee. "Hot damn, Red, we ain't gonna have to ask 'im. We ain't gonna have to saddle our troubles on that there young'un. He's sayin' he's gonna throw in with us."

McClain cast Olerud a sour look. "I heard 'im, you old goat, but he ain't heard what kind o' troubles we got." He took a swallow of his drink, then looked at Bill. "Okay, gonna tell ya, an' don't want no snap decision to go out that door an' start shootin'. Want you to give it some thought, talk to us 'bout it an' let us make the decision whether to do what you figger'll work."

"Fair enough. I don't want to start a war with anyone without knowin' why, an' then I'll do some careful plannin'."

McClain glanced at his best friend, got a nod and turned his look back to Tenery. "A few months ago, Rourk rode into town at the head of about fifteen or twenty men. After havin' a drink here, he told 'em to git on with what they'd planned. They left, an' must've spread out in the town, goin' to one or two stores each." Red shook his head. "Didn't know what they were about 'til they come back in, had a drink an' headed back to the ranch Rourk took over."

Hans stood, arched his back apparently to get the kinks out then again sat. "Them riders o' Rourk's told the store owners they'd come in every two weeks expectin' to get thirty dollars from each store; and if anyone bucked 'em, they'd find out what would happen."

"Why didn't y'all tell 'em all to go to hell? Get together and blow 'em to kingdom come?"

"Tenery, you notice only two or three of 'em come in town at once?" McClain asked.

Bill nodded.

"Comin' in like that kept us from killin' 'em. Also, you notice that pile o' ashes over yonder the other side of the hotel?" At Bill's nod, he continued, "Them ashes used to be another mercantile store, b'longed to Kirk Holbert. Rourk made him pack up an' leave town the next day; at the same time, he come around to each business in town an' told us it'd happen to us if we even had a town meeting."

Tenery shook his head. "Still don't see why y'all didn't fight."

McClain's faced flushed redder than his hair. "Dammit, Bill, we wuzn't afraid for ourselves, we wuz afraid for our friends. He told us if a single one o' us bucked him, he'd burn out and kill one o' our friends.
. . ."

"Young'un, nary a one o' us has been afeared for himself," Olerud said. "You see, from the day Roland Horn, Penny's pa, brung us in here we been like family. We been afeared fer our friends, shakin' in our boots we'd do somethin' to git one of them

218

or maybe their whole family hurt, killed, burned out or all o' them things."

Tenery took a swallow of coffee and stared at the table a few moments. "I understand. Now we gotta figure what to do 'bout it." He shook his head. "Want you to know somethin': I never in my life set out to kill a man, but maybe that's the only answer. Somebody's gotta kill Rourk."

McClain chuckled. "Gretchen Thoreson, the widder woman who owns the bakeshop across the street yonder, danged near saved us the trouble. He's lyin' up yonder in the hotel, both laigs shot out from under 'im."

Bill squinted at his almost full glass of whisky. "What'd he do to make 'er do that?"

Red looked at Olerud, got a nod, and said, "I'll tell you only so much, no more."

Tenery chuckled. "Hell. Know she must've had a good reason, but yeah, go ahead tell me."

McClain skirted the reason the Easterner figured he had some sort of claim on Gretchen, but told about him getting drunk and threatening to kick her door in. He pulled his shoulders up in a shrug. "Reckon the poor woman wuz frightened outta her wits. When he actually did kick her door, she unloaded a double-barreled, twelve-gauge Greener at 'im. Cut his laigs slam out from under 'im; he's been lyin' up yonder in the hotel ever since. He ain't able to git out an' about yet, but Charley Farnum, the hotel owner, told me the only thing he's done since he's been in that room wuz to write a letter to New York City 'bout two, maybe three weeks ago. Farnum put it on the stage for 'im."

Tenery frowned. "You say he wrote a letter to New York?"

Red nodded.

Tenery's deepened frown drooped his eyebrows over his eyes such that he could hardly see. "Damn! Wish that hadn't happened. Bet money he sent to New York for more men."

"Aw hell, Tenery, you reckon that's what he wrote that letter for?" Even the idea of what Bill suggested caused McClain to flush even more. He glanced at Olerud. "If what Tenery's sayin' is true, we got more trouble than we had 'fore Gretchen shot 'im."

Bill shook his head. "Don't see it that way. Yeah, it'll make our problem harder, but if I come up with a good plan, we'll take care of it all during the same fight."

Despite their solemn conversation, McClain chuckled.

Tenery frowned and twisted to stare at the saloon owner. "What the hell you see funny 'bout him gettin' more men?"

"That ain't what I wuz findin' funny, lad." Red laughed out loud this time. "He ain't got a gun. After Miz Gretchen shot 'im, but before we had 'im carted off to the hotel for the doctor to fix up, I took 'is gun belt off, wrapped it around his holster an' brought it with me here. It's over yonder behind the bar."

Bill nodded. "Make sure he doesn't get another one when he heals enough to ride outta here. How much longer you think he's gonna stay cooped up in that hotel room?"

Olerud frowned and gave Tenery's question some thought. "Doc says he figgers another week an' he'll be able to ride."

Bill thought on that a few moments. "Good. That'll give me time to get back to the ranch, get to feelin' better, think on the town's troubles, come back in an' have a meeting with every man in this town."

McClain opened his mouth as though to say something. Tenery shook his head. "Not gonna hear any argument 'bout the meeting. I'm gonna ride in, tell you to gather the folks we gonna meet with, then eliminate any troubles you folks have — got it?"

The old liveryman cackled and slapped his knee. "Hot damn, Red, I done told you we needed this here young'un to hep us.

Now he's gonna do it."

McClain frowned, picked up the bottle and held it toward the lamp to study its contents. "We done polished this bottle off. I'll git another." He stood.

Bill put a hand on Red's arm. "We've had enough whisky. I'm gonna head back to the ranch in the mornin', gonna get a night's sleep 'fore I put my mind to what to do 'bout Rourk."

He stood and twisted his holster around for more comfort. He looked at Red a moment; then nodded. "When the men come in for their drink 'fore goin' home each night, don't make a big deal outta it, but let them know you'll be callin' 'em to come over soon. That'll give 'em time to think on it awhile an' maybe get ready for a fight. Don't b'lieve any of 'em would figure a meeting would be for any other reason." He headed for the door.

Even though Tenery had been gone for less than an hour, Penny pulled the kitchen curtain aside and stared up the trail leading to town.

During the next three days she repeated the action often enough to cause Rufus to comment, "Dammit, girl, you gonna wear that there curtain out pullin' on it that way.

Why, hell, I betcha you done pulled it aside every danged hour since that boy left here for Elkhorn."

Penny shot him a hard look. "Gonna tell you somethin', Rufus Bent: he's my man, I've laid claim to 'im an' he ain't fought the bit even once." She nodded. "Yeah, I mighta been lookin' too often durin' those first two days, but this is the third day — he said he'd be back in three days. I'm gonna keep lookin' for 'im."

Rufe looked at the woman he'd helped raise from a little filly. He'd been standing inside the door, preparing to go back to the bunkhouse; instead, he crossed the kitchen, put his arms around her shoulders and pulled her to his rugged old chest. "Honey, it's still mornin'. He wouldn't have left the hotel 'til only a couple hours ago. It'll take 'im most o' the day to ride back out here." He chuckled. "Give 'im 'til late afternoon, then start lookin' for 'im again — I'll stand right there with you and help pull the curtain aside." He shook his head. "Truth be known, I been lookin' down the trail for 'im too."

She twisted her head to look up at him. "Rufe, how'd this happen so quick? I've knowed a whole bunch o' strangers to ride in here, met some in town at the dances an' never met even one o' them I'd give a second look 'til Bill Tenery rode in here. Don't reckon I done much more than look at 'im an' he took my heart." She shook her head. "Never figured it'd happen like that. Reckon I always thought my man would court me for a considerable time: he'd tell me how he felt; I'd study on it for some time an' tell 'im I felt 'bout the same way, an' then we'd decide we'd see a preacher man."

Rufus held her slight form close to him. "Almost daughter o' mine, sometimes I reckon the man upstairs looks down on a young'un an' a mighty pretty little filly an' says to himself, 'Better make them two know *reeeal* quick what they got right before their eyes, make 'em reach out an' take what I know is theirs.' "

Instead of going back to the bunkhouse, he steered her to a chair and pushed her into it, and poured them each a cup of coffee. "You want me to stay up here with you 'til we see that young'un ridin' in?"

She looked up at him. "Would ya, Rufe? Know you ain't sent the boys out to do any chores in this weather. Just keep me company."

He stared into his coffee cup a moment, then pinned her with a look that said he was going to tell her something she had to accept. He chomped down on his chew a couple of times, still looking at her.

"All right, Rufe, you might as well get it said. You been thinkin' an' chewin' pretty hard."

He pulled his lips into a grimace. "Know by now you can read me pretty good." He nodded, and said, "Tenery went into town to find out what the troubles are. When he comes back he's gonna put his mind to seein' what they gotta do 'bout it, then he's gonna go back in there an' help 'em to solve whatever's botherin' 'em — that's gonna mean gun help. You know that, don't you?"

She nodded. "Know it, but been tryin' to make believe it didn't have to happen that way." She blinked back tears. "Oh, Rufe, he's already been shot up somethin' awful since he got here. Don't think I could stand it if he got shot again."

"Honey, I figger when he comes up with a plan, its gonna be one he figgers will keep everyone as safe as possible."

She sniffled. "Yeah, Rufe, but it's that 'as possible' that's worries me."

Only a few miles northeast of the ranch on which he'd made himself a prisoner for almost ten years, Yancy Tetlow rode slowly, leading his packhorse. He gazed at the mountains and off to the east at the snow-covered plains as though God had only that morning put it all there for him to admire.

Mm-mmm. Reckon I done lucked into bein' made a friend o' one o' the finest families in this here country. Gonna find that boy an' bring 'im home, then we're gonna all be family agin. He shook his head even though no one could see him. *Who woulda ever figgered a old Tennessee farmboy turned outlaw would ever git a chance to have a home like Mr. Chance an' Miz Betsy done give me?*

As happy as a man could ever think to be, Yancy hummed to himself awhile, then wondered how far that town of Elkhorn stood from where he rode. He decided he didn't care as long as he found Billy. Heck, he might have to ride to Billings, or even Miles Town up yonder in the Montana Territory, but however far he had to ride, or however long it took, he'd stay on the trail. Billy was up yonder somewhere.

He'd counted the gold eagles Chance had given him for the trip several times. It came to almost two hundred fifty dollars. He'd never, not even in his outlaw days, had as much money. He made up his mind he'd save as much of it that he just flat didn't need to live on so he could give a whole bunch of it back to the man who had given him a home. Aw hell, he'd given him more than a home — he'd given him a mighty nice family at the same time.

The third day on the trail, he got the feeling between his shoulders that he better move over against the mountains and stop dreaming of what a wonderful world he rode in.

He had penetrated the Crow lands. He respected them as one of the tribes that would fight you right down to your socks. He didn't mind fighting them. He had gone with Mopeah and his band on several raids over the years — but then he always had a few Shoshone to fight alongside. Now he rode alone.

He searched out across the snowfield, hoping the Crow were as smart as the Shoshone and would stay in camp in weather such as what he rode in now. He chuckled. *Hell, only an old ex-outlaw is dumb enough to be out here alone in this weather.* He thought that, but didn't relax any of his senses.

That night, he found a tumble of boulders in which to make camp. He rode out from it and searched for any chance a fire could be seen. Even though he thought there was no chance his fire could be seen, he'd keep it small.

The next morning before rolling his blankets, he slipped to the side of one of the huge rocks to search across the lands. He wasn't alone.

Two warriors rode about four hundred yards from where he stood. His first thought was to dart back into the rocks, get his rifle and wait for them to make a move toward him, but hopefully away from him.

He had no doubt they were looking for trouble. He'd bet the whole poke Chance had given him they were hoping to find an old buffalo. Here in the dead of winter food was probably getting pretty low in their winter camp. He figured it that way because Chance had cut out a few head of cattle for Mopeah to take to the Shoshone reservation.

He stood against the boulder, as still as the rock itself; any movement and they'd spot it. They might think it an animal of some sort, and that would be worse than letting them know he was a man — they'd try slipping up on an animal with the chance it would be large enough to make a few meals back at their winter camp. He would stay as he was, hopefully blending in with the rock, and maybe they'd ride on. He hoped in vain.

They apparently swept the plains with a

look; then turned their attention toward the mountains. Almost past him they abruptly kneed their horses directly toward the rock he stood by.

Yancy didn't wait. He darted into the jumble of boulders, grabbed his Winchester, stuffed two handfuls of cartridges into his pockets, jacked a shell into the magazine — hoping they'd not heard the sound — and went back to peer around the huge rock. They came at him at a dead run.

He drew a bead on the lead rider, took a deep breath and squeezed the trigger. That rider threw up his hands and fell off the side of his horse.

Tetlow moved his rifle's barrel a hair and held the sights on the second rider. He squeezed the trigger; at the same time the Indian kneed his pony to the side. His shot missed.

The Indian was now too close for Yancy to use his rifle, so Yancy draw his Colt — too late. The warrior was already almost on top of him, the knife in his right hand ready to swing. Tetlow gauged where the Indian would land, stepped to the side and pulled his bowie knife at the same time.

Tetlow wished he wasn't wearing his heavy sheepskin; then he grunted. Hell, the warrior had on as much clothing. And even though most would consider Tetlow fat at first glance, Yancy knew he was as light on his feet as most men. The warrior ran at him, swung his knife and missed. Tetlow stepped in close and sliced. He missed as well.

The two men backed off, circled to look for an opening. Abruptly, the Indian feinted toward Yancy's knife hand, then stepped to the other side and swung. For a fleeting instant his blade hung in Yancy's coat. Tetlow, his knife held straight out ahead of him, pushed it into the warrior's side. He jerked it clear and swung at the Indian's neck — at the sliver of flesh only barely above the top of the warrior's buckskin jacket. His blade made solid contact. Blood spurted over his knife hand. He moved back a step, ready to swing again. He could have saved the step. The warrior's head lolled off to the side, his neck cut at least halfway through.

Yancy stood there, waited for the Indian to fall. He finally toppled to land at Tetlow's feet. He stepped in, wiped his blade on the warrior's coat and sheathed the big blade. Then he looked between the boulders to the Indian he'd brought down with his rifle. That Indian lay where he'd fallen.

Tetlow swept the snowfield with a look, searching for any dark, moving object, thankful for the white surface. Finally satisfied he had this part of the world to himself, he walked to the man he'd shot, collected his weapons, went back to the one he'd used his knife on, gathered *his* rifle and knife, and put them all by his pack saddle. Then he made a fire and fixed breakfast.

While drinking his second cup of coffee, he studied the man he'd knifed. Unlike many white men of the day, he didn't think of the Indian as savage. He'd grown to know the Shoshone as a feeling, human people. He thought if he'd known the Crow as well, he might consider them as he did Mopeah's people.

Finished with breakfast, he saddled, loaded his packhorse. Again looking at the stiff bodies, he wished he had a shovel to dig a hole to put them in. He mentally shook his head. Hell, if he'd had the tools, he couldn't have dug, the ground was probably frozen halfway to Hades. He thought on it a moment, went to the man he'd shot, dragged him into the jumble of rocks beside the other dead man and stacked small boulders over them. Satisfied he'd done all he could for them, he climbed on his horse, gathered the lead rope of the packhorse and rode out.

■ ■ ■ ■

The morning after Tenery had laid it out for McClain and Olerud, the old liveryman watched Bill ride from his stable. He went back to his living quarters, banked the fire in his potbellied stove, glanced at the empty stalls and headed for Red's saloon. Tenery's horse had been the only one he'd taken care of for two or three days.

When he pushed through the saloon door, Red was about to place the coffeepot back on the stove. "Pour me one too, McClain." He walked to the bar and picked up the cup Red put in front of him. "Don't know when the last time was that I felt so good; even slept good last night."

McClain cocked his head to the side and grinned. "Reckon you think you done cornered all them good feelin's. I wuz 'bout to tell you the same thing." He nodded. "Bet we both got to feelin' good for the same reason."

Olerud pulled his face into a sober look, squinting one eye about half closed and shaking his head. "Red, reckon I feel sorta guilty 'bout feelin' so good, but hell, we been needin' somebody to kick us in the hind end, tell us what we had to do. But we

232

wuz lucky enough to have someone tell us *he* wuz gonna figger out *how* to git it done."

McClain stared at his friend for a long moment, then said, "Olerud, it ain't been but a few days since I give you hell for even thinkin' 'bout draggin' that young'un into our fight. But I gotta tell ya, since he's done took the bull by the horns, I been feelin' mighty good."

Olerud pulled a plug of Brown's Mule from his pocket, offered Red a chew; at his head shake, opened his pocketknife and carved off a slice for himself and tucked it into his cheek. He chomped on it a couple of times before saying, "Red, reckon we better not wait'll the townsfolk come in for a drink; think maybe we better give 'em more warnin' than that."

"What you figger on doin'?"

Olerud pulled his hat off and scratched his head. "Gonna go to *them,* tell 'em what's done been happenin', give 'em a longer chance to think on it."

McClain stared at the far wall, frowning; then he nodded. "Good. I'll do the same, an' when you come in fer yore drink each night we'll tell each other who we done seen."

Hans chewed furiously for a moment. "We got it to do, Red, but remember: Rourk's sittin' up yonder in that hotel room, an' it looks down on the street. He's gonna git the idea we're up to somethin', an' if one o' his men come in town, he's gonna let 'im *know* we're up to somethin'."

Red chuckled. "Charley Farnum tells me that ain't a danged one o' Rourk's men been up there to see 'im."

Olerud shook his head. "That don't mean one o' 'em won't go up there. We better play our cards close to our vest." He took a swallow of coffee. "Bein's you done got mighty friendly with the widder woman, you better tell *her.* Tell 'er to keep them guns loaded, but to stay outta the fight if it comes into town."

"What the hell you mean, I 'done got mighty friendly' with 'er? I ain't got no friendlier than anybody else."

Olerud laughed and slapped his thigh. "Hot damn, knowed I'd git ya with that one." He sobered. "But, Red, I'm tellin' ya right now, if'n I wuz twenty, thirty years younger, danged if I wouldn't be sparkin' 'er myself."

McClain gave him a sour look.

About sundown — if there had been any sun — hoofbeats sounded toward the stable. Penny stood and hurried to the window.

234

Rufe got there about the same time and pulled the curtain aside. Penny looked at her old foreman. "He look all right to you?" Her words came out as though she was short of breath.

Rufe nodded. "Yeah, he's all right. He's gonna take care of his horse and go to the bunkhouse. When he doesn't find me there, then he's gonna come up here." He chuckled, more from releasing nervous energy than finding anything funny. "Reckon I better set that jug o' rye on the table. You git some cups out. Figger he's gonna want a mighty strong cup o' coffee."

Penny gave him a knowing look. "Rufus, I declare I b'lieve you find excuses for him to come up here just so you can take a drink."

He shrugged. "Better to have a reason than have you nag me 'bout drinkin' too much."

"Rufus Bent, I've never nagged you 'bout drinkin'. Fact is, you hardly ever take a drink but what I have one with the two of you."

The kitchen door opened; Tenery stepped through it and quickly closed it behind him. He looked at them and grinned. "Dang it, reckon y'all are gettin' used to seein' me ride in. You don't even come out to greet me anymore."

Ignoring his statement, Penny scanned him from head to toe. "Seeing as how you got back in one piece this time, reckon I can put the bandages away an' take the hot water off the stove."

Tenery grimaced. "Heck, Penny, it's not that bad."

She pinned him with an accusing look. "Bill, do you realize this is only the second time you've come home without a bullet hole in you?" She nodded. "If you'll think on it a moment, what I said 'bout the bandages an' hot water wasn't so much a joke as the truth."

Tenery glanced at the table and grinned. "See y'all were watchin' for me — you already got the cups out, an' that jug o' Rufe's sitting there on the table."

He'd been holding a gunnysack in his right hand. He swung it up and placed it on the table. "Thought Rufe might be gettin' mighty thirsty so I brought four more jugs." He looked at Penny. "If you'll pour us some coffee, let's sit an' I'll tell y'all what I found out in town."

He pulled Penny's chair from the table and held it for her to sit, then took a chair beside her. "First off, I want y'all to know it was like I figured; there's not a coward in that town. The reason the townsfolk let

Rourk's bunch buffalo them was all out of love for their neighbors."

Then he told them what he'd instructed McClain and Olerud to get done while he was healing at the Saddle Horn, as well as about Gretchen Thoreson shooting Rourk.

He shook his head. "I gotta give it some serious thought — don't wanta go back in there half-cocked an' get a bunch of those folks hurt."

He told them about the probability that Rourk had sent to New York for more men. "I gotta figure that he did, an' if so, then I better think along those lines. Better to overestimate an enemy than to sit there an' let them overrun us with a superior force."

As serious as the conversation had been going, Penny laughed. Tenery looked at her and growled, "What's so danged funny?"

She pulled her laugh down to a smile. "You, Bill. If I let myself think it, You sounded like you were talkin' to a bunch of soldiers, the way you were taught at West Point."

He took a swallow of coffee and gave her a grim smile. "Penny, that's the way I *am* lookin' at the problem. That way we're a lot less likely to get people hurt."

Rufe had been sitting quiet, but abruptly he sat forward, poured them all a shot of rye and looked at Tenery. "How many men, growed men, you figger is in that there town — fightin' men is what I'm talkin' 'bout."

Bill thought a minute, frowned, then shrugged. "Countin' boys who been using a rifle since knee-high to a frog? Reckon the total would come to 'bout forty. Why?"

"Jest thinkin' . . . we could leave 'bout twelve men here to guard the ranch — keep Rourk from burnin' it — an' I could add 'bout six men to what you figger the town's got —"

Tenery cut in. "Forget it. Not one man from this ranch is gonna go in there. 'Sides that, I want ta make danged certain we don't lose a cow or get one buildin' burned. My opinion is that if I work out a good plan, forty guns are gonna be plenty."

Penny sat there staring at him, her face pale. "You're gonna go in there, put yourself in the front of 'em — an' get shot full o' holes again."

Bill shook his head, then chuckled. "Lordy day, girl, you make me out to be a total danged fool? When I figure how to fight 'em, I'm gonna figure how to keep me safe also." He knocked back the drink Rufus had poured, stood and stepped toward the door. "Reckon I'm gonna get on down to the bunkhouse, pull up beside that potbellied stove and get warm and read the paper that came in from Billings while I was in town. Then I'm gonna crawl into my bunk an' get a good night's sleep."

Yancy Tetlow, holding close to the foothills, looked for a place to make camp, a place he could defend. He had a hunch he was close to that town he'd heard of, Elkhorn was its name. He rode over the swell of a hill, and a town lay before him. He hoped it was Elkhorn. If it wasn't he'd somehow ridden by it. He urged his horse down the hill, down the lonely trail. Passing several stores, he pulled rein by the livery, the only building he'd bet on in his identification of what it was.

He climbed stiffly from the saddle, limped to the big door and opened it. By the time it swung open far enough for him to enter, his muscles loosened up. An old puncher hobbled toward him from the back. "You got a stall I can put my horse in?"

"All I got is stalls — all empty. Put 'im in any you want an' come on back to my office. I got a pot o' hot coffee sittin' back yonder on the stove."

Yancy studied the old man and figured he liked him; he was right hospitable. "I'll shore be beholden to you for a cup o' hot

Arbuckle's; been ridin' since sunup — if they *wuz* any danged sun."

Olerud laughed. "Name's Hans Olerud. Go on back there an' pour yoreself a cup, I'll take care o' yore hosses," he said as he led the horses into two large stalls.

He'd finished about a half a cup by the time Hans came in. The liveryman studied him a few moments, then asked, "You gonna git a hotel room tonight? You don't, you're welcome to sleep in the hayloft."

Yancy grinned. "Man, I been sleepin' on the cold ground for quite a spell. Figger I'm gonna git me a room fer tonight." His grin widened. "But I'm tellin' you right now, 'fore I git me a room, I'm gonna find the saloon an' knock back at least two or three drinks, thaw me out a little."

Olerud poured the coffee he'd only that moment put in his cup back into the blackened old pot. "Come on. I'll show ya the saloon an' give ya the name o' the jasper what runs it. He's my friend." Hans said that last proudly.

For some reason, Yancy felt good about this town. He'd wait to ask about Billy until after he'd swallowed a couple of drinks.

Hans shrugged into his sheepskin and he and Yancy went out the door together.

As they strode to the bar, McClain studied

the man with his friend. He looked fat, but as lightly as he stepped, Red quickly changed his mind. That man might be bulky, but he sure as hell wasn't *fat*. He reached for a bottle of bar whisky but before he could pour, Olerud said, "Put that danged rotgut back on the shelf, this here man's been in the saddle since daybreak. Give us some o' yore good stuff."

Red grinned to himself. Hans asking for the good stuff was as good a recommendation of the stranger as he could want.

"Howdy, stranger, what in the name o' tarnation you doin' ridin' round in this weather?"

Yancy grinned. "Jest ain't got much sense, I reckon." He held out his hand to introduce himself but Olerud took care of that. After getting McClain's name, Tetlow asked, "They been a man through here in the last month or so by the name o' Bill Tenery? I'm lookin' fer 'im."

The friendly light went from Red's face, and Olerud moved a couple of steps to the side.

"You gunnin' fer 'im?" Red bit the words off as though they were made of steel.

Yancy frowned and studied the two men a moment; then shook his head. "Pull in yore horns, men. I helped raise that there boy.

He's s'posed to have gotten home some time ago. We been lookin' fer 'im to ride into the ranch, but he ain't showed. His pa sent me to look fer 'im." He nodded. "That's 'zactly what I'm doin'."

McClain's face didn't relax. "What's his pa's name?"

Tetlow didn't like all the questions, but figured he'd answer one or two; then they could go to hell. He pinned Red with a look that would pierce an oak door. "Don't know as how all that's any o' yore danged business, but his pa's Chance Tenery, helped build the railroad down yonder the other side o' South Pass City, an' now has a ranch jest this side o' the Shoshone reservation." He clamped his jaw tight a moment. "That there's all I gotta say."

8

McClain's expression changed from hard and bleak to amused. A slight smile crinkled the corners of his lips. "Mr. Tetlow, you done found 'im — sorta."

Yancy, still feeling hot blood behind his eyes, pinned Red with a look that demanded answers. "What the hell does that mean, 'sorta'?"

Olerud laughed. "Git the burr out from under yore saddle, Tetlow." He chomped on his tobacco a couple o' times, spit and got a nasty stare from McClain. "Means 'zactly what he done told ya. You *sorta* found 'im 'cause he ain't here right now. Figger 'nother two, maybe three days he'll be back." He frowned. "At least that there's what he told us."

"Where's he gone fer these two, three days?" Yancy demanded.

"He's been spendin' 'is time out yonder at Miss Penny's Saddle Horn Ranch." Olerud shook his head. "Ever' time that boy gits shot, he goes out yonder fer her to doctor 'im back to health."

"Ever' time he gits shot? What you mean? Somebody hereabouts been shootin' at my boy? Who the hell's been doin' that? I figger Billy can outfight any two men anywhere you want to dig 'em up."

Olerud cackled and slapped his knee. "Ain't no question this here man knows Bill Tenery," he said to Red. He turned his look back on Tetlow. "That boy done 'zactly like you said — he's outfought two men twice, but took lead both times. Miss Penny's done nursed 'im back to health each time, an' each time she's tried to talk 'im outta comin' back to town." He grimaced. "But what I seen o' that boy she might as well have talked to one o' those big rocks out yonder in the mountains. He's got a haid danged near that hard."

Yancy studied the old man a moment, then nodded. "Yep, that there's my Billy. He ain't never took to doin' like he wuz told." He laughed. "Shore woulda liked to been hidin' somewhere an' watched 'im at that there Army school when they started tellin' 'im how the coyote ate the rabbit. Bet he bucked like a raw bronc."

McClain shook his head. "Don't think so.

That boy's got a good head on 'is shoulders. Think he only bucks when he knows a man is wrong." He poured them another drink, and glanced at a window. "It's gettin' might nigh dark outside; too late to head for the Saddle Horn. Why don't you git yore hotel room an' come back down? We'll have a few drinks."

Yancy stared into his drink, frowning. This was the first time he'd been in a town in about ten years. It was mighty nice talking to people; besides, he couldn't head out until daylight. Riding at night in this country could be right dangerous. So he nodded. "Reckon I'll do that. Ain't talked to no one for quite a spell now. Reckon I'll enjoy it."

Before he left to get a room, Olerud told him there was a man on the second floor of the hotel who'd been shot in the legs and to steer clear of him. "I'll take yore rifle outta its scabbard an' put it in my office."

Yancy had more questions about this town and its inhabitants, but thought to save them until later. He headed for the hotel.

McClain watched the door close behind Tetlow, and knocked back the rest of his drink. He stared into his empty glass a moment then looked at Olerud. "Reckon we done seen all the folks in town 'bout the meetin' we gonna have when young Tenery comes back to town — all 'cept one, an' I'm gonna go see her right now."

Hans frowned. "We ain't gonna let no woman help us fight! You know danged well they ain't one single man hereabouts who'd allow that." Then with a smug look, he said, "Why don't you use it as an excuse to take 'er over to the café fer supper?"

Red stared at his friend a moment. "Why, dang you, you meddlin', broke-down old cowboy, I — I, well hell, reckon that's a mighty good idea. Gonna do just that." He shrugged into his coat and pulled his hat down on his head. As he stepped toward the door, he said over his shoulder, "Take care o' the bar for me while I'm gone. In case Tetlow gets back before me, buy 'im a drink or two on the house."

He hadn't been to see Miz Gretchen since she fixed him dinner. He thought he'd waited long enough that she wouldn't take it wrong for him to visit. He angled across the street to her bakery thinking he'd better check with Cody and see if he'd heard anything about the replacement door he'd ordered for her.

He opened her door to warmth; Gretchen was in her rocker. *She looks mighty pretty sitting there.* "Howdy, Miz Gretchen. I been waitin' to see when Cody would get your door, but figgered I had a good excuse to come see you this time without that."

"Mr. McClain, you don't need an excuse. You just come on over anytime an' we'll have a cup o' coffee."

"Well for goodness' sake, ma'am, I woulda been over here 'fore now if I'd knowed that."

She picked up the coffeepot and another cup.

Red shook his head. "Ma'am, we ain't gonna drink yore coffee. Want you to come with me to the café an' we'll have supper together. What I gotta talk 'bout'll wait 'til we get back here."

She frowned. "Sounds serious."

Red nodded. "Reckon it is, but that's what I gotta talk to you 'bout. You hungry 'nuff to eat now?"

She smiled. "If I wuzn't, Mr. McClain, I'd say I was." She swung her coat over her shoulders and let him help her put it on. "Let's go have supper."

Unusual here on the frontier, the café had individual tables. Red held Gretchen's chair for her to be seated, sat in the one next to her and slanted her a questioning look. "Ma'am, last time I seen ya, thought we agreed to eliminate the mister an' missus. Reckon I'd feel like we were friends if we did."

"Well, goodness, Red, I surely want to be friends. Runnin' a business, I don't get to visit with the ladies much." She nodded. "All right, first names it'll be." She leaned closer to him. "You said we had somethin' right serious to talk 'bout. Let's hear it — then we can talk 'bout things that'll help us to know each other better."

Red nodded, wondering how to tell her that they were soon to make a decision about the town's troubles. He decided to say it straight out. He told her about Bill Tenery, about his determination to force the issue with the Rourk bunch. Then he cocked his head to the side and studied her a moment. "Gonna tell ya, Gretchen, I want you to keep every gun you got loaded an' where you can get your hands on one of them in a hurry. He shook his head. Now I ain't tryin' to scare ya, but I want you to be ready in case any o' that crew tries to come in your place — that is, if we have to fight 'em in town — hope we won't have to, but I want you to do exactly what you done to Cord Rourk."

The lady who ran the café interrupted, "I'll tell you what we have tonight, then you can decide which one of the two things you want. I got venison stew or beefsteak. You can have biscuits with both. I got some eggs too."

Red looked at Gretchen.

"Stew sounds good to me. I don't ever take time to fix any. Seems like most o' my time's taken up with doughnuts an' cookies."

McClain looked at the lady. "Make it two, an' coffee when you get time." He shifted his look back to Gretchen when the lady went to the kitchen.

"Like I was sayin', anyody tries to come in yore shop once the dance has started, you blow 'em to hell." His face heated, he thought it had to be red as his hair, but he had to say what he felt. "Gonna tell ya, if the fightin' happens here in town, I'm gonna git over to you quicker'n scat. I'll be there to protect you if it works out that way."

She must have been holding her breath. She exhaled. "Red, I'm surely glad you offered that. Most o' the women here have their men to watch over 'em an' don't have to worry 'bout defendin' themselves with a gun." She smiled. "Think now I can feel like a real woman; like I got somebody lookin' out for me."

"Ma'am, don't know why you wouldn't always feel like a *real* woman. You're as much woman as I ever seen." He nodded.

"An', yes'm, you can figger on me to take care o' you." His face flamed like a ripe tomato.

Gretchen lowered her eyes to look at her plate. "Tell you, Red, I take what you jest said as nothin' more than you wantin' to be my friend — my real friend. Don't be embarrassed 'cause you offered. I can tell by the way you're blushin' that you probably think you said too much." She shook her head. "You said what I needed to hear to make me feel safe. Thank you, Red."

He felt like his chest would explode, felt like he thought a child would feel on Christmas morning, then something bubbled out of his chest: a rumbling laugh. "Well, dang it, Gretchen, if you wuz a man, I'd say let's have a drink to seal our friendship, but of course you ain't. We'll have a swallow of coffee instead."

His laugh was contagious; hers followed his. "Red, we'll do nothin' of the kind. I have a bottle at the bakery." Now it was her turn to blush, and she did so very prettily to Red's thinking. "I confess, every once in a while when I'm feelin' extra lonely or quite tired, I take a little nip. Them times ain't happy ones. Makin' a friend *is* a happy one an' soon's we finish supper we're gonna go to my place an' have a little nip together."

Even though he had come to see her on a sober subject, the evening had turned into one of the happiest he'd known for many a day. He would make it a point to come see the pretty lady as often as he could break loose from his saloon. Olerud would tease him mercilessly — but to heck with it, let the old man have his fun. If he got too nosy, Red figured he'd make him pay for it by having him take care of the saloon while he was gone.

The next morning, Tetlow thought to head out at once for the Saddle Horn, then decided that Red and Hans might not have had breakfast yet, and that he would enjoy eating with his newfound friends. He'd enjoyed the drinks he'd had with them the night before. He'd buy breakfast. They hadn't let him buy but one round the night before.

He knocked on the door twice before Red pulled it open. "Damn, man, you shore do git up early. It's only six o'clock."

Yancy chuckled. "Reckon I fergot you townsfolk sleep to might nigh lettin' the mornin' git away from you. Down on the ranch, I'da had five or six steers branded by this time o' day."

Red grimaced. "Aw hell, Yancy, come on

in. I live in the back, so I got the coffee 'bout ready to boil."

"Bet you ain't eat yore breakfast over at the café in a while. Figgered I'd treat you an' Hans to a meal, then I better hit the trail. Gonna see my boy right soon."

Red went to get his coat, saying, "Let's go wake that brokedown old puncher. Bet money he ain't still asleep."

The three of them had their meal and talked, drank a couple cups of coffee until Yancy paid for their breakfast, saying, "Reckon I better git gone if I'm gonna git out there in time for the noonin'."

They shook hands. Red stopped Tetlow as he stepped toward the door. "Want you to tell Tenery we done talked to every man in town. They know 'bout the meetin' an' they all said as how they wouldn't miss it; fact is, they seemed right anxious to find out what he has in mind."

Yancy nodded. "I'll tell 'im."

When he and Red had gone to the livery to get Olerud, Yancy had saddled his horse and walked both it and his packhorse to the café. He stepped off the boardwalk, toed the stirrup, lifted his hand in a choppy wave and headed out.

■ ■ ■ ■

Standing in his room, holding the curtain open only a crack, Rourk peered across the street at the café. He pulled his brows together in a deep frown. *Who was that stranger? Why all the sudden activity of people visiting each other? What could they be up to? My men had told every damned person in this worthless little town to keep to themselves.* He wished one of his men would come to town to see him. He needed to talk.

He limped — more of a waddle than a limp — to his bed and sat on its edge to think. Maybe it would be better to wait and talk to Whitcom when he got here with more men. He pondered that thought awhile, then decided not to do anything until his New York cohort showed up. His frown deepened. Hell, there wasn't a man he'd first brought out here that he trusted. His jaw clamped. He shook his head. He didn't trust Whitcom either, but he'd withhold paying any of the new bunch until they'd done what he needed doing.

He stared at the wall a moment, not seeing it. He didn't want to destroy the entire town, only that woman, McClain, Olerud

— and maybe that cowboy he'd only moments ago seen them with. No, that man looked like he was traveling, leaving town. He'd had a packhorse.

Tenery had worried the problem to a frazzle. He could think of nothing better than to gather the town's menfolk, ride out to Rourk's ranch, kill all they could get under their guns and burn the ranch to the ground. He tightened one corner of his cheek. Hell, he might get a bunch of the men killed if he did that. He cast that thought aside — but maybe he'd go back to it later.

In the four days he'd been back with Rufus, he'd done every odd job around the place that he could identify as needed doing, however slight. He thought better when busy, but Bent dogged his footsteps, trying to get him to get back in the bunkhouse and rest; let his body heal.

The morning of the fifth day, he had the fire in the forge burning to his satisfaction, had shaped a new shoe for his horse's front left hoof and was straddling the stallion's leg, ready to nail the shoe on, when Rufus came fuming into the stable. "What're you doin', boy? You gonna come down with a chest cold if you don't git back in that bunkhouse."

Bill pulled a nail from between his lips, drove it home and repeated the action until he had the shoe tight. Then he took the rasp and shaped the hoof to the nail. When he had the task looking as good as he figured he could get it, he dropped the leg and looked up at Rufus. "Bent, you ever figure I might *need* to be doin' some good, hard labor? It's good for me, will get me back in condition." He shook his head. "I don't b'lieve I ever let myself get so soft before. But I'm tellin' you right now, I'm 'bout back to where I want ta be. Another three or four days an' I'll be ready to fight a bear." He grinned.

Bent grimaced. "Well, I done what Miz Penny told me to do. But like every other time I done what she said — it ain't done one damned bit o' good." He frowned and cocked his head to the side. "You come up with what you gonna do in town?"

Tenery shook his head. "Not one thing that I can feel assured I won't get any o' those men shot all to hell."

Rufus raised his eyebrows. "They ain't a man here worth a damn who wouldn't figger that freedom from payin' them Eastern punks part o' their hard-earned money wuzn't worth any price."

Tenery nodded. "Yeah, but every time I think I have it nailed down, I think o' the little kids who might lose their daddy." He shook his head. "It always comes down to that, an' I don't think I could look in the mirror to shave if I did that."

"It's gotta be done, an' you might not ever git another chance, what with Rourk shot up an' his men stayin close to his ranch. Think on it, then make up yore mind." Rufus twisted to face the door and headed for the house to see Penny.

Tenery scowled at his retreating back. He knew Bent was headed to tell Penny that he'd carried out her orders — and that it had done no good. He chuckled deep in his throat.

Cold though the weather was, he'd worked up a sweat working on his horse's footwear. He shrugged back into his coat and went back to the bunkhouse. He picked up a book from one of the hands' bunk, sat on the edge of his own bunk and had read two pages when the sound of a horse approaching brought a questioning frown to his forehead. As far as he could figure, Bent hadn't sent any of the Saddle Horn riders away from the ranch. He thought to stand and have a look-see, but shook his head. Whoever it was would either come to the bunkhouse or go to the ranch house. He settled onto the bunk.

He sat there a few minutes, read another couple of pages, but the question of who had ridden in kept shoving into his mind. He reckoned he'd better take a look or he'd never get back into concentrating on what he read. He opened the door just in time to see a rather fat man come out the big house's kitchen door ahead of Bent. Rufus' right hand hung close to his handgun.

Tenery scowled. That man ahead of Rufus tickled his memory; then a knot formed in his throat and his chest tightened. He swallowed a couple of times, memories reminding him how much he missed the home folks. "Yancy! You finally left the ranch. What the hell're you doin' up here?"

While Bill still had the words in his mouth, the rotund man broke into a run — and he *could* run. He got to Tenery, opened his arms wide and gathered the ex-soldier into a bear hug. Bill pounded Tetlow on the back while the rotund man pummeled his back and shoulders.

Finally they stood back from one another. Tenery stared at his old friend. "Bet Papa sent you to look for me."

Yancy nodded. "Boy, you done treated yore folks mighty bad. We all been worried sick 'bout you. Bet yore ma, pa, Mopeah, Adam an' his wife, Mornin' Star, an' me done looked up the trail dozens o' times each day since you said you wuz gonna leave the Army." He shook his head. "I done taught you to treat ever'body better'n that. Fact is, we all done taught you better'n that."

The joyful swelling of Bill's chest became a giant hollow space, but the lump in his throat got larger. He frowned. He *had* treated them badly. Every day, he'd thought to write, but each time something seemed to get in the way, or he'd pushed the thought aside in favor of another task.

He stared into Yancy's eyes, nodding slowly. "Yancy, I know I've treated all o' you somethin' awful, but I b'lieve Rufus standin' there behind you will tell you I *do* have some o' that time covered with a good excuse." He shook his head. "And I gotta admit I had time to write 'fore now, but was usually miles from any town an' didn't have paper or pencil." He shrugged. "Probably not much excuse but those are the reasons."

He shifted his look to Rufus. "Reckon y'all exchanged names up yonder at the house, or you wouldn't have brought Yancy outta there without a gun in his back if he said he was *lookin'* for me."

Rufus nodded. "You notice I walked behind him. He wuzn't gonna git a chance to harm you."

Tenery chuckled. "Yeah, reckon you could say I figured pretty early why you walked behind him." He slapped the old outlaw on the shoulder. "Let's go back to the house, let Penny pour us a cup o' coffee an' bully Bent into sweetenin' it with some rye."

Yancy nodded. "Beginnin' to wonder didn't you folks in this part o' the country ever take a drink."

Sitting at the kitchen table, Bill brought Penny and Bent up-to-date about meeting Tetlow and the escape from The Hole. He told them everything he could think of that had been part of his life, including the Military Academy, his getting disgruntled with being put behind a desk, resigning his commission — everything up to the day he rode into Elkhorn. He swept them with a look that said they knew as much about him as he himself did. Then he pinned Tetlow with a "don't argue with me" look. "Gonna tell ya, Yancy; I got somethin' I gotta do 'fore I leave here." He nodded. "Gonna get it done first, then I'll ride down to see the folks. Got a lot to tell 'em."

Penny locked him in a straight-on look. "Gonna tell *you,* big man, you ain't goin' down there without me — you might ferget to come back." She cast Yancy a chagrined look, blushed a deep red and shifted her gaze to her empty cup. She mumbled, "Reckon Bill should tell ya why I said that. Know I sounded like a brazen hussy."

Tetlow, a slight smile breaking the corners of his lips, shifted his look from Tenery back to Penny. "Pretty lady, don't reckon Billy needs to tell me nothin'; them words o' yore's done told me ever'thing."

Tenery, trying to hold back a smile, forced his face into a solemn mask and looked at Penny a moment. He shook his head. "Been thinkin' 'bout that. Reckon we could hunt us up a preacher man 'fore we leave here, or we could get married like the Shoshone do."

Penny's face lighted up with a big smile. "Oh, Bill, that sounds so romantic. Let's get married Shoshone fashion."

Yancy broke out into a belly laugh; laughed until tears streaked his cheeks. He finally sucked his laugh down to a heavy chuckle. "Careful, pretty lady, if Billy agrees to that, you two'll already be in double harness." He let his chuckle die down. "You better hope he don't agree with you right now." He shook his head. "Kinda figger you gonna want a preacher man."

A puzzled frown creased Penny's forehead. "A preacher or maybe a war chief to say some words over us, but whichever it turns out to be, *I'm gonna be the happiest brazen huzzy you ever did see.*"

Bill thought they'd had enough fun at Penny's expense. He explained the Shoshone marriage agreement to her, then shook his head and said, "We'll get us a preacher."

She grinned. "You think you scared me, Bill Tenery? Gonna tell ya right now, we're only one word from bein' married the Shoshone way. You say it's all right, an' you're gonna be in deep trouble 'cause I'm gonna hold you to it."

Bent and Tetlow glanced at each other, grinned, and then pinned Penny and Tenery with a smile. They said in unison, "Ain't no doubt who's callin' the shots here."

Bill smirked. "Not a one o' you know how tempted I am to makin' us married. Hell, if I remember it right, Ma an' Papa did it the same way."

Yancy nodded. "You remember it right, Billy. Know how happy we all wuz when Adam drove their wagon onto the reservation." He grinned. "Fact is, the whole danged Shoshone tribe held a celebration fer almost a week. Old Chief Washakie joined in."

He picked up his coffee cup to refill it; then, a totally innocent look wiping out any hidden intent, he blandly said, "Shore would be nice if I had somethin' to sweeten this here drink with."

Rufus, flushed a deep red, stood and pulled a bottle from the cupboard.

Yancy, a slight smile breaking his lips at the corners, nodded his thanks when Bent poured a healthy slug of rye into his coffee. He turned to Tenery. "When we goin' in town to finish yore business?"

Bill studied the man who'd helped raise him and shook his head. "*We* aren't goin' in. *You're* gonna stay right here with Penny an' Rufe." He shook his head. "Not gonna go home an' tell 'em you got shot all to hell."

"Billy, you ain't never told me what to do. You ain't gonna start now. I'm gonna be right there alongside you when you open the ball," Yancy stated firmly.

Tenery stared at the rotund man a moment, jerked his head in a nod, then cast him a wintry smile. "Started to say it'd be your funeral, but I won't put it that way. I want you to lead the way back onto Papa's ranch. Fact is, I'm gonna be right proud to have you sidin' me. Gonna seem like old times.

"Haven't made up my mind how to fight that bunch yet; looks like I'm gonna have to have two plans — the second one'll be if Rourk has sent for more troops. Kinda hope he has, that way we can get rid of all our troubles at once."

Despite those sitting around the table, Tenery's mind shifted to taking care of Rourk. If he *had* sent for more men, he wondered how many he could count on. He decided maybe fourteen or fifteen at the most. He added that to those left of the Easterner's original bunch, played that figure against the number of towns people he thought would join him and nodded. If he had to, he might be able to split the town into two groups; one to guard the town, and one to attack Rourk's ranch. He pulled his lips into a grim smile. He felt closer to solving how to fight.

"What in the world are you thinking, Bill? For all practical purposes you left us several minutes ago. You might as well have been back in Washington," Penny accused.

He frowned, then nodded. "Reckon I was somewhere else, mentally." He cast her a smile. "But I b'lieve I'm a little closer to comin' up with how to use the men we have."

Penny's face hardened. "Gonna tell ya right now, cowboy — you're stayin' here 'til I say you're well enough to go off an' get yourself shot again."

Tenery chuckled, then laughed outright. "Penny, if I thought I was gonna go off an' get myself shot again I b'lieve I'd send Yancy in to tell 'em 'bout the plan an' I'd stay here."

Rufus shook his head. "Now I'm tellin' y'all like it is: you folks just heered the biggest bunch o' bull you ever gonna hear." He turned his eyes on Bill. "Son, if I thought we could keep you here, I'd go in your place."

"Aw hell, Rufe." Yancy looked at Penny. " 'Scuse me, Miss Penny, reckon I fergot myself. Anyway, Rufe, they ain't a man in this Wyomin' Territory what could keep that man outta a fight long's there was one goin' on somewhere."

"Why do you say that, Yancy?" Penny's expression said she was afraid of the answer.

Tetlow looked at Tenery, then rested his look on her. "Miss Penny, when that boy wuz growin' up, Mopeah had to dang near sneak his warriors outta camp when he wuz gonna go raidin' the Crow. Billy wuz jest flat set on goin' with him every time." He rubbed his jaw, frowning. "You see, Miss Penny, Mopeah made Billy a Shoshone warrior when he was only twelve years old." He chuckled. "Reckon that boy took bein' a warrior a mite serious."

Settling into his favorite subject, he told them about Mopeah, Chance and Billy fighting a bunch of Lakota Sioux, and Billy accounting himself as a warrior in that skirmish.

He started on another of Bill's escapades but Tenery cut him off. "Folks, you sit here an' listen to Yancy tell whoppers 'bout me an' we'll be here 'til daylight." He shook his head and frowned. "Never seen a man who liked to talk as much as he does. Why, he even introduced himself to Pa as Friar Tuck when they first met. He's mighty good at spinnin' yarns."

Penny studied Tenery a moment. "Bill, I don't think Yancy would have to stretch facts much indeed to talk about things you've been doin' all your life."

"Ma'am, don't reckon I'd have to stretch nothin' if I wuz talkin' 'bout Billy Tenery. That boy wuz jest flat built to barge into all kinds o' trouble."

Tenery stood. "Reckon I'm gonna go to the bunkhouse, finish readin' that story I started when Yancy showed up with his tall tales." He tipped his hat to them and left.

He'd not cleared the door before Penny turned to Yancy. "Now I want to hear all about Bill."

Tetlow grinned. "Wuz hopin' you'd ask." He settled into his chair, then frowned. "Reckon if I'm gonna tell ya 'bout 'im, I better git a full cup o' mud. 'Course I'm gonna sweeten it a little with some more o' Bent's rye."

Rourk spent most of every day standing at his window peeking around the edge of the curtain hoping to see a couple of his men ride in. His hope was in vain. He kept thinking his legs would heal enough for him to ride, but every time he pushed his luck on stretching them out, bending them to the way he'd have to sit a saddle, the pain pulled him to the floor and he'd have to crawl to his bed, pull himself onto it and lie there sweating and panting, knowing he was a long way from getting out of his room. Then he'd curse a blue streak, all the while including Gretchen in his tirade.

Tetlow had been gone almost two weeks. Several times each day Chance and Betsy went to the door, opened it and searched the landscape to the north. Chance tried to make his wife believe he looked to see if the men had come in off the range, but finally she pinned him with a look that said he didn't fool her one iota. "Chance Tenery, when Yancy finds our boy, we'll see him ride in with Billy in tow — not until then, so why don't you relax and let time take care of it?"

Not feeling much like a grin, he crinkled the corners of his mouth. "Reckon I don't relax for the same reason you don't. Honey, you walk to the door an' look for any sign of them as often as I do."

She crinkled her brow in a worried frown. "Oh, Chance, you suppose Yancy mighta had to ride all the way to Billings, or maybe Miles Town?"

Chance nodded. "Figure if he gets to Miles Town, he's gonna think 'bout givin' up on his search — then he's gonna go on even if he has to go all the way to Chicago."

"That's a mighty big town to look for one man in. How far do you think he's gotten by now?"

Chance steered Betsy to a chair. "Tell you for a fact, honey, I don't b'lieve he's gotten much farther than that town to our north, Elkhorn. It just seems like forever to us. It's a lot harder to wait for news than it is to try to find the news."

He changed the subject. "Morning Star showin' any signs that she's gonna have that baby soon?" He chuckled. "If she doesn't do it soon, I b'lieve Adam's gonna go crazier'n a rabid skunk."

Betsy looked at Chance, her look saying that she knew he was trying to get her mind off of Billy and Yancy. "Husband of mine, Adam was the same way with their first two babies." She laughed. "I think if they had a dozen children, he'd be the same way."

"Tell you one thing, Betsy, those babies don't look anything like Adam. They look like full-blooded Shoshone warriors already."

She nodded. "Hope this one's a little girl. Think that's what Morning Star *and* Adam want too." Almost before finishing her sentence, she went to the door and looked to the northeast. Chance shook his head and pulled one side of his mouth down. He knew she couldn't help her actions. He knew because his emotions were tied to the same string.

In the back of his store, Trent Cody sorted the mail the stage had delivered only moments before. A caged-off corner of the store served as the post office. He flipped one envelope over to see who it was addressed to. He frowned. Cord Rourk was the addressee. The letter came from New York.

He slipped the letter into his coat pocket and told his wife he had to see McClain and for her to handle the store. She nodded while he opened the door and left.

He ran across the trail, but still felt chilled to the bone in the short time it took to enter the saloon and shut the door behind him.

Red bellowed from behind the bar, "Ain't time fer yore evenin' drink, Cody. What brings you out in the cold this soon?"

Trent reached into his pocket, pulled out Rourk's letter and handed it to McClain. "Figgered you an' Olerud oughta take a look at this, then let's talk about it."

By then, Red's eyes had focused on the envelope. He frowned. "Run down to the livery an' get Hans. You're right. We need to talk 'bout it." Before he finished his sentence, Cody had left for the livery.

McClain stared at the letter, felt bile rise to the back of his throat at the thought that more of that city slime might be coming out here. He had no doubt this was in answer to the letter Farnum said he'd mailed for Rourk. The thought entered his mind to tear it open and see what it said. He mentally shook his head. To open it and see what it said would be a crime. He'd wait until Cody and Olerud came back. The three of them would have to determine what to do. He wished Tenery was in town.

He continued to look at Rourk's name scrawled in large letters. Angry bile continued to flow under his tongue. When Olerud and Cody walked to the bar, Red slid the letter across the polished surface without a word.

Hans stared at the name on it, chomped down on his chew a couple of times and spit into the spittoon at the corner of the bar. He picked up one of the glasses McClain had put in front of him and Cody. He took a swallow of his drink and looked from Red to Trent. "Let's open it; see who sent it to him an' what it says."

Cody shook his head violently. If he hadn't had such a thick neck, Olerud figured his head would come loose. "Nope. We open that letter, the U.S. marshal would be lookin' fer us."

Hans stared at the handwriting a moment, then a sly look slid over his face. "Red, you got any glue back there in yore office?"

A puzzled frown creased Red's forehead. "What the hell you need with glue?" He shook his head. "Naw, I ain't got any use fer that kind o' stuff."

Olerud shifted his eyes to Cody. "You got any in the store?"

"Maybe a couple o' bottles. Why?"

A grin split Hans' face from ear to ear. "You go git a bottle, bring it back to me, then you head back to yore store." Cody shrugged, shook his head and left.

As soon as Trent closed the door behind him, Olerud looked into McClain's eyes. "Put a kettle o' water on to boil."

"Got one on already." The puzzled frown disappeared. A grin replaced it and Red chuckled. "We gotta send Trent back to his store 'fore we do what I know damned well we gonna do." Hans' laugh drowned out any noise Red's chuckle might have made. Cody came back in the door, slammed it behind him, shivering, and came to the bar. He handed Olerud a small bottle of glue.

McClain poured them each another drink, grunted that it was on the house, then pinned Trent with a straight-on look. "Want you to leave this here letter with us a little while. We'll give it back when you come over for your 'fore supper drink. It'll be just like you left it with us."

Cody stared at Red, shifted his look to Olerud, then shook his head. "Ain't gonna ask neither one o' you what you got in mind

271

to do with that letter." He glanced at the boiling kettle of water, quickly shifted his look from it, said he'd be back for another drink later and left.

Red frowned. "Anybody come in while we're takin' care o' this little job, we gotta git it outta sight in a hurry."

"Hell, McClain, you ain't had a customer all day; same as me. Too cold."

Red nodded. "Let's git on with it." He didn't need those words, he already held the envelope over the steam.

A few minutes later, about a quarter of an inch at a time, Red peeled the envelope flap back until it was opened all the way. He pulled the letter from the envelope and held it across the bar so he and Olerud could read it at the same time. The heavy saloon door opened.

McClain shifted the letter to his left hand, put it under the overhang of the bar and asked Tom Lease, a Rourk rider, what he'd have.

"Whisky, a whole glass full. Gotta knock the cold outta my bones."

Red filled a glass, put it in front of Lease, and before he could turn back to Olerud, the Rourk rider downed it and held the glass out for a refill. While he poured the second drink, only to make conversation, he said,

"Mighty cold to be ridin' round the countryside. You come in to see yore boss?"

Lease shook his head. "Hell no. Not any of us would spend our time looking to see *him*. A whole bunch of us needs tobacco. We drew cards to see who'd come to town for it — I lost." He knocked back his drink and said he was going over to the store, tossed a coin on the bar and turned to leave. He looked over his shoulder. "Soon's I get our tobacco, I'll be back for another drink, then I'm gonna head back to the ranch. You can sack me up 'bout six — no, make it eight bottles o' whisky to take with me."

As soon as he cleared the door, Olerud grinned at Red. "Don't seem as how them men're gettin' along with their boss very good, does it?"

Red frowned, shook his head and glanced to where he'd put the letter. "Better wait'll Lease leaves town 'fore we finish what we started." He took out a gunnysack and put the whisky in it that Lease had ordered.

They had not long to wait. Lease came back through the door with a sack slung across his shoulder. He knocked back the drink Red poured, tossed Olerud a coin with the explanation he'd left his horse in the livery, paid McClain and left. Olerud watched him from the window as he collected his horse and rode out of town.

"By golly, he didn't go up to see Rourk."

Red had read the letter while Hans was spying on Lease. "Think maybe this letter tells us. Here, read it."

The old man took the letter, held it out at arm's length, then pulled his glasses from his pocket. "Danged eyes ain't what they used to be." He held the one page so he could see it, read, then looked at McClain. "Red, this here may be bad news for us. Wisht that boy would come to town soon; he needs to know this."

Rourk had watched his rider go into the saloon, stay a few minutes, come back out and go across the trail to Cody's store. "Dammit, get through with what you doin' and come on up here to see me. I have things I want you to do." His mumbled words fell into the empty room.

He stood at the window peering around the edge of the curtain. After a few more minutes, Lease came out carrying two sacks. Rourk grunted, satisfied that his man would be in his room in only moments. He waddled toward the door to open it when Lease got there. He cursed. His legs refused to work like they had before that woman shot him. One more step, and he stumbled;

he had to grab the doorknob to keep from falling. He cursed again and waited to hear Lease's footsteps in the hall. He waited. No footsteps.

He frowned and went back to the window — and watched his rider head out of town. He mentally added Lease's name to those he'd get rid of when Whitcom got there with more men. The fact was, he planned to get rid of the entire bunch he'd initially brought out here. He stumbled back to the side of his bed and sat on its edge. He'd have to be able to ride before the new bunch arrived. He had to make sure they did things the way he wanted. He planned to meet them out at his ranch. Having them all in town at once might start an all-out war with the townspeople.

Tenery sat at the one table in the middle of the bunkhouse looking at Bent lying on his bunk. "Rufus, you reckon you can remember every grown man in town?"

The ranch foreman nodded. "Yep, reckon I could remember every man on the four ranches within thirty miles o' here too. Why?"

Bill frowned, then pinned Bent with a look that didn't even see him. His mind had locked on the word "four" when Rufus mentioned the ranches within a half day's ride. "You say there's four ranches? About how many riders do each of them have?"

Bent's brow pulled two deep furrows in his forehead. He thought a few minutes, then shook his head. "Don't know, young'un, I'd have to write 'em down when I put my mind to it."

"All right, get a sheet of tablet paper and put your mind to it. I want to know how many grown, fightin' men we got in this area. Then I'm gonna ask you to send riders to each ranch. I want them at the town meeting — or at least someone that can rep for them."

"You figgerin' to get all them folks into the towns folk's fight?"

Tenery nodded, slowly. "Rufus, I'm figurin' everyone in fifty miles should have an interest in the welfare of the people, the businesses an', well, everything in that town — same as we do. What you think?"

Bent grinned. "Jest wish I'd thought of it myself. Danged tootin' they got the same interest in that town as us. Without it, we'd all have to ride over a hunnert miles to buy provisions." He went to a shelf above his bunk, pulled a yellowed Indian Head tablet from it, pulled a pencil from his shirt pocket and sat across the table from Bill. "This here's gonna take me some time. Writin' ain't the best thing I do."

"Take your time. I still have a good bit o' plannin' to do on the way we're gonna fight." Before he could speak again, Cookie yelled that supper was ready.

9

When Charley Farnum brought him Rourk's letter, Cody put it to the side instead of putting it with the mail and took it with him when he went to the saloon for his evening drink. Tenery stood behind the bar. Cody handed him the letter. "When you an' Olerud finish with it, get it back to me. The stage'll be in tomorrow an' I gotta get this letter on it." He swept the room with a look. "Where's McClain?"

Tenery grinned. "He went over to the bakery." He chuckled. "Think he's sorta sweet on Miz Gretchen, but too danged bashful to say anything."

Cody chuckled. "Tell ya, Tenery, if I wuz single an' hadn't met my wife, I'd be standin' in line to spark her. She's a mighty fine-lookin' woman."

Bill nodded. "She is that, Trent." He and Olerud were the only ones in the saloon other than Cody. He looked at the letter again and said, "I'll bring this back to you soon's we get through with it."

Cody nodded, knocked back his drink and left. As soon as he'd cleared the door, Olerud took the letter and held it over the kettle's spout. He soon had the flap open. He removed the sheet of paper and held it so he and Tenery could both read it.

"Hmmm, he's askin for fifteen or sixteen men, sayin' he'll pay 'em a hundred a month." Tenery grinned and looked at the old man. "That's not much pay for a man who's lookin' to die." He squinted toward the wall, not seeing it. "We're gonna have enough men to handle those already here *and* those that'll get here — if the ranchers will spare a couple or three men apiece."

Olerud nodded. "They will. What one don't have they'll be another who can make up fer it." He took the glue bottle, smeared glue across the back of the envelope, folded the flap back in place and rubbed his thumb across the edge, saying with a grin, "Good as new, huh?"

Shaking his head and smiling, Tenery looked at the old liveryman. "You'd have made a damned good pirate, Hans." He reached under the bar and brought out a bottle of McClain's good stuff. "Think we've drunk enough coffee today to float one of the Navy's battleships. What say we have a drink of Red's good whisky?"

"Well, hot dang it, I wuz beginnin' to wonder if you'd done quit drinkin'. Thought maybe them do-gooder women from back East done got ahold o' you."

Bill laughed. "None o' them got ahold of me, but bet you a painted pony we got some women like that in this town."

Hans knocked back his drink, picked up the envelope and headed for the door. "Better git this back to Cody 'fore he thinks we decided to keep it. 'Sides that, he's most likely gettin' ready to close fer the night."

"I'll have you another drink poured when you get back. I'll put some money in the till so Red won't think I'm tryin' to get paid for stayin' here."

Before Olerud got back, McClain pushed through the door. The red of his face would put a ripened tomato to shame.

"Your face that red from the cold, or Miz Gretchen act like she might like you to come over more often?"

"Aw hell, Tenery, if they wuz a woman within a hundred miles who'd have you, bet you'd go sparkin' too."

Hans opened the door, came in and quickly closed it behind him.

"Know what, McClain? There *is* a woman

like that — a whole lot closer than a hundred miles, an' I guarantee you I'm not gonna let somebody get there before me." Bill nodded. "You decide you've gotten to know Miz Gretchen good enough to start sparkin' her?"

McClain frowned. "Don't know. She acts like she likes to have me around, but maybe that's 'cause we done got to be friends." He shook his head. "Shore don't want to mess up a good friendship."

Tenery nodded. "Know how you feel." He took a swallow of the drink he'd poured before Red came back. He gave it a few moments' thought, then shrugged. "Tell you what. Why don't you ask Cody what kind o' woman stuff she buys, you know, like perfume, stuff like that. Buy somethin' special for her and give it to her next time you go to see her."

"Now why didn't we think o' that?" Olerud grimaced. "Hot dang it, McClain, ain't no wonder we're still single. We jest flat don't know how to go 'bout sparkin' a woman." He squinted out of one eye at Tenery. "I see a woman what I figger to court, reckon I'll jest talk to you 'bout it 'fore I mess things up."

Red looked at their drinks and poured one for himself. "Hell, you old goat, ain't a woman in the whole territory what'd have you. Tenery ain't gonna have to trouble his head 'bout helpin' you."

Olerud's face turned beet red, showing through the years of sun browning and wrinkles. "Wh-why, goldang it! If I wanted to find me a woman, bet I could do it."

Bill chuckled. "Come on, McClain, you're 'bout to cause the old man to have a heart attack. Stop makin' 'im so mad." He looked at Hans. "You give Cody the letter?"

Olerud nodded, then said, "Wisht we coulda kept it a few days — at least 'til the next stage come through — to give us a little extry time."

Tenery looked at Red. "Now why didn't we think of that?" He took Hans' bony old shoulder in his right hand. "Was Cody ready to lock the door when you left over there?"

Olerud nodded, then grinned. "Yeah, he locked it right 'hind me." His grin turned into a full-fledged laugh. "Figger I'll be waitin' outside his door in the mornin' when he unlocks it. Bet money I kin talk 'im into losin' that letter 'til the next stage comes through — that'll give us a extry week."

Olerud's money would have been safe. Cody agreed to "lose" the letter until after the stage came and went later that day.

Along with Cody's agreement to hold the letter Hans had to slosh through melting snow and ice — the long-looked-for thaw had set in. A Chinook wind flowed down the mountains.

Out at the Circle-R, Fran Martin cornered Tom Lease after breakfast. "Know you've heard the drippin' off the roof. Be time those merchants got some business; then *we* can get back in business."

Lease stared at the one man in the entire Rourk bunch that he respected. "Fran, I don't know that I want to 'get back in business.' " He shrugged. "Reckon I'm getting soft, but each time I've taken money from those townpeople I've felt dirty." He shook his head. "Don't know what's happened to me, but it sort o' started before I left New York. I saw good, honest people workin' to make a living — an' they woulda made out pretty good if we had let them alone."

Martin chuckled. "Our conversation last night have anything to do with you feelin' this way? You know, the idea Rourk may be sendin' for more men."

Lease stared into Martin's ice-blue gaze. "Could have." He shook his head. "Know I'm not a coward, but if I'm gonna die, I want ta go over the divide with as clean a feeling as I can."

"You ever wonder how we got to doin' the things we did back East? You know, robbing stores, people, drunks; then the same insurance racket we been doin' for Rourk."

"Yeah, insurance — give us a cut of your take or we burn you out, that is if we don't kill you and your family first." Lease nodded. "Yeah, I've given it some thought. We got into it because there were no jobs, at least none we'd take because the money didn't come in fast enough."

Martin smiled, letting his lips only crinkle at the corners. "What you figure on doin'? You gonna go back to New York?"

Lease shook his head. "No way. Figure I'm out here where nobody knows me, maybe I can learn how to do a day's work."

Martin had had some thoughts along the same vein. He smiled. "You ever think to take on a partner?"

Lease stared back into Martin's cold eyes. He nodded. "Yeah, but there's two things wrong with that thought. First, I don't know of anyone who would hire two men who didn't know what work was; and second, I don't know of anyone dumb enough to pay us while we learned."

Martin pinned Lease with a questioning

gaze. "You got any o' that money left these merchants been paying us?"

Lease nodded. "Most of it. Why?"

"Me too." He chuckled, something he seldom allowed himself to do. "Know what I'm thinkin'?" He didn't wait for an answer. "I'm wonderin' what cowboyin' would be like."

Lease stared at his friend. "You're crazy! Hell, man, that's *hard* work — on top of that, I don't know one end of a cow from the other."

Martin shrugged. "Just wondered how serious you were about workin'."

Lease thought a few moments about Martin's words. Finally, he pinned the quiet man with a look that Martin thought to be on the verge of satanic. "Tell you what I'm thinkin' " — he nodded — "an' yeah, it's crazier than anything I ever thought of."

Martin sighed. "Okay, let's hear it."

"Don't laugh. Everybody in this bunch has been thinkin' the gunfighter was hidin' out somewhere; nobody would say that he was most likely out at that girl's ranch — well, I think that's precisely where he is."

"What the hell are you talkin' about?"

"Well, I figure to hunt 'im down, an' if he doesn't shoot me soon's he sees me, I figure to talk to 'im."

Martin shook his head. "Tom, if you're thinkin' what I think you are — I know damned well you've lost your mind."

Lease grimaced, then shrugged. "Then I reckon I've lost my mind. Figure if I'm gonna make a break from what I've done all my life, I might as well do it even if it hurts." He chuckled. "Think it'll hurt pretty bad if cowboyin' is as hard as I think it is. Most of the men I've seen who do that for a livin' are damned rugged folks."

Martin said, "You mind me taggin' along? What I hear about that gunfighter, you might need me along to help you convince 'im that you're downright serious about what you propose. If everything happens the way you figure, I'm tellin' you, I won't be turnin' back when the going gets rough, even harder than either of us can imagine."

Lease shook his head. "Nope, don't mind you 'taggin' along'; fact is, I was hoping you would." He sighed. "I haven't told you the whole dumb idea."

"Well hell, I've listened to this point, tell me the rest of it."

Lease chuckled — nervously. "Just like all o' us, I've been collecting money from the same merchants. I been thinkin' 'bout goin' to see 'em an' give back what I got left. That'll leave me with what I came out here with — 'bout two hundred dollars."

Martin's eyes thawed to a soft blue. "Reckon I'll still tag along."

Penny sloshed down to the bunkhouse, calling for Rufus to come to the door, she wanted to ask him something. After a few moments he stuck his head out. He shrugged into his coat. "What you need, little one? Know it must be important for you to have trudged down here in that mud."

"Gotta ask ya, Rufus, didn't Bill say he'd probably be back by last night?"

Bent frowned, obviously thinking. He nodded. "Yeah, seems like that's what I heerd 'im say. You gettin' worried?"

She nodded. "Yeah. Most times I don't reckon I'd worry, but he seems to have a talent for gettin' into trouble."

He looked over his shoulder, then turned back to her. "Most o' the men're still in their bunks or I'd ask you in. Go on back to the house, I'll be up in a minute, ain't no need in you standin' out here in the cold."

She turned and headed back to the warmth of her kitchen. As soon as she got inside, she took two cups from the cupboard, filled them and sat. In a few moments, Bent came in.

He looked at the steaming cups of coffee and sat across from her. "Want ta tell ya, little lady, that boy can take care of himself, so quit worryin'. I figure if anything *had* happened to 'im, McClain or Olerud woulda come out here to tell us. I b'lieve they had so much to talk about, he stayed another night."

She nodded, then said, "Rufus, I didn't start worryin' 'til after our nooning, but even if he did stay an extra night, he shoulda been here by now."

He cocked his head, then grinned. "Bet that hoss I hear is our boy now."

Penny jumped to her feet, turning her chair over when she stood. She went to the window, pulled the curtain aside and peered out. Not stopping to put on her coat, she hurried to the back door, opened it and yelled, "Bill Tenery, you get yourself up here to the house soon's you take care of your horse!"

Tenery glanced toward the house, nodded and rode into the stable. *Reckon this is the way it's gonna be when we get married. I gotta be careful about worrying that little lady,* he thought.

He stripped his horse, hung his saddle over the stall wall and headed for the house.

When he went in, he glanced at the table.

Only Rufus and Penny had a cup of coffee in front of them. He grimaced. "Damn, reckon I'm deep in the doghouse or you'da had a cup of hot coffee waitin' for me."

Her mouth a straight-line slit, her jaws knotted at the back, she stared at him a long moment. "Get your own."

He pursed his lips in a silent whistle, then turned his look on Bent. "Reckon around here a man is judged guilty before he has a chance to tell his side of the story." He had untied the top leather thongs holding his sheepskin together. He flipped them back over each other, knotted them, pulled the door open and left.

Bent stared at the girl he'd helped raise, then he did something he'd only done two or three time ever before. "Penelope, reckon you've played hell now. You've hurt that boy's feelin's. He's a right prideful man. Don't know as how a man or woman could ever get away with treatin' 'im like you jest done."

She stared at him, the hot look in her eyes warming to a scared one. "Reckon you're mad at me too, Rufus. Don't remember the last time you called me Penelope. Y-you think he'll leave, ride on down toward the Shoshone reservation?"

He shook his head. "No, don't think he'll

do that 'til after he finishes the job he started around here, but once he gets that done, I figger he'll hit the trail." He shook his head. "Don't blame 'im one damned bit neither."

She pulled her coat from the wall peg and shrugged into it.

"Where you goin'?"

"Down to the bunkhouse. If he don't come out an' talk to me, I'm goin' in."

Bent stared at her a moment. "You ain't goin' inside o' the men's place, that there's their home. Ain't no feeemale gonna go in there an' undo their privacy. Them men are probably lyin' round in their long johns."

She'd taken on that thin-mouthed stubborn look again. She shook her head. "Don't care, Rufus. I'm gonna make that hardheaded man listen to me, gonna tell 'im why I acted like I did."

He studied her a moment. "An' why the hell *did* you act that way?"

She turned and gave him that straight-on look she usually saved for when telling him the truth. "Gonna tell ya, Rufe, I'd done got so danged scared I couldn't even spit, then when I seen he was all right I had to let off my nerves bein' tied up in knots." Her shoulders slumped. "Reckon I let it all off in anger."

Rufus gave her a hard look. "Figgered as much. Yore ma used to do that to yore pa. I cornered her after I seen 'er do that a couple o' times, an' I jest flat told 'er how the cow ate the cabbage. She listened, never done it agin."

"You tellin' me how the cow ate the cabbage, Rufus?"

He nodded. "Reckon that's what I'm doin', little one."

"You gonna keep on callin' me Penelope?"

"Only when you act like a hardheaded mule."

She finished putting on her coat. "Goin' down there an' talk 'im into comin' out an' listenin' to me."

"Don't you even think 'bout goin' in the bunkhouse!" Rufus warned again.

She chuckled. "I won't, but he don't know that. If I threaten to go in there, I'll bet a painted pony he'll come out."

He nodded. "Go ahead. I'm gonna sit right here an' drink my coffee."

She sloshed back through the mud and stopped outside the bunkhouse door. Placing her hands on hips, she called, "Bill Tenery, come to the door, I gotta talk to ya!"

No answer.

"Bill, you come out here, or I'm comin' in."

This time she got an answer. In only a moment he stood in the door.

"Miss Horn, you come in here an' I'll turn you over my knee. That's somethin' I figure your folks didn't do enough of when you were growin' up."

"Wh-why, you wouldn't dare." She studied the hard look he gave her and thought maybe he would. "Oh, Bill, please come back up to the house. I-I-I was just so worried I reckon I let it all come out in anger. Please come on back an' let me make it up to you."

His hard looked softened, then he smiled. "If we were married I guarantee you one thing — I'd show you how to make up for it."

She gasped. "Bill Tenery, if the men heard what you just said, what will they think?"

His smile changed to an outright laugh. "They're gonna think the same thing I mean." He nodded. "All right, let me get my coat. I'll be right up."

She went back to the house, and even before she shrugged out of her coat, she took a cup from the shelf and poured him coffee. She looked over her shoulder at Bent. "Know what he said?"

Rufus shook his head.

"He said he'd turn me over his knee if I dared come in there." She stared at Bent a moment, sort of breathless as she shook her head. "Never figured 'im for a wife beater."

Bent chuckled. "That boy's a good poker player. He wouldn't have touched you, but he sure as hell bluffed you outta doin' what you wuz tryin' to bluff *him* with."

She stood there a moment, anger washing over her again, then she grinned. "Gotta remember that. He ain't gonna outbluff me agin."

Rufus gave her a sober look. "Don't bet on it, little one; 'sides, I wuz you, don't reckon I'd take a chance. Figger you'd be wrong more often than you'd be right."

Stomping, then scraping outside the door announced that Tenery had arrived. He opened the door and came in. Penny noticed him look at the table and the third cup of coffee, and a slight smile broke the corners of his lips.

Penny felt anger push into her head again. She breathed deeply, pushed the anger down and speared him with a look. "Don't push your luck, cowboy. You won that one, but don't bet on the next one."

He raised his eyebrows, wiped any expression from his face, shrugged and said, "Don't know what you mean, ma'am." He pulled a chair out for her to be seated, and walked to the other side of the table and sat where the full cup steamed.

Obviously to break the chilled and tense atmosphere, Bent stood and pulled the jug from the cupboard. Spiking each cup of coffee, he said, "Reckon you found out what you went in town fer?"

Tenery nodded. "An' a lot more." He took a sip of his coffee, then pursed his lips. "Hot." He then launched into all that happened in town. "Reckon we're not any worse off than I've been thinkin', an' the good thing about it is, I know what to figure on now." He chuckled. " 'Specially with those two pirates buyin' a week or two more time."

"Still don't know where you gonna set the fight up. Where you figger would be the best place — out at the Circle-R, or in town?" Rufus carved himself a chew from the plug of Brown's Mule, put it in his mouth, worked it around until he settled it between his cheek and gum, then looked at Tenery, obviously waiting for an answer.

Tenery stared into his cup a moment, nodded and said, "Been thinkin' 'bout that. If we can get the extra men, an' keep Rourk's old bunch out at his ranch, it'll be a lot safer for the town folks, especially the women an' children." He grimaced, then added, "If we get enough men from the ranches, we might have enough to leave a few in town to safeguard the homes and businesses, take the rest to the Circle-R, kill everyone we can get in front of our guns — and end the whole thing right then."

Penny stared at him a long moment. "Bill Tenery, there ain't a soft spot in your whole body." She shook her head. "Don't you figger to give 'em a chance to surrender?"

His eyes locked with hers. He slowly waggled his head. "Kill 'em now, or we'll have it to do later." He shrugged. "Might as well get the job done all at once." He cocked his head and looked at Rufus. "You got anybody out doin' anything?"

Bent shook his head. "Did have, but they done come back. They wuz breakin' ice along the crick so's the cows could drink."

Tenery stood, checked his handgun to make sure it sat snugly against his thigh, and nodded. "Horses comin', sounds like more'n one. Stay in here, Penny. Rufe, you got a rifle in here?" At Bent's nod, he said, "All right, stay in here an' cover me. I'll see who came out in this cold to see us." He put his coat on, hooked it behind the grip of his handgun and stepped out the kitchen door.

He stared toward the two men riding into the ranch yard, along with a pack horse. He frowned. They looked familiar. He squinted; yep, they looked damned familiar — they looked like two of Rourk's riders. They had their hands crossed, gripping the saddle horn. "What're you men doin' out here?"

The one with the hard-looking expressionless face speared Bill with a questioning look. "We never met before, but I have to believe you're Tenery, the one my bunch calls the gunfighter."

Tenery nodded. "That's right — now give me your names."

The man who'd been talking said, "I'm Fran Martin, my partner here is Tom Lease." His voice came out soft but loud enough that Bill had no problem hearing. Martin pinned Tenery with a strange look — questioning yet a glance at his hands crossed on the saddle horn put doubt into his expression. "Mr. Tenery, we've come out here to ask a favor of you. We have something to offer in return."

Bill studied them a moment. They were hard, tough-looking men, but they looked him in the eye while Martin talked. "All right, one at a time, climb from your horses, leaving your hands out where I can see them."

The one called Lease left his horse first, turned so Tenery could see his hands; then Fran Martin did the same.

"All right, you say you want a favor and you have something in return. Reckon we could stand out here in the cold and talk, but I'm gonna ask you to step into the bunkhouse where it's warm. Don't either o' you put your hands close to the buttons on your coats." He flipped his thumb toward the door to the bunkhouse. "That way."

Tom Lease chuckled.

"What the hell's funny?"

"Just thinkin', Mr. Tenery, I was about to say that you could trust us, then realized how ridiculous a statement like that would sound. But despite the irony of it, we would like to sit and talk awhile." He pulled his mouth down at the corners in a grimace. "Fran and I talked long into the night a couple nights ago, an' we came up with an idea. Hope you'll listen to what we have to say."

Bill raked them then their horses with a searching look. "Looks like you men are packed for traveling, bedroll, everything a man needs for the trail."

Martin nodded. "That's what we want to

talk about, Mr. Tenery."

"You men leavin' Rourk?"

Lease said, "Yes," while Martin nodded.

"All right, let's go inside. Y'all walk ahead of me."

Inside, Tenery asked five men playing penny ante to break it up for a while, that he needed to talk to the two men who had come in with him. A few men still ate lunch.

Lease, Martin and Tenery sat. "Now tell me what this is all about," Bill said.

In a hopeful but doubtful voice, Lease said, "We want you to teach us how to cowboy."

It was all Bill could do to hold a straight face. He glanced at their hands folded on the table in front of them. "Turn your hands palms up. Let me see them." They did as he said. The two pairs of palms looked soft enough that they could have belonged to a woman. "Good Lord, either o' you ever done any work — real work?"

Martin shook his head. "No, sir. Can't say that either of us can make that claim — but we want to learn, don't want any pay while we learn, just want what most men never get — a second chance."

"What do you mean, 'a second chance'?"

Lease glanced at Martin, who nodded. "I'm gonna lay all our cards on the table,

Mr. Tenery. Fran and I have spent a lifetime doin' things that any real man would say is flat-out crooked. We got to talkin' and found that we were both fed up with what we've been doin'. Don't think 'til we came out here we ever got close enough to real people, family people, working people, to realize what a sorry life we were leading." He shrugged. "Thought if we had a chance, which we never really had while in New York, we might be able to make somethin' outta ourselves." He shook his head. "No, we don't think to ever get to having a lot of money, nothing like that, but maybe we might get to where we could look in the mirror when we shave without feelin' shame."

Tenery wouldn't make it easier for either of them. "So, sitting drinking coffee one night, the two of you decided to quit Rourk an' find a better life?"

Martin shook his head. "No, Mr. Tenery, we both been thinkin' 'bout this a long time, we just didn't know the other ever had the same thoughts."

"What about the money you been takin' from the town's businesses?"

Lease's face lit up like the sun had only then come from behind a cloud. "Tell you, Mr. Tenery, when we came through town,

299

we both of us stopped by the stores we been takin' money from and gave back every cent we got from them."

"So, what are you going to live on 'til you find somebody dumb enough to give you a job?"

Martin, his face red and even harder than Bill had seen it, said, "We both of us had some of our own money when we came out here. B'lieve we have enough to live on 'til we get a job, even if we have to swamp out saloons."

Tenery allowed a slight smile to crinkle the corners of his eyes. "If I take you on, you can bet your soft butts I won't let up on you — hell, I won't even let you quit. I'll blow you to hell 'fore I let you snivel outta doin' your job."

For the first time Martin relaxed. He laughed. "Mr. Tenery, there's no way you'd shoot either one of us without giving us a chance. You might kick us out the door, tell us to get gone — but you wouldn't shoot us."

Bill chuckled. "You're right, but I gotta tell ya, I don't own this ranch, I'm not even the foreman so I don't have the authority to hire, fire or do a damned thing around here." He shook his head. "But I might take you on under my wing, to see if you have the makin's of honest men."

Lease looked at him squinty-eyed. "You mean that? You really mean it? You don't have any reason to put trust in either of us. We've told you what our lives have been." He shook his head. "There aren't many in this world who would put any trust in either of us."

Tenery swept his glance across them. "You know who'd be the loser if I can't trust you?" His face felt like a dry lake bed in August. "I'd be the winner all the way. If I give you a chance and you double-cross me, you'd always remember you had a chance and threw it away." He looked over his shoulder at Tetlow lying on his bunk. "Yancy, come over here for a moment."

Tetlow grunted, swung his feet off the side of his bunk and walked to the table. "What you want, Billy?"

"Tell these men what you were doin' for a livin' when you helped us get outta Jackson's Hole."

Yancy looked at Tenery a moment, shifted his gaze to the two men sitting there and nodded. "I wuz a outlaw, had been one most o' my life, robbed stages, banks, stores." He shrugged. "Reckon I took what I could get away with from anybody who looked like they had anything. Didn't never kill nobody, though, so when Mr. Chance, Bill's pa, give me a chance to go straight — I took it. Ain't robbed nothin' since." He leaned his head back, squinted toward the ceiling a moment, obviously thinking, then said, "That there wuz might nigh ten years ago."

"Tell 'em how much hard work you had done before Pa took you on."

Tetlow grinned. "Don't reckon I ever done a day's work after I left my uncle's farm." He chuckled. "But I'm gonna tell ya, since I joined up with Chance Tenery's ranch, I ain't had many days when I felt like I hadn't earned my keep. I'm standin' right here, lookin' you in the eye, and tellin' you: I been mighty proud o' every one o' them days."

Martin stared at Yancy a long moment. "Mr. Tetlow, I thank you for telling us that. I hope I'll be able to say the same someday."

Yancy laughed. "Tell me that after dark someday when you been in the saddle since before daybreak an' know you're only gonna get three or four hours sleep before you haveta do it all over again."

Neither Martin nor Lease joined in Tetlow's laugh. Martin nodded. "That's what I would hope to tell whoever would listen, Mr. Tetlow."

Tenery had been sitting there, quietly studying the two men. At the Academy and in the field of combat, he'd had to make quick judgments of men and their character. He'd seldom been wrong.

He turned his eyes to Tetlow. "Crawl back in your bunk. Gonna talk to these men awhile longer." He turned his attention back to Martin and Lease. "What about the men you've been ridin' with? You gonna be able to turn a gun on them if you have to?"

Lease looked at the coffeepot sitting on the big potbellied stove and licked his lips, then nodded. "Mr. Tenery, I can't say that either of us have been riding *with* any of that bunch. We pretty well stayed to ourselves." He shrugged. "Don't see that as a problem though. Most o' them left in that bunch'll soon be gone anyway." He glanced at Martin and got an almost imperceptible nod. "We figure Rourk has sent for a whole new crew. Neither of us have anything to base that assumption on, but that's what we believe. If he has, I think their first job'll be to run us off — or kill us."

"That why you're cuttin' out?"

"No, sir. We both think we can match up with any of 'em with guns." He shook his head. "We're not scared of 'em."

Tenery allowed a slight smile to crinkle the corners of his eyes. "Noticed you lickin' your lips for a cup of that hot coffee. Bring your bedrolls in, get your cups an' help yourselves."

Martin pinned a long, penetrating look into Tenery's eyes. "Thank you, sir."

Tenery grinned. "Wait'll the end o' the first day's work, then thank me — an' it'll be like you spiked it out: no pay 'til I see you can earn it." He flipped a thumb toward the bunks. "Find one with nothin' on it. I'm goin' back up to the house, tell the boss what I've just done here on her ranch."

McClain looked at the array of stuff Cody had put out on the counter. He pushed back his hat and scratched his head. "Hell, Trent, I don't know what no womenfolk use. Why don't you tell me what Miz Gretchen usually buys fer herself?"

Cody picked up a bottle of toilet water. "Every once in a while this's what she gets fer herself. Seems to like it more'n any o' these others; it's called Magnolia. I ain't never smelled it, but she likes it."

Red chuckled. "When I go over there for doughnuts an' she walks by me, she always smells good."

"Sounds like you done made up your mind to start sparkin' 'er."

"Aw hell, you an' that danged busybody old man been talkin', ain't ya?"

Trent looked McClain in the eye. "Red, reckon ever'body in town knows you want to court Miz Gretchen — ever'body 'cept you an' her, that is." He shook his head. "Naw, me an' Olerud ain't been talkin' 'bout y'all."

"You got anythin' to wrap this perfume in?"

"Only thing I got is brown paper."

Red nodded. "That's good."

A few minutes later he was headed toward the bakeshop. Hans had agreed to take care of the saloon for him.

He made sure to clean his boots of mud before he opened the door and went in. He couldn't decide whether he liked the smell of baking things or the meals Miz Gretchen cooked. He finally figured he liked them about equally.

She came out of the kitchen, wiping her hands on her apron. "Red, I was beginning to think you'd forgotten the way over here — it's been two days."

"Aw, ma'am, reckon I jest don't want to make a pest of myself. 'Sides that, if I get Hans to watch over my business any more often 'fraid he's gonna begin to think he owns it."

She stood back and studied him. "You know, if you worry with that package any more than you have been since comin' in here, whatever's in it won't be any good."

He held it out to her. "Thought you might like this. Cody says this's what you buy ever' once in a while."

She tore the paper off and tears flooded her eyes. "Oh, Red, it's just what I like. Haven't been able to afford it since that bunch of Rourk's have been takin' money from me." Then, to Red's surprise and embarrassment, she threw her arms around his neck and hugged him. She pulled her arms down and stepped back, her face flushed bright red. "Oh my goodness, what'll you think of me?"

As hot as his face felt, he knew it must match hers in color, but he couldn't let this opportunity escape — he might not have another. "Ma'am, what I think of you is that you're a mighty fine woman, an' I been wantin' to do that ever since we sorta started seein' each other." He studied the toe of his boot and shuffled it around a moment before looking her in the eye. "If you won't think I'm thinkin' o' you as anything but a lady, I shore would be obliged if you let me have another hug."

She studied him a moment. He wondered if his words had offended her, then she smiled. "You big bear of a man, if you don't put your arms around me an' hug me tight, I think I'll just flat bust. I been wantin' that hug longer'n you."

She held her arms wide. He stepped into them and put his arms around her waist. He held her tight to him, didn't want to let her go, but she caught his forearms in her hands and pushed them loose. "Guess you think I'm just a brazen woman what wants a man, but, Red, I needed to feel you close to me, been needin' that since before you fixed my door." She shook her head. "You ain't gonna let this run you off, are you?"

He shook his head, slowly. "Ma'am, ain't nothin' in this whole territory could run me off."

"Well, if you think you could eat warmed-ups, reckon I'll mix up some biscuits, put the stew on to warm, fix some fresh coffee an' we'll have supper."

"Aw, I figgered to take you to the café," he said, smiling, "but to tell you the truth, I'd druther eat your warmed-ups than anything they fix down yonder at the café."

She pulled a chair over so he could look in the kitchen and told him to sit while she got things ready.

They ate and talked; sat there in comfortable silence; talked a while longer; and finally Red thought he'd better get back to his saloon. Before he left, she stood close and asked him for another hug. She didn't push his arms away this time.

His walk through the mud to his business might as well have been on the paved streets of New York.

As soon as he went in and closed off the outside wind, Olerud studied him a moment. "Yep, reckon you done agreed with yoreself that yore gonna spark that there good-lookin' woman. 'Bout ready to march you over yonder with my handgun stickin' in yore back an' tell 'er you done come courtin'."

Red pinned Hans with a look that would have pierced an inch-thick steel plate. "Know what, old man? They ain't a tongue-waggin' woman in this town more of a busybody than you."

Hans slapped his knee, and laughed until tears rolled down his cheeks.

Red pulled his mouth down in a grimace, shook his head and said, "Looks like you done took over my business, so pour me a drink — a full glass."

When Hans handed him his drink, he gave McClain a look that begged him to ask what he knew that the saloon owner didn't. "All right, you old goat, looks like you gonna bust wide open if I don't ask what's happened while I been gone. What is it?"

Olerud sobered, then stared at him. "Jest gonna tell ya." He poured himself a small glass of whisky, looked at it a moment, then knocked it back. "Two riders come through town while you wuz over there gallivantin' with the widder woman. Know who they wuz?"

Red shook his head. "Hell no, I don't know who they wuz, but I reckon if I wait long enough, maybe 'fore I die of old age you'll tell me."

Hans gave him a jerk of the head that would have been a nod for most. "Yep, jest 'bout to do that. It wuz two of Rourk's men, with a packhorse trailin' behind. Looked like they wuz gonna cut outta here fer good."

"Hmmm. That *is* news, old-timer. What you figger they wuz up to?"

"Jest gonna tell ya that. One of 'em wuz Martin, you know, the quiet one, the one what's been collectin' money from you. Know what he up an' did?"

McClain stared at Olerud a long moment. "Reckon if I wait long enough, you're gonna tell me even *that*."

"Danged tootin', an' you gonna be mighty pleased. He come in here, I figgered maybe to git some more money from you" — he shook his head — "but, Red, that there wuzn't what he wanted at all. He took a sheet o' paper outta his pocket, showed me how much money he done got outta you, counted out a bunch o' double eagles and give 'em to me, sayin' as how he figgered you an' him wuz even. Said he wuz leavin' town, turned hisself around and walked outta here."

"You tellin' me he give back all the money I done give 'im?"

"That's 'zactly what I'm tellin' ya. I couldn't b'lieve it, but you know what made me b'lieve it?"

"Reckon you gonna tell me *that* also if I wait long 'nuff."

Olerud nodded. "Shore am. Well, after that quiet man done give me yore money, that tall lanky drink o' water Martin seems to partner with — he's the one been takin' *my* money — well he done the same thing for me."

McClain took a goodly swallow of his drink and pinned Hans with a questioning look. "He say if the other folks wuz gonna get back their money?"

"I asked 'im that," the old man replied. "He told me that him an' his partner wuz the only ones decided they wuz gonna try to be decent people from now on."

Red shook his head, stared at the pile of double eagles, knocked back the rest of his drink and held his glass out for Olerud to fill. "Well I'll be double damned. Either of 'em say where they wuz headed?"

"Didn't say. I didn't ask."

McClain again looked at the double eagles. "Put mine in the cash box. Anybody else come in while I wuz gone?"

"Yep, one o' the punchers from the Circle-Y an' one from the B-Bar-B come in, said as how their bosses figgered to keep half their crews at the ranch, an' send the rest in to help us with the Rourk fight. Both said they wuz keepin' half o' them at the ranches in case any o' those renegade Crow figgered to attack their respective home ranches." Olerud poured himself a cup of coffee. "That's gonna give us six more fightin' men."

Red frowned, obviously thinking. "Know what, Hans, we're gonna have enuff men to leave the town pretty well protected if that boy decides to have us attack the Circle-R." He smiled. "That takes some o' the worry off my shoulders."

Olerud again laughed, slapped his knee and said, "What yore really sayin' is that maybe you can stay in here an' keep Rourk's bunch away from Miz Gretchen."

McClain gave him a sour look.

Rourk's men sat around the only table in the bunkhouse. Jim Sore stared at the two bunks Martin and Lease had occupied. "Anybody see 'em leave?"

Ben McCall nodded. "Yep, they made no secret of it. Martin said they'd talked it over an' decided they had enough of this life. Thought they'd see if somebody would give 'em a job."

Sore snorted. "Scared, just plain scared. Neither of them had the guts to stay here and face what Rourk's gonna do when he gets well enough to come back out here."

McCall chuckled. "If there was anyone scared, I don't have to look any farther than you, you gutless bastard. You've had your chances to call Martin's hand several times. You yellowed out every time."

Sore jumped to his feet, his hand flashed under his coat — then stopped in mid-motion. He stared down the muzzle of McCall's handgun. He moved his eyes to look into those of the man he hated.

Ben's eyes, cold as a frozen lake bed, reflected the smile that showed no humor. "One of these days, Sore, I'm gonna let you finish getting your gun out, then I'm gonna send you to hell." He slipped his .38 back into its shoulder holster. "Fact is we can try it now."

Sore again sat. "Not now, McCall. I'll name the time and place."

"Nope. I'll do that, and 'til then I'll make damned sure you're not behind me. You get that advantage an' I figure I'd be a dead man."

Sore's eyes dripped poison, but he stayed in his seat.

McCall flicked a glance at the others sitting there. "Gonna ride in, see how Rourk's doing. Reckon I'd like one of you to go with me."

Steve Bartlet nodded. "I'll go. Don't give a damn how he's doing, but we might find out what he's planning." The corners of his lips crinkled. "Wonder if he knows Lease and Martin have left?"

"I figure he sees about everything that goes on in that town. He stands behind the curtain in that hotel room and watches who goes and comes," McCall said.

Bartlet swept the men sitting there. "Any of you need anything, tobacco, whisky?" He shrugged. "Anything 'cept a woman — I find one I'll keep 'er for myself."

In only a few minutes, Bartlet and McCall had made a list of what the men wanted and were headed for town. McCall, short and blocky, slanted the black-haired Bartlet a look across his shoulder. "We're going to Rourk's room to see what his plans are. We keep our guns in their holsters."

"Why do you say that about our hand-guns?"

" 'Cause I b'lieve he doesn't have one and he'll try to have one o' us give 'im ours. Don't do it. I don't trust 'im far as I could throw this horse."

"You have him spiked out about the way I think most of us have." As though to re-assure himself, Bartlet slipped his hand inside his coat, moved it under his left shoulder, rubbed the grip of his .38 and brought his hand back out.

They topped a rise outside of town. Mc-Call studied the now-muddy street. "Not many people out and about. Thought since the thaw almost everybody would be catch-ing up with what they let go during that freeze." He looked to the side. "Think I'll have a drink before we do any shopping, then we'll go see Rourk, not that I give a damn how he's doing, but I want to see for myself."

Bartlet nodded. "Same here." He frowned, then hesitantly asked, "You ever think about doing the same thing Martin and Lease did?"

McCall shook his head. "No. I never thought to do the *same* thing. I think they're gonna stay out here and work for a living." He laughed and shook his head. "If I leave, I'm heading back to New York."

Bartlet nodded. "Me too. Ain't no way I'm gonna stay in this backcountry." He reined his horse to the tie rail in front of the saloon. "Let's get that drink."

When the two men closed the door behind them, McClain took the Greener off the end of the bar and slipped it under the ledge of the smooth surface.

The stumpy one Red recognized as Ben McCall held up two fingers. "Give us two water glasses of that rotgut you hand across the bar."

"You don't like what I serve, go somewhere else." McClain gripped the twelve-gauge in a pistol grip, holding it barely below the bar top. He nodded. "Might help you make up yore minds, I done doubled my price on this here stuff you call rotgut."

Bartlet sputtered. "D-d-damned if I'll pay fifty cents for any kind of whisky."

"Wuz hopin' you'd say that. Now git gone."

Bartlet's hand swept for his coat, but he'd forgotten to unbutton it. Red brought the double-barreled Greener to the top of the bar, fired, and moved the gun to point toward McCall. "Got another load here. You want ta try yore luck?"

The stumpy thug held his hands wide of his coat. "What the hell's gotten into you, McClain? All we wanted was a drink."

"You still want a drink?"

McCall stared at the body of the man he'd ridden to town with, swallowed a couple of times and nodded. "A big one, reeel big."

Keeping the Greener in a pistol grip with his right hand, Red poured what the stumpy one asked for. "Two dollars."

"Two dollars? Hell, I can buy a gallon o' this stuff for that much money!"

McClain grinned. "Reckon you better go buy it then." He made as though to turn, then twisted back. "Oh! Reckon I oughta tell ya, that drink you ain't drunk yet? Well, damned if it ain't done gone up to four dollars."

McCall looked at the drink which he had yet to touch and shook his head. "Damned if I will." He stooped to open Bartlet's coat.

"Leave 'im like he is. I'll take care o' his money, gun an' gittin' 'im took outta here. Now git gone." While talking, Red picked up the drink he'd poured for the stumpy one, put it on his side of the bar and wriggled the shotgun's barrels toward the door.

McCall, his face a frozen mask, stared at the bartender. "I'm leaving, McClain, but I'm telling you, this ain't the end of you and me."

Red smiled. "Never figgered it'd be. Next time I see ya, reckon I'll jest start shootin'. Ain't gonna wait fer you to open yore coat."

McCall spun and, looking over his shoulder at Red, crashed out the door. He bumped into Olerud, who was running to enter about as fast as Ben tried to get out. He backed out of the way and stared at McCall's back. "Damn! Wonder what built a fire under his butt?" He pushed the door open again and went in. A few feet from the bar, he stumbled over something soft and looked down, Bartlet lay there sprawled out, a hole big enough to put both fists in opened his chest. Olerud raised his eyes to look at Red. "Reckon you done put that there extra Greener to use. What caused you to open 'im up like this?"

Never breaking the stern, thin-lipped look on his face, Red said, "He allowed as how the whisky I serve is rotgut."

"Damn, McClain, I ain't never figgered it wuz the best a man could buy, but remind me to not ever complain 'bout the way it tastes." He glanced at Bartlet's now stiffening body. "What're ya gonna do with 'im?"

"First, I'm gonna take that shoulder holster an' gun off him, then I'm gonna see if he's got a money belt with some o' the money he's been takin' from us in town and then I'm gonna find out who that person is an' give it all back to 'im."

Olerud shook his head. "Red, that ain't what I'm askin' ya. What I want ta know is: what the hell you gonna do with this here body?"

McClain shrugged. "Gonna wait'll Miles Mabry comes in, pay 'im whatever he charges to bury folks outta whatever money Bartlet's got on 'im, then have 'im cart the body outta here."

"Gonna leave 'im there 'til then?"

"Yep, figgered to do just that. You got any better idea?"

Olerud shook his head. "Nope, long's you git rid o' him afore warm weather sets in an' he begins to stink. Long's I can stand the smell, I'll still come in fer a drink."

Red began to relax, a slight smile softening his face and crinkling the corners of his lips. "Hans, take care o' the bar. I'll go round up Mabry an' have 'im come git rid o' that trash."

Olerud grinned. "Now you're talkin' like

my friend — settling down some. Tell me what happened."

McClain took a few minutes to lay out what caused the whole thing, then went to go get Mabry. While he was gone, Hans stripped Bartlet of his gun and money belt, and emptied his pockets. He made a pile of everything on the shelf behind the bar.

When McClain came back with Mabry, he said McCall was still in town; he'd seen his horse at the hitch rail in front of the hotel. "Reckon I better not get too far from that scattergun 'til I'm sure he clears town."

Olerud nodded. "Gonna stay here with ya 'til *I'm* sure he's gone."

At the light tap on his room door, Rourk unconsciously reached for the gun under his left shoulder. When he found only his shirt, he cursed between clamped jaws. "Who the hell is it?"

"McCall. You gonna let me in?"

"Yeah, it's unlocked. Come on in."

McCall came in, closed the door and glanced around. "Hmmm, all the comforts of home, huh?"

"Don't get smart, Ben. What did you come in here for? Not a one of you have been up here since that woman shot me."

McCall smiled without any warmth and said, "Wouldn't be up here now except I wanted to see how you thought to keep operating." He walked to the window and pulled the curtain aside. "You see about everything that happens in this town right from this window, don't you?"

Rourk nodded. "Most."

"So you saw Lease and Martin ride through?"

"Yeah, thought at the time they'd quit an' were headed outta here. We lose any more o' that bunch I brought out here?"

McCall stared at him a moment. "I rode in here with Stan Bartlet; he never made it any farther than the bar."

"He quit too?"

Again McCall pushed that cold smile out. He nodded. "You might say that. McClain blew 'im half in two with a charge of twelve-gauge buckshot." He shrugged. "Reckon we don't have many left. How you gonna handle this town without enough men?" He waited for Rourk's answer, studying the ranch owner all the while.

Rourk's expression changed subtly. A sly look changed his eyes.

"I've given that some thought. I think if I double up on the jobs you men're doin' we can take care of it." He nodded. "Fact is,

I've been thinkin' 'bout findin' some more men."

McCall pinned him with a "don't lie to me look." He walked away from the window. "You've sent to New York, haven't you?"

Rourk's head shake was too quick; his eyes shifted to look at the door, not looking into McCall's. "No, no. Don't know where I'd find more. Don't know anyone back in the city that would come out here."

McCall chuckled inside. The ranch owner was lying through his teeth. He'd found out what he wanted to know. He walked to the door.

"Wait a minute before you go, there are a couple of things I need you to do for me."

His hand on the doorknob, McCall stared at Rourk. "Yeah, and what would they be?"

Rourk stood. "First, I want you to rent a wagon and take me back to the ranch — can't ride a horse with my legs like they are," he admitted. "Second, I need your handgun, somebody took mine when I got shot."

A deep chuckle rumbled from McCall's chest. "Rourk, I don't give a happy damn if you have to walk to the ranch; an' as for me givin' you my shoulder gun, you gotta be crazier'n an outhouse rat. Get somebody else to give you a gun." He was about to

321

step through the door when he decided he'd leave the ranch owner with another thing to worry about. He gave him a straight-on look. "And I'm gonna tell ya right now, I got my money like all of us do. Got mine in my money belt; gonna go by the ranch, get my bedroll and head for Billings come daylight." He laughed. "Seems like you're gonna need every damned one of those men I figure you sent to New York for." He closed the door softly behind him and headed down the hall.

When he walked out of the hotel, from the corner of his eye he saw a man push his shoulders against the wall and step to the side. He held a shotgun and the man was McClain. The Greener pointed straight at his gut. "What's got into you, Red?"

McClain grinned. "Jest figgered since I got one o' you an' the money he done stole from us, I'd take a little more of it back. Turn yore back to me."

McCall thought to try for his gun, then realized he'd be making the same mistake Bartlet had made — his gun was buttoned inside his coat. He put his back to McClain, then it felt like his head exploded. That was the last thing he remembered.

Red stared at the stumpy man lying at his feet. He yelled over his shoulder, "Farnum, come out here, I need some help."

In only a moment the hotel owner pushed through the door. He stared at McCall and turned his eyes on Red. "What happened?"

McClain pointed the shotgun at McCall. "Decided to start takin' back some o' the money they been takin' from us." He waved the barrel of the Greener toward the unconscious man. "Real careful-like, reach inside his coat an' take his shoulder gun, then go through his pockets an' take anything he's got in 'em — and see if he don't have a money belt. I'm gonna stand here 'til he comes to, tell 'im how the cow ate the cabbage an' send 'im on his way."

Farnum carried out Red's orders and when he handed everything he'd collected to the saloon owner, he gave him a straight-on look. "I wuz you I'd send for Tenery, but first we better get most o' the men to circle Elkhorn an' shoot any o' that bunch that even looks like they gonna come in town. Remember, they took all this money by threatenin' to kill our families an' burn our businesses."

McClain jerked his head in a nod. "Figger you're right. We better keep this man in town 'til Bill can get in here. Don't want to give 'im a head start on what we get ready to do." Juggling the armful of McCall's stuff he frowned. "Think I'll lock my saloon and go get Tenery myself. I'll watch this trash 'til you can go over an' get Cody to come help tie him up. Y'all put 'im in the hotel cellar 'til we get back."

Tenery worked as hard, maybe harder than Lease and Martin while he showed them how to do jobs close in to the ranch house, but he had to chuckle to himself at the end of each day. They dragged themselves to the bunkhouse, waited for supper, then fell into their bunks — but, to their credit, neither of them complained, and they waited for him with saddled horses each morning.

At the end of the week, he noticed they stayed up later, joined in the banter with the other men, and sat in on the penny ante games. He nodded to himself; they would make it.

He'd ridden back to the cookshack for his nooning when Bent fell in alongside him. "Rufus, want you to pick out one o' our best hands and have him start teachin' those two city men to rope and herd." He chuckled. "You might even put 'em on a couple o' skittish broncs."

The sound of a horse approached. Tenery glanced past Bent, down the trail from town, frowned and shook his head. He'd never seen McClain ride to the edge of town, let alone out in the country like this. "Hey, Red, what ran you outta town? Never saw you on a horse before."

McClain rode to them, threw a leg over the pommel and slipped to the ground. "We got trouble in town, Tenery, an' I gotta take credit fer causin' it."

"Tell me about it."

Red nodded. "First off, reckon we're wantin' you to come in town with me." Then he launched into what had happened in town, and that he, Cody and Farnum had McCall tied up in the cellar of the hotel. "Didn't want to give 'im a chance to git out yonder to Rourk's place an' bring the rest o' that bunch down on us; figgered you'd know what to do now."

"You spread the word to the rest o' the men in town?"

McCain nodded. "Left Olerud an' Cody to do that; told 'em to station men around the town an' to shoot anybody who came in from the direction of the Circle-R."

Tenery shot the big saloon keeper a slight smile. "Don't know what the hell you need with me; sounds like you already got things done."

Red nodded. "Figger we're okay fer now, but they's gonna be a whole new bunch o'

325

that there trash gonna come to these parts mighty soon — that's when we gotta have you. Me an' Olerud read a letter Rourk sent to New York."

Tenery turned his eyes to Rufus. "I'm gonna get my gear, rifle an' bedroll. Keep those two men busy, work the hell outta them 'til I get back. Gonna be gone awhile." He stepped toward the bunkhouse, then reversed himself. "Better tell Penny I'll be gone a few days."

The look Bent gave him was hard enough to shatter a rifle slug. "You damn sure better; you don't an' I'll guaran-damn-tee ya they ain't gonna be room in this whole danged territory fer any o' us with all the hell she's gonna raise."

Bill looked at McClain. "Get yourself a cup o' coffee. I won't be long." He headed for the house.

When he tapped on the door, Penny opened it and stood in the way until he put his arms around her and gave her a light kiss.

"You been spendin' all your time with those two men o' Rourk's, then come up here to tell me you're gonna go back to town with McClain an' all I get outta you is a hug 'bout like you'd give your sister."

"Yep, I'm goin' back to town with Red,

an' yep again, I gave you a sisterly hug. Any more than that an I'd be takin' a lot more time than I figure I better take right now. McClain's already started the ball. All hell's gonna break loose soon an' I need to be there."

So soft he had to strain to hear, she said, "You gonna go in there an' get yourself shot agin?"

He shook his head. "Don't figure on it, little one. We'll have enough men, an' we'll know what to expect. I hope to get this job done without anyone getting shot."

"What about those men Tom Lease said he an' Martin figgered Rourk sent for?"

"They had it figured right. McClain said he an' Olerud knew for a fact he'd written for more men. That's why I want ta get in there now, see if I can get rid of the ones he's had with him."

"What're you gonna do, Bill, invite 'em to saddle up an' get gone peaceable-like?" Her mouth set in a straight line. Her jaws knotted. "Why don't you invite them to have a drink with you? I'm sure they'd figger that wuz right neighborly of you."

He stared at her a moment, shook his head and said, "Aw hell." He spun and left, not seeing the hand she held out to him, or the tears flowing down her cheeks.

When he got to the middle of the yard, Bent stood there holding the reins to his horse. "Saddled 'im, rolled your blankets, filled the magazine of your Winchester an' packed trail gear on a packhorse. McClain sounded like he'd like to get gone soon's possible."

Tenery nodded. "Soon's Penny gets over her mad at me, tell her that I'll be back as soon as we get rid of the *whole* Rourk bunch." He pinned Rufus with a look that he thought still carried his anger. "She wouldn't listen, even though we knew this was gonna have to be done sooner or later." He toed the stirrup, swung aboard, looked at Red and nodded toward town.

They rode stirrup to stirrup, neither of them saying much. Bill kept his thoughts on the problem. He thought back to what he'd said to Penny, and realized he might have hit on solving part of the problem — he'd get rid of the men Rourk had brought with him before any others could get here.

Night was two hours old by the time they rode into town. They went directly to the livery. Olerud stood to the side when they climbed from their horses. Red slanted him a look. "Still got McCall in Farnum's cellar?"

The old man nodded and grinned. "Don't

b'lieve that Farnum boy ever 'sperienced nothin' like that 'fore. I left 'im sittin' on a keg in the cellar, holdin' a scattergun on McCall even though he wuz tied up tighter'n a throwed calf."

Tenery looked at Red. "Figured to stop at your place an' let you buy me a drink before I did anything, but reckon I better get to the hotel an' see how Farnum's doin'."

McClain nodded. "I'll go with you. Open the bar later."

In only a minute, they stood next to Farnum, who still held the Greener on McCall. To Tenery's thinking, the hotel owner had a bulldog look about him. He wasn't about to let the city man even wriggle as though to get out of his bindings. He slanted a look across his shoulder. "Ain't let 'im hardly move since Red left to go get you."

Holding a chuckle inside, Tenery nodded. "You did good, Charley." He turned his look on McCall and frowned. "Think we better keep 'im tied, keep 'im here 'til I decide what to do about the rest o' that bunch."

He turned as though to leave, then said, "You two bring 'im with us, I figure to have a drink while I think on it."

10

While Red unlocked the door to the saloon, Tenery and Farnum held McCall between them. Once inside, they shoved him to the floor between the bar and the back shelf. Bill stared at him a moment, then cast McClain a grin. "Pour us a hefty one, Red, I'll pay for 'em."

With a glass full of McClain's best in front of him, Tenery gripped it in a cold hand and walked to the nearest table. He sat and pondered what to do about the rest of Rourk's men.

Abruptly, he went to stand over McCall. "How many men are left out at Rourk's place?"

The city thug gazed up at Tenery, no fear in his look. "You want ta know that, I'd say ride out there and count 'em."

"An' I'd say you're diggin' a deeper hole for yourself. Was thinkin' of sendin' you outta here with a horse 'tween your legs."

He shook his head. "You just this minute changed my mind. You gonna leave here walkin'." He grinned. "Gonna sit down and enjoy my drink 'fore I ask you again. You give me an answer an' I might let you keep your sheepskin. Every time I ask you an' I don't get an answer, you're gonna lose another piece of clothing." He went back to the table, picked up his drink, and stared at the wall, wondering what to do next.

Standing behind his second-floor curtain, Rourk watched McClain and Farnum take McCall down. A rush of pleasure flowed from his chest to his head. The bastard deserved whatever they gave him.

Then his thoughts turned to how many men he had left. Until Whitcom got here with those men he'd asked him to bring, he would need every man still at the ranch, but hell, it seemed like they'd all deserted him.

He shrugged mentally. The townspeople had not caused him any trouble since he'd had to hole up in the hotel — if they continued as they had, he figured he could wait for help to arrive. But whatever happened, he had to get out of this hotel room, had to get back to the ranch — yet he had to have help to do it. He needed a wagon to haul him out of town. He couldn't straddle a horse.

Penny stood there, her hand held toward the man she loved, beseeching him to wait, to listen to her, to let her explain why she'd acted as she had, that her anger had been triggered by fear; fear for him. She slowly let her hand fall back to her side. The sound of horse's hooves leaving the ranch yard brought a tremulous breath along with deeper sobs. She couldn't let him leave like this.

She grabbed her coat, hurried to the door — and met Rufus on the way in. "Wait a minute, little miss. You ain't gonna foller that there man. He's got some serious things to take care of an' they ain't a damn thing you bein' with 'im is gonna do but get 'im killed, maybe both o' you catching lead. Now sit down. I'll pour us a cup o' coffee, an' you can cry yore heart out on my shoulder."

Before he could turn toward the stove, she was in his arms. "R-Rufe, I never knowed it'd be like this, never knowed lovin' a man could hurt so much."

He stroked her back, crooning meaningless sounds. "Penny, for every hurt you're havin' right now, you're gonna have a whole bundle o' happiness later. Now you git to the table an' sit." He took her arm and steered her toward a chair. "Gonna spike our coffee a wee bit. Figger that'll make us both feel better." Then he mumbled, "Reckon I wanted to side him in this here fight bad as anybody, but he got right proddy when I said so. He said we had to keep enuff men out here to protect you an' the ranch."

She sniffled and took the empty cup in her hands. "Rufus, he's lettin' the other ranchers send men to help, why don't he want us?"

"Aw, honey, it ain't that he don't want us." Bent poured coffee and reached to the top shelf for his bottle. "He wants us all right, but he knows this here ranch is the one Rourk has figgered to take over as his. Bill Tenery ain't gonna stand fer such." He tilted the bottle of whisky over their cups. He pulled his chair away from the table and sat. "Now you sip on that drink. I'll do the same, an' then we're both gonna feel better."

Lease walked alongside the man he'd partnered up with. "How you feelin' about our decision to get outta that crooked game we were in?" He chuckled. "We've both had time to feel the pain of real work." He grinned. "And I *do* mean pain. There were a lot o' days I thought we'd lost our minds."

Martin smiled. "Tom, I have to admit I was sorely tempted the first few days to say 'to hell with it,' an' go back to our old ways." He shook his head; then chuckled. "But you know what? Every day I feel more like a *real man*. Fact is, I been finding myself sorta lookin' forward to each day's work.

He shrugged. "We're both learnin', we're both getting muscle where we never had any before." He laughed. "And to top all that off, when I look in that shard these men call a mirror, when I see myself in that glass, I ain't ashamed o' the man I'm lookin' at."

Lease shot his partner a quizzical look. "Man, I don't think I ever heard you say so many words all at one time, but I have to admit, you've put it right on the line. I feel the same way you do."

Martin frowned and shook his head. "You suppose these people are beginning to trust us?"

Lease shrugged. "Don't know, Fran, but the way I've got it figured is that they are tolerating us, an' will continue to do so until we mess up — an' as these Westerners would put it, I guaran-damn-tee you I ain't gonna mess up."

Martin shot him a smile. "How long 'fore

you figure we can call ourselves Western-ers?"

"After what we've just told each other, I'd say we can start right now."

They laughed and slapped each other on the shoulders like a couple of kids.

Tenery stared at the wall for several minutes. Regardless of what McCall said as to the number of men still at the Circle-R, Bill thought he had it honed down real close to the right number; considering Lease, Martin, Sore and now the man lying behind the bar, he thought at the most there might be no more than eight men out there. If he played his cards right, he figured he could get rid of them without having to kill them, or them him. But remembering that they'd now gotten townsfolk's money back from four of them, he wanted to handle the eight such that all, or at least most, of the money could be reclaimed. He'd have to give it more thought.

While sitting with a drink in front of him, he shuffled several ideas through his mind and cast each aside. He'd probably get some family men hurt with most of his ideas.

Then he toyed with luring Rourk's men out of the ranch house and having men stationed alongside the trail to ambush them. He shook his head — he couldn't accept shooting men without giving them a chance — but he kept going back to the idea. Damn! There had to be another way. Finally he thought he might be able to whittle them down two, maybe four more men, but he'd be cutting the time for the arrival of the new bunch from New York down to almost nothing. Could he gamble on getting the job done before they arrived?

He lifted his glass to his mouth. He had emptied it without realizing he'd taken a swallow of it. He held it out for McClain to fill. With a full glass in front of him he pinned a quizzical look on Red. "You think you, Cody, Olerud and Farnum can keep that man another four, maybe five days? That'd mean feedin' 'im, guardin' 'im while he goes to the outhouse . . ." He shrugged. "You know what I'm askin' you to do. If you can, I think we can get more of the folk's money back to 'em."

McClain gave him a straight-on look. "Tenery, they ain't nothin' me or any o' the others wouldn't do fer these here folks. Why, hell, we're all like family in this here town." He nodded. "Yep, we'll hang onto him long's you say." Red chuckled. "Where you been the last few minutes? Hell, you been starin' at that there wall like you wuz in another territory."

Bill nodded and let a sheepish grim slide across his lips. "Reckon I got lost in tryin' to figure out what to do next, an' *next* is far as I got, but if this works, I b'lieve we can take care o' the rest of it. One good thing, I think we have enough men to do the job."

McClain glanced at the window, then pulled his huge old silver railroad watch out and stared at it.

Olerud cackled and slapped his knee. "Tenery, you gotta let that man go. He's settin' there like he's got a whole bunch o' hornets in his pants. He's itchin' to git over to see Miz Gretchen."

Bill felt a pang of guilt as to the way he'd ridden away from Penny. He nodded. "Get on over there an' see that pretty lady."

McClain went through the door like a scalded cat, leaving behind a hard look toward Olerud. In only a few strides he opened the door to the bakery. Gretchen, sitting alone, rocking back and forth in her rocker, jumped to her feet. "Oh, Red, I'm so glad you came over. I saw what happened in front of the hotel, and maybe a half hour 'fore that I heard what sounded like a shotgun blast from your place." She blushed. "I wuz awfully worried 'bout you 'til I seen ya come out an' lean aginst the

337

wall to the hotel." She shrugged. "Well — anyway you know why I wuz worried."

He stood only a few feet inside the door, looking at her, thinking how lucky he was to have a pretty woman like her worry about him. Why heck, after thinking on it, he reckoned the last person to worry about him was his dear old mother back in Ireland. When he'd left the Old Country to come to America to work on the railroad he'd thought, even said, that he would return home "one of these days." That had been years ago. He knew now that he'd never go back.

He walked toward her. Thought as he had so many times that he didn't want to mess things up between him and this pretty lady. His steps, in his mind, were timid — but he got to her, put out his arms to hug her and quickly dropped them back to his side. She saved him the feeling of getting rebuffed.

"Oh come on, Red, give me a hug; a good tight one. I b'lieve we done got past that stage where we have to wonder if it's all right."

He stepped close, pulled her to him and did exactly as she'd said. After moments that seemed all too short, he relaxed his arms and stepped back. "Heck, Gretchen, reckon I cain't make myself b'lieve a woman pretty an' nice as you, could ever like me enuff to want me near her."

She chuckled deep in her throat. "Big man, after that first hug you gave me, wantin' to be near you changed to how *much* I wanted to be near you. Sittin' in here alone as I'm wont to do, an' thinkin' 'bout ya . . . well, I reckon I decided it was a whole lot o' *much*."

She blushed, right prettily to McClain's way of thinking, then she said, "S'pose you think I'm right brazen to be tellin' you this?"

He stared at her a long moment, then shook his head. "No, ma'am, we ain't neither one o' us young enuff to be tellin' each other nothin' but the truth." Abruptly, he thought how that might sound. "Aw, Gretchen, I wuzn't meanin' you're gettin' *old,* I wuz jest sayin we ain't kids no more."

She laughed. "You know what, big man? I wouldn't want to go back to bein' a kid. I kinda like the way things are right now."

He held his arms out for another hug.

Tenery looked at Olerud. "What I want you an' the other townsfolk to do, in addition to keepin' McCall here, is to make sure when any o' that bunch comes to town that you have somebody watchin' them from the time they arrive, keep a long gun sighted on 'em 'til I can make sure I've got 'em where *I* can get a gun on 'em. I'll take it from there."

Olerud frowned, gave Bill a straight-on stare. "You ain't got a gut in yore head, Tenery. You done got the hell shot outta you doin' somethin' we shoulda been doin' fer ourselves. Don't know what you got in mind, but tell me, then we can take care of it."

"Nope. Just want y'all to make sure I don't have to take care o' more'n one at a time."

In the main room of the Circle-R ranch, eight men slouched; some stretched out on the floor, and others draped into or over chairs. Wes Benton went to the cabinet, pulled a bottle out and held it up to the light. He shook his head and said, "Empty." He frowned. "Been three days since McCall an' Sore went to town for whisky an' tobacco. Wonder what the hell's happened to 'em. Ain't any women in there to take up their time."

Tell Bailey swung his legs off of the chair arm. "You think maybe they cut out of here like Lease an' Martin done?"

Grant Watley shook his head. "Naw, don't think the money we gave 'em to buy us stuff

340

was enough to make 'em take it an' run."

"Wasn't thinkin' of the money we gave 'em." Bailey scanned the room full of men. "They, like all of us, ain't had nothin' to spend money on. Bet they got within fifty dollars of what they took off them hicks in town." He shrugged. "*That's* plenty for them to leave with."

Watley stood, reached under his left arm to make certain his handgun was in its holster. "Think I'll ride into town, see what's holding 'em up." He glanced at Bailey. "How 'bout ridin' in with me?"

Tell nodded. "All right." He glanced at the window. "Getting late. We might as well stay in town tonight 'less you want ta get to your bunk late."

While they shrugged into their coats Slim Ketchum stared at them a moment. "You think maybe them town people got up enough guts to buck any o' us?"

Bailey shook his head. "Never would think that. They're probably spendin' time talkin' to Rourk," he said and chuckled, "if they ain't spendin' all their time hangin' over the bar in McClain's saloon." He shifted his eyes to Watley. "Let's go."

Tenery was pouring himself a cup of Red's coffee when he heard Trent Cody yell from the roof of his store, "Riders comin'; two of 'em, comin' from toward the Circle-R."

Bill looked at Olerud. "Get down to the livery. Don't do anything except put their horses in a stall." He swung his look to McClain. "Red, check your guns, make sure they're loaded an' where you can get your hands on 'em real sudden. I'm gonna stand back there against the wall." He chuckled. "If I'm the first one they see, they might start shootin' 'fore we have a chance to get my plan in action." Olerud went out the back door, headed for his stable.

McClain broke the action of his scattergun, checked the load and snapped it closed. Then he inspected his handgun. Tenery went to the back wall and stood in the shadows. They waited.

In only a few minutes, hoofbeats sounded, then stopped. "They'll be takin' their horses into Olerud's now. Stand fast, men, they'll be here in a minute, we know they're gonna stop for a drink before they do anything else." Tenery thumbed the thong off the hammer of his Colt, eased it in its holster and placed his shoulders against the wall. He had settled there when the big wooden door swung open; Rourk's men, two of them.

They walked to the bar, held up two

fingers and swung their looks to see the entire room. Somehow they missed seeing Tenery standing against the wall and pinned McClain with a look. Bailey frowned. "We expected to see McCall and Bartlet; they rode in a couple days ago. You seen 'em?"

Red nodded. "Yep, they come in, decided to stay awhile." He grinned. "Fact is, McCall's down in my cellar. He wuz gonna stay in the hotel's cellar but we figgered he'd be more at home in mine." He made as though to take a bottle from under the overhang of the bar; instead his hands came out full of a twelve-gauge Greener. "Y'all stand jest like you are right now an' I won't cut you in two."

They had both unbuttoned their coats when they came through the door. When they walked to the bar they had put their hands on it. Tenery spoke to their backs. "Do like McClain told you, an' we'll let you walk outta here in a couple o' days." He laughed. "And when I say 'walk,' that's exactly what I mean."

Each of them made as if to turn toward Bill. "Don't! Either or both of you turn toward me an' I'll load you with .44 lead." He walked closer to them. "Sink to your knees, and keep your hands in sight above your heads. Then spread-eagle, flat on your stomachs. Do it. Now."

They did as Tenery ordered. He waved his handgun for Red to come around the bar, then studied the two men lying there. He wanted to get their guns but didn't want McClain getting close enough that they might surprise him. He decided to have them stand again. "Changed my mind, both o' you get to your feet." He stood back from them while they carried out his orders. "Now walk toward the bar, put both hands on it and lean forward. Now work your feet back until you got most o' your weight on your hands; do it 'til you damn near fall on your face."

Finally satisfied they couldn't grab for their guns without falling, he went to their backs, felt inside their coats, and pulled a .38-caliber Colt from each. He slid the guns across the bar. "Get back there, McClain and put those pieces with the rest of them you been collectin'."

He turned his attention back to the two men. "Stay like you are 'til I tell you to straighten up." He ran his hands down their legs, behind their backs and around their waists, until he was satisfied they had no more weapons. Then he said they could stand erect. "Now I want two things: first, shed those clothes — all of them. Then I want you to tell us who you been takin' money from since you came to our town."

Bailey twisted to look at Tenery. "What the hell you mean, take *all* our clothes off?" He shook his head. "It's cold in here, gunfighter, damned cold."

Tenery allowed his lips to crinkle at the corners. "You don't do like I said, real sudden, you're gonna be a lot colder, like cold an' dead. Now shed 'em, all of them."

After a few minutes they stood there in their long johns. "Now untie those money belts." He looked across the bar at McClain. "Come around here an' empty their pockets, pull their pants over their boots, take the loot behind the bar and keep it separate."

After only a few minutes, Red again stood behind the bar. Tenery grinned, gave McClain a "well done" look, then told the two thugs to put their clothes back on.

By the time they were dressed, Olerud came bursting through the back door. "Hot dammit, knowed I wuz gonna miss the fun." He grinned, looked at Red, then turned his look on Bill. "From the looks of it, y'all didn't need no help." He moved his look to across the bar and obviously took in the two revolvers and the money belts. "They very heavy?"

McClain nodded. "I figger we done got most o' what's been took." He swung his look to the thugs. "How many men y'all got left out yonder at Rourk's place?"

They only stared. Red chuckled. "Ain't talkin', huh?" His chuckle changed to an outright laugh. "Bet by the time the gunfighter gits through with you, you gonna be singin' the answer to what I asked you from the top o' the highest buildin' in this here town."

Each of Rourk's men cast worried looks toward Tenery. He held back a laugh. They knew him only as the gunfighter. They didn't know whether he would torture them to get what he wanted. He allowed himself to show a cold smile; no humor reached his eyes. "McClain, don't push 'em to answer that. I figure I'll have a lot more fun gettin' what I want." He nodded. "Yep, I learned some things from the Comanche and Apache that I ain't had a chance to try yet."

Red and Olerud figured what he was doing. Olerud shook his head. "Naw now, gunfighter, don't reckon either one o' us cottons to that sort o' thing. Wh-why hell, we ain't no savages. Know the places you been an' the things you done it ain't gonna bother you none to pull their toenails out — you know what I'm talkin' 'bout."

Tenery nodded, then holding his face stiff as old leather, looked at the two men. "Yeah, I know what you're sayin', but when I allowed as how I'd help you, reckon I figured whatever I decided to do y'all would back me." He shrugged. "You give me a hard time on this, reckon I might sweep the two o' you in with them."

McClain shook his head. "Aw hell, don't think either of us wants to buck you." He nodded. "Yep, you go ahead an' do things your way."

All the while Olerud and McClain talked, Tenery kept his eyes on the two thugs. When they came in from outside, the cold had painted their faces a rosy red. Now, with each word said by Tenery, color had slowly drained from their faces. They now had a pasty, biscuit-dough tinge to them. He hoped he didn't choke trying to hold back a deep-chested laugh. He looked at Olerud. "You got some rope we can tie them up with? I need to think on what I'm gonna enjoy most when I start to work on 'em."

"Yeah, I got —"

Watley cut in, "Aw hell, gunfighter, there's six of us left out there. We'll tell you anything you want to know."

Tenery kept the cold stare, but told Olerud to get the rope anyway, that he figured to keep them tied tight for awhile. "Still figure to have 'em walk outta here; one at a time." He dropped his Colt back into its holster, gently. "Now, get the rope."

With them firmly tied and in the cellar, Tenery left Olerud to make sure the prisoners didn't get free of their bonds. When Bill and Red got back in the bar area, Tenery allowed himself a *real* grin. "Damn, never thought up 'til now what a bad hombre y'all figured me to be."

"Tenery, I gotta tell ya, I don't know how I kept from laughin' 'til I jest flat fell out in the middle o' the floor."

Tenery chuckled deep in his chest. "That old man is priceless. I never thought he'd pick up on what I intended so quick."

"Bill, that old man's the best friend I ever had — an' I never had him pegged as bein' dumb."

Tenery glanced at the loot stacked behind the bar. "Six to go, McClain. We been lucky so far. I b'lieve we might take two more of 'em; figure that many will come in next time."

"What're we gonna do if they all come in at once?"

"Fight. They come in a bunch, that's gonna be *their* intent, an' the fact they haven't had any o' y'all buck 'em so far, I think they're gonna figure on an easy time of it."

A worried frown creased Red's forehead. "Them six I ain't too worried 'bout — but what about the sixteen Rourk's done sent for? You figger we gonna have enough men to take care o' them?"

His face feeling like sheet steel, Tenery gave McClain a straight-on look. "Been givin' that a lot o' thought, Red." He shook his head. "I haven't come up with anything that'll keep us from gettin' some o' you hurt. Yeah, I b'lieve we can whip 'em, but it ain't gonna be easy."

Red pinned him with a "no nonsense, no give" look. "Tenery, we ain't fought so far 'cause we wuz fearful for each other. Now we got somebody to show us how to do it, you gonna find they ain't a damned one o' us gonna show the white feather." He nodded. "Yeah, some o' us might get hurt, might even buy the farm, but what's left's gonna be able to be free to live like we want."

The ex-soldier knocked back his drink, held his glass for another, then said they'd better organize men to keep watch on the prisoners. "An' although the ranch help hasn't gotten here yet, I want you to have every man in town to come over here. I want them to understand what to do whether we're gonna fight six or sixteen. Get them over here right away." By the time he got the last word out, McClain was headed out the door.

Tenery went behind the bar, poured a fresh cup of coffee, looked at the several piles of loot and felt a wave of satisfaction flow over him. Even if they had to take on the six, he felt confident the town's men would win that fight.

Two days later, Slim Ketchum glanced across the Circle-R main room. "Benton, I got a bad feelin' about Bailey an' Watley. They said they were gonna stay in that town overnight." He shook his head. "Up 'til now, haven't thought that there was enough guts in that whole town to tie into us; beginnin' to change my mind, 'specially since that gunfighter showed up. 'Til now I been thinkin' that woman out at the Saddle Horn was the one who sent for 'im." He shook his head. "You think maybe the townspeople sent for him?"

Benton stared at the cup of coffee sitting in front of him. "You sayin' you an' me should ride in there, see what's goin' on?"

Slim shook his head. "Not sayin' that; what I *am* sayin' is that all six of us needs

350

to ride in there. From what I've seen, the six of us can beat hell outta all those hicks put together." He swept those in the room to make sure they were all listening. "Gather 'round, men, we gonna decide what to do."

They pulled in closer to him. They talked, argued, thought to split up, threw that idea out, then decided that they would ride in tightly bunched. "I think if we stay together we can throw the fear of God into 'em. They might be able to get enough men together to fight two of us, but six of us?" He shook his head. "Hell no, I b'lieve they see a clump o' us, ridin' in together, if they got time, they'll run like a flock of sheep with a wolf in their midst." He scanned the other five men. "What do you men think?"

Ketchum studied the others' faces while Wes Benton talked. At first he saw doubt, then when it was apparent that they'd all six ride together, the doubt faded. He held back the chuckle that bubbled inside. The age-old adage came to his mind: "in numbers, there's strength."

He stood, looked down on the tightly clustered group, then nodded. "All right, take care of your weapons, make sure you got plenty of cartridges — no need to take bedrolls with us; we get those hicks taken care of, we'll stay in the hotel." He chuckled.

"Hell, we might even look in on *the boss* while we're there. Not that there's a one o' us who gives one happy damn how he is, but it'll be another chance to let 'im know he ain't *the boss* anymore." They all thought the idea was funny and laughed.

He gave them a cold smile. "Let's get ready. Saddle up."

Tenery had finished one cup of coffee and drunk half of another by the time McClain glanced at all in the room, then looked at Bill. "Reckon we're all here. How you figger to take 'em on?"

"We still got a man on the roof to warn us?" At Red's nod, Tenery pinned each man, one at a time, with a hard look. "We're through givin' in to that bunch, men. When you leave here, the next time I see you, I want you to be carryin' a rifle, an' I don't want to see a one o' you without it until this is over." He looked at McClain. "You tell 'em we expect sixteen more of 'em after we take care o' this bunch?"

"Yeah. We know what we're facin'."

Tenery nodded. "Good. This time, men, I figure we're gonna have two, maybe all six of Rourk's men ride in here. Regardless, we'll take care of it the same way." He pointed at three men. "Want you men an'

Olerud to get inside the livery, two in the loft and two beside of the big doors. Get with it."

He looked at Cody. "Take three over to your store an' place them at the windows and door. While we're all together, don't want any of you opening fire 'til you hear me cut loose." He chose to put men in the four buildings at the north end of town, and six more on the roofs behind the false fronts. "Gonna be cold up there, men, but we gotta do this right. We do, an' I b'lieve we'll get back most of what they took from you." He turned his eyes to McClain. "Every hour or so, swap out the men inside with those on the roofs." He nodded to them. "Good luck. Let's do it."

When they scattered to take up their stations, Tenery went to the livery, got his rifle from Olerud's office and went back to the Red Dog. McClain, two other of the townsfolk and himself manned the watering hole.

Twice in the next four hours, Red went out and sent men to swap positions with those on the roofs. He came back in and shook his head. "Bill, I don't figger any of 'em gonna come in today. It's gettin' sorta late."

"McClain, we're gonna stay just like we are 'til 'bout ten o'clock," he replied, "then

353

I figure it's gonna be safe to call it a night."

At the same time he told Red that they'd hold their positions, a yell came from across the street at store-top level. "Riders comin' — a whole bunch of 'em."

Tenery grabbed his rifle. "McClain, I'm goin' down to the livery, gonna face 'em 'fore they can get off their horses. Remember, don't fire 'til I do. If they got any sense we ain't gonna have to shoot any of 'em."

"Boy, you ain't goin' out yonder in the open. You do, they gonna kill you deader'n hell."

Bill stared at the saloon owner a long moment. "Gotta stop 'em outside — in the open. Now y'all keep your rifles trained on that bunch while I tell 'em how the cow ate the cabbage." He pushed through the door. Following him out were McClain's words: "You dumb, crazy bastard."

Tenery walked to the livery stable, stood by the side wall out of the wind waiting for them to ride to the front of the big double doors.

He took a deep breath, smelling the scent of pine, mountain spruce and grass dried on the stem. Of all times for his thoughts to turn to Penny . . . but he'd hoped she'd be sharing that fresh scent with him.

The slosh of hooves broke into his

thoughts. His stomach churned; he felt as though he'd vomit his lunch, then felt like a big hollow below his ribs. *Damn, Tenery, b'lieve you're just what Red said you were: a dumb, crazy bastard.* He shrugged mentally. Hell, nobody said we could live forever.

He waited for the sound of hooves to stop, then stepped around the corner of the building. Three riders had already stepped to the ground and had their coats unbuttoned. "Y'all stand just like you are an' none o' y'all'll get hurt."

Apparently stunned, they stood motionless for a moment. "There're rifles pointed at you from ev—"

Before he could finish his sentence, two of them reached into their coats. Tenery swept his hand for his holster; his Colt came out of it and spewed fire at the two standing on the ground. They dropped. The remaining four frantically tore at the buttons of their coats. Voices from windows and rooftops yelled for them to freeze. They did.

Tenery stepped closer. "Smart; damned smart. Now sit there, hands stretched toward the sky." They did as he told them. He walked to the two men on the ground and toed them, onto to their backs. Both stared at the sky through sightless eyes. He gazed at those still sitting their saddles.

"Gonna have you, one at a time, turn your left side to me and step from the saddle." Not taking his eyes from them, he yelled, "Olerud, send two men out here!"

He waited for the big doors to swing open, then, not looking at the two who came out of the livery, said, "Any o' these thugs even bend their elbows as though to lower their arms — shoot 'em." With their rifles covering the four, he looked over his shoulder. "The rest o' you c'mon out. Olerud, you know the drill, go through their pockets, then take their money belts to Red's place."

He centered his look back to those still sitting their saddles. He pointed his .44 at the one closest to him. "Reeeal slow-like, get off your horse, then lie down, facedown with your arms stretched straight out above your head."

"Hell, gunfighter, that ground's so muddy it's soupy!" the outlaw protested.

Tenery chuckled. "Couldn't have planned it any better if I was in charge of the weather." He swallowed the chuckle, hardened his voice. "Get on your stomach."

Using all the care he thought would keep the town's men safe, he had the last of Rourk's men get to the ground, searched each of them and removed everything from their pockets and waists — guns first. He put each man's stuff in his hat and had Olerud put their name on it.

Finished with that task he stared at them a moment, then shifted his gaze to those standing with their rifles pointing at the now-prone men. "One of you go to Cody's store. Bring enough rope to tie all these men hand and foot."

About a half hour later, the four stored in McClain's cellar and the men from the rooftops and inside the businesses stood lined up along the bar. As soon as Red had a drink in front of all who wanted one, Tenery walked behind the bar to stand alongside the big bartender. "Listen up, men. This went smooth and easy today, but I don't want any of you to think the next time's gonna be this easy. First place there'll be almost three times as many of 'em; second place, they won't be sittin' atop horses. I figure they're gonna be comin' in on a stage, two stages if I got it figured. We're gonna —"

"Hell, Tenery," Farnum cut in, "don't know what you need us for."

Olerud put his two cents' worth in. "Reckon as how he's gonna need us, 'cause one o' these here days he's gonna get 'nuff sense not to do damn fool things like he done a little while ago."

Tenery pulled the corner of his mouth down in a grimace. "Tell you how it is, men, I was scared spitless, but we needed to get those men out in the open. Once they got in the stable it would have been a lot harder, an' we'd have gotten men hurt." He shrugged and shot them a grin. " 'Sides that, I'd already sent every one o' you to take up station elsewhere. We'll have it planned better the next time."

He took a swallow of the drink McClain had put in front of him, then slanted a look at the big man. "Red, I want you to make sure there are at least three men guarding those we have stashed in the cellar." McClain nodded.

"Also, we gotta all put our heads together an' come up with some way to turn 'em loose." He knocked back the rest of his drink and stared into the bottom of his now empty glass. "Wish we had time to get a U.S. marshal in here 'fore that new bunch arrives."

"Hell, Tenery, one marshal ain't gonna be able to handle all the men we gonna have by then — if we don't have to kill most of 'em." While talking McClain poured Bill's glass full.

Most of the men knocked back their drinks and made as though to leave. Tenery held up his left hand; his right held his fresh drink. "Stand fast, men, there are a couple more things we gotta settle 'fore you go back to your stores." He took a swallow of his drink, then flicked his thumb toward the back of the bar. "Red an' Olerud have put that stuff in piles and written who each one of them were taken from. You know who's been takin' your money so I want each of you to file down that shelf and take what's yours. Don't leave here 'til we've done more talking."

While they walked along the back of the bar, Bill packed his pipe and lit it. As soon as the last man had his money, Tenery told them to gather around. "Now I'm gonna tell ya like it is. When that new bunch comes in here, we won't know they've arrived until we see 'em. It's gonna be too late to do anything 'bout it then 'cause we'll be scattered all over town. I want us where we'll do the most good; fact is, I'd just as soon we didn't have to take 'em on in Elkhorn; wives and kids might catch lead." He shook his head. "Don't none of us want that."

Cody scowled. "Bill, you sayin' we gonna leave the town unprotected?"

Tenery shook his head. "Not sayin' that at all." He stared over the crowd's heads at the back wall, thinking. He brought his look back to focus on the men. "Way I have it figured, we'll have enough men to protect the town *and* attack those we let go to the Circle-R." He downed his drink and poured a cup of coffee. "Y'all come back over here 'bout seven in the mornin'. I'll have it figured what we're gonna do by then." He nodded, then grinned. "Go ahead, take your recaptured loot to your family, let your wives stash it away somewhere. Know damned well there's not a one o' you who can't use what you have. Go on now, get on home — or wherever you're goin'."

As soon as the last man cleared the door, Bill looked at Red, who stood there, shuffling from one foot to the other. "What's the matter, McClain?"

The big man frowned, studied his hands a moment, then looked at Tenery straight on. "Tell ya what's got me worried. I done told Gretchen I'd make damned sure when hell broke loose that I'd keep 'er safe, that I'd be there for her."

Bill allowed a smile to crinkle the corners of his eyes. He nodded. "Don't see as how that's gonna be a problem. There are a couple more widows here in town. They don't have a man to watch over them either." He stared at the wall a moment, then nodded. "Might be a good idea for you to see them an' make sure when we ride out those ladies go to the bakery. You can see that nobody bothers any of 'em. I'll leave one more man with you." He swung his look to Olerud. "What the hell you grinnin' at, old man?"

The livery man chuckled. "Jest thinkin', Bill. I knowed McClain wuz gonna want ta look after Miz Gretchen. Also knowed you wuz the man to run this here show, but what I didn't know wuz the way the town's men wuz gonna fall right in line with what you're sayin'." He laughed. "Fact is, even them what ain't never been in the army act like you're their Officer in Charge, or maybe the top NCO in the bunch."

His face not showing any humor, Tenery stared at the old man. "Hans, when you an' McClain asked me to do this, I figured there had to be only one man running the show. If there's another man with the experience to do the job" — he grimaced — "hell, he's welcome to it."

Before he finished having his say, Red and Hans were both shaking their head. "No, Tenery —" McClain cut his sentence short and cocked his head. "Sounds like two, maybe more horses jest pulled up to the hitch rail." He put a Greener on the bar in front of him. His finger still rested inside the trigger guard when four men pushed into the room, all from two of the outlying ranches: Gordy Saturen, Hitch Bandy, Tobey Warren and a puncher whose name he didn't know but who he'd seen him in the saloon. "You men come in to help fight them city boys, or you jest come in fer a drink?"

In one voice, they answered, "Fight."

Red put the shotgun under the ledge of the bar. "What'll you men have?"

They ordered, and while he poured their drinks he made them acquainted with Tenery. Then, just so there wouldn't be any doubt, he told them that Tenery was in charge of the fight.

Saturen chuckled. "Hell, don't make us no nevermind. We figgered if y'all would share your fun, we'd join in." He shivered, knocked his drink back and held his glass for another. "Cold ride in." He gulped at his drink as soon as Red filled his glass. "They'll be 'nother five men here by noon tomorrow."

Olerud chuckled. "Hot dang it, I knowed y'all out yonder would back our play." He glanced at Tenery. "We gonna have all the men we need, young'un."

Bill nodded. "Glad to see it."

Hans took on a solemn look. "Gotta tell

362

ya somethin'." He nodded toward Tenery. "You gotta watch out fer that there man when the screwdy-roo starts; he always tries to hog all the fun. Yep, you gotta dang near shove 'im aside so's you can git part o' the action."

"Why, you broke-down, stove-up old varmint, think just for you sayin' that, I'll put you right out front when we go in on that bunch," Tenery said.

Olerud laughed, slapped his thigh and shook his head. "Naw now, that don't worry me a'tall. You gonna get yore share o' the fun."

Bill swept the four new men with a look. "In the mornin' most o' the men're gonna meet in here while we talk 'bout what we're gonna do. Like for y'all to be here." Then he told them that Rourk was staying at the hotel and to put a chair under their room door because the New Yorker was without a handgun and would probably try to get one any way he could.

Saturen laughed. "Hell, Tenery, all he's gotta do to have mine is to walk straight down the barrel of it." He shook his head. "Naw, ain't nobody gettin' my gun — not even a friend."

Bill chuckled. "Way I had you men figured." He frowned. "Reckon I better tell ya right now: Charley Farnum says the rooms to you are on the house, so when you get there, just sign in and get your keys."

Hitch Bandy smiled. "Now that there's mighty nice o' him; the boss give us hotel money so I reckon we kin jest buy a few more drinks."

They all laughed.

Penny waited a couple of days. From the moment Bill rode out to fight what she considered hers and the town's responsibility, her nerves and her temper stretched beyond what she thought she could tolerate.

She stood at the kitchen window and stared down the trail toward town. Someone walked from the corral; Slim Cannard. She nodded to herself. He was the puncher who had brought Bill to the Saddle Horn that first day. He might feel that he should have been chosen to go into town with the man they had all learned to call "friend." *That* made up her mind.

She stepped to the kitchen door, opened it and called for him to come to the house. Without missing a step, he changed course and answered her call.

When he got there, he removed his hat and looked questioningly at her. "Yes'm.

What you need?"

Penny said, "My mind's made up, Slim. I'm goin' to town; gonna see what Bill's doin' there; an' if he's figgerin' on another one o' his dumb stunts, I'm gonna stop 'im. Want you to go with me."

"Aw, Miss Penny, you gonna git Rufus madder'n all kinds o' hell. First he'll land right straddle o' me; maybe even fire me right here in the winter; then I figger when he gits tired of whippin' up on me he's gonna get reeeal serious when he starts on you."

Her mouth set in a stubborn straight line, her jaw knotted, she shook her head. "He's jest gonna have to get mule-headed; he ain't gonna change my mind."

Cannard jammed his hat back on his head. "Gonna tell ya, Miss Penny, Rufe can fire me if he wants, but you gonna need somebody with you. Don't want you ridin' that trail to town all alone. Wh-why hell, a mountain cat, bear, danged near anything might git after you." He nodded. "Yes'm, no matter what happens I'm goin' with you.

"Leastways I figger you've gonna hire me back after Rufus fires me." He grinned, then laughed. "*That's* gonna be more hell raisin' than when he hears I'm goin' to town with you."

"Get your bedroll, rifle an' plenty of cartridges. When you're ready we'll ride."

He nodded, spun and went to the bunkhouse. A few minutes later, almost running, he came back; his bedroll hung from his shoulder, saddlebags were in his right hand, his left clutched his rifle.

On his heels, Rufus Bent turned the air blue with his cursing. "Dammit, I done told you if you take another step, you're fired — don't come back to this here ranch."

Penny stepped into the fray. "He ain't fired. If you done fired 'im, I jest now hired 'im back. I'm goin' to town, gonna see what's goin' on, *I'm the one who told 'im I wanted him to go with me — so now get off'n his hind end.*"

Rufus stopped in mid-stride, drawing his shoulders up around his neck in obvious anger and frustration. "I'll go with you."

"No, you won't. You're the only one I've got who knows what needs to be done here on the ranch." Her mouth softened. She glanced from him to her boots, scraping melting snow into a slushy pile. "Rufus, I do everything you say. You've kept this ranch runnin' jest the way Papa woulda done it. I need you, Rufe; you've been like my papa to me — but this is somethin' I jest plain gotta do. My man's in there. I gotta know he's all right."

She watched him study her. His shoulders lowered and the red receded from his flushed face, then it softened. He nodded, turning to Cannard. "Dang you, young'un, you take good care of her." His voice grew husky, and pushing soft words out as though past a lump in his throat, he said, "She's all I got in this world, young'un. Don't you let 'er git nowhere near where there's shootin' goin' on."

Cannard nodded. "You can bet a painted pony on that, Rufe. I'll bring 'er home safe. 'Course, I'll probably have Tenery along to bring us both home safe, 'cause by then we gonna be rid of Rourk." He again nodded. "Now you quit yore worryin', we're gonna be all right." He turned his eyes on Penny. "You ready to ride, ma'am?"

She nodded, toed the stirrup and rode out alongside her youngest rider.

McClain glanced at the empty shelf in back of the bar area, turned his look to Tenery, then grinned and nodded. "Tell ya, Tenery, I'm shore glad to git rid o' all that money. Every time I looked at it I got worried so much I got the miseries; hell, any man on the run coulda come in here, seen I wuz alone an' taken every penny of it." He grimaced. "Danged tootin', reckon I wuz some amount more than worried."

"Red, I didn't feel all that good 'bout it sittin' out there in plain sight either." He frowned. "How 'bout you pourin' me a fresh cup o' coffee, then goin' over to Miss Gretchen's place an' tellin' her what we got planned — an' that you'll be there with 'er, the other two ladies, an' at least one of the other men." He grinned. "Don't figure you mind runnin' that errand, 'specially considerin' that it'll be Miss Gretchen you're gonna see. Go ahead. I'll watch the bar for you." He didn't have to say it twice — Red was already gone.

About the time McClain cleared the front door, Grant Watley strained against the ropes on his wrists, twisted his head, putting a heavy strain on his neck muscles, and said, "Ketchum, all we gonna do is make our wrists raw an' bloody trying to get outta these ropes. Know how I'm thinkin' to play this hand?"

Ketchum's voice came from in back of him. "Nope, don't believe I know, but I know damned good and well you're gonna tell me, so go ahead."

"All right. In the first place, I b'lieve with the gunfighter leadin' these folks that they're gonna take care o' that new bunch Rourk's bringin' in — but there's gonna be a bunch o' killin', and most o' those getting killed will be Rourk's men."

"Yeah, how's that help us?"

"The way I have the gunfighter figured out is that he's gonna let us go; probably no money, maybe no horse, but he ain't gonna kill us. I b'lieve he ain't as bad as McClain was makin' 'im out to be."

"Damned if I'm ready to stake my life on what a soft touch he *might* be. If I can get outta these ropes, I'll untie the rest of you and climb outta that cellar window and get gone; might be able to steal a horse to ride out on — but, like you, *I'm getting outta this dump of a town.*"

Watley frowned, then asked, "You figure to go back to New York?"

Even though Watley couldn't see him, Ketchum frowned. He thought, *Yep, why not?* Then he said it.

"How we gonna get there, broke and no guns? If we had even one handgun we could hold up a store, or someone — but we ain't gonna have a damned thing to do anything with, and we sure as hell won't have train fare."

"Tell ya, Watley, before I grew up, I rode the blinds, slipped into empty boxcars, rode the rods, I ain't forgot how."

"You ever remember that it's still winter, colder'n a well-digger's butt in this Montana Territory? Hell we'd freeze to death."

Watley tightened up inside. Some, even most of these bastards had no fight in them, didn't even seem to want to make the best out of what little they had. "If you have a better idea, tell me what it is. If not, I'm gonna play it my way."

In the saloon, one floor above the cellar, Olerud shut the door behind him, looked around and said, "Bet you McClain's done hooked you into takin' care o' the bar while he goes over to Miz Gretchen's."

Tenery chuckled, then shook his head. "I knew he was itchin' to get over there, so I volunteered to take care of things. He'll bring her up-to-date on what we figure to do." He poured Olerud's drink, gave the old liveryman change for the cartwheel with which he'd paid for his drink, cocked his head and frowned. "A couple o' riders — at least, sounded like more'n one horse — just pulled in to the tie rail."

Olerud knocked back his drink, and nodded. "Figger it's more from the ranches." He was right.

Two men came through the door, both

looking half frozen. One said, "Howdy; they's three more be here in a hour or so." He stared at Bill. "Reckon you be Tenery?" At Bill's nod, he continued, "Done heered a lot 'bout ya. Liked all I heered." He shucked out of his coat. "Might's well give us both a whisky — tall glass, *full.*"

Tenery poured, and when the puncher reached for his pocket, he shook his head. "On the house. Red said to tell you the whole town appreciates y'all comin' in here to help us."

The cowboy frowned, pulling his mouth down as though trying to figure how Mc-Clain could afford to give his whisky away. "Hell, Tenery, he'll go broke that way. Better let us pay our way."

Bill chuckled. "Don't think so. If he doesn't do it, I'll solicit every businessman in town to pick up part of the tab."

Across the trail, in the bakery, McClain finished explaining that he would be here with her and the other ladies who would join them when the new Rourk group got in town.

Gretchen studied him a moment. "I'll take what I can get, big man. I was hopin' you an' me could be here alone, jest talk, get better acquainted."

Red laughed. "Gretchen, much as I'd like that, it's probably better we ain't gonna spend all that time alone. Much as I like holdin' you close, an' much as you seem to like it, I'm fearful how much we might like it — mess up a good friendship; shore as hell don't want that to happen."

She stared at him a moment. "You ain't figgered out that there's not one thing in this world that's gonna mess up what we done found?"

Red twisted the cup of coffee she'd brought him around on its base. He knew what she offered him, wanted it, but he wasn't willing to take the chance. He wanted a whole lot more, and for a much longer time than what *might* happen if they gave in to their desires. He shook his head. "Ain't gonna . . ." He stopped, listened, then gave her a questioning look. "Hosses jest pulled up to yore hitch rail. Most who would ride in here would make their first stop over yonder at my place." He shook his head. "Don't know of no woman who'd be ridin' a hoss to town in this weather, or any reason they'd be comin' to town. Do you?"

"Don't know, Red, they's so much goin' on 'round here these days I quit tryin' to guess about anything." She opened her mouth to say more when Slim Cannard opened the door and held it for Penny to come in. "Howdy, Miz Gretchen, I done brought you some company while I go lookin' fer Mister Tenery." He hadn't looked at Red until then. He crooked his mouth at the corners in a slight smile. "Howdy, Red, bet Tenery's over at yore place; you reckon so?"

McClain nodded. "That's where he is, but it ain't gonna do no good fer you to go over there to bring him over here. I left 'im in charge 'til I git back. 'Fore you go over there . . ." He stopped, pulled his mouth down at one corner in a huge grimace. "Sorry, Miss Penny, fergot my manners, reckon I'll say 'howdy' now."

"Reckon I can say my howdy to you, Red. What's goin' on? Bill gotten himself into anymore trouble?"

McClain shook his head. "Not yet, but while I got you both here, gonna tell y'all what's 'bout to happen."

Gretchen pulled chairs to the table and poured the coffee.

Penny, not having taken her eyes from Red, said, "Go ahead, tell us what's 'bout to happen, an' what you mean by that 'not yet.' "

McClain took his time, told them what they expected would happen, where Tenery wanted all the unattached women, how he planned to keep them safe and that he didn't know how Bill planned to deploy the men — but that they had plenty of men to do whatever was called for. He thought to tell her how Bill had faced up to the last of Rourk's original bunch, then clamped his mouth shut. It was obvious that the ex-soldier meant more to her than only being another rider. Yep, he'd best not tell her too much.

"You had your mouth fixed to say more, then cut it short, Red. What were you gonna say?"

Red's face heated up. He knew it must be redder'n a dusty day's sunset. His mind searched for the way to answer her. "Wuz gonna say, Miss Penny, hope you brung yore bedroll with you, 'cause Miz Gretchen's gonna have her place full."

"You already as much as said that, now why don't you go back over there an' tell 'im I just come to town?"

McClain shook his head. "Ain't gonna put more worry on his shoulders. He done told me he wouldn't stand fer you bein' here for 'im to worry 'bout, said you got madder'n hell, but he didn't give in to yore gettin' mad. Said he jest rode off."

He grimaced. "Ma'am, I tell 'im bout you

ridin' in here, an' that you brung one o' the riders he figgered to help guard yore ranch, he's gonna have a big mad settin' right on top o' the worry he's already got." He shook his head. "No, ma'am, I ain't gonna do that to 'im."

Penny's eyes puddled. She seemed to melt right before his eyes. "Know you're right, Red. Reckon I never think of other people, always do what I want to do, then somebody with sense tells me what I'm *gonna* do — an' I realize I ain't nothin' but a selfish woman."

Slim had been sitting quietly, taking in all that was said. Then, not being able to hold his opinion in, he shook his head. "No, ma'am, you ain't no selfish woman. Don't know much, maybe nothin' 'bout women, but I'm here to tell ya; the way you act 'round that there man ain't selfishness, it's what I figger a woman in love with a man would do."

Penny's face bloomed like one of the roses his mom used to grow. Aw, hell, he'd opened his mouth and said too much, Slim thought. "Reckon I done embarrassed you, ma'am. Shouldn't of said nothin'."

Penny stared at him a moment, then nodded. "Yeah, Slim, you embarrassed me, but reckon you explained it to these folks right well." If possible she blushed even more. "I done told 'im how it was with me, an' he said as how he felt the same. So when all the trouble's over reckon we gonna do somethin' 'bout it."

She stared at the wall a moment, then switched her look back to Slim. "When you get to the saloon, tell Bill I sent you in should y'all need more help. Don't even hint I'm in town too. I'll stay here with Gretchen; know I'll be safe here, he ain't gonna allow for no unsafe women."

Slim let out a deep sigh of relief. He'd been picturing the amount of hell Tenery was gonna give him. He'd dodged that butt chewing — for now. He grinned to himself. He was glad to put it off, but he knew he'd get one sooner or later. Later was better.

Red stood. "Reckon I better git on back over there, see what's happenin'. Maybe Tenery's done got it all thought out what we're gonna do." He grinned. "Gonna tell you one thing, Miss Penny: when this is all over, Tenery's gonna be a damn good bartender; he's already got a whole bunch o' practice." When he went out the door he felt Gretchen's eyes follow him. In a way, he was glad Miss Penny and Cannard had showed up. He might not have been able to push his feelings to the back of his mind otherwise.

When he went into his own business, he felt safe. When Tenery held up an empty glass toward him, with a questioning look, he nodded.

Tenery filled it, set it in front of him, then told him about the arrival of the ranch hands. "We're gonna have plenty of men, Red."

McClain grinned. "You got one more. Miss Penny done sent Slim Cannard in since she wuz afraid you might need more men. Think maybe he stopped to git a bite to eat 'fore he come over here."

Tenery thought about that for a few moments. Sending Slim to town must be a peace offering in that they had parted in anger. He nodded. Yep, that had to be it; besides, if they handled Rourk's men the way he figured they would, Penny, the ranch and the hands would be safe.

Tell Bailey was the first to work his hands loose from the ropes. He bent, untied his ankles and took care of each of the other men. "I've been thinkin' about what we're gonna do when we leave here."

Watley rubbed his chafed wrists a moment, then asked, "Okay, what you come up with?"

"One at a time, we'll go through that window. Then we're gonna go down to the livery an' hope that old reprobate's already come here for his drink. He has, we're gonna look in his office for weapons; whether we find any or not, we'll take horses and put this damned town behind us. We might be able to sell 'em when we get to Billings for enough to eat on, and at least pay partway on a ticket home." He looked at Watley a moment. "What do you think?"

"Think maybe you've got a good plan, Bailey. We'll try it your way."

Tell pushed upward on the window; it didn't budge. He tried again, still no movement. He put his head close to the glass, checked the frame then shook his head. "Damned thing's nailed shut."

He stepped back, studied it, swung his head to look at all of the cellar, then shrugged. "One thing for sure, we can't go through the saloon with no weapons." He grimaced. "Looks like we gonna have to break the glass."

Ketchum shook his head. "We do that, we're gonna have everybody from upstairs down here with drawn guns."

Bailey drew a crease between his eyebrows. "Think I got an idea. You reckon if we took our coats off, held 'em over the

378

glass and hit the coats it'd make less noise?"

They all swung their eyes to look at one another, and apparently agreed. Watley put it into words. "We ain't got much choice — seems like the only chance we got."

Bailey went to the corner of the room and picked up a length of board that had been left there. "All right, shuck those coats, men." He stepped back and studied the window a moment. "Tell you what I plan. I'm gonna hit your coats reeal light at first, then a little harder 'til we hear or I feel the glass give, then we'll take the coats away from it an' peel that glass outta the frame — okay?"

They nodded. Ketchum and Watley collected coats; three of them held them to the glass; and Bailey, taking care with each stroke, hit them three times before he heard a slight tinkle. He gave each side of the window another two taps and stepped back, grinning. "Careful now, put your coats on. Be very quiet, pull those pieces of glass outta the frame, then lay them gently on the floor to the side."

Only a few agonizing minutes later, he told them to start squeezing through the window. In less than five minutes, the last of them had squeezed to the outside.

McClain drank his drink, held his glass for Tenery to refill, took a couple of swallows, and frowned.

Tenery chuckled. "What's the matter, Red, your whisky so bad even you don't like it?"

Red shook his head. "Don't get smart, Bill. Naw, I wuz jest wonderin' when somebody last checked the prisoners."

He'd not gotten the words out of his mouth before Olerud cocked his head. "Don't b'lieve they's gonna be much need to check 'em; a whole bunch o' hosses jest left my stable headed away from town. Figger they done took some o' my hosses." He said that last while heading for the door. Tenery ran to the stairs leading to the cellar.

He opened the door, glanced at the empty floor below and yelled over his shoulder. "Gone!" He made a dash for his coat and, while pushing his arms into it, looked at Hans. "You tend the bar. Gonna see if we can catch 'em 'fore they get to the Circle-R. They probably have guns out there. They do an' we got a fight on our hands."

Everyone ran from the room, pulling

handguns and checking the loads while they headed for the livery. Tenery checked them while they ran; all had their rifles tucked under their arms while they checked their handgun cylinders. Thank the Lord they hadn't left them in their saddle scabbards — but also thanks that he'd never seen any of the New Yorkers carrying rifles. He figured they'd catch them before they could get into and out of the ranch house. *Then* let them try to again escape. The advantage rested with those who had rifles.

They threw the gear on their horses, toed the stirrups and ran hell for leather from town. "Rein 'em in a little, men!" Tenery yelled. "We don't want ta kill our horses. Still think we'll catch 'em 'fore they can get outta that house. Know that's where they're headin'."

No one said anything else until they swung around the brow of the hill which sloped down to the house. Tenery motioned them to rein in. When they stopped and gathered around him, he squinted toward the house. Horses were tied to the hitch rail in front. "We got here in time, men. Now I want you to space yourselves such that we have the house surrounded as best we can with what we have. Anybody who steps out the door o' that house, shoot 'em. I don't mean shoot to wound, I mean shoot to kill — got it?" They nodded and began to circle the ranch house.

McClain stood close to Bill and cast him a worried look. "Know you got some damn fool thing you're figgerin' to do, Tenery, but I ain't gonna let you do it. You done took enough lead fer us in that town."

Bill gave him a hard look, and shook his head. "Nope, not gonna do anything — right now. We still got too much daylight left, but if we still got 'em nailed down here come dark, I figure I might sashay down yonder an' take a look-see."

Red said, "Knowed danged well I oughta stay close to you. Why don't we sprinkle a few shots through them windows, let 'em know we're here?"

Tenery shook his head. "Thought o' doin' that, but we do an' we'll drag this fight out more'n I want to." He chuckled. "McClain, you know how danged cold it gets out here after dark?" He shook his head. "I've already tried that. If we let 'em try to get away, we might drop 'em all 'fore we freeze solid."

Red nodded. "I'll circle round an' tell the men what you jest said." He shrugged. "Don't know why I didn't think o' that." He chuckled. "Reckon that there's why you're in charge an' I'm not." While leaving to tell the men, he looked over his shoulder and winked at Tenery.

Bill watched McClain walk away, then stared at the house. As best he could remember there should be six men down yonder. Angry blood pushed to his head. He'd had enough. Those bastards had tried to kill him, done almost as bad to the townsfolk; and they'd probably go back to New York and do the same things to their own. Music he'd heard the Mexicans had played at the Alamo came to mind — "Show No Mercy." His face felt like a dry creek bed in July — hard. He nodded to himself. That was the way he intended to play his hand 'til this thing ended. He glanced at the hitch rail. A man made a dash for it. Lazily, Tenery put his rifle to his shoulder, aimed and fired. One down, five to go.

Another ten minutes and McClain circled the hill to his side. "Got one, huh?"

"Yeah, but if I remember correctly, we still have five to go, an' they know we're here now, so it's not gonna be easy."

Red nodded. "Yeah, and we still don't know if they got rifles."

One of the men in the house answered that for him by firing out the window.

The sharp crack of the shot told Bill it was a rifle. He looked at McClain. "We know now." His face hardened. "Red, I don't figure to leave a damned one o' those men alive when we leave here." He shook his head. "Know that sounds mighty hard, but I had enough. I've had to kill Indians who never did a damned thing to me." He slanted his head toward the house. "Those men down there have given me more than enough reason to kill 'em — *that* I'm gonna make sure of 'fore I leave here."

McClain only stared at him. He'd seen the boy face guns before, in his saloon, but he'd never seen how hard he could be when having time to make a decision which would have been tough on most any man. Now he knew why the Army wanted to keep him.

Tenery slanted him a look. "Better take up station away from me; it'll leave less of a hole for them to slip through in case they try it on foot." He glanced toward the mountains to the west. "Gonna be gettin' dark soon, and I don't want *any* of 'em leavin' here walkin' or ridin'. We still got sixteen more to get rid of after these."

Darkness settled in. Tenery looked to his left, then his right. He couldn't see any of his men, so it figured they couldn't see *him*. He stared at the field ahead of him. Most of the snow had melted, but it would still be sloshy in the dark places where the bare ground showed through the patches of white. He nodded to himself; that should camouflage any person trying to slip up on the ranch without him having to get on his stomach and crawl — or damned near swim to the house. Yep, he'd give that idea a little thought.

About three minutes later he figured he'd give it all the thinking he wanted to waste. He placed one foot into the mush, withdrew it and was satisfied with the small amount of sucking sound it made. He moved toward the house, slowly and near silently. He'd done this more times than he wanted to think about while scouting for one general or the other.

He glanced at the windows; all dark. He wished he hadn't warned them that there were men surrounding them; now he figured they'd have someone at the windows and they had enough men to cover. He slowed, thinking to drop to his stomach, shook his head. Nope, he'd rather die dry and halfway warm than wet and cold. He only slowed his pace such that it was hard for him to see any movement of his legs — and movement was what they'd be looking for.

When finally he brushed against the wall he stood to the side of one of the front room windows. *What the hell you gonna do now, Tenery? You can't see any more than they can. Wish I had some way of setting something on fire to show me something to shoot at.*

He stood there in the dark, his guts tight, threatening to empty his stomach. His thinking threw an unceasing string of blame on his own stupidity. Then, one of the windows blossomed with rifle fire. Almost before the sound of the shot died away, shots from the periphery of the yard winked toward the house. Rifles answered. Tenery stared at each window. The window he supposed to be the one from the kitchen remained dark.

He nodded, hoping he guessed right, hoping all of those in the house were in the front room. He'd soon find out.

He waited for the next volley. As soon as the exchange of fire started, he pulled himself to the window's ledge, kicked his legs and catapulted into the dark room.

He lay there on the floor a moment, muscles pulled tight to brace against the tearing, sledgehammer blow of a leaden slug tearing at his body. It didn't come.

He stood, careful to not make more noise than the sound of gunfire shaking the room in front of him. Abruptly, all firing ceased. He froze. Waited, hoping gunfire would again erupt. He had only a moment to wait.

With the first shot he ducked into the front room, illuminated only with the dim light the gunfire provided. He slipped to the side of the door, stood there a moment; then, moving very slowly, he thumbed the thong from his handgun, moved his hand along his waist to make sure the extra handgun he'd tucked behind his belt was still there. He'd kept the thong tight against the hammer of his Colt to guard against losing it while trying to get into the house. All gunfire ceased.

He stood there. *Hell, don't stop now.* Without flashes, he had nothing to shoot at.

Abruptly, his own men again commenced firing — then those in the room opened up. As soon as he could bring his .44 to point at the flashes, he thumbed off shots, emptied his right-hand revolver, holstered it, made a border shift and commenced to empty his backup at the flashes.

Curses, now from only two windows. "What the hell you doing? You shootin' at *us,* you dumb bastard."

Tenery fired at the sound, then trained his handgun on the flash and sound of the only other gun still shooting. Then, nothing; no sound, no flashes — only darkness and quiet.

He stood there for what seemed like eternity. He listened for groans, anything at which he might fire another shot. Not even heavy breathing broke the quiet of the room. *All dead,* he thought. He fired another shot, this one toward the roof, expecting a shot in return. Nothing.

He went to the window and yelled, "Come on in, men! We got 'em all."

In only a few moments, men streamed into the room, some from the front, some through the kitchen. McClain headed the bunch.

"Tenery, knowed damned well you wuz gonna pull some damned fool stunt, an' you went well beyond what I thought. Hell, ain't nobody got the imagination to come up with anything as dumb as you always seem to come up with — an' each time damned if you don't top out on what nobody's able to predict."

Bill, his knees feeling like water, slipped down the wall. Then sitting on the floor, he watched while one of the men found and lighted a lamp. He slanted McClain a wry grin. "Red, go ahead, pour it on. I don't know of anyone dumb enough to top this." He pinned him with a hard look. "You better not tell a soul in town what happened out here — got it?"

McClain nodded, but his look showed wonder, at both the total disregard for life and the boundless stupidity that Tenery seemed to dredge up from somewhere.

Red stared at Tenery. "You know that there girl in town's gonna be mad enuff to spit soon's she hears 'bout this."

"Just what do you mean, 'that girl in town'?"

McClain gulped, swallowing twice. Why the hell couldn't he keep his mouth shut? He had promised not to say anything about Penny being in town; now he'd let it slip. " 'Reckon I meant Miss Penny, out yonder at her ranch."

Tenery shook his head. "Nope, Red, don't think that's what you meant at all. Penny's in town, isn't she?"

McClain stared at the floor, then locked eyes with Bill. He nodded. "Yep, reckon I let it slip. I promised that girl I'd keep my mouth shut. Me an' my big mouth ain't never learned to jest quit talkin' when I'm ahead." He again nodded. "Yes, she come to town with Cannard. She made 'im come with 'er after buffaloin' Rufus." He shrugged. "Think maybe they had 'bout as big a scroody-woo out yonder as you could have without a shootin'. Rufus give in, though, 'cause she'da come alone if nobody came with 'er."

Tenery pinned McClain with a look that would have penetrated a granite mountain, then his look softened. He put his hands flat on the floor and pushed to his feet. "Aw hell, Red, I know how hardheaded that woman can be." He chuckled. "Know how hard it is for you to keep your mouth shut too." He frowned, obviously thinking. "We'll make believe you never told me. *I'll* be the one to go see Miz Gretchen when we get back, an' *I'll* just happen to find Penny there."

McClain's face lighted up as though he was a kid and Bill had only then given him a piece of hard candy. Then the light in his expression faded, he grimaced. "Thanks, Tenery. Shore don't want that there pretty widder woman gettin' mad at me. Gonna need to keep 'er my friend."

Tenery nodded, then glanced toward the stable. "A couple o' you men get down yonder an' put lead ropes on those horses so we can get 'em back to town with us."

Cody frowned. "Ain't we gonna stick

391

around 'til mornin' an' bury these men you done took outta the fight?"

Bill's face hardened so he could hardly see past his slitted eyelids. "Not buryin' a damned one of 'em."

"What about those men we been figgerin' gonna show up in the next few days?"

Tenery's face still felt like dried leather as he replied, "Let 'em walk in here to the stink o' dead bodies — might make 'em think maybe they should grab a handful o' the next stage outta here. Might give us an edge."

Chance moved closer to Betsy, put his arm around her shoulders and rubbed them a moment. "You're thinkin' 'bout Billy, aren't you?"

She nodded. "Wonderin' how far Yancy's had to go to find 'im. He's been gone a pretty good spell. I'd have thought he'd've caught up with him by now."

"It's a big country, honey. I think he mighta had to go as far as Miles Town, or maybe farther; he did and I b'lieve we're lookin' for 'im back too soon." He chuckled, although his phoney show of amusement was only to make his wife feel better. "Yancy don't get back here soon, danged if I don't think we'll have to rope an' tie that big

Shoshone Mopeah." He nodded. "Yeah, danged if I don't b'lieve he'd head out leavin' his wife to have that baby all by herself."

"Chance Tenery, you know that he knows we'll be right there with 'er when she starts labor." She nodded. "Heck, he'd leave her with us as quick as he would his own mother and father." She snuggled closer to him. "Know what I know?" Without waiting for him to reply, she continued, smiling, "That big warrior thinks as much of Billy as he does his own children."

Chance only smiled and nodded. "Yeah, you're right about that. And once in a while I think about that boy bein' a homeless orphan when we took 'im in — but, Betsy, he's as much ours as though he'd come from your womb. Yep, he couldn't be more ours than he is."

Betsy sat back, wide-eyed. "Don't you get any ideas about headin' out to look for Billy *and* Yancy. Tetlow's gonna find our boy, so you stop worryin'."

A belly laugh bubbled from Chance. "Yeah, I'll stop worryin' 'bout the same time you do." He shook his head. "But, no. I'm not gonna head outta here lookin' for 'em."

If Penny looked down the trail toward the

Circle-R once an hour, she walked to the window and looked every few minutes. Gretchen stared at her a few moments. "Shore is heck to be in love, ain't it, Penny?"

"You know what? I b'lieve if I'd known how much pain it could cause a woman, I'd have stayed clear of all men. Jest flat didn't know it could be so hard."

Gretchen laughed, then shook her head. "Ain't neither one o' us would give one second of this anxiety if it meant takin' another man who ain't the man we done chosen. Honey, we got us two shore 'nuff *men*."

Penny nodded. "I only wish they weren't so danged *much* man. Maybe we wouldn't worry so much." She went back to the window, looked out into the dark; she couldn't see — but listened for the sound of horses' hooves. No sound disturbed the quiet.

She turned from the window, picked up the coffeepot, put it back on the stove without pouring and cocked her head. "They're back — they're back, Gretchen!" She twisted as though to head for the door. Gretchen took her by the arm.

"You let them men put their horses away, get to Red's place and have a drink — then I think one o' 'em'll come tell us what happened." She grinned, then laughed. "They're all right, though; I know, 'cause it sounded like they brought a whole bunch o' horses back with 'em; Hans Olerud's horses, if they didn't get 'em back, they'd still be chasin' that bunch o' city thugs."

Penny again picked up the coffeepot, sighed, poured her coffee and sat. She stared at her friend a moment, then shook her head. "You ain't gonna cut me any slack, are you?"

Gretchen shook her head. "Not where it comes to stickin' yore nose into men's fightin' business."

Olerud stood in the doorway of the saloon. He counted the horses Cody led into the maw of the big stable. All of his horses were there, but where were those who had stolen them? He knew the answer, but hesitated to believe his neighbors would have come back before burying them. He thought about that a few seconds, then nodded. There was one damned hard man in that group. *He* would leave 'em right where they fell.

Tenery led the group he'd left town with out the door of the livery and to the door of the saloon. Olerud counted them. They were all there, and none of 'em limped, or leaned on a friend for support — they were all right.

When Tenery stood in front of the old man, he said, "Got your nags back. Seems like you'd be appreciative enough to have us a drink poured."

"Well, gosh-ding it, Tenery, I'm a old man, don't move very fast anymore." He chuckled. "Aw hell. I had to stand here an' count y'all, make sure they wuzn't nobody missin', or bein' carried." He nodded toward the bar. "C'mon in. I'll have a drink settin' in front of each o' you 'fore you can say scat."

He squinted one eye, cocked his head and looked at Tenery. "What you do with them who wuz ridin' my hosses?"

"Left 'em all sittin' around Rourk's place, reeal comfortable. They're all right." His face took on a no-give look. "Not a one of 'em's gonna give us any more trouble."

By then, Olerud stood behind the bar and had a bottle tipped over a line of glasses. He looked toward McClain. "These here drinks are my part o' the party." He swiveled his head to see all in the room. "Thanks, men, you're 'bout the best family a man could have, even if he got the chance to pick each one o' you."

Tenery walked behind the bar. "You men, go see your families, let 'em know you didn't get hurt, then come back over here.

Gotta tell ya how we're gonna take care o' that new bunch that'll be here, by my best guess, in two or three days. We're gonna be ready come hell or high water — an' every danged one of us'll be okay. Promise your wives what I just said."

They knocked back their drinks, looked tiredly at him and left. "Clean those weapons while you're gone." Bill had to lift his voice only a little to make sure they all heard.

He twisted to look at McClain. "Now I'm gonna go see what that young lady has to say is her reason for causing me more worry." He tossed off the drink he held, stepped toward the door and practically walked into the bottle Red held in front of him.

"You better take this an' give it to Miz Gretchen. Tell 'er I said it's to make sure she has a drink fer us men when we git time to git over there." He laughed. "Bet she an' them other women we gonna have in there with her might even take a nip, 'specially after we take care o' Rourk's new bunch."

Tenery wrapped his fingers around the neck of the bottle at the same time McClain told him to remember he hadn't said a word about her coming to town with Cannard.

Penny had been looking out the window

every few seconds to check when Red might come over; instead, Tenery came out the door of the saloon. She gasped. Surely he wasn't coming over here. Then his steps put the lie to her thought. "Oh my goodness! Bill's on his way over here! May I stay outta sight in yore room 'til he leaves? He's gonna be madder'n a skunk-sprayed coyote if he sees me."

Gretchen nodded and pushed her toward her bedroom. "Stay in there. I'll let you know when he leaves."

Tenery came in, handed the bottle to Gretchen and explained why McClain had sent it. She smiled. "He knows danged well they's a lady or two who might take a wee sip with you men."

Abruptly, Bill took an exaggerated sniff, sniffed again, then looked at Gretchen. He forced his face into the hardest look he could muster past his wanting to laugh. "Where's Penny?"

Gretchen stared at him wide-eyed. "What do you mean? Reckon she's out yonder at the Saddle Horn."

Tenery pinned her with a squinty-eyed stare. "Miz Gretchen, there's not a woman in this town uses the same perfume that Penny orders outta New York. Add to that the fact that every scent you women use takes on a special, personal scent; I know Penny's been in this room less than a very few minutes ago. Tell 'er to come outta wherever she is."

Gretchen seemed to wither — her shoulders slumped, she grimaced. "Come on out, Penny. I tried."

Bill, holding his face rigid, stared at the only door she could come through into the room. She came through the door, obviously thinking she would catch hell for not staying at the ranch; her eyes showed it; they were wide, she was a little pale, but she had a stubborn set to her mouth. "Bill Tenery, you get jest as mad at me as you want to, but I stood worryin' 'bout you long's I could. I jest flat had to know you hadn't done some stupid thing agin."

He gave her that frozen look as long as he could hold it then let his face soften. He held his arms wide. "Come here, little one, come here where you belong."

If there had been room to work up any speed in the room, she would surely have done so, but Tenery thought she tried. She literally fell into his arms before they tightened around her. "Oh hell, Penny, you think I could be angry for you caring enough to put yourself in a dangerous situation when I'm the reason for it?"

He glanced over her shoulder toward Gretchen. "Reckon she told you how it is with us?"

Gretchen laughed. "If she didn't, I ain't dumb enough to not recognize the symptoms. Go ahead, git yore huggin' done, then we both want you to tell us what happened out yonder."

Bill held Penny to him as tightly as he dared when among others, turned her loose, asked Gretchen to pour him a drink from the bottle Red had sent over, and then told them what happened. If any of those who had gone with him had heard this story, they would have thought he related a fight they had never seen — and probably wouldn't. "Hell, I don't reckon a man could want any better bunch of fightin' men around him than that bunch." He shook his head. "I'm here to tell you, when that bunch sets their minds to get after it — they *really do get after it.*"

Penny stared at him a long moment, then shook her head. "Bill Tenery, you should've quit when you were ahead. I've seen the hands out at the barn shovelin' manure that was less smelly than that story you jest laid out fer me an' Gretchen. Now tell us what *really* happened out there."

Tenery's face warmed, then got hot as a

six-shooter that had fast-fired every chamber. "Well, what I just now told you is almost . . ."

"Don't make it worse."

Gretchen, who apparently had been taking in the back-and-forth exchange, put her two cents in. "Red's been tellin' us 'bout you for quite a spell now. What you jest spouted fer us to b'lieve ain't near 'bout the man I been hearin' 'bout since you come to town."

He squared his shoulders, sucked in a deep breath, and gave them each in turn a straight-on look. "You women have the only story I'm gonna tell ya. Now, I'm tellin' ya to get off my back. Those men went out there and did the job I figured them to do — they did it well."

The two women stared at him a moment, then turned their eyes to each other. Both shrugged. Then Gretchen grinned. "Don't worry, honey, I'll git the story outta Red. I don't figger he's ever been known to keep a secret, an' I never heard anybody say he'd lie." She nodded. "He'll tell me."

Tenery had no doubt but what she was right. McClain just flat couldn't keep his mouth shut, especially when there was a good story to be told. He pulled Penny to his chest again, told them he had called a town meeting — a "man" town meeting — and had to go. He wasted no time getting out the door, then sighed in relief. Those women were tough.

When the door closed behind him, Penny said to no one in particular, "Wonder what damned fool thing he pulled out there. Know it wuzn't very smart, an' also know danged well we been listenin' to the biggest fairy story ever told."

Rourk watched the whole episode unfold, except for the way his men had escaped the saloon. But he did see them ride out of the livery with the stolen horses. He didn't give a damn whether they got away or not — they were crooks who were cowards. Those he had coming in were crooked also, but could fight. He nodded to himself. That was what he needed — someone who could and would fight.

He stood there, his legs paining all the way into his stomach, but he wanted to see how many of the townspeople came back from the chase he'd seen them start.

He saw them, and counted them. They, all of them, came back with the horses, and there were no men lying across the saddles of the stolen horses. *What I expected,* he thought, but felt no sorrow for any of those he'd brought out here. At the core of his emotions was hatred. That damned Tenery — he'd started the entire unwinding of all his plans. When this was over, Tenery was the one man he wanted to see stretched out with enough lead in him to sink one of those Navy ships he'd looked upon before leaving New York.

He went back to his bed and, ticking off one finger at a time, counted the days since he'd written Branch Whitcom in New York for more men. He frowned. By his estimate they should be getting here any day now; he really had thought they might have gotten here before now.

He thought to attack Farnum when he brought his meal up, take his gun and get out of this town until Whitcom could get here.

He mentally shook his head. He'd better wait'll after his man from the East got here, let him and those he brought with him clean up the mess he was certain Tenery had caused out at the Circle-R. He knew damned well they hadn't stayed out there long enough to bury those they'd killed and he knew they'd killed them all.

Also, if he had to stay in the woods until he could set up a plan as to how to take on Tenery and the townspeople, he'd better wait until the weather warmed a bit. He didn't hanker to be any more uncomfortable than was necessary.

He nodded, even though no one could see him. Yeah, he would stay right where he was until he had some certainty that he would have a halfway decent chance of being warm and well fed. He stretched out on his bed. He'd wait.

Yancy Tetlow had surges of guilt. He knew how much anxiety those folks north of the Shoshone reservation must be feeling, how they must be constantly looking down the trail for him to lead Billy home, but he knew there was nothing he could do to shake that hardheaded boy into leaving the task he'd set for himself.

He gave himself a satisfied grin. Hell, he fit right in with this bunch of Saddle Horn cowpokes. He shrugged. He reckoned maybe the hands on any ranch would be pretty much the same; hardworking, hard drinking, honest and loyal to the brand they rode for. He pushed any guilty feelings he had to the back of his mind — he might as well because he would have to play the hand Billy Tenery dealt him.

Branch Whitcom pulled out his huge silver

pocket watch and saw the time was pushing toward sundown. He snapped the cover closed, wondering who he'd stolen it from — and couldn't remember. He frowned. How the hell long would it take to get to that hick town Rourk was in? He shrugged. It didn't make any difference, there was nothing he could do to hurry the trip, but he and his men had been bounced around in the stage for what now seemed most of his life. He wondered if the bunch in the stage behind fared any better.

The stage company had to send two of its vehicles to accommodate the number of men he brought.

Rourk's letter had said that he was holed up in the hotel waiting for his legs to heal from getting shot by a woman. Whitcom let a cold smile slide across his face. Cord hadn't changed one damned bit. Someday he would be killed by a woman he'd done wrong. Whitcom couldn't understand a man who let women govern his thinking and actions like Rourk did.

He swept those in the coach with him a thoughtful look, frowned and wondered if they shouldn't have bought long guns before leaving Billings. That town they headed for might not have enough in the stores to sell them sixteen rifles. He pulled his shoulders

405

up in a shrug. Hell, they'd have to make what they had take care of the problem. He couldn't see that it would be that great a task; they'd probably get it taken care of in one afternoon, spend the night drinking, collect a month's pay from Rourk and head back to New York. How the hell much longer would it take to get to Elkhorn?

About the time Whitcom had that question in mind, Tenery made sure everyone in the room had coffee or whisky in front of them. Trying not to be obvious, he counted the men he could count on. They would all stick. There were forty-two hard-jawed, grim men in the room.

"Hey, men, lighten up, let's enjoy tonight; 'sides, I b'lieve I got it figured where we can cover the town an' the ranches without anybody gettin' hurt bad, less o' course you do some damn fool thing like some o' us been known to do."

McClain bellowed loud enough for the people in Billings to hear, "Yeah, y'all try to act like that damn fool talking to you, well dammit, you gonna get yore head blowed off! Jest act like you got a gut in yore head an' you gonna be all right."

Tenery slanted his friend a sour look. "Just for that remark, I'm gonna make damned sure these men drink enuff o' your *free* whisky for you to have a severe pain in your money belt."

Bill made sure every man had his drink of choice in front of him, and called the meeting to order. One by one, he selected those he wanted to stay in each building, then said he wanted all of the family members to stay in town.

He looked at Cody. "Trent, b'lieve your store is the only buildin' in town set up outta that mountain stone. It's gonna be the safest in town, so that's where I want your loved ones. Gonna be crowded." He nodded. "Know y'all noticed I put an extra couple of men in there with the women and children. Don't want any o' that bunch gettin' close to where they'll be holed up. The rest o' you will have two, maybe three men in each buildin' with you. We're gonna have eighteen men go to the Circle-R. I figure that's twice what we need to take care of that bunch.

"Somethin' you all gotta know: those city thugs are fightin' for money, you men're fightin' for your families. *That makes each one o' you, as fightin' men, worth any three of 'em.*"

"Hot damn! Shore am glad Tenery didn't have a family to fight for out yonder at the

Circle-R; hell, we'da had to hunt up some more men fer 'im to shoot." McClain quickly sat after that outburst, but not before Bill pinned him with an iron stare.

Olerud stood. "Tenery, them men're gonna come in here on the stage, the way I got it figgered. They gonna have to git to Rourk's place an' I ain't got enuff hosses fer all o' 'em."

Bill frowned. "Rent 'em a wagon." He stared at the wall a moment. "Figure they gotta take Rourk outta that hotel room; he won't be able to straddle a horse." He nodded. "Yeah, they're gonna need a wagon — maybe two. Go down yonder to your wagon yard, pick out the two in the sorriest shape you got an' make sure they're right handy to your livery. Better do that right now; take a couple men to help you."

His look followed Olerud and two men out the door. He swung his head to take in the room. "Somethin' else I want every man in here to make sure of: *we don't want any o' those thugs fired on while they're still in town.* I want the fight to take place where we can control it. I want it out of town, out in the country, where the terrain will be in our favor. Rourk's ranch buildin's will be almost as good." He grinned. "I'd even like to get 'em bottled up in that ranch house once more; *we'd* sure as hell take care of 'em there."

McClain put his foot in it again. "Men, don't none o' you give 'em a chance to git holed up in that there house agin. Hell, we'd miss out on all the fun. Tenery's got a selfish habit o' hawgin' all that stuff when he gits the chance."

Bill's look this time surpassed his last steely gaze. "Know what, Red? You keep on lettin' your mouth overload your rear end, I'm gonna make damned sure you get all the *fun* you can handle."

McClain chucked up a huge belly laugh. "Tenery, you ain't worryin' me none a'tall. Hell, you couldn't stand it if you thought anybody wuz cuttin' you outta the action."

Bill shot him a wry grin. "McClain, you were there; you saw how long I shook, how sick I must've looked after I realized what a dumb thing I'd done." He shook his head. "Don't figure on me bein' that stupid again. 'Sides, way I got it thought out, you an' me — we got us some marryin' to get done."

"Bill, I ain't even said nothin' to that pretty lady 'bout such yet."

Tenery chuckled. "Well, I'm tellin' you right now; you better get with it or I'll guaran-damn-tee ya there's a cowboy right here in this bunch who'd be glad to take your place. That's a mighty pretty lady."

Red slid a searching look at each man in the bunch, finally nodded as though satisfied he could handle it if someone pushed in on what he now considered his territory. "Ain't worried, Tenery."

Bill thought to tell them he had said all he had to say, then thought of a couple more things. "Men, if we can, I want to catch them out 'tween here an' the Circle-R — not gonna warn 'em, just gonna cut 'em down."

He swung his gaze from the shocked looks of the men in front of him and gave Cody a straight-on look. "Trent, I don't think those city men gonna come in here with long guns. Don't know how many you have in stock, but I want you to hide all but maybe one or two. Don't want long-range fire at us," he said, shaking his head, "that is, not any more than we have to handle."

Cody shook his head. "Hell, Tenery, you ain't gonna give 'em no chance a'tall."

"Didn't figure on it." He frowned. "Reason I say to let them have maybe one or two rifles is that you know danged good an' well out here — where we got Indian trouble, those ridin' the owlhoot, an' others who're just flat-out out to get somethin' for nothin' — there ain't a general store anywhere that won't have at least two or three long guns. I want to keep any of that bunch from gettin' suspicious. And remember, Rourk's probably gonna be with 'em; he'll know danged well you stock at least a few rifles."

Cody stared at Bill a long moment, thinking Tenery must be the hardest man he'd ever known. The look on every face standing there reflected the same thought.

"Okay, men, let's break it up for tonight. When you get around in the mornin', I want each o' you family men to take up stations like we've talked about — an' stay where you're assigned 'til we can all gather in here an' celebrate — wives included."

From his second-story window, Rourk had watched the town's men and ranchers gather and disperse for each meeting. He had no doubt but that his and Whitcom's job had increased in difficulty at least tenfold, but every time he had the thought, Tenery and hatred took over his mind.

A hot red film enveloped his thinking; the fact was he didn't think — he only *felt,* and every sensation absorbed his body and mind in emotion, emotions that precluded thought.

He wanted Tenery. If he could face him,

his own confidence pushed the idea that regardless how fast and accurate Bill Tenery could get that side gun into action, his own quickness and deadly aim would prevail. Once the gunman was out of the way, the townspeople would fold.

He nodded to himself. Yeah, he'd have that woman's ranch *and* the town.

The next morning, McClain, Olerud and Tenery, having already been to the café and eaten breakfast, sat at a table in Red's bar drinking coffee. Olerud frowned. "Today's Sunday, ain't it?"

"Yep. Comes every week, you old goat. What you figgerin' now?"

The old liveryman ignored McClain's sarcasm. His frown deepened, "Way I got it figgered is, the stage, maybe two of 'em, 'll be here soon after our noonin' time today. They're already a day late."

Tenery nodded. "B'lieve you're right, old-timer. Think soon's the men have their breakfast an' come over here I'll take 'em out the back door, go to your stable, saddle our horses and have 'em set up somewhere 'tween here and the Circle-R."

He twisted to look at McClain. "Gonna send Cannard over to the bakery; want you with me."

Red's mouth worked as though to say something. Tenery gazed at him steely eyed. "No loose jawin', McClain; we're gonna do it my way."

Red looked squinty eyed at Tenery a moment, then nooded. "Why you gonna take 'em out the back way, Tenery?"

"I —"

Olerud cut in. "You red-headed smart aleck, if'n you'd jest not be so quick to unhinge yore brain from yore tongue an' listen to other people onc't in a while, you'd know danged well why."

With a self-satisfied look, the old man said, "We all know danged good and well Rourk stands up yonder in that there window an' watches ever'thing that goes on along the main street." He nodded. "Tenery takes everbody outta here the back way, that city thug cain't see us an' he can get outta town an' set up without Cord Rourk even guessin' we're ready fer 'im."

"Knowed all along what Tenery wuz doin'; jest wanted to see wuz you smart 'nuff to figger it out." While talking, McClain stared steely eyed at his old friend as though daring him to refute his statement.

Olerud cackled, and slapped his knee. "Hot dang it, you ain't knowed no such." He laughed again.

■ ■ ■ ■

Through the early morning hours, the town's men and cowboys drifted into the saloon. When each of them came in, Tenery handed them a cup of coffee; and after they drank, he told them to go out the back door to the livery and make certain their rifles were clean and that they had enough cartridges for a good fight. "And be danged sure you got enough warm clothes on. We might be out yonder more'n one day *and* night."

Rourk watched them gather at the saloon, but every few minutes, his legs would tire, then pain, and he'd shamble to his bed and sit a few minutes before stumbling back to the slightly pulled curtain.

His failing to see anyone leave Red's place caused him no wonder. They might have gone back home, or to their businesses while he sat. He gave nothing much thought except the thought that he might soon have Tenery in front of his gun.

About eleven o'clock, Tenery swept the men sitting patiently on their horses, waiting for his leadership to tell them what to do. Damn! What a troop these men would make

414

for the Army. He would be proud to command or ride with such a bunch.

He motioned them closer. "Men, I've been thinkin' 'bout what we're about to do. Told you I wanted every saddle emptied." He shook his head, "After thinkin' 'bout it, unless they force it, I think I got a way to end all this without killin' those men regardless how much they might need it."

He packed his pipe and lighted it. "All o' you know where the trail winds through that pile o' boulders out yonder 'bout four miles? Well, that's where I figure we can set up. Y'all fire one round, empty two or three saddles, an' we'll have their attention — then I figure I can get them to surrender, but I'm tellin' you right now *I'm* gonna take charge of Rourk. Don't want a one of you pointin' your long gun even close to him — he's mine."

He swept them with another hard look. "All right, let's ride; and when we get out there, gather around again and we'll pick out the safest place for each one of you. Let's go."

They rode without much conversation; except for McClain. He joked and laughed, and in general, his voice rumbling through the tightly bunched riders seemingly kept their nerves loose. Tenery gave a silent prayer of thanks. Men who were too keyed up were apt to do foolish things, stupid things, and he wanted none of them hurt if he could prevent it.

He chuckled to himself. Who the hell was he to judge anything they did as stupid? He should be able to judge, he was the one who originated that kind of stupidity.

After about an hour's ride, they pulled rein at the rocks. Bill climbed from his horse, walked among the rocks, sighted through spaces between them and chose the best places he could find for his riflemen. He placed each of them, and said loud enough for all to hear, "All right, men. Don't fire until I do. One volley, then hold your fire an' we'll see how my plan works from there. Get comfortable. Don't know whether they'll get here today — but think so."

Back in Elkhorn, Penny glanced at the three men Bill had left to guard Gretchen, two other women and herself. Tenery and Red had said that McClain would be one of those left behind — but at the last moment, Red had walked across the trail and told her he just flat couldn't let the others do more than him. He said he had to go with them. He didn't put the blame on Tenery.

Gretchen had studied him a moment and decided she couldn't strip him of the degree of pride she'd have to, to make him stay with her. Now she and the women looked at the men who'd stayed behind. They were all good men.

Penny edged to Gretchen's side. "You reckon our men're gonna want ta get married soon's they get back?"

Gretchen sort of smiled. "If I learned anything in the short time 'fore my man got 'imself killed, it's that a man ain't got much patience where gettin' his wants put off is concerned. Why?"

"Well, jest got to thinkin'; Bill's folks settin' down yonder close to the Shoshone reservation, lookin' for him to show up any time, sweatin' bullets for 'im to do so — they ain't gonna look with much favor on me holdin' 'im up. Fact is, they might not like me a'tall if I do such."

She shook her head, and knowing her face must show the misery she felt, said, "Don't know as how I could do nothin' like that even if I made up my mind to not like 'em, an' I danged sure ain't even had such a thought."

She frowned, tried to think clearly; then nodded. "Reckon I better give some thought as to how I'm gonna get 'im headed that way without a preacher man sayin' them words over us. Know danged well ain't neither one o' us got the patience to put off what a man an' woman in love's gonna want ta do right sudden when they know they're alone, an' they ain't nobody a-lookin' on."

A gurgle of a laugh bubbled from Gretchen; then it erupted into a full-out belly pushing laugh. Obviously trying to talk between laughter, she pinned Penny with a knowing look. "Tell you how it is, honey; I bet this here bakery, an' they ain't no doubt in my mind, y'all gonna find a way to get mighty close to each other without neither one o' you havin' any reason to pull a whole bunch o' guilty feelin's under yore covers."

Penny looked at her friend; then dropped her gaze to the floor. Her voice so soft she hardly heard it herself, she said, "Gretchen, if Bill wuzn't such a gentleman, he coulda already made a soiled dove outta me." She shook her head. "An' I'm gonna tell ya somethin'; him bein' a gentleman ain't gonna hold me back fer very long." She shrugged. "Ain't fair, but reckon it's me that's gonna have to make me stay a lady."

Tenery again checked where each man lay. Assured that they were as safe as any location he might put them in, he turned to Mc-

Clain. "Wonder what Olerud promised those two men driving the wagon?"

Red shrugged. "Reckon he didn't have ta promise 'em no more'n we knew we'd git outta this — a decent, peaceful life."

Tenery stared down the trail, deep creases pulled between his eyebrows. "Hope to hell when the shootin' starts they got enough sense to lie down in the boot; they might not get hit that way."

This time, McClain, sober-faced, stared into Bill's eyes. "Them men, each one o' them, been through the War 'Tween the States, Indian fights; you name it, they're jest as good fightin' men as we got with us — an' they ain't dumb."

Somewhat satisfied, Tenery turned his eyes back to the trail. If both drivers would stop the wagons as soon as the fight started, maybe all of the city bunch would throw down their weapons at the same time — *if* they threw them down.

The sun, having shed its meager heat on the now-drying ground, slipped toward the horizon. Melted snow had pulled back from rocks in the trail that had been covered only two days ago. Tenery's glance swept the surrounding terrain, in most places it had fewer holes and rocks than the trail. *Gonna be a rough ride for those men, who probably had never seen anything but cobblestone streets.* He chuckled to himself. Damn, but he'd like to see them bouncing around on those wagons.

He pulled his watch and checked it; four-thirty. He shook his head. "Men, get as warm an' comfortable as you can. If they don't show by dark, I think it might be after ten tomorrow 'fore we do see them. Don't b'lieve they're gonna come along today. After dark we'll put some coffee on; y'all can eat those sandwiches the ladies fixed for you."

He walked by one of the men and heard him ask the man next to him, "You scared, Joe?"

Whoever Joe was chuckled. "Damned too-tin'. Been in these things 'fore, an' I'll tell you right now, I been scared each time — but mostly it's the waitin'. Once things git started we won't think 'bout it 'til it's all over." All he got out of the man who asked the question was a grunt.

About ten o'clock, they'd had coffee, and were wrapped in their blankets. Tenery squatted by McClain. "I'm gonna stay awake for awhile, listenin'. I don't hear anything by midnight I'll catch a few winks." Even though black dark surrounded him, and he knew Red couldn't see, he shook his head. "From then 'til daylight we won't have to worry 'bout them comin' at us. No need for anyone to stay awake." Red's answer was to roll tighter in his blankets.

Tenery sat on a boulder that lay by the side of the trail, looked at the Big Dipper occasionally to estimate the time; then he'd stare at the velvety sky, a sky so big it engulfed the world and let the distant, cold starlight get a little closer. Finally, he gave it up and crawled into his blankets.

About an hour before daylight, Tenery wakened, got the men out of their blankets, had a couple of them fix breakfast — fried bread, bacon and beans — then he told them to get back to the places they'd been in the day before. Now they had more waiting to do.

Rourk stood by the curtain in his room. He expected the stage in today, in fact he'd been looking for it for two days, it never came in when scheduled — but it damned sure should get to Elkhorn on this day.

Every few minutes he'd look at his watch. Farnum had brought his breakfast, he'd eaten, then gone back to the window. He glanced at his watch again; it was pushing up to eleven-thirty. He frowned, cocked his head and listened. One stage, then another, pulled to the side of the trail in front of the hotel — right below him.

He nodded, a cold, satisfied smile pulling at his lips. His men would off load from the stages in only a few minutes; they could get him out of this room he'd spent so many miserable days and nights in, they'd go to the ranch and he'd tell them what the game was and how he figured for them to play it.

He leaned out the window. "Hey, Whitcom, I'm up here. Have a couple men help me downstairs, then we'll head for the ranch."

The New Yorker cocked his head to look up at Rourk, and nodded. When both stages unloaded, he motioned his men to stay where they were while the two he selected to get Rourk went upstairs.

The two empty coaches and their drivers reined up the trail to the stage station. Supported on each side by Whitcom's men, Rourk came out the hotel's front door. He frowned. The town was strangely quiet. Usually by this time of day there would be wagons, horse traffic, women hurrying to Trent Cody's store, punchers headed for the café — but there was none of that.

He shrugged. As cold as the weather had been, then the thaw, and now puddles from one side of the trail to the other, he thought the townspeople were waiting for a little more drying. He glanced at the men Whitcom had brought with him. "Don't know if McClain's opened his saloon yet, he's kinda sloppy about that, but if he has, we'll have a drink before we head outta here." He got total approval of that idea — but there was a padlock on the door when they got there.

Rourk looked at Whitcom. "Never seen this place locked from the outside before." He shook his head. "Strange." He raised an eyebrow. "What the hell, I got whisky out at the Circle-R; we'll be there soon."

He shuffled toward the livery. "Don't believe that old bastard who runs the stable's gonna have enough horses for all of us. We'll have to take a couple of wagons to get out there." All he got for that statement was groans. They must have had enough bouncing around in the stagecoaches; now they had to endure more of it. When he assured them his ranch wasn't but seven or eight miles from town they settled down a bit.

He swept the men who had come to help him with a questioning look. "Any o' you men bring rifles with you?"

Whitcom cocked his head to the side. "What do we need rifles for? All of us have our handguns."

Rourk pulled his mouth down in a grimace. "Out here, people don't fire from very close; an' don't cut 'em short on that, they hit what they shoot at — from a long way off." He looked toward Cody's general mercantile store. "We better have your men get some o' those long guns."

Whitcom shot Rourk a look of disgust. "Good, damned good, Rourk. I don't b'lieve a one of 'em could hit anything past twenty or thirty feet with a rifle, but if you say we need 'em, we'll get 'em. But you're gonna pay for 'em," he stressed.

They spent only a few minutes in the store, just long enough to get the two rifles Cody had in stock. Rourk spent more time selecting a revolver to once again fill the new shoulder holster he also bought — the only one Cody had in stock. With it snuggled under his arm, he felt dressed again.

The livery proved to be of little help. There were two worn-out wagons and a couple of seemingly out-of-work cowhands who said they would drive 'em out to the Circle-R for "eatin' money," as they put it. Rourk offered them fifty cents for the job, but Whitcom, red faced, gave the Circle-R owner a hard, straight-on look, and said. "Rourk, these men said they needed eating money, by damn, you're gonna pay them more'n that. You're gonna give 'em a couple days, or more days-dollars."

Rourk didn't like the way Whitcom inserted his will into everything that came up, but he agreed to pay the men two dollars for the trip.

The slim, lanky one of the two said as how that would be enough, but that he wanted the money up front. Rourk dug in his pocket and handed the two men their money.

After glancing down the trail and listening, Tenery frowned. He had never fired on anyone from ambush, and the way he'd set his men it was sure as hell an ambush. He grimaced, then yelled, "Changed my mind, men. Want McClain to do the talkin' 'cause he's got the loudest voice. Don't want any o' you to open fire unless I do. We're gonna try to get outta this without gettin' any o' those city fellers hurt, an' damn sure don't want any of us gettin' shot."

He begged cigarette papers from one of the men and fashioned himself a quirly, thinking he might not have time to smoke his pipe. He drew a long coal on the end of the ragged job he'd made of rolling the smoke, then said, "If we can get those

425

wagons stopped without having gunfire, I'll take it from there unless one o' those men insist on swappin' lead with us."

Red bellowed loud enough to be heard up in the Montana Territory, "Knowed it; knowed it all along. Told you men Tenery wuz gonna hawg all the fun if we let 'im." He drew his lips down in a grimace. "What damned fool thing you gonna pull this time, Bill?"

Staring into the distance, Tenery frowned; then shook his head. "Not gonna do anything stupid this time, my friend, but I think I can get the job done without any killin', get rid of Rourk an' send those men back where they come from."

McClain only stared at the man they had all come to rely on for leadership — and friendship.

"All right, men, stay where you are. Figure it won't be long now," Tenery said.

Tenery's estimate proved correct. Less than fifteen minutes, and the rattle of wheels grinding against rock, the wood-rending sound of wagons flopping into chuck holes and the cursing of the drivers trying to get the wagons on level ground again broke the quiet.

Tenery held his hand out to his side, palm down, waiting for the lead wagon with its load of men to pull even. Then he signaled Red to call for the drivers to rein the horses to a halt.

"Pull them horses in — both wagons — you men ridin' in 'em keep yore hands high." Red bellowed. "Grab fer a handful o' that there blue sky. Don't none o' you do anything foolish an' ain't nobody gonna git hurt."

Every man did as told. By Tenery's guess, they had no choice. They had nothing to shoot at. He stepped into the trail, yelled over his shoulder for his men to stay where they were, and told them to drop any man who looked like he was going to try his luck.

He swept both wagonloads of men. "Gonna tell you like it is, men. Every one of you is covered by a long gun, in the hands of men who know how to use 'em." He had thumbed the thong off the hammer of his .44 before he stepped onto the trail.

"I want each o' you to veeery carfully lift your handguns outta those shoulder holsters you wear and drop them over the side of the wagons onto the ground — all 'cept you, Rourk. Want you to keep yours until I tell you different. All right, do it."

Reluctantly, using only their fingertips, the men from New York lifted their weapons from under their arms and dropped them.

Many of the expensive weapons splashed into muddy holes.

Tenery, keeping his eyes riveted on those in the wagons, yelled, "McClain, come out here. Count the men, then count the weapons on the ground, including those two rifles. When you got 'em all accounted for I want to know."

Tenery kept the Circle-R owner under his gaze, knowing he'd left him with a weapon, and knowing the thug would try a sneak draw if he thought he could get away with it. Tenery's fingers never left caressing the walnut grip at his side.

Finally, McClain glanced over his shoulder. "All o' them guns you want counted are here, an' the numbers match the number o' men except for Rourk's handgun. What you gonna do now?"

His face feeling like a dry lake bed after six months of no rain, Tenery stared at the crippled Circle-R rancher. Except for Indians, he'd never set out to deliberately kill a man. Now that had changed.

"Have a couple men lift Rourk outta that wagon. Set 'im on the ground facin' me. I'll take it from there." He turned a hard stare to the man about to be lifted from the wagon. "Rourk, while you're getting settled on the ground, don't make even a twinge toward your armpit. You do, an' I'll blow your brains all over this part of Wyoming — got it?"

A triumphant look came to Cord Rourk's face. His eyes squeezed down to slits; his thin-lipped mouth pulled into a sneer. "You think to try to beat me in a fair, stand-up, head-on gunfight, Tenery? Hell, back in New York, I eat boys like you for lunch."

"You ain't in New York now. You're in the West."

Rourk gingerly placed his feet on the ground at the side of the wagon. "When I beat you, gunfighter, what do you intend to do then?"

"You beat me, I'm tellin' my men right now to let you go, but to make sure you and all these men with you leave Wyoming. You don't, an' I'm tellin' 'em to hunt every one of you down, don't give any of you a chance; to shoot you on sight."

Tenery's gut muscles tightened. His shoulders ached. He'd never seen Rourk pull a gun, but he'd bet he was good, very good, or he wouldn't have been able to control the numbers of men he'd had with him.

"Go ahead, take your sheepskin off so you can get to your suit coat, but do it very slow-like."

Almost as though he relished every moment of this, Cord Rourk seemed to make a production of worrying each tie on his sheepskin loose. Finally, after what seemed a lifetime to Tenery, the rancher shrugged out of his outer garment. He passed it to his left hand and leaned as though to place it on the ground in front of him — and his right hand streaked under his suit coat.

Every motion, every sound slowed in Tenery's mind. He'd been expecting any kind of sneaky move. Rourk's hand had time to grasp the grip of his revolver when Tenery's hand flashed to his side. He wasn't aware of his palm slapping the walnut grip of his Colt, wasn't aware that it was in his hand, wasn't aware that his thumb eared back the hammer. It was there and it bucked in his hand twice.

Rourk had his gun out. It jumped, bucked, spewed smoke and lead.

A hot streak burned Tenery's side. At the same time, a red stream spewed from Rourk's mouth, his gun bucked again, but it pointed toward the ground, and kicked up muddy water from a pothole close to his feet. A stream of curses bubbled through the red froth streaming from his mouth. He died cursing, hating Tenery to his last breath.

Tenery's glance swept the city men. "Who

is in charge of these men?"

Whitcom nodded. "That'll be me, cowboy. What do you think to do with us?" His voice showed no fear.

Bill studied the man, figured him for a hard man, but one that said it like it was. "If I turn you loose and you climb aboard a stage an' head back East, I figure to let you an' your men head out."

He realized he held his .44 at his side, smoke still trickling from its barrel. He slipped it gently into its holster. He nodded. "Know that man lying yonder must have promised you somethin' to come out here, so I'm gonna let you go through his pockets, his money belt, take what he might have to pay your men." He chuckled. "Hell, it might not be enough to buy you breakfast — but take it."

Whitcom stared hard-eyed at Tenery and nodded. "You've said how you think to play the hand, cowboy. I don't ask more than that of any man." A cold smile flicked his lips. "Get us back to your town, an' we'll catch those vehicles from hell you call transportation back to Billings, an' get outta your life."

Tenery nodded. "That's all I ask. Now check Rourk for whatever he might have stowed on 'im."

Whitcom jumped to the ground, bent over the body of Rourk, and soon had him stripped of any valuables. He hefted the money belt, shot those who had come West with him a satisfied look, and said, "Looks like we're gonna have a payday, men." He again looked at Tenery. "You gonna let us empty our weapons of cartridges and keep them?"

Tenery wagged his head from side to side — slowly. "Don't push your luck, city boy. You got your pay, and more importantly, you have your lives." He looked over his shoulder. "McClain, collect all those weapons lyin' in the trail. Some o' you will be pleased to have 'em."

He grinned, really feeling like smiling wouldn't hurt, "Y'all don't want 'em, there'll be some in town who will." He sneaked a hand to the side he'd felt burn when Rourk fired. His fingers came away sticky and wet, but knowing they'd freed the town from Rourk's dastardly scheme, his side didn't hurt nearly as badly as he expected.

All five women in Gretchen's bakery vied for position at the window, each looking, hoping to hear the sound of horses returning with all riders sitting their saddles.

Cannard, one of the men left to guard the women, shook his head. "You ladies get yoreselves a cup o' coffee an' set there on that bench. When them men git back to town, I'll tell you if all them saddles are full — like they oughta be — now set down."

Even as he spoke, the sound of a large bunch of horses, accompanied by the rattle of wagons, broke into his words. All five women dashed out the door and ran toward the livery. Slim stood there only a moment longer than the women.

Tenery glanced at the stage station, then turned his look on Whitcom. He grinned. "Looks like you lucked out, Whitcom. The stages you boys rode in on are still sittin' there. You're not gonna wait 'til mornin' to get gone — you're gonna do it right now."

Whitcom sighed, then pinned Bill with a resigned look. "Tenery, as much as I dread that ride back to Billings, I'm gonna be damned happy to shed the sight o' this town." He smiled, as close as Bill thought he ever let himself do such, and said, "As you Westerners would say, I ain't a damn bit sorry to leave. Ain't never gonna come west of the Mississippi again."

Tenery found himself liking the cold-faced man.

His eyes hunted and found the one person in the world he wanted to see among those gathered in front of the livery. He couldn't have missed her if he'd tried. Her skirt lifted to an unladylike level between her ankles and knees as she ran toward him. She looked him over from top to bottom, then climbed to the saddle behind him.

"That scratch along yore side must not be bad, or you wouldn't be ridin' straight up." She tightened her arms around his waist. "Does it hurt so bad we cain't git married 'fore we leave for your folks' ranch?"

Tenery let out an exaggerated groan. "Reckon if you treat me reeeal gentle-like, I can stand at least one night o' marriage."

"We'll take it one night at a time — for the rest o' our lives." She tightened her arms around him.

He groaned this time too — but only because he twisted in the saddle trying to gather her into his arms.

ABOUT THE AUTHOR

Jack Ballas served in the U.S. Navy for twenty-two years, and received twelve battle stars for his service. In his younger days, he ran a honky-tonk saloon in the South (with the help of a twelve-gauge shotgun), rode the rails, and found himself lost deep in the Everglades. He was taken in by a band of Seminole Indians, whom he credits with saving his life. Ballas now makes his home in Fort Worth, Texas.